Fighting Behind the Lines
A "Nelson's Men"
Series about the Korean War

Book Two

Dennis Kennelly

Fighting Behind the Lines
Copyright © 2017 by Dennis Kennelly
ISBN 978-0-9986953-2-7
Library of Congress: 2017903672

La Maison Publishing, Inc.
Vero Beach, Florida
The Hibiscus City
www.lamaisonpublishing.com

"Success consists of going from failure to failure without loss of enthusiasm."

Winston Churchill/Quotes

From the Author

Although a work of fiction, this story reflects the time and attitudes of world events. Actual time frames and depictions of noted military and political leaders are facts. My story and its characters are a product of my imagination.

A fascinating aspect of the beginning of this war is the lack of a consistent historical depiction as to how this happened and, not only why it took America by surprise but why it took so long for America to come to South Korea's aid.

But the story of Korea goes much deeper, as it reflects on how America viewed it's standing in the world at the end of WW2 and how that morphed into its present day Super Power role.
Korea set the stage for America to fill a void that no other country could and had a cascading effect on American foreign policy to the present day.

Long forgotten, the men who fought here wondered why. They were not viewed as heroes. They didn't win. They fought to a tie, a truce. It wasn't even considered a War: just a police action.

Some police action! Tell that to the families of the dead and wounded.

Deaths:
Total In-Theatre - 36,574
U.S. Wounded in Action - 103,284

Somehow I hope to bring some recognition of the valiant efforts these men made in a long ago fight for our country.

Prolog

**North Korea Began the Invasion of the South at 0400 – (4:00 am)
on June 25th, 1950.
This book opens on Day Three of the Invasion –
Tuesday, June 27, 1950.**

America is still undecided about what to do.

The rapid advance of the invasion force has not been fully digested by the US military nor America's political leaders. Communications have broken down within South Korean military forces to such an extent that entire divisions are unaccounted for and their whereabouts unknown.

One thing is clear. North Korean troops are on the outskirts of the South Korean capital of Seoul. The second point that's beginning to dawn on a few American generals is that the overwhelming firepower and training of this enemy will be difficult to stop.

As head of Intelligence of Eighth Army (G- 2), Colonel Nelson foresaw these events and continually lobbied, albeit unsuccessfully, for increased military arms for South Korea, particularly, heavy artillery and anti-tank weapons.

His assessments of South Korea's inability to repel an invasion were now beginning to be recognized by General MacArthur's headquarters.

Nelson's clandestine listening Posts had done their part in warning of impending attack. Three of the four Posts still have not been heard from after having been ordered to withdraw to fallback locations on the eve of the assault.

The Post, positioned and hardened as the primary block to the North's main line of attack down the Uijongbu Corridor, performed its role and delayed the enemy's advance for two full days. After abandoning The Post, the men assumed their secondary role as gorilla's, fading into a near prepositioned hideout to further harass and delay this onslaught so that America could have the time to clearly see what this aggression meant to the whole of the Asian sphere of America's influence.

The Post men waited in hiding for orders at the mountain lair known as the Peak. Other of Nelson's men picked up the slack.

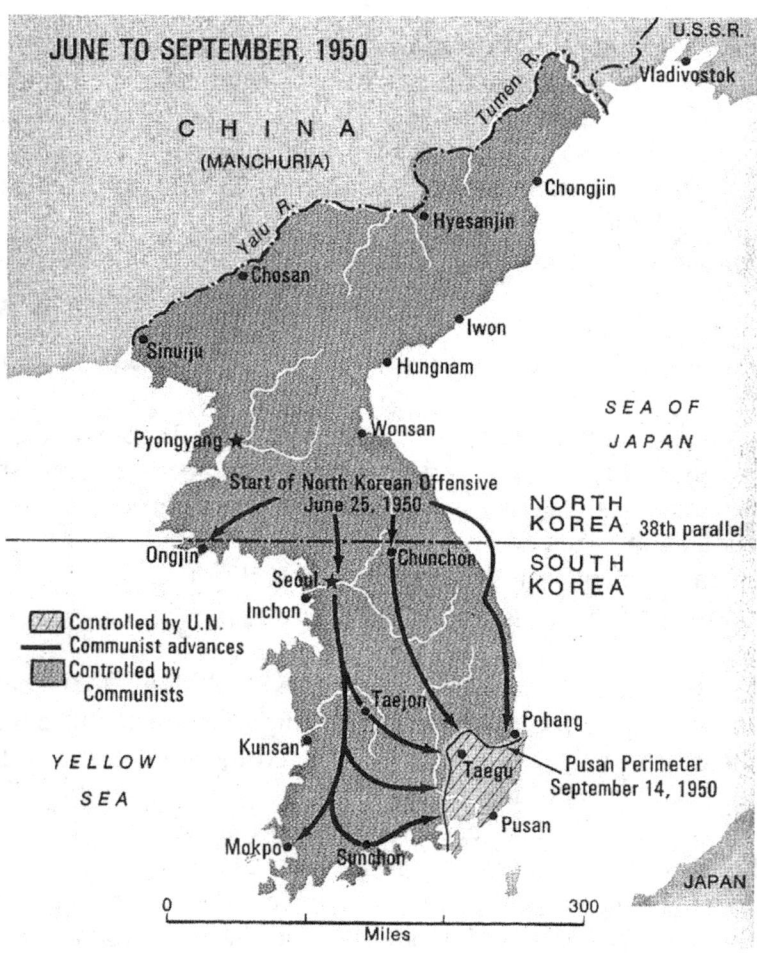

Chapter One

**Tuesday, June 27, 1950   Day Three of the Invasion
Aboard USS Juneau – Sea of Japan - Off the East Coast of
Korea — 0500 – (5:00 am)**

*The USS Juneau (CL 119) was a Light Cruiser that had never
seen war. That was about to change. The first USS Juneau (CL52)
was also a Light Cruiser that was sunk at the Naval Battle of
Guadalcanal in 1942. All seven hundred men but ten, perished. This
loss included the five Sullivan brothers. Their death on the same
ship henceforth changed how family members could be assigned
throughout all the Armed Services. Never again would family
members be allowed to serve together on the same ship or in the
same unit.*

Rear Admiral J M Higgins was sipping coffee and reading the flash dispatch just received from Naval Forces Far East Command, Admiral Turner Joy, his boss. He read it again to make sure he understood it, then glanced at the positioning chart at his side. The map showed where the ship was in relation to the Korean coast and was updated every hour.

He passed the dispatch across the table to the ship's captain. "Jesse! This brings us to the fight. Read it. When you finish your coffee, I want you to go to general quarters and announce this message to the crew. Then I want flank speed with a heading towards the town of Yangyang on the coast."

"Sir, don't you want to wait for that destroyer due here later today?"

"No, Captain. I think at flank speed we will arrive just before dawn. Catch them bare-assed. Teach them a thing or two about sneaking up on nice people."

"Will you accompany me to the bridge, Admiral?"

"Captain, I wouldn't miss this for the world."

After they had been announced on the Bridge, the sailors went back to regular station. The captain turned to his executive officer.

"Number One! Sound General Quarters! This is NO drill!"

"Aye, Captain, sounding General Quarters!"

The alarms sounded along with the loudspeaker notice, "This is no drill! I Repeat, this is no drill!"

They had practiced for many days. Their timing was excellent today. Captain Jesse C Sowell was pleased. He and this crew had been together for almost a year. He liked the men, but he really loved this ship. She was fast, and man did she pack a punch.

Everybody had settled into their battle stations. The captain picked up the ship's intercom speaker phone.

"This is your Captain speaking. The President of the United States has just authorized the Armed Services of the United States to assist the South Korean Government in repelling the invasion of the North Korean Communists. Gentlemen! We are going to war today!"

He paused, waited for the crew to settle down.

"I want you to think about the rich heritage of the ship you sail. Her namesake fought with great valor, amassing many victories before her heroic ending. Within a short time, our moment will arrive, where, we too, will test our strength and determination to defeat a powerful enemy who is hell bent on destroying the things we hold sacred. To that end, we are approaching the coastline of South Korea and intend to interdict the coast road where the invading Army is driving south, unopposed."

He paused.

"In other words, we're gonna shell the crap out of them!"

A huge roar erupted around the ship.

After things had quieted down, he continued.

"Let me remind you that the North Korean's have naval forces; destroyers, PT boats and submarines. Probably mines and certainly planes. The Russians supplied these arms to this enemy and trained them well. This is a formidable enemy. Be wary! All right men, prepare for heavy and prolonged shore bombardment. Good luck and God bless America!"

He gave the order for flank speed and heading. The ship shuddered as it increased speed and heeled to starboard as it turned and headed toward the Korean coast.

Later, on the bridge, as the ship neared the coast, the Admiral and Captain stared out onto the black sea.

"How close do you want to take her in, Captain?"

The Admiral didn't much care about the answer. He was just killing time. The water was deep right up to the beach. They could lay off a mile and bring their 12 - 5" guns to fire, point blank. That would be foolish, as better results would be gotten from five to seven miles out.

"What would you suggest, Admiral?"

3

He looked up at the Captain and saw him smiling. The Admiral smirked, realizing the Captain was playing an officer to superior officer joke on him. He liked the younger man.

"Number One! Initiate plot to five miles north of Yangyang and seven miles east. Then reduce speed to ten knots and turn southward to parallel the coastline. Advise me on ETA to that point."

"Aye, Captain!" He gave a few commands then went to the plotting table. "Captain. ETA in fifteen minutes."

Korea – Kimipo Air Field – Five miles Northeast of Seoul – 0530 – (5:30 am)

The fire on the tarmac was like a beacon to Sergeant George Lopez. He had come so far. It was both frightening and exhilarating. His Post #1 team had been ambushed before they could withdraw on the eve of the invasion. The lone survivor, out of the ten men team, had escaped south during the last few days. He hid among the advancing enemy as they chased the retreating ROK Army past him. Crossing two rivers and finally passing in front of the attacking forces. Now he faced his goal of reaching fellow American troops at the Kimipo airfield. He was scared.

Two hundred yards from one of the airfield perimeter defense positions, he couldn't tell who they were. His fear of the ROK troops was well founded. His belief that a ROK unit dug in around his Post had turned and killed his entire team as they were about to leave, told him that he wanted nothing to do with Korean troops, North or South.

He knew this base. Had traveled down here many times to pick up supplies when Billy couldn't or won't deliver supplies up to his Post. Knew there weren't many American soldiers stationed here. Billy was the guy he needed to find because Billy knew him. Sure, Billy had given him a lot of shit, always. Now, he'd take that and more, just want to get safe.

Almost transfixed watching the big transport burning, it was disheartening. He started thinking. Was Billy still here? Are Americans still here? Can I get through this perimeter without being killed? Finally, his intuitive side kicked in. Find a way! Like you always do! Something always shows up. Right? Find it!

Chapter Two

Tuesday, June 27, 1950 Day Three of the Invasion
Aboard USS Juneau – Sea of Japan - Seven miles Off the East
Coast of Korea — 0630 – (6:30 am)

The Admiral was curious, "Captain, any worthwhile targets in this harbor?"

"Only the harbor itself, Admiral. But we'll make a mess of the town as well. The aerial recon photos don't show anything of worth along this stretch except rolling trucks and tanks heading south. Rail tracks alongside the coast highway need to get mashed up. That's it. It'll be a good start for the third day of the invasion."

"I agree, as long as we're shooting at them and they're not shooting at us."

They felt the ship lurch as it made a hard turn to Port and slowed. The executive officer spoke into his headset. "Firing officer, commence main gun plot."

The bridge on this new cruiser is spacious and quiet. As the six big double barreled five-inch gun turrets started to turn towards land, the mechanical sounds of them moving into firing position were ominously noticeable.

The admiral and captain were on the starboard side, looking at the mainland, binoculars at their eyes. It was still dark. Low clouds and intermittent rain were perceptible. Outlines of the mountains behind the coastline were taking shape as the early dawn began.

"Captain, I just got word from our signals lookout on #2. He's got a Morse code flashing light message from that mountain top."

He pointed. "It's just south of this town. US Army, they say. They want us to confirm receipt, should we?"

"Were they specific? Who are they?"

"Yes, sir. They say they're Eighth Army, post four, their commander is a Colonel Nelson in Japan. They signed off with Jack, JP, Phil, Greg."

Admiral Higgins spoke up, "I know something of this colonel. He's G-2 of the whole Eighth Army. A big shot."

"Okay One, tell him to confirm message. After he finishes, have him come in. I want that message sent off to Far East Fleet Command, ASAP."

A few minutes later, the Officer of the Deck came in. "Sir! All hands are below decks; guns are clear to fire."

The Captain turned to his Number One, "Okay One, commence firing!"

The executive officer spoke into his headset, "Fire control! Commence fire! All guns!"

Korea – High on a Mountain on the East Coast – South of the Town of Yangyang – 0650 – (6:50 am)

"Damn! What a show!"

The bombardment had been intense and continuous along a long stretch of coastline within their sight. Destroying tanks, trucks and much everything that was on the road, the road and the railroad tracks. As the sun rose, the shadows of the big ship gave way to its distinctive look of a major ship of the American Navy. The men were awed at its look of power. The sight of its destructive capability was inspiring.

"I guess we're in the war now, Jack. About goddamn time!"

"JP, we, meaning us, have been **IN** the war for a bit now. But I agree, it's time we had a helping hand."

7

"You're the master of understatement, Jack. Ya think they'll be back?"

"JP! I'll bet everything I have that not only will they be back, but they're also gonna bring lots of friends!"

"What about us?"

"We got this far with no help. Maybe Colonel Nelson can pull a magic act of sorts. But we can't count on anything or anyone, just ourselves. Meanwhile, the Gods of war have given us an opportunity to get some needed supplies. So let's saddle up, get down to that wreckage, and resupply. We need flashlights, ammo, food and, God be merciful, a radio."

"I'll get Phil and Greg. Are you sure you want to go down there in daylight?"

"I don't see any movement down there. Yeah! Now's the time. Let's hurry. It'll take us an hour to get there, maybe twenty minutes to scrounge. That's asking a lot, but I'm counting on them being really screwed up from this surprise."

JP went off to gather the other two men. Jack wondered if this was a smart move. Decided he had little choice. They were starving. Pretty much out of everything. Losing six men of his command at the ambush had toughened his resolve to bringing the rest of his men back safely.

Korea – Kimipo Air Field – Five miles Northeast of Seoul – 0700 – (7:00 am)

"Captain, the truck is loaded! We're ready to go!" Said Billy, extremely anxious to leave. Working like a man possessed the last few hours, he had packed the truck and its trailer with his mechanic's tools, spare parts and food. Arnie, his helper, did most of the heavy lifting. He too was worried about the fast approaching enemy shelling. The lack of heavy weapons of the ROK troops at the airfield and the haphazard digging in and around the airport perimeter didn't instill much confidence.

Last night's strafing attack by North Korean fighter planes and subsequent destruction of the big C-54 Skymaster transport, still burning on the tarmac, confirmed, that this airfield was a mighty dangerous place to be hanging around.

Since Colonel Nelson authorized the reposition of the three men to Suwon Airfield some twenty miles farther south, Billy and Arnie, felt the nearness of safety and wanted to move out as fast as they could.

Billy thought about his buddy calling him from Suwon last night. What incredible luck! Telling him that a P-51 fighter had been found under a tarp, at the very back of a hanger that was being emptied of US Army surplus ammunition for distribution to the ROK Army. He didn't know what to do with the plane and wanted Billy's advice. Billy knew exactly what to do.

It was his ticket out of here. He wasted no time in convincing the captain, "Wild Bill," a three-time Ace flying P-51s against the Germans, to call Colonel Nelson so they could go there and get that plane flying. He was an ace mechanic, and Wild Bill was a great fighter pilot. A few Aces are a hand you need to bet on, and Colonel Nelson pushed in his chips, approving the new mission. Billy hoped the plane didn't need too many parts because he didn't have many.

As he walked back towards the barracks to find Wild Bill, Billy wondered where the hell the Captain was. We gotta go now! He whispered to himself.

Behind him, he heard. "Billy! Is that you?"

He jumped when he heard the voice. It came from the side corner of the barracks he was near.

"Holy shit! Who the fuck are you!?"

Emerging from his cover, a disheveled soldier called out, "American! Post #1, Sergeant George Lopez." A Tommy gun hung at his side pointing at the ground.

Billy relaxed, vaguely recalling the name.

Just then, Wild Bill came through the door and saw the two men walking towards each other. Looking closer at the unknown man's uniform, or, for a better description, his rags, he knew he was an American soldier.

"Damn!" Said Wild Bill, looking at this stranger. "You look like shit!" Turning to Billy, "You know this tramp?" He grinned.

Now, with recognition, Billy ran to George and grabbed his shoulders. "Come on George! We're just leaving! Got grub and water in the truck." Billy surprised himself at his emotional caring for someone other than himself. He fought hard to shake off this new feeling, not wanting to go too far, as he steered George towards the truck, "What happened? Where's the rest of your team? How'd you get here?"

Wild Bill was right behind them. "Shut up, Billy! Can't you see this guy can hardly walk? You guys go in the back. Get him fed and let him rest. I'm in the front with Arnie. Let's go!"

The twenty-mile trip would usually take about an hour. Not today. Good thing Kimipo airport was on the south side of the Han River because the main bridge out of Seoul was packed with fleeing hordes of all ilk, civilians, soldiers, animals and vehicles. All approaches to the bridge were jammed solid. None the less, their pace was a crawl.

Only one road led south out from the airport. It connected to the only main road heading south, just below the Han River Bridge. It seemed like the entire population of Seoul was leaving at the same time…because, with artillery rumbling in the far distance, panic had set in.

The people of Seoul realized they waited too long. Reality kicked in and hope faded. Their President had lied to them. Their Army wasn't strong. America wasn't coming to rescue them.

Riding in the back of the truck, Billy listened to the artillery in the distance, won't be long now, he thought. Watching George eat like a starving man, he saw relief in his eyes. Something happened inside him. He jerked. Not liking this new sensation and wondered. He wanted to find out what happened but decided to keep his mouth shut. Something new for him. He felt the answers he would get would probably scare the shit out of him.

Later, they arrived at the road junction south of the Han River Bridge.

"I bet you wish you were on a plane right about now, Captain."

"Two freak'n hours! To go five miles! Yeah, Arnie! I'd give a lot to be flying over this crap!"

"Once we get past this intersection and onto the highway, it should speed up."

"You're an optimist! Just look at the crowd on the bridge. I bet it's been that way all night."

They watched a ROK company pass in front of them, heading south.

"Looks like the Army's not going to defend the city."

They started to move into the crowd, slowly edging in just behind the ROK unit.

The explosion made both of them jump in their seats. They turned to see the center of the long bridge enveloped in a tremendous cloud. Debris flew hundreds of feet in the air.

"Holy shit! We're being bombed!" Shouted Arnie.

"Oh my God! I can't believe it!" Wild Bill just stared at the scene.

"Should we get out of the truck!? We're a pretty good target."

Everybody on the road started to run in all directions, dropping their belongings. Some fell and were trampled. Panic all around.

"No Arnie! We're not being bombed. I heard no plane. That bridge was purposefully destroyed by the ROK. I guess the Commies are close."

"With all those people on it! There must be a couple a thousand! They even have their troops on it!"

"I don't have an answer, Arnie. It looks like somebody panicked. Let's just get the hell out of here!"

They made quick progress for a while. The crowds watched them pass as the people huddled in ditches just off the road.

Chapter Three

**Tuesday, June 27, 1950   Day Three of the Invasion
Korea – On the East Coast - South of the Town of
Yangyang – 0930 – (9:30 am)**

They made it halfway back up the mountain. The weight of the salvaged booty slowed them. They moved in silence. They hadn't eaten much in three days, and it showed. Finally, Jack ordered a break. The men dug into the food supplies they'd found.

"Why aren't we heading south, Jack? Isn't it dangerous going back to our hideout?"

"Dangerous? What'da you mean, JP?"

"What if somebody saw our signaling this morning?"

"Did you see anyone alive down there? Besides, what makes you think we should go south? Maybe we should go west? I have no idea! I know heading south right now in daylight is dangerous. Let's find out what the hell is going on first before we make our next move."

"You're right, Jack! Shit, you've always right." Lamented JP with a smile.

"That's why I'm a first sergeant, JP."

Phil finished a can of some unknown contents. "This stuff smells awful, but it's not bad, kind of like it. How's yours, Greg?"

"I don't know. I was so hungry I didn't stop till it was gone and I'm still hungry."

Jack stood up. "Come on; we'll eat more at the top. Got a ways to go."

They continued going higher. Phil spoke.

"I used to hate Navy guys, 'squids,' I called them. Thought they were just wusses. After seeing what they did down there, though, I've got a whole different attitude."

Jack looked back at Phil. "You were in Europe. How in the hell were you supposed to know anything about the Navy? I Island hopped in the Pacific. Let me tell you; those Navy guys were worshiped."

"So they helped you out?" Phil asked.

"They saved our asses. That's what they did! And oh, what you saw down there is nothing. That ship was a cruiser and a light cruiser at that. It didn't have big guns."

"Jesus! You mean they have bigger guns?"

"Phil, where've you been? Don't you read?"

"Hey, come on Jack, I read tech stuff, that's it. I hate reading about anything else."

Greg had heard this back and forth before and could see it was going to escalate. "Cut the shit will you guys! I want to hear more about these big naval guns, Jack. I don't know anything about naval guns either."

The men kept climbing. They were renewed by the food and the spark of hope they felt after seeing the destruction of the enemy by their Navy.

Jack spoke loud over his shoulder.

"OK! Let me tell you about my first battle. I was fresh out of boot camp and shipped out on a Liberty ship. That was the worst thing I ever experienced and I've been through a lot. We hit a storm. Me, and everybody else thought we would die. Some wanted to; we were so sick. Anyway, we finally stopped at some island called Saipan. This is '44. The Marines had landed a few days before. Apparently, they needed help from the Army. They sure did as it turned out. We scaled down thick rope ladders into landing craft in the dark. The noise from the Navy ships shelling the island was deafening. I couldn't see shit except for flashes. We landed at sunrise and proceeded up this valley. I think we got a few miles in and then ran into to this ridge."

"Jack! We're curious about navy guns, not your history of combat experience."

"Shut up, JP! I'm telling a story. You guys are all ignorant about what happened in the Pacific. I'm telling you this because this new war looks pretty similar. So shut up and listen."

They kept climbing.

"We advanced on this ridge with tank support. They cut us up real bad and had to fall back. My LT called in an air strike. The planes bombed and strafed that ridge for a good ten minutes. We started out again. Lost four more tanks and a lot more men. Those bastards were in caves, in the ridge, not on top of it. The planes did zilch."

He turned to see that he had their attention and kept climbing.

"Then a Navy guy shows up. Says he's a spotter for the **California**, a battleship off the coast. He does his thing. Tells us to hunker down. A few minutes passed. Then, what sounded like a train passing over my head, I felt this tremendous explosion. This spotter called back some corrections, then said to fire for effect and then told me to bury my head. Shit rained down. Never before or since, have I ever experienced anything that even came close to that bombardment! The ground shook, like an earthquake. The sound was deafening. I thought I would die!"

He stopped and turned to them.

"Maybe five minutes later it ended. I was groggy. When I looked out, there was no more ridge. I mean, that fifty-foot high rock ridge was not there anymore. Totally gone. I exhaled in relief, not believing my eyes. The spotter told me that they were big sixteen inch naval guns, nine of them from that one ship."

Greg was impressed, said so. Then added. "I hope I get a chance to see something like that."

JP stopped and turned to Greg. "You're an idiot, Greg. You know, if you get your wish, it means we're in deep shit. I don't want to see anything like that, ever!"

14

Jack shook his head in disgust. "Guys! My point is that we have incredible firepower available to help us survive, even if we're in a bad spot. It should give you assholes some comfort."

JP shot back, "The only comfort I'll feel is if *I'm on* that battleship firing those guns."

Chapter Four

Tuesday, June 27, 1950   Day Three of the Invasion
Japan – Russian Embassy – 0900 – (9:00 am) – Military Attaché
Colonel Andrey Markovich's Office

"Colonel, I have a very upset American Colonel named Nelson in front of me. He says he must see you on an extremely urgent matter. He wants to meet with you, now. Sir, what shall I do?"

In English, "Of course, please escort the good Colonel to my office, immediately."

On the second floor, the front office was grand. More fitting an ambassador's office or a ballroom than a military attaché's office, but it was in keeping with the Russian style of opulence. The entrance doors were thirty feet away from his desk. It allowed Andrey to take the measure of the man as he approached. He didn't like what he saw. Decided friendly might be best to start.

"Jim, how good of you to visit," he called to him as Nelson approached. "I do hope you enjoyed our little May Day party a few weeks ago, so glad you came. Can I get you some coffee? Please sit, tell me what's so urgent."

Colonel Nelson came to attention in front of Andrey's desk and saluted, didn't wait for a return salute. He kept standing.

"I'm here on my own, Colonel, unofficially. Eighth Army doesn't know anything about this, yet. I hope they never find out."

"Jim, is this about this civil war that the South Koreans just started?"

"You know me for how long now? More than five years, right? You probably know more about me than I do. So cut the crap! I know what's going on and you know what's going on." He paused. "But here's the thing, something happened yesterday. Something really big. And your government is involved. But you know what's worst? I'm very pissed off about it!"

"What are you talking about?"

"I'll tell you a little story that some friends of mine told me. It happened just last night, south of a town in Korea called Cheorwon, where someone blew up two bridges."

Andrey noticeably blinked.

"That was nothing. These people also discovered a big house nearby with a special unit guarding a Korean general. It had a barn out back that was being used to torture American soldiers. They witnessed three men being brutally killed. That's bad, but what's atrocious Colonel, were the three officers who were conducting the torture. One was a Korean major, he was multi-lingual, he enjoyed the physical stuff, you know, like cutting off fingers or, like he did to one man, skinned him alive."

Andrey turned ashen.

"Another Korean officer was a captain; he was kind of a go-between, didn't speak English, but was fluent in Chinese and Russian."

"And that brings me to why I'm here. Because the third officer was a Colonel, a Russian Colonel!"

"No! That can't be! We wouldn't be part of anything like that!"

"Shut up! There's more!"

"The Russian died quickly, my friends assure me, and he had not participated in the torture. The Korean officers died less swiftly and revealed further information. This particular unit is called **Grey Dragon**. They were given orders to harshly question all enemies with potential information and to severely deal with all Americans. The general in the house was this unit's leader and was killed along with all of this unit, unfortunately, before he could be questioned."

Nelson was beet red, face bulging with anger.

17

"Lastly, and most interestingly, the Korean captain revealed, when answering the question about who this general reported to, said he didn't know. But he said this general often complained about this idiot Chinese general he had to deal with, and then this captain mentioned that the Russian colonel also complained to him about his asshole Russian general that he had to write reports for."

Andrey was shaken, disbelief, yet knew what Colonel Nelson had just told him was true.

"Here's what's going to happen, Colonel. You're going to cable your bosses in Moscow and relate exactly what I told you happened. Somebody over there is going to get to the bottom of this and find out who is running this unit and they're going to shut it down!"

He took a step back and stared hard at Andrey.

"Because if they don't, I'm coming after them. I'll find out who they are."

It was then that Andrey did a strange thing. He leaned forward and put his figure to his lips to signal to Colonel Nelson not to speak any further. Andrey then pointed to his ear and then pointed to his lamp to indicate a listening device was planted there.

"Jim, this talk has made me feel ill, I think I need some air, come with me out to the veranda."

They moved through the expansive doors; Andrey closed them behind him.

"I'm sorry, Jim, everybody is monitored, I must be careful. What you have told me is disgusting and deeply insults me. I knew about the bridges being blown but nothing about anything else. That's odd that no mention was made in the cables about a Russian colonel or a Korean general being killed, that's big news. Somethings wrong here."

"So you know nothing about this operation, or who runs it?"

"Korea has become, how do you say, fucked up. Many hands in the pot, all stirring in different directions. I'm on the outer circle and not privy to the core. It's like trying to look into an erupting volcano, look over the edge too far and you lose your head."

"Can you find out?"

"So, I gather my good friend Howie over at CIA knows nothing of this?"

"NO. I didn't want a lot of publicity in case I had to deal with this myself."

Andrey nodded, understanding.

"I have a few friends I still trust, so yes, I think I can discover what this outfit is up to and who's in charge. I tell you, Jim, I want to know for me, not you, because if I can, I will kill this bastard myself."

"I just want it stopped Andrey; I don't care how."

"There's only one way to stop this, Jim. Now listen to me. Until we speak again, don't do anything stupid. I'm on this now as my top priority. But if something should happen to me, like a car accident or if I'm suddenly recalled to Moscow. Then you'll know I failed and you're free to start your private war."

"Don't fail, Andrey. I've become fond of you."

"Now that we're friendly again, I need to ask you something that's been on my mind for many years. Right after the war, I know that Donovan wanted you so bad in his OSS. I think he wanted you to take his place and head up the whole operation. Why'd you turn him down?"

"Andrey, you never stop, do you?" He turned to leave.

"Jim, before we go in. I'll need a week or so; I'll contact you. When we go inside, I'm going to make a fuss in the office. Put on a show for the monitors. Pay no attention. And Jim, thanks for coming here, I want to work with you in the future. Our countries should be friends, not enemies."

"I agree Andrey. You be careful. Okay, now you can start calling me that capitalist pig nonsense."

Chapter Five

Tuesday, June 27, 1950   Day Three of the Invasion
Korea – The Peak – 1100 – (11:00 am)

Rusty, Red and Tully sat under a tree in their mountaintop clearing. All first sergeants, Rusty, the recent commander of the clandestine Post and Red, his longtime friend and second in command, had embraced Tully and his volunteer Ranger squad on the eve of the invasion. The Rangers had fought with valor but suffered severe casualties. Tully had proved his leadership and was now a trusted member of Rusty's inner circle.

The rain last night had abated and turned to just cloud cover. The temperature at this 3000-foot elevation was pleasant, and the view of the two valleys this hideout straddled was almost scenic.

The location was established when the Post team began building their compound some nine months ago. It was their first fallback position hideout should they have to abandon The Post. Well stocked, it also contained the Top Secret VLF (very low frequency) communication equipment.

This VLF technology performs much like the old Morse code telegraph apparatus except it is wireless. Signals travel line of sight via a cone shaped sending/receiving unit. The signal expands over distance and can cover hundreds of miles. Towers were built high on mountains down the length of South Korea, terminating in Pusan, at the tip of the peninsula. This allowed easy transmission to Japan and Eighth Army Headquarters at Colonel Nelson's office. Since the signal expanded, the sender only needed an approximate location of the cone receiver. The signal shot like a rifle, but after a few miles, it acted like a shotgun blast. It only needed low voltage electricity, be it a battery or a portable foot or hand cranking power generation unit.

"I think we should wait till early dawn tomorrow before we head out. Our mission last night really pissed our northern invaders off. They're still trying to figure out how it happened and where we came from. I'm sure they got patrols out, searching everywhere."

"I agree, Red," Rusty said. "With the rain washing away any tracks, though, I think we're safe here. For now anyway."

"I disagree!" Tully stood up and started pacing. "I think we should move now. Here's the rub. I figure they started their search first thing this morning when it stopped raining. Starting at the house and moving south towards us. Red's right. They've pissed. After blowing two bridges and killing a general along with his whole unit, they want us real bad. They won't stop. They'll cover every inch of this valley until they find out where we've hiding."

Rusty shook his head. "They'll never find this spot. The rain washed away any sign that we came up here."

"It doesn't matter if we left a sign or not, they'll follow any trail or path that could have been used. It's only logical that we came from one of these mountains. Let's not forget these are not stupid people."

Red leaned in then turned to Rusty. "He's got a good point. As much as I'd like to rest up another day, I'd hate to be trapped here."

"Besides," Tully added, "making our way at night is maybe more dangerous. Even the high foothills are tough to navigate, and we'll make no time. Another option would be to hug that road, but it would be like rolling the dice every few steps. We could stumble into anything."

"Okay, okay. I get it." Said Rusty. "But I think we shouldn't go down this valley at all. They're looking for us there. We should leave by the way we came and proceed south down the Uijongbu Valley. What do you think?"

21

Red and Tully looked at each other. The expression on each face told Rusty that they hadn't considered this option.

Red spoke.

"That does solve an immediate problem. It's a great thought since we know that valley pretty well. But we don't know what's happening there. How far has the North progressed? The ROK had a few defensive positions further south of the Stream. Have they been overrun? The big question is how do we get from the end of this valley to the western edge of the other valley? You know, the place where we're supposed to meet that ROK unit Colonel Nelson set us up with to join. That's probably twenty miles or more away."

Tully, still on his feet looked at Rusty. "Your idea is spectacular. Red is always the voice of reason, but if we're dead who cares. What's the expression, **live for today for tomorrow is unknown**, or something like that? I didn't even think of going back into that valley. I don't know this area. Shit, I hardly know what country I'm in. But Red raises a serious point. So let's talk about it."

Rusty looked at Red then Tully.

"I think we can all agree that it would be safer to go down our valley that we know. Its forty miles either way. But Red's right. This choice brings with it the additional distance we have to cover to get to the meeting location. It adds twenty miles over mostly open terrain. But that open plain we have to cross is mostly just rice patties. The rainy season has just started and they're not flooded yet. So it'll be pretty easy going, especially at night. That's the only time we could do this without being spotted. The other thing in our favor would be where the enemy's focus would be. I'm sure, by that time, Seoul will be captured. They'll be concentrating on their end game. They want to totally destroy the ROK forces south of them. It'll give us an edge."

Tully looked at Red for confirmation. Red acknowledged.

"You have a way of making something complicated seem simple. We should move now."

"OK," Rusty said as he stood. "Let's get everyone moving!"

Suwon Airport – Twenty miles South of Seoul – 1200 – (12:00 pm)

Frustrated by the stop and go trip along the crowded road, Wild Bill was at the end of his rope. The ROK soldier at the airport gate didn't speak English. They didn't have any papers. With rifle pointed at them, he made them pull off to the side. Captain Stands started screaming at him. Finally, a US Army lieutenant showed up.

"What's up, Captain?"

"Are you shitting me, Lieutenant!? I've been ordered here. I've been on that fucking road for six hours! What the fuck is going on!? Let me on this base before I get out and kick the shit out of you!"

"Hold on cowboy. I'm following orders too." He glanced at the driver's uniform, saw Arnie's Eighth Army patch. "What's in the back?"

"Two guys with a secret weapon. What do you think we got!?" He barely contained himself.

"Sorry Captain. Big things are going on here and everybody's on high alert. What're your orders?"

Wild Bill changed his expression. "What big things?"

"My platoon only came in a few hours ago, for security. Lots of ROK brass just arrived. Civilian big shots too. The South Korean President is here. We're expecting a plane with some US Army brass pretty soon. That's why I'm here."

"You know what's up?"

"You're kidding, right? Who're you supposed to report to?"

"Uh, no one. I'm to take charge of a warehouse. An Army storage building."

23

"I saw some US troops near two hangers at the southeast end of the tarmac."

"That sounds right. Can we go in now?"

"Sorry for the delay but we weren't expecting any American troops at the gate." He moved off towards the gate and waved them through.

Arnie drove through the central part of the airport towards the hangers in the corner.

"Over there, Arnie," The Captain pointed, "American troops by that second hanger."

They pulled up in front of five soldiers sitting on crates in front of the open structure and got out. Billy came around from the rear, became the point man.

"Hey, I'm looking for Gene, Sergeant Hays. He around?"

A corporal sitting at the far end responded.

"Yeah, he's inside," pointed to the open hanger, "We're all on break."

"Lazy bastards!" Billy muttered under his breath. "I'll find him."

He led the way into the hanger. Off to the right, he saw a hammock and two guys lying against some crates.

"Gene!" Billy yelled. "Get your ass up! You son of a bitch!"

The guy in the hammock stirred.

"I'd know that obnoxious voice anywhere. Hi, Billy!" He struggled out of the hammock and walked up to him.

"Damn, don't you look like shit?" Said Gene with a smile.

"And you look fat and ugly."

They embraced.

"Thanks, Gene. I owe you for saving my ass!"

Gene backed up. "What're you talking about?"

"Jesus, Gene! If you hadn't called me about this P-51, I'd still be in Kimipo. Probably getting overrun about now. Maybe dead."

Wild Bill stepped forward.

"I love reunions, but I want to see this plane. Gene, have you inspected it? Any major problems?"

Gene turned and saw the captain's bars and wing insignia on Wild Bill's utilities and did a double take.

"No, sir! I just removed the tarp. Besides flat tires, she's intact. I didn't get into her. Let me show you."

Gene led the men out and over to the next hanger with closed doors.

"That hanger you were in seems pretty full. Aren't you supposed to give the ammo and stuff to the ROKs?"

Gene looked at the captain and stopped walking. A blank expression on his face.

"Captain. No offense! But if I knew you better, I'd tell you to go stick it."

Wild Bill stood still, didn't react. Gene had a look, and he continued.

"My men have had four hours of sleep since we got here yesterday morning. Worked like dogs to load trucks from this hanger." Pointing to the hanger they were approaching.

"We've got nothing here. No forklifts, no roller lines for crates. Nothing. It's all grunt work. We had a platoon of ROK troops helping us empty this hanger. They left a few hours ago. We're expecting another ROK unit to come and help empty the second hanger. But they haven't shown up yet."

"I tend to get ahead of myself sometimes, Gene. Hence my nickname."

Gene was surprised at the captain's remark but responded.

"Billy's not gifted in human talk and interactions. He never said who you were?"

"Captain Bill Stands at your service. Commonly known by friends and foe alike as *Wild Bill.*"

"You're the Ace! Right? Holly shit! I thought you looked familiar. I'm honored."

"How in the hell do you know me?"

"You were already famous when I joined your squadron in Carentan, France. It was three weeks after Normandy and I was scared shit. I was just a maintenance grunt. You'd become a double

Ace by then. The ground crew all wanted to work on your plane. Yeah, you were something. Still are, I guess. How come you're still a captain?"

"Small world." The Captain ignored the question. "Let' just see what we got here, Gene. I hope **he'll** fly."

As Gene and Billy approached the large hanger doors, Billy leaned into Gene, "You know, he got his third Ace."

"Damn!"

They each grabbed a side and slid open the doors.

The vast empty hanger revealed the plane in the back. Surrounding it, stacked high along the back and side walls, were crates.

Pointing to the stacked boxes, Gene said, "We left these crates because they all belong to the P-51. Bombs, rockets and fifty caliber ammo. Some parts too."

Taking the sight in,the Captain stopped. He hadn't seen this amount of munitions since....well, he couldn't remember.

"Yeah! Now that's what I'm talking about!"

Billy walked to the plane and did a quick look. "Arnie, get that ramp over there in the corner," he pointed.

Arnie pushed the ramp up to the engine. Billy ran up and opened the engine cowling.

"Good news! She's got an engine!"

Relief flooded Wild Bill's face. He knew the main reason a fighter would be left behind was that it had been stripped, usually, to take its engine.

Wild Bill called back up to Billy. "Okay, Billy, now it's time for you to get **Him** running. I don't fly no woman. This war machine will henceforth be named **Just Due**."

"Bring in the truck, Arnie. Put the nose over there." Billy pointed. "Oh! Go wake up George!"

Chapter Six

**Tuesday, June 27, 1950   Day Three of the Invasion
Japan – Eighth Army Headquarters – 1300 – (1:00 pm)**

As Colonel Nelson entered the building, he met his Executive Officer, Major Hank Jarvis.

"Glad you're back, Colonel. Shit's hit the fan. Our new orders have brought every Tom, Dick and Harry out of hibernation. Everyone wants direction. We're kind of in the dark as to what to tell them."

"That's okay Hank. I'm good with dark."

They proceeded to the large conference area that had been converted into a War room when the invasion began three days ago. It seated fifteen men, jammed in at desks around the room and at a large center table. Wires hung from the ceiling to the center table where banks of phones were manned. Right now there were twenty-five men in the room.

Nelson entered the chaos. Phones are ringing. People yelling. He stopped and thought, God, I'm made for this! Okay, Colonel, now do what you do. Kick ass and save lives!

"All quiet!" Nelson yelled.

The sergeant next to him realized that nobody heard him. He saw the serious look on his commander, pulled out his forty-five pistol and fired into the ceiling. "Commanding Officer here! Attention!"

Colonel Nelson jumped, as did everyone. The room fell silent. He put his hands on his hips.

"Listen up!" He scanned the room.

"Everybody else can panic but NOT YOU! Right now you're reacting. That's unacceptable. Our job is to anticipate! Stay calm and plan. You wouldn't be in this room if you weren't the smartest people in the Army. So act like it! Men's lives depend on you!"

He turned to the sergeant who fired the pistol and said so all could hear.

"I like your style sergeant. However, in the future, I suggest you use a whistle."

You could feel the room relax. He addressed them again.

"Right now, Eighth Army is not the center of this conflict. *Only* air and naval forces have been authorized to attack the North Koreans invading the South. And even that is restricted to action *below* the 38th parallel."

He paused for effect.

"But this will all change. We are effectively at War. It's political right now. We just can't come out and say it. I think this delay in our full involvement is because our President wants world opinion to be on our side. This may take a few days. But whether we're supported by the United Nations or not, we're going to war! This, I assure you!"

The only sound in the room were beeps from unanswered phones.

"Now! Addressing something closer to home; Eighth Army is, as some describe, outliners to our Emperor."

The room stirred at this remark. All knew the ambivalence felt between commands.

"General MacArthur has his ways. But he is Eighth Army's ultimate boss. Despite his foibles, let me remind you that he is one of the most brilliant generals of all time. That being said, I know we have issues with his staff. They have never fought with us, and they don't know General Walker and certainly they don't know us."

Hands behind his back, he paced in a thoughtful manner.

"None of this bullshit matters. You will do your job. You will work with anyone. Asshole or savior. The sole purpose of what we do is to give our troops the intelligence we gather and guidance to help them defeat the enemy. Period!"

He paused again for effect.

"Today, you're gonna get more tools to do just that. Eighth Army, meaning General Walker, has ordered that his Army needs a fully manned Headquarters Staff. Peacetime regulations be damned!"

A big cheer went up. "About time!" somebody yelled.

"You men from our individual division's G-2 staffs here today are now officially attached to Eighth Army HQ, G-2 Staff, under my command. Other staff officers from all the divisions, whether it be planning, logistics or personnel are being pulled together. We're all part of a unified command structure under Colonel Harris, Eighth Army's Executive Officer."

Nearby, a major, raised his hand. Nelson pointed to him.

"Sir, I'm with General Dean's 24th Division. General MacArthur's chief of staff, General Almond, has indicated to us that we might be attached to General Church's command when he assumes control of all forces in Korea today. What does that mean in this new structure?"

"Great question, Major! What it means is that the higher ups don't know what's going on. They're playing it safe. We haven't committed ground forces yet, but we have advisers there. The military follows their bosses. Nobody wants to make a mistake. So nice and easy does it. I'm not privy to General Church's orders, but I'll bet he's the advance team. You know, check out the situation on the ground. Try to get the home folks to defend themselves. But the situation is already apparent to anyone that has been focused on events. We must come in to save this country from being overrun. That means troops on the ground or we use an Atomic Bomb. What do you think?"

He looked around the silent room.

"But you, Major, are now with Eighth Army HQ. Whether your division gets reassigned or not, it will come back under our wing sooner or later. Notwithstanding this temporary transfer, we, meaning Eighth Army, will assist in any way to help the command structure on the ground, whatever it is."

He raised his voice to the room.

"Am I clear?!"

The room responded with a resounding, "Yes, sir!"

Chapter Seven

**Tuesday, June 27, 1950   Day Three of the Invasion
Korea – The Post Men – Somewhere South of the Peak
– 1830 – (6:30 pm)**

With Tracker and Snake at point, the men made their way south. A Native American from the Chippewa tribe, raised around Lake Superior, Tracker made a name for himself early on. He was gifted. The local police utilized his skills to hunt down escaped felons and other bad folks. He had another gift that nobody understood, least of all himself. An ability to enter a trance like state and perform feats directed by Spirit.

While he and Snake got along, they were not close. They shared being under Rusty's command at the Post for nearly a year but the last few days brought them as close as they'd ever been. Still, they remained fiercely independent.

Snake also got his name for a reason; but it was acquired more recently. Forward scouting missions in Europe had earned him the moniker that stuck. As a young boy living in Mexico, his parents had escaped a harsh life and were lucky to find an American family in Laredo, Texas, that needed help on their farm in exchange for food and shelter. As he learned to speak English, he discovered that not all white people were inhuman.

They hugged the high foothills and made decent time. Nine miles they figured, and no enemy contact. They were feeling pretty good.

"What's that?" Snake pointed off towards the central valley. Birds circled about a mile away.

"Somethings dead, Snake."

"Shouldn't we check it out?"

"Why? This valley has lots of death in it now."

"I know, but there's something about this. I think we should."

"Okay. We're far ahead of the men. We can take a detour. Let's hustle over."

Dropping their packs to the side as a marker, they moved down the rocky terrain into some high grass. Near where the birds circled, they smelled it first.

"I thought so." Said Tracker, as he came upon the bodies.

"Dios mío! Qué horror!" Snake was shaken as he gazed at the fifteen soldiers lying face down. "They're all shot in the head." Snake yelled. "Those...." he couldn't finish. He made the sign of the cross over the men and whispered a prayer.

Tracker bent low and walked amongst the dead. He looked at their patches and checked for officers. He saw a partial armband on a soldier. The body's awkward fall hid it. He turned him to see it and stared with recognition at the Red Cross medic patch. He remembered watching this man administer the fatal morphine to his dying soldiers at the Ridge so they wouldn't be tortured.

"Shit!" Tracker called over to Snake. "These guys are all from the Ridge, Captain Hui's men."

Tracker vividly recalled the battle. Was it a day ago? Time seemed to morph into a cloud. He remembered leaving the Post to help the ROK troops on their flank and tell them they had to withdraw. He remembered the fight at this Ridge, meeting Captain Hui and his dying men.

"Red bastards!" Snake growled.

"Let's go," said Tracker, "nothing we can do here."

"They're just regular soldiers! Why'd they have to kill'em?"

Tracker came over to the visibly shaken Snake. "We've killed many, you and me. Mostly because we had to. But sometimes hate and revenge takes over. I know I'm guilty of that. It's human, Snake; we fuck up. Let it go."

"No! This is wrong! I'll remember this horror until I die!"

When they returned to the pathway, Rusty was resting by their packs. The men were strung out on the path behind him, sitting or lying down.

Rusty knew by their expressions that what they found was bad. He'd seen the birds. Knew there was death to be found. He didn't say anything, just looked at them. Tracker came over to him and sat down. Snake went off farther up the path, away from them.

Tracker sat silent for a moment, looked at Rusty.

"This North Korean tribe has adopted some of the worst practices of my ancestors. That's over a hundred years ago when we were savages." He looked at Rusty, wondering if he thought that way about him. "They don't take prisoners. But if they do, and if there's time or any reason, they torture them. I'm disgusted. Even the Japs took prisoners." On reflection, he added, "Well, sometimes they did."

"How bad is it, Tracker?"

"Captain Hui's soldiers. Fifteen. Back of the head. Execution. No officers."

Rusty took it all in. He was stoic. "I'm starting to hate these Commie bastards. Let' saddle up. You and Snake take the point again. We don't have much light left, and I want to get to our Depot."

Tracker nodded. "It'll be close; it's only a mile or so, we'll get there just before total dark." He left to meet up with Snake.

Rusty walked down amongst the men, checking with each. He found his combat medic, Marty, sitting with his two wounded patients, Joe and Mario.

While assaulting a North Korean General's H Q building, Joe and Mario had sustained life threating wounds. Mario, a newly arrived Ranger, acclaimed mountain climber and preeminent stealth killer, was stabbed in the gut by this general before killing him.

33

Joe had saved Tracker in that same battle because of his heightened sense of immediate danger that nobody could explain, and nobody in the future would fail to ignore. He had jumped into this burning house and killed the solider aiming at Tracker. He was dying of smoke inhalation when, in an effort to escape the smothering smoke, he charged the front door he thought the North Koreans were about to enter, and fell through a grenade hole in the porch floor, hit his head and passed out. He required a long line of stitches across his forehead that looked like the top of his head was affixed to the rest of it; Frankenstein-like.

"How're they doing Marty?"

"Bitching and moaning like new recruits in boot camp."

Joe jumped on that last line. "It's the company, Rusty. He's like a mother hen."

Mario was quick to follow. "He even came over to watch me piss. Claims he was checking to see if this knife wound would bleed. I'm starting to think he may swing both ways." He had to laugh after the words left his mouth. They had just popped in his head. He couldn't believe he had said them.

Joe and Marty also laughed but not Rusty. With a solemn look, he turned to Marty, "So, do you?" Held it for a second then burst out laughing. "Sorry, Marty just couldn't resist."

Marty served with Rusty at the Post for the last year. An Army combat Medic, he'd seen extensive action on the Pacific Island of Okinawa. Stationed near Hiroshima after the war, he set about helping the locals and was instrumental in establishing a mini Army Hospital for their care. Colonel Nelson soon learned of his accomplishments, on and off the battlefield, and elicited his joining his Post team by promising a supportive role for him to enter Harvard Medical School after a year of service in Korea. As an accomplished alumni with a Doctorate in History, Nelson was 'somebody', and Marty jumped at the chance.

Tully came up to them, somewhat agitated. "Are we having a party?"

"Relax, just checking on these two. They're in good form."

34

Rusty looked back at Marty.

"Kidding aside, I want your assessment."

"You know, I'll get even with you," said Marty as he looked over the two, then back at Rusty. "Mario's recovery is nothing more than a miracle. I can't explain how Tracker's treatment at the scene, using that hot bayonet to cauterize that deep knife wound, was so utterly effective, but it was. No bleeding and only minor muscle pain. He's ready to go on any mission."

Rusty looked over at Mario, sitting there with a big ass grin on his face.

"That's what Rangers do!" Tully said and beamed, realizing his soldier was out of any danger.

Now looking at Tully, Marty quipped, "Maybe it's true what they say about Rangers," he paused, "you know, like they're really not human."

That got a grunt out of Rusty and a dirty look from Tully.

"Anyway, Joe's stitches are holding up. He's not wobbly like he was earlier. He still has a minor concussion, so he's somewhat restricted. He shouldn't be exposed to any artillery barrages."

Joe still had a migraine that he hadn't told Marty about, but his sense of humor wasn't diminished. He leaned in and raised his finger to Rusty, "I'm trusting that you're paying attention to doctors' orders."

"Enough of this fun." Rusty said as he stood and headed back to the front of the column. Tully caught up with him.

"Are we near your depot hideout?"

"I told you it's not a hideout. It's well hidden, but it's nothing like the Peak. We have some weapons, ammo and minimum supplies here, nothing else. It'll be okay to stay the night but no longer. We got another mile or so."

"Can we communicate from there?"

"No. We don't have a line-of-sight shot to a tower. Now, go back. We'll stop when we're close. We'll need to reconnoiter the area before we go in."

35

Later, the fading glow from the muted, cloud covered sunset revealed outlines only. Tracker stopped. He was just outside the Depot. He heard nothing. He twitched. Leaning over to Snake's ear he whispered, "Something's wrong. Tell Rusty that this looks like a trap. Come back to this spot."

Minutes passed. Snake returned with Rusty and Tully. They huddled, whispering.

"I got a feeling Rusty. Not sure why."

"Best be safe, Tracker. Never known you to be wrong. Okay! We'll play it like an ambush of an ambush. We'll circle the depot from behind. Everybody light. Snake, take Tully back. Tully, tell Red he's the fire brigade if things go sideways. You bring up Dean, Ben and Marty for this position. Snake, you get Mario and Frenchy and head out to the right. I'm with Tracker circling to the left."

"My pale face chief not thinking right," whispered Tracker. "I want Foxy. Tully can come, but you stay here."

Foxy was a half & half. Dad was American with Nordic features and Mom, first generation Korean. Well educated, from Chicago, he served in Europe from Normandy to the end and spoke fluent Korean.

"He's right," Tully said to Rusty. "You stay here and direct Red if shit happens."

"Ok. Bring the guys up," said Rusty.

The men came, formed a skirmish line around Rusty. Foxy, paired with Tracker and Tully, set out to the left, hugging the cliff. The second team of Mario, Snake and Frenchy crawled right.

Dean, the Ranger sniper, was positioned off to the right of Rusty. He continually scoped the area. Off to the far right, he saw something. He refocused. Zeroing in, he couldn't find anything. He kept at it. Going back and forth with his scope, he stopped again and signaled to Rusty that he saw something over there. He pointed.

Rusty acknowledged with a hand gesture.

The subsequent silence was deafening. Then Dean saw a flash of movement.

Off to the left, a grunt was heard. Not loud, but it was heard in the quiet night as if someone fell or was hit by a baseball bat.

Having taken out the two man on the far right ambush edge, Snake and Mario circled further to the rear of the Depot. Frenchy moved straight ahead, going deeper into the site.

"Halt!" A loud Korean word sounded at his front.

Frenchy turned and yelled back in Korean, "Grey Dragon here!"

Mario and Snake, out of sight, slid off to find the voice.

The voice came back to Frenchy. "Stand! Your men too."

"I'm alone here." He stood. "My men are scattered, looking for deserters."

"You're…" a shot rang out. Frenchy dove to the ground. A few more shots rang out. He couldn't figure from where. He lay still.

"Frenchy!" Came Mario's familiar voice, "You OK?"

"Damn! You took your sweet time!" He called back. "Who the fuck shot that prick?"

Behind him, Dean responded. "Sorry, Frenchy. It looked to me that he didn't buy your bullshit and was about to blow your head off. Maybe I should've waited?"

Frenchy realized his fortune. "No, no! Safe is always best. Thanks!"

Mario called back. "We got the other two with him."

Frenchy landed at Normandy with the 5th Rangers at Omaha and fought through Belgium. Growing up in Champlain, NY, on the border with Canada, where French and English were interchangeable, he spoke French early on. He was not formally educated but had a gift of hearing and understanding languages, particularly if a woman was involved. His liaisons during and after the war enabled him to speak German, some Russian, a good deal of Chinese and he was almost fluent in Korean.

Tully came from the left dragging a body. "This one's still alive."

Foxy followed and joined the men now in the depot area.

"Where's Tracker?" Asked Rusty, having just joined the group.

"He thought there might be more men further back by the cart path." Foxy replied.

"You let him go alone?" Rusty was annoyed.

Foxy didn't like the implication. "I take it you've never seen Tracker in action. I have. I'll attest that he's a one man wrecking crew that prefers to do his thing alone."

Red came up to Rusty. "I put out pickets around the perimeter while you guy's been discussing the weather. What's the situation?"

Mario spoke, "We got five."

Tully added, "We got three. This one," he pointed, "is still breathing."

Rusty grabbed Foxy's arm. "See what you can get from him. I don't like this situation. Make it fast."

Dean came to the backside of the Depot. "Not sure what was supposed to be here, but there's nothing but some empty boxes in the ravine. Is this the Depot?" He moved past the men, came up to Frenchy and tapped him on his head. "Glad it's still there." He quipped.

"Qui! I've grown much attached to it. Thanks!"

"Tully! Red! Come here!" Rusty called. He saw some of the men settling in. He didn't like it.

"We're not staying here. Got to move fast. I think it's a bigger trap than we thought. Red, I want you to take a team to guard our western flank, along that cart path. Take the machine gun and the bazooka. Wait an hour, then follow."

Every team member had memorized the detail map location of this area.

Rusty continued. "Tully, you'll lead the rearguard team as we follow this ridge. When you get to the next high ridge, about a mile south, set up an ambush line. If they get through Red, you're our last guard. We'll proceed another two miles and wait for you."

Red pushed Tully's arm. "Don't you be shooting my men by accident. Nobody's getting through us."

"Then somebody better be singing something American," was Tully's response.

Tracker came in out of the dark just then. "I hope we're moving chief. Got two more trying to flee. Spirits tell me bad things coming to us."

Rusty rarely knew when Tracker was real or was faking his Indian Tribal heritage stuff. He did know that he rarely was wrong. He listened.

"OK." He called to Red and Tully. "Let's get moving." Rusty was nervous, felt jumpy. Not a familiar feeling.

Foxy came over to him. Rusty was abrupt. "Did he say anything?"

"Oh yeah! He just told me this is a trap, a big trap. A full platoon is involved. More squads are at the ready, standing by, near the main road, two miles away."

"Shit!" It was much worse than he thought.

"Red! Tully! Come!" He yelled.

They heard his urgency, came running.

"Big change!" Rusty huddled with them. "Forget what I said. We're staying here and fighting. A large force is approaching. If we don't stop them now, they'll keep pursuing us, bring in more troops to help. I think their main force is about to capture the Capital and nobody gives a shit about what's happening with stragglers, like us, in the rear. We need to stop these guys. Now!"

"Good!" Said Red. "Never fought a rear action I liked. As you said before, Rusty, an ambush of an ambush. Let's fuck'em at their own game."

Tully was relieved he wasn't in charge of protecting their rear. His strength was attacking, and said so, "I'll take a small team to their rear. How big is this force anyway?"

Rusty smiled at the Ranger. "Only you would ask about the strength of the attacking force after you volunteered."

"That's why I'm here." He looked at Red, then Rusty. "Someone's got to save you sorry ass Army guys."

Red slapped Tully's back, "I love this Ranger!"

Rusty looked at them. "Here's my plan."

A few minutes later, the teams moved out. The ascending larger crescent Moon shimmered a slight light through the patchy clouds.

South of the Cart Path

Red's team entered the rice paddy south of the cart path and moved west towards the expected enemy approach. The water was only a few inches deep. They found a berm twenty-five yards off the path and got behind it. Red organized the men.

"Ben, take the machine gun to the west edge. You're our flank guard. You engage the center first. Marty, you're with him. Go! Larry! Over there". He pointed.

"Arron! Come with me." They settled into the water of the rice patty as Red got the bazooka set. "Arron, I know you can't hit a goddamn barn door from ten feet away, so just load this mother and duck."

"Can't help it if my training was deficient," Arron whispered and smiled to himself, knowing Red had instructed all the men a few days before.

This was a diverse team that had not worked closely together before. Ben was a new Ranger arrival who was morose, combative and often said he was cursed by death claiming his close friends throughout his life, particularly during the war and more recently over the last few days. When his best friend, severely wounded, was rescued in the middle of a difficult battle by flying Ace, Wild Bill Stands, his spirits soared, felt his curse was broken. He had hope and started to smile.

An oncoming dim light appeared in the distance.

On the North Side of the Cart Path

Tully's team ran down the cart path until they saw a distant light. They veered off the path and continued through the knee-high grass, then waded into the rice paddies. He waved the team to stop. Well to the rear of the other teams, he bet this spot would be beyond the enemy's rear column when the ambush was sprung. He disbursed his men but kept Frenchy at his side. He paused a moment, thought about *"his men"*. No longer distinguishing between his Rangers or Rusty's Army Post men, he thought, no, they're not *my* men. I'm just in charge of their lives for the moment.

Tully's group held the best stealth team. Snake, the ghost. Mario, shadow of the ghost. Tracker, a wisp on the tail of a ghost.

He leaned in close to Frenchy, whispered, "You may have to give your finest Korean performance if we're spotted."

Frenchy whispered back. "I'm a gifted actor! And shit! Did you think I might speak French to them?"

They waited.

The Depot

This area was isolated, like an Island amongst rice patties with a foreboding mountain at its rear. The cart path from the main road meandered through the rice patties then straightened out to the Depot and then curved south, hugging the mountains edge.

The terrain offered excellent cover. The fast rising foothills lacked trees and high bushes, but the rock outcroppings provided great protection and a good field of fire.

Rusty set his binoculars down next to him, disturbed by what he had just viewed. Armored vehicles were not what he expected. Not tanks, they looked like half-tracks. Bad enough, he thought. The subdued moonlight hid details, but he could see two vehicles, troops in front and behind the first half track, but it was a bad angle. He couldn't see beyond that second half-track.

"Dean!" Rusty called over to the sniper. "Are you seeing this?"

"Of course! My scope is much better than your piece of shit. What do you want?"

Rusty realized how tense he, and probably everyone else had gotten. This was now a life and death situation. His ambush plan could quickly turn into their death trap.

"Can you see beyond the second vehicle?"

A moment or two passed.

"No! Can't see clearly, but there are silhouettes. I think troops. The front elements are approaching your ambush start. Do you want me to go as planned?"

Dean's shot was to be the signal to start the ambush at a given point. He was tasked to take out the leading officer. His kill priorities descended from there. With his experience from landing with Tully's platoon at Point De Hoc, Normandy, to the end, he needed no micro direction. If records were kept, he probably was the best American sniper in WW2. A self-contained person, he was thankful for his British Sniper training in England, since his American Army offered none. He had saved many of his friends.

"Yes! Don't miss!" Rusty came back with a tone reflecting the anxiety he felt.

Dean grunted back. "You don't know me well. Relax, I've seen much worse. You've got Rangers here!"

Joe, not far away, heard the exchange. He called out, "He's much better than he looks, Rusty." He raised his voice, "Does anyone have odds yet?" He paused, "Long has it's less than ten to one, we're good." His Brooklyn accent came out. It usually did when he was anxious.

Moose, the huge Ranger, readied his BAR to take out the lead element. Laid out next to him was ten of his twenty ammo box loads for fast loading.

Foxy crawled forward, away from his assigned position. He saw a gap that could be trouble in their defense. He found a place.

South of the Cart Path

Arron reacted at the sound of the tracks. "Holy shit! We got tanks, Red!"

"Quiet! I don't know what we got here. It doesn't matter if it's the fucking Queen Mary. You just load and duck. Got it?"

Arron feared tanks more than anything. He wanted to run.

It Began

Dean's shot rang out above the vehicle noise. The officer on the lead half-track fell back.

Red was tracking the first half-track with his bazooka. At Deans shot, Red fired. Swoosh! The rocket hit dead center of the half-track and exploded. Big and bright.

Firing from the ambush teams started with the first shot. But Tully's team remained quiet and moved out of the rice paddies onto the cart path and came at the enemy's rear.

A ten man enemy squad trailed the second half-track. Diving at the first shot, the enemy crawled forward seeking more cover from the half-track. The noise was intense. Ben's machine gun was firing into the soldiers between the half-tracks. Heavy firing was being returned to Red's team by four of the prone rear guards.

Men in the second half-track swung their heavy caliber machine gun to answer the attack from Red's position as well and immediately started shooting.

Tully's men ran forward to within twenty feet of the prone troops and ripped into them with their Tommy's on full auto. Tully kept running, grabbed a grenade off his belt, dropped to his knee ten feet from the tracked vehicle, pulled the pin and lobbed it into the open compartment where the machine gunners were firing. A rocket swished out the front of the vehicle and went north. Tully went flat and rolled. He heard the dull sound of his grenade going off in the compressed area where the gunners were.

Frenchy landed next to him with a thump. "You Ok?" He asked, not waiting for an answer he continued. "The rear guard are dead."

A soldier appeared coming around the rear edge of the vehicle and was knocked flat by a burst from Mario, crouched behind Tully and Frenchy.

Tully turned to Mario, signaled him to move forward along the north side of the vehicle. Snake followed. Tracker moved into the rice patty on the north side going forward.

Following Rusty's plan, Red's team stopped firing after the initial action if Red determined his part was over. Red was to move closer to the Depot, to cover Rusty's flank. The move was also intended to minimize a friendly fire accident with Tully's team attacking from the rear.

The fire from the burning first half-track had set the enemy soldiers in silhouette.

It wasn't fair. But Rusty was relieved. He didn't want fair.

It didn't take long till the firing stopped.

Shouting repeatedly in Korean, "Surrender!" a few soldiers stood with arms raised. They were brought forward by Tully, Mario and Frenchy. Frenchy directed them in Korean.

A few shots rang out behind them in the column. All ducked.

They heard Snake yell, "Just cleaning up! No worry!"

Tracker emerged from the shadows totally soaked. He held his hatchet at his side. "No one left in the patties." He said as he passed the group.

Relieved that his decision didn't kill them all, Rusty surveyed the aftermath for a moment and made his homage to the war Gods and carried on.

"Foxy! You and Snake find out what you can from these bastards. I want to know if they killed those ROK prisoners."

"Where's Red?" Rusty yelled, realizing Red's team hadn't come in.

"Here!" Red called, as he joined the gathering.

Rusty turned to him. Saw that behind him, Marty and Arron were carrying a body.

"NO!" He screamed.

The men reacted, running to help. There was nothing to help but take the body.

Marty called out like he was crying. "I couldn't save him!"

Red grabbed his shoulders. "Marty! Ben was shot through the neck! Only God could've saved him!"

Off to the side, away from the group, Snake stood with his Thompson pointing at the five squatting prisoners. Foxy knelt, interrogating them. Snake was surprised they responded to questions. Flashing through his mind, like a lightning storm, were the images of the dead ROK soldiers he found. He saw that these guys were scared, but resigned. Hardened soldiers, he thought, they'd seen much death. He wished he could understand what was said. Then they all bowed at the last question and murmured something. Foxy rose.

"Did they do it?"

Foxy knew what he meant. "Yes. Orders were their excuse. Said they were sorry."

"Believe them?"

"No! Got to tell Rusty some info. Be right back."

Foxy found Rusty standing over Ben's body. Came right up to him. Rusty turned to him with a blank look.

"You okay, Rusty?"

"Yeah." He lied. "What'd you get?"

"The rest of their unit moved south for the push on Seoul. They didn't alert anyone. Out of radio range."

They both jumped at the burst of automatic fire at their rear. Men hit the deck.

Foxy knew.

"Sorry!" Snake yelled as he came from the firing. "They tried to escape."

Rusty shook his head. He'd seen this before. Turning away from them he walked slowly towards the Depot.

Joe came over to Marty. Knelt next to Ben. Dean followed. "We'll bury him." They said in unison.

Behind them, Arron said, "When we buried our Confederate soldiers on Yankee soil, we sang a song for them. I think we should do the same for Ben. I'll help bury him."

Dean, Ben's fellow Ranger said, "Ben's from Baltimore. But I'd like to sing a song for him. What did you guys sing?"

"*Oh Shenandoah* is what we sang, do you know it?"

They dug a shallow grave and sang a verse for Ben. It wasn't just for Ben. They hadn't yet mourned their other friends.

Both Tully and Red realized how demoralizing a loss could have on a leader in the midst of a great victory. Rusty showed the signs. They gathered around him. Ben was a Ranger. Tully's guy. So he spoke first.

"I've told you this before, Rusty, but you need to hear it again. You saved our asses here. We could all be dead now, but for your leadership. You've done this a few times since I've been here. You're good. Red and me make you better; don't forget it."

Rusty nodded. "Thanks. Now, let's get the hell out of here."

Chapter Eight

Tuesday, June 27, 1950   Day Three of the Invasion
Suwon Airport – Twenty miles South of Seoul
– 1900 – (7:00 pm)

Wild Bill spent the entire day avoiding contact with anybody of rank, and that hadn't been easy. Two US transports had arrived sometime after he was in the hanger inspecting his new baby, *JUST DUE.*

The planes brought many officers, generals on down. He didn't want to be questioned about why he was here. He had his orders and had his plane. All he wanted was to contact his boss, *my favorite Colonel*, as he called Colonel Nelson, and get the hell out of here. But he couldn't.

The primitive airport control tower was packed with the new arrival of staff officers trying to establish contact with their headquarters in Japan. As it turned out, the airport had no means of communicating with Japan. The line to the Korean Cable relay station in town was disabled, and nobody seemed to know how to fix it. He was appalled by this lack of functioning equipment. Abandoned trucks, folk lifts, and jeeps lay idle everywhere. The radar in the tower didn't work. He learned much by wandering the airport.

Chaos is what he found. Thousands of ROK soldiers milled around, seemingly, without leadership. On his return, he did find an organized effort around the hanger next to his. Gene was yelling directions to a platoon of ROK soldiers loading boxes onto three trucks in front of theirs.

He waved to him as he entered his hanger through a small door on the side of the building. Gene didn't respond.

His hanger was dark except for the small lights at the back around the plane. Men were talking, then a curse, and another. They didn't hear him. Parts were strewn around. A man's legs showed, resting on the canopy, his body was hidden in the engine. He heard banging noises from the far side and more curses.

He yelled, "Billy! It's not running! What the hell is going on!?"

A body came out of the engine. Billy was covered in oil. "Captain!" He had this guilty look like he'd been caught at something he did wrong.

The Captain glared at him.

That got Billy more uptight. He jumped onto the ladder, rushed down to him, blabbering all the way. "I haven't stopped since you left. This bird is screwed up. Been sitting for a year! I haven't found out why it was left yet. I know there's a reason." He kept talking. "Arnie and George have been at it too. They drained and cleaned the gas tanks. They're working on cleaning the machine guns."

"Stop!" Wild Bill realized Billy didn't get his humorous side. He knew he could be excessive sometimes in his demands. "You're doing a good job, Billy! Just anxious to get him going. Any idea when?"

"That's what I've been trying to tell you. He's almost ready for an engine test. That's when I can find out what's wrong. All this other shit needs to happen first before we test."

"So! When?"

"Got a few more hours of stuff to get done tonight. Tomorrow we'll test."

"Good. Because we've got to get out of here soon."

Billy reacted, looked scared. "What'd' ya you mean?"

"Shit's following us, Billy. We need to move faster." He looked around, puzzled.

"Where's George?"

"Here!" George came out from behind the plane.

"Damn! You look a whole lot better than this morning!" Gene had found him new fatigues and boots.

"Feel better too! Nothing like food and some sleep."

"Come with me. Let's sit in the corner. I want to hear your story."

Over the next hour, George recounted his last three days.

Japan - Eighth Army Headquarters – Colonel Nelson's Office – 1930 – (7:30 pm)

Major Jarvis started his first briefing. A new experience. Since the invasion, activity had increased to such a level that Colonel Nelson decided he needed to maintain an overview of events and not be bogged down in the minutia of daily activity. Doubling of his staff left him no choice.

"Stop! Hank! No details. I only want to know what you think is important. Big picture and oddball events. Things you're not sure of, you're the boss. I trust your judgment. My only exception relates to the Post Teams. I want to be involved directly. On everything! I will take calls from them. They are my personal responsibility. Do you understand this?"

"Yes, sir." He shifted in his seat. "I'll start over."

"Good." He didn't know the major well. He was handpicked a year ago to replace his retiring second but had had little interaction with him over the dull period. Jarvis was exceptionally gifted. Brilliant, was the word often used in his file. Nelson's mentor, General Bill Donavan had recommended Hank Jarvis, and Nelson didn't hesitate to bring him in as his Executive Officer. Though he liked Jarvis, Nelson held many aspects of his command close and hadn't fully included him until now.

"General Walker has set a meeting with all staff for 0800 (8:00 am) tomorrow in the new Staff HQ at the recreation building. They've been working on setting it up since early today."

49

"Are you prepared?"

"Not yet, but I will be."

"We'll meet here at five am to review what we've got. Bring the team."

"Right." Major Jarvis fiddled with his notes, not quite prepared to finish the briefing, then started.

His presentation ended an hour later. Alone, Nelson thought it had been a hell of a day. News of contact with survivors of Post # 4 brightened his spirits. At least that's something. Nothing from the other Posts. Damn. Well, at least Eighth Army is making moves. Yeah, he thought, we're coming, and soon. But it sure as hell going to be bloody. We're not ready. But we'll get ready! And damned fast. He finished his thoughts, determined them to be mostly positive.

Korea – On the East Coast – South of the Town of Yangyang – 2100 – (9:00 pm)

In the interior of the funnel top of their mountain hideout, the men, fed and rested, talked.

"How's that radio going, Phil?"

"Can't find the problem, Jack. It got bounced around a lot. Didn't see any damaged tubes, think it's a connection somewhere. I'll try again tomorrow."

"You know this radio?" Asked Greg.

"Oh, yeah. German. Came out at the end. Best portable radio in the war. Those Nazi's were good. We were very fortunate this didn't get brought to the field earlier in the war, it's that good."

"Who're we gonna call anyway?" JP asked.

Jack had to laugh. "Anybody, asshole! Maybe that Cruiser if she comes back. Maybe the Marine landing force that shows up. How the hell do I know?"

Undeterred, JP went on. "I mean, do you have a plan? Waiting doesn't seem like much of a plan."

It was so dark; nobody could see five feet. Jack spoke to the voice. "I told you we're winging it. My plan is to keep us alive until we can figure out what's next. So stop asking me!"

Greg was working his new found Russian assault automatic weapon. "Seems simple enough. You ever fire one of these, Jack?"

"No. We didn't meet any Russians in the Pacific. I've only seen photos. Only know the Russians made a million or so of them. Don't know anything more about it."

JP chimed in, always ready to lodge a complaint. "Heavy weapon with this drum magazine. Must be 100 rounds in here. Funny looking shells too, smaller than our regular stuff. Wonder if it has stopping power?"

"You're an ass! It killed six of our guys, didn't it?"

"I wasn't thinking. Sorry, Jack." He paused, then JP continued. "Hate to give up my Thompson. How about I keep mine? You guys give me your ammo. That should be enough for me."

"That's it! You stop this crap! We don't have enough Tommy ammo between us to give you two magazines. We're not going to die because you ran out of ammo with your favorite weapon. Get it?"

Greg filled the intermittent silence. "I kind'a like the feel."

"It's what we got. Be thankful we've got something to shoot."

"Jesus! I'm with you, Jack!" Greg had the last word of the evening.

Chapter Nine

**Wednesday, June 28, 1950 – Day Four of the Invasion
Korea – The Post Men – Twenty-four miles northeast of Seoul
–0400 – (4:00 am)**

Sensing movement, Joe stirred. It was Marty.

"Sorry."

"Sorry, is if I shot you. Why're you up?"

"Couldn't sleep."

Joe got up, moved to a nearby rock and relieved himself. "What's wrong, Marty? Is it Ben?"

"Don't know. Yeah! I think Ben dying in my arms triggered this feeling. Weird. Never felt this way before. Got this black cloud in my head. Don't think I'm gonna make it to medical school. Don't think I'm going home at all."

"Oh, that shit!"

"What're you saying?"

"Jesus, Marty! We're in a freaking mess. Don't you think we all feel this way?"

"Do you?"

"I consider myself sane. Well, maybe mostly. But yeah, I'm not sure this is gonna work out. But I didn't think I'd survive Flatbush Ave either. And then there was Okinawa. Shit, I didn't think I would see another day, and that was day, after day, for three months. I don't know what to tell you other than it's out of your hands. Do your best, but if it's your turn…"

"Joe, I'm scared; I hate to admit it, but I don't want to die now."

"Marty! Snap out of it! Natural you feeling like this. Rusty said you defended an aid station about to be overrun by the Japs. Do you remember the fear you felt? But you stayed and fought. Stick with that, because that's who you are!"

The rest of the men stirred, did their morning thing, got organized. A new day.

"Tracker! Come here!" Rusty sat with Red and Tully.

"You think we can make this next ten miles within these rock foothills? Or should we go higher?"

Tracker looked stoically at him. "Paleface Chief, you think I foresee future? It's been seven or eight months since I scouted this area. From here to the end of the mountain break, there is no tree or bush cover. The ravines, ridges and gorges are the only cover. It should be enough for us. As far as making it? I can only guarantee success if I scout ahead."

Tully jumped in. "You fucking Indian scouts led Custer to his end. Be more careful this time."

Tracker wasn't fazed. "Not my Tribe. Besides, Custer was an ass." Tully had to laugh.

"I want Snake. You follow in an hour."

Rusty looked at Red and Tully. They nodded, but Rusty added. "OK, Tracker. But I want Joe with you."

"You think I need a good luck charm?"

"Thought maybe you could use a little extra help."

"Okay. Joe's good. He has Spirit."

They moved out.

Suwon Airport – 20 miles South of Seoul – 0530 – (5:30 am)

At the front door of their hanger, Gene yelled in, "Got hot chow by the tower! Good too!" He disappeared.

53

Billy was the first to move. "Let's go guys; I'm starving."

"Hold up, Billy. We'll go together. Need a volunteer to stay and guard my plane."

George spoke up. "I got it! Bring me back something."

The Captain turned to him. "Remember, no one goes near that plane. No one!"

For emphasis, George picked up his Thompson, held it in one hand by his side. "Roger that, Captain."

Walking across the tarmac toward the tower, activity around them was impressive. It seemed like thousands of ROK soldiers were being lined up, armed and directed to nearby trucks.

"Hope they're going north. What d'ya think Captain?"

"Not a clue, Billy. The only thing I see on these guys is defeat. You notice that they all have different unit patches? Not a good sign."

The chow line wasn't long. The field kitchen was restricted to US soldiers and ROK top brass. The only two tables, off to the side, were settled by high-ranking US officers, including a general. The rest of the soldiers had hot trays on their laps and coffee cups on the ground. They sat on a nearby stack of machine parts and boxes.

They found an open area and sat on the ground leaning against some crates.

"I haven't had a hot breakfast like this in a long while." Said Arnie, between mouthfuls.

The captain was more concerned with the officers at the tables. He'd spent all of yesterday avoiding them and now they were twenty feet away. Shit, he thought, this was dumb. Should've taken off my bars.

Captain "Wild Bill" Stands stood out like a lighthouse at midnight. His large frame of six two, coupled with his blonde hair and Hollywood looks made him an immediate beacon to be inspected. And he was.

A colonel got up from one of the tables and came over. "Captain, the general would like a word with you."

Nelson followed him back, did a perfunctory salute and was asked to sit. The general eyed him, gazed at his Eighth Army patch, his pilot wings and scruffy look.

"Who the hell are you and what are you doing here?"

"Strange circumstances bring me here, sir. I'm Captain Bill Stands, Eighth Army Intelligence."

"You didn't answer my question, Captain. What are you doing here?"

"Sir, I'm under orders to tell no one of my mission."

"What? I'm General Church! I command every unit in Korea. Don't get insubordinate or I'll throw you in the brig! What's your mission!?"

Wild Bill had a premonition something like this might happen. He relaxed in his chair and composed his thoughts, stared at the general.

"Sir, I venture to say that you've got a lot on your plate. Like a whole country. My mission here is secret. If anything, it's to help you if I'm successful."

He paused, seeing the general relaxing his posture, Wild Bill continued. "I can't take orders from you. You're not in my command structure unless you relieved General Walker as the new Eighth Army Commander. Have you?"

"You're a cocky son of a bitch, aren't you?"

"No, sir. Just a good soldier following orders, sir."

"You better be who you say you are. You're dismissed!"

Walking back to the hanger, Billy, unnerved by what he witnessed, said, "Captain! You seemed to have really pissed off that general. Are we in trouble?"

Feeling carefree, Wild Bill laughed. "Trouble! From that general? No Billy, trouble hasn't arrived yet."

Billy expected the captain to elaborate, but he just kept walking, smiling. Damn, he thought, this guy *is* Wild. Never seen an angry general before and the captain doesn't seem to give a shit. Damn! What the hell did I sign on to?

Chapter Ten

**Wednesday, June 28, 1950 – Day Four of the Invasion
Japan - Eighth Army Headquarters – New Army Staff
Headquarters in the Recreation Building
–0800 – (8:00 am)**

First Meeting

Dictated by the political demands to reduce costs, four years ago the Army changed its long-held doctrine to have General staffs at the Army and Corps level. Those functions reverted to division level.

Until now.

General Walker disobeyed the Joints Chief of Staff order yesterday.

Before then, Eighth Army Headquarters Staff consisted of thirty men of rank. In a moment, he was going to address over two hundred men of his new HQ staff.

The Rec building was the biggest on the base. In just a few hours, it had been transformed into a working grand ballroom hub. A maze of dangling wires from the ceiling to tables, phones and teletype printers everywhere. It was crude but fully functional.

At the hour, General Walker walked into the assembled staff. He looked not as he was. Short and stout of frame, he didn't look commanding. If you thought that, well, you would be like many Nazi's that died before his brilliant tactical leadership of General Patton's Third Army's leading spear Amour Corps Commander. He was, in WW2, one of the most fearsome of American Generals. Flexible, bold and intuitive.

"I don't give good speeches." He paused as the group murmured. "But I call it as I see it."

Walking to the side, he composed his thoughts.

"You're the brains of this **Eighth Army**! I don't care what division you're from! This Army commands many divisions, and you serve them all. That's right! I said you serve them all. And you will!"

He paused.

"We face a daunting task. We're not at total war yet. Our men have not been committed to the ground yet. That will change. When the balloon goes up, I expect Eighth Army to respond immediately. That's your job! We need to stop these Commies from taking this country. You've been at it for one full day. I hope it's been productive."

Colonel Harris joined the general at his side.

"This is your new boss, Eighth Army Executive Officer, Colonel Harris. Before I turn this over to him, I want Lieutenant Abraham Zelts to stand."

From the back of the hall, a young man rose. He looked dumbfounded. "Here, sir!"

"You were in charge of loading the first ship of munitions we sent to Pusan the day after the invasion. Is that right?"

Ramrod straight, he answered. "Yes, sir!"

"You added four bulldozers and two cranes that weren't authorized. Why?"

Nervous, he promptly replied. "Sir! I went to Pusan a month ago. Knew the port was a mess, that they would need heavy equipment to unload and move our munitions. My orders said munitions and supplies. I interpreted supplies to mean equipment as well, sir."

The general now looked around the room and said, "That's what I want from each of you! Think! Anticipate! Be flexible! It turns out that, without that equipment, it would have taken two more days to get those munitions to where it was needed, and we'd still require the machinery for follow-on shipments!"

Abraham noticeably relaxed. Thank God, he thought.

The general focused back on him. "For your initiative, Mr. Zelts, you've been promoted to Captain, effective immediately."

Clapping began, then exploded. Rare to see a young, lowly staff officer achieve recognition.

Colonel Harris took charge. Each section reported.

Chapter Eleven

**Wednesday, June 28, 1950 – Day Four of the Invasion
Korea – On the East Coast – South of the Town of
Yangyang – 1030 – (10:30 am)**

The morning passed slowly. Intermittent rain added to the men's moodiness and discomfort. No slickers or shelter from the elements made the waiting that much worse. Stoppages of rain brought some activity, but usually, the next cloud came along all too quickly, preventing completion of a task just started.

As usual, JP was restless. Griping since he awoke, he finally settled into a mumbling silence, seemingly talking to himself but not getting any feedback.

Since they got back from their scrounging yesterday, Jack had been studying an enemy map taken from a dead officer. It was detailed, covering the coast all the way to the city of Pusan, some hundred miles away, right to the tip of the peninsula.

Jack couldn't figure out what to do. Kept rattling around the options in his mind. Do we go over the mountains to the west? But we don't have maps there. Where would we come out? Could we even do it? Do we follow the coast south through enemy lines? For a hundred miles! Damn, I believe in luck but not miracles. Do we wait for something? Like another ship with a rescue party? You're kidding! Nobody is coming for us! Whatever happens, we're gonna do it ourselves. But what?

Jack decided to share his dilemma with the men, if for nothing else than to pass the time. They talked awhile, exchanged some ideas then lapsed into silence as the issue went unresolved.

Minutes passed, then JP jumped up. "I got it! It's so simple!"

They had witnessed JP's performance in the past and just stared at him as if he were an idiot.

"We'll hijack a boat!" He yelled.

Jack, stunned, did a double take. Greg and Phil frowned, they knew nothing about boats. But Jack did. He knew a lot about boats.

"Jesus Christ!" Jack said. "I know you almost a fucking year, and that's the first damn intelligent thing that's ever come out of your mouth!"

"Really?" Shocked, JP thought he was making a joke.

Jack grew up in Warwick, Rode Island. The harsh mill town was situated right on Narragansett Bay, one of the most beautiful places in the world to sail. He loved sailing. From age five, he sailed with his dad on their twenty-foot sloop every chance they could. When he reached twelve, his dad let him take it out by himself, although he often had his best friend, Steve, with him.

Steve was the reason he joined the Army, not the Navy, which had been his first choice. They were promised that they could serve together in the same unit, the Navy couldn't promise that. The Army was true to its word. They landed together on Saipan. Steve was killed on the second day.

The rain paused again. Jack took out the map, now searching with different eyes. Sure enough, he found a small hamlet in a cove only a few miles south of them. Got to have a boat there, he thought.

"I got a plan!" He said excitedly. "JP! I could kiss you! But you're not my type."

Unusually, JP didn't know what to say.

Greg was not so stunned, "Where're we gonna get a boat?"

"There's a fishing village not far from here. That's where."

"How do you know they got a boat?" Greg persisted.

"It's a fishing village! They've got to have a boat. Pretty sure anyway. Tonight, we'll go steal ourselves our escape boat."

"You know anything about boats? Sure as shit, none of us do." Quipped Greg.

"Oh yeah, I do." He filled them in on his sailing experience.

"Phil! You haven't said a word. You Ok?"

"Just frustrated. Can't find the problem with this radio. Every time I get it out of the case it starts raining. Water's not good for these things. If I find the problem now, I'm not sure it will work because of the moisture."

"We didn't have a radio before, at least we have a chance for one now, so don't give up. What do you think of our plan?"

"Don't know! Kinda feel like that saying, jumping from the frying pan into the fire. But if you think it's the best way, I'm on board, literally."

"Your idea JP. Why're you looking so down?"

"Because I was just being my wiseass self. Really, I was just trying to be funny. Boats scare the shit out of me Jack. I get seasick at the thought of being on the water."

Jack acknowledged with a nod, "Then it's unanimous."

Looking around at his team. "No other way makes sense to me. We go today. Start down around five thirty. That'll give us two hours of light and a half hour of twilight. We'll have a sliver of a new rising Moon if there are no clouds. That should put us at the village around nine or so, give us time to reconnoiter. We'll make our move around midnight."

"You sure about this, Jack?" Asked Phil.

"Yes! Are you worried we may have to do some night work? You have done it before, haven't you?"

"Yeah, a few times. Never liked it, though. Slitting throats is not my thing."

"Never met anyone who thought otherwise. Kill or be killed, right?"

Greg and JP shared Phil's feelings. All three answered in unison. "Right."

61

Suwon Airport – Twenty miles South of Seoul
– 1400 – (2:00 pm)

Gene came into the hanger looking worried. Wild Bill was sitting on a crate studying maps.

"Hey, Captain! Just got word that Kimipo fell last night. Looks like Seoul's gonna surrender today."

"Not like it's a surprise, Gene. You almost finished?"

"Yeah, got another hour or two. How's the repair going?"

"Slowly but surely. Do you know what you're doing after you're finished passing out the ammo to the ROK's?"

"Yeah. A captain came by telling me we're to join General Church's men, assemble by the control tower late today."

"Hope you guys are leaving soon. It's gonna get hairy around here in a day or so."

"Shit, I hope we're out of here tonight. Gotta get back, see you later."

Wild Bill decided he couldn't wait any longer. He had to get hold of Colonel Nelson. Not wanting another run-in with the general, he had put off going to the newly erected communication center. Every half hour he had peered out of the hanger checking on the activity around this center, hoping the general would leave the airfield on a sightseeing mission. But he hadn't. A steady stream of ROK officers going to and fro was all he saw.

The Captain yelled as he stood, "Billy! You any closer to testing him?"

"Yeah! Almost there. About a half hour…maybe."

"Got to go make a call, be back in a few. Don't start him until I get back."

Surprised by the absence of ROK troops, he walked to the new radio center. It wasn't far away, near the control tower, it was a hanger, three hangers up across the tarmac from him. The weather was dark, heavy air, with low clouds and light rain. Same as it's been all morning. A sudden break in the cloud cover, with the sun shining through would occasionally occur, surprising the onlooker and lulling him into thinking the rain pattern had stopped. It hadn't.

The big hanger doors were open. Tables set up on the side and back. Makeshift desks were strewn about with men sitting on crates speaking on phones. A teletype machine off in the corner was clanking away. Lots of small groups were milling about.

He saw no general. That's a break, he thought. He spotted a lieutenant who seemed to know what was going on and went over to him. It was the same Lieutenant he met at the gate yesterday.

"Hey Captain, you find your guys?"

"Yeah, thanks. Now I need to call my boss in Japan."

"See that big console? Tell the sergeant operator who you want; he'll get you a phone."

After a short wait, he was directed to a phone station, sat on a crate and picked up the phone.

"Major Jarvis!"

"Captain Stands calling for Colonel Nelson."

"About damn time. What's your situation?"

"Who the hell are you and where is Nelson?"

"Right. You're true to form, Captain. Colonel Nelson is unavailable now. I'm now operational officer for G-2. Our staff has gotten much larger, but I'm tuned into your situation. Did you get the plane?"

"It's being worked on as we speak. Don't know if he'll fly yet. Still at the airfield with a gaggle of General Church's crowd. What're my orders?"

"What'd you do to the general to piss him off so much? His executive officer called earlier checking on you. Said he wanted to put you in charge of a shit cleaning operation. I spent twenty minutes with this guy. Told him to back off, that you were under personal orders of General Walker."

"Just a minor misunderstanding about chain of command. What's my orders?"

"Get that bird up and out of there, ASAP. Go to Taejon. That's our assembly point. It has a cable station. Ever fly in there?"

"Know where it is but never been."

"It's worse than Suwon. Much smaller but it'll handle the P-51. We're sending up supplies and fuel from Pusan. You need to move fast, Captain. Seoul just surrendered."

"Call you when I get there. Tell my favorite colonel to get more P-51s. Even though I'm here, one just isn't enough."

The sun had just popped out of the clouds as Nelson left the hanger and started across the field. He heard the engine, turned around, looked up and saw a plane diving right towards him. He dove to the ground, listened to the machine gun fire and watched as the bullets came right over his head. They stitched their way along the tarmac, hitting two men, knocking them off their feet. The bullets raced towards his hanger, but the pattern angled right, over to Gene's hanger. The truck in front was riddled. It and the hanger exploded. The sides of the walls blew out, and the roof collapsed. It burst into flames. Another enemy fighter strafed the only plane visible at the airport; a transport sitting on the northern section of the airfield turned it into an inferno.

Thankfully, clouds rolled in and it started pouring. Wild Bill lay still, somewhat shaken by his near death. He waited for the next pass. After a few minutes, surprised at no follow-up, he got up.

A fire engine pulled up to the burning hanger as men ran by him. Bodies were lying in front of the structure, mostly around a destroyed burning truck.

The Captain felt lucky to be alive. He was angry. He almost bought it. Couldn't imagine not dying in a plane. That's how he wanted to go. Not on a goddamned tarmac!

He found Billy and his crew dragging bodies away from the wreckage, trying to help the wounded. But there were only bodies. He had passed the two dead men on the tarmac. A sergeant and a corporal. Yeah, he thought, could've been me.

"Sons of bitches!" Billy yelled as he pulled Gene's mangled body away from the burning truck.

"Sorry, Billy." The Captain laid a hand on his shoulder, "Come on. Nothing more we can do here."

Korea – The Post Men – Fourteen Miles northeast of Seoul – 1630 – (4:30 pm)

As Tracker predicted, the terrain changed from easy to something close to impossible. Stark and desolate, ugly brownish gray rock ridges and ravines splayed out from the mountain like spokes on a wheel. Their route south looked ominously like crossing the ocean swell in near storm conditions, with each ridge revealing the next trough and the next wave to surmount. Some ravines were twenty feet deep and long while others were shallow but short. Flat areas didn't exist, even the wide ravines undulated. The biggest obstacle was that there was little solid rock. It seemed as though the mountain had had a recent landslide. The surface consisted of loose rocks of all sizes, and there was a total absence of trees or bushes.

The going was less than slow, more like a crawl. Each man carried a minimum of a hundred and fifty pounds on their backs, plus weapons, plus three canteens of water. It was brutal, exhausting and painful. Men tripped and fell often. Adding to the misery, it rained hard.

The three point men were in line, twenty feet apart with Tracker at the center, Joe in the lead and Snake at the rear.

"Hold up! Joe! Come in!" Tracker yelled over the sound of the heavy rain. Turning around, "Snake! Come in!"

They huddled.

Tracker had been here before. "There's a hamlet about a mile to our west. We should check it out before going farther. I'm not sure we could go much longer anyway, we should take a serious break."

"I've done some crazy damn trekking before but this…I vote yes, we stop." Joe leaned against a boulder.

Snake had already removed his backpack and crumbled flat against the angle of the ridge. "Good!"

"I'll tell Rusty. Stay awake!" Said Tracker.

Rusty was in a foul mood. He had fallen so many times he didn't know where most of his pain came from. Everything hurt.

Soaked to the bone, hungry for something hot and depressed about the lack of progress, none the less he kept up a good façade. He knew the men felt the same and they weren't bitching. Well, most weren't.

He took Trackers advice well. Told Foxy to go back with him and scout that area. They'll spend the night where they had stopped.

Returning, they found Snake curled up asleep on his side. Joe was eating out of a can. Joe greeted Foxy.

"Nice of you to join the front line troops. Did you bring a tarp?"

"I brought hope. Hope you don't choke on that can of shit you're eating. And hey, you lucky dog, your weather out here is so much better. Glad I came!"

"Why are you here?"

"We're gonna scout that hamlet. Might need my language skills. But first, I'm taking a break."

He took off his gear, collapsed on some rocks and fell asleep.

Twenty minutes later he awoke with a start, looked around at Tracker. "You ready?"

"No. But I guess we should go before the sun comes out." It was still pouring.

"Mind Snake, Joe." Snake hadn't moved a muscle.

"Break a leg!"

They moved off down a ravine to the rice paddies three hundred yards distant. Easy going downhill with no load but still they slipped and fell a few times. They walked the patty edge until Tracker signaled the direction of the hamlet. There was no direct path. They entered the patties; the going got slow. The ground in the patties had still not turned to thick mud yet, but the water was six inches deep.

Visibility was hindered by the heavy rain, but for them, they finally appreciated it for its cover. They bent low when they saw the roofs, then stopped. Foxy spied the area with his binoculars, saw no movement on this side. They moved closer.

"I'm going to check out the other side. Move in closer. Look for my signal."

Foxy went one hundred feet west to where he had a full view of the hamlet. He counted twenty houses. Concrete with straw roofs, the size of the houses looked to be about a thousand sq. ft. The town was laid out like a horseshoe, eight each on the east and west sides, with four larger structures at the south end. The layout was somewhat haphazard with no straight lines. Some houses were set far back from the main street while others had a small front yard. All had extensive gardens.

He didn't need his spyglass to see a Russian scout car parked in the square. Shit! He thought, now what? He went back to find Tracker. He found him behind a cart, fifty feet away from the first house.

"There's a Red scout car. Probably three or four men. What'd you think?"

"Foxy, I act. You think."

"Shit, Tracker. Talk to me."

"We came to scout. We have. Let's go back."

"Why are they here? It doesn't make any sense. Why only a few men? There must be a hundred people in there! They should have at least a squad. Something's not right."

"What'd you want to do?"

He made up his mind. "I'm going in to find out. You stay here."

The rain hid any noise of his movement, not that he made any, but he welcomed any help. Making it to the first house, he listened under the open window but heard nothing. Moving to the next house down, he did the same. It was also silent. On the third house, after doing the same thing, he decided to go in. The dead man lay in a pool of his blood, throat cut. An older man, maybe fifty or seventy, hard to tell. Still warm. Mud tracks and water on the floor. Two, maybe three people, he thought.

Continuing south, he checked each house for noise, not bothering to enter. Where are they? The rain was the only sound he heard. It was loud enough to hide most any racket he might make banging into something.

Crossing to the last house, he spotted another scout car on the side of the house across the street. Oh man, did I just screw up! He stayed still at the last house, thinking of what to do next. Leaving now seemed like a pretty good idea. Then he heard a muffled shot but couldn't tell from where. He moved to the far end to see the southern row of houses.

"Anything?" Came from his back.

Foxy almost jumped out of his skin at Tracker's little joke. "You asshole!" He whispered.

"I heard the shot."

"We have more company."

"I know. They're in the far corner house."

"How do you know?"

"Been doing serious work while you were checking empty houses."

"How many?"

"Not sure, eight or nine maybe. Other people in there too, locals. Many villagers in the two houses across the way, tied up I think."

"Any guards on them?"

"Didn't see any."

"Let's go!" Said Foxy, resolved to prevent the slaughter of the townspeople.

They darted across to the south row of houses, working their way to the enemy occupied house at the other end. Two open windows and a back door. Foxy looked in the first nearest open window, an empty bedroom. Voices came from the next room, but he couldn't hear clearly.

"Let's take them from inside." Said Foxy.

"No. You go in; I'll take the door."

"OK. The door opens out."

"No shit. Two minutes." Said Tracker, as they set their watches.

The voices were louder and clearer as he climbed through the window. He moved to the open door, transferred his Thompson to his shoulder, removed his holstered .45 and got ready.

68

Someone was being questioned while others were chatting in relaxed banter.

On the mark, .45 outstretched, Foxy walked into the room and said in Korean, "Move and you're dead!"

Tracker was at the rear door with his .45. He moved in and to the side for better coverage.

Everybody froze, like a still picture. An officer standing next to a guy tied up in a chair, face bloodied, head down. Three soldiers sitting in chairs on the side wall, four soldiers sitting on the floor, leaning against the front wall. A dead civilian was sprawled out, face down, on the floor in the center of the room, blood seeping from numerous wounds, most notably from his head, which had a large hole in its back.

"Anymore of you?" Nobody responded.

He went to the standing captain and knocked him out with a sudden swing to his head with his pistol.

"I'm going to start killing you one by one until you tell me. If you lie, I'll kill all of you. Now, are there more men?"

A sergeant sitting in a chair shook his head, no. Then said, "This piece of shit officer made us come here. He wanted revenge on his hometown. He is the one who killed these people."

"How many did he kill?"

"Ten, I think."

Tracker disarmed them, piling the weapons in the corner. Foxy had them all sit in the front corner. Then he went to the man in the chair. Unconscious, he untied him and laid him on the floor. Severely beaten, his face was a pulp, eyes swollen shut, unrecognizable. He needs Marty bad, he thought.

"Where's your unit, Sergeant? When are you expected back?"

"South, near Seoul. Tomorrow morning."

"Do they know you came here?"

"No. The captain lied about our mission. This was personal for him."

In English, he called over to Tracker, "OK, now shoot them in the head."

None of the prisoners flinched. "Good, they don't understand English."

"Damn! I thought you meant it." Said a smiling Tracker.

Foxy went to free the townspeople and came back with a roll of thick twine. They tied the soldiers, hands in the back, around their ankles and sat them along the side wall. Then they were gagged. The captain was left tied up lying on the floor.

"The villagers felt sure he was going to kill everyone, Tracker. Said he had gone crazy. He'd been away ten years after he ran off. Blames everyone for not protecting him from the Japanese. They don't understand it. Just think he was nuts. They don't know who this stranger is. He just showed up this morning asking for help. Then these guys showed up. The town people are very grateful that we saved them. Told me that they'd prepare a feast for us tonight in our honor. I told them about the rest of the men. They smiled more, said they feel even safer. We're welcome to stay as long as we want."

"Oh man!" Tracker looked up. "Thank you, Spirit! Hot food and a dry floor!"

"I'll get Rusty." Foxy went to the back door, turned back before he left. "I told the folks not to come down this way. And Tracker! Don't eat any mushrooms." He laughed as he left, thinking of Tracker's experience eating hallucinogenic wild mushrooms at the Peak two days ago.

Later, the men gathered around a table that was filled with hot foods of all sorts. The families had brought in trays and bowls soon after they had arrived; started the cooking fire for warmth and giving thanks to them for saving their lives. Then they left them to eat, get dry, and rest.

Chapter Twelve

In a single column, Jack led the men down along the ridgeline. It was a challenge in the torrential rain. The debris on the road from yesterday's shelling had mostly been pushed aside allowing unobstructed vehicle movement. Traffic was light with no foot soldiers in sight. Jack's first look at this cove made him wonder why this little hamlet was spared destruction. He'd seen this before, thought it was a random act of mercy or just somebody screwing up. No matter why he concluded, we're just goddamned lucky.

Situated on a small bluff across from the village, a hundred yards away, Jack spied the town layout, small wharf and yes, there was a boat; two in fact. One was a fifty-foot shrimp boat of sorts with big outriggers at the sides. In front of it was the one he got giddy about. Perfect, a thirty footer, an open fishing boat with a small pilot house at the stern and one main mast forward. He could see the sail furled on the boom, ready to be raised by a simple pulley. Got to have an engine.

"We're in luck boys." He happily told his men. "Our ride out of this shit is waiting for us!"

"Is it big enough?" Asked a jumpy JP. "I mean…for the ocean?"

"Plenty big. Just gotta get it! Don't see any movement anywhere. We'll wait a few hours."

The time passed. The night was black and rain hammered down. The wind was light out of the southeast. They crossed the tracks and road, went down the embankment to water's edge, and then followed it to the wharf. They crept all the way down and past the shrimp boat. Eerie, no people, no lights, only the sound of the rain. The men got on the gently rocking boat. Old but solid, simple, almost primitive. She had a deep hull; the deck had two raised hatches for storing the catch below. Jack directed the men to positions. Greg on the bow line, Phil on the stern and JP in the center. Jack went to the boom, untied the lines holding the wrapped sail and gathered the boom lines.

A searchlight broke the blackness as it beamed off the breakwater from the ocean side. A boat was coming into the cove.

"Get cover!" Whispered Jack. "No shooting!" Jack got to the seaside gunwale, readied his new Russian weapon.

The throating, distinctive diesel engine sound of the gunboat passed within twenty feet of them as it proceeded to tie up at wharf's end, behind the shrimp boat, some sixty feet away.

Jack called out. "Stay behind the hatches." He motioned to Phil to go forward.

A little later, Jack saw three men walking off the patrol boat and into the village. He assumed they were officers. Would they stay? Almost midnight, pretty late to make a house call. So what're they doing? Not a God damned clue, he said to himself, irritated.

Jack entered the little pilot house, scanned the controls, steering wheel, ignition switch, two levers, no gages, no compass. "Great!" He said aloud to himself, then thought, if we get outta here, it's dead reckoning all the way. No problem! Getting out is the problem.

He weighed the options. Wait, maybe they'll leave soon? Try to sneak out under their noses? Attack and blow it up? He thought enough. Time for action. He crawled out, went to his men. They huddled at the first hatch.

"We're gonna sneak out of here. If I can start the engine we'll power out, if not, I'll raise the sail. As soon as the engine starts, let the lines go. Otherwise, I'll signal from the mast. Get ready on the lines."

JP vomited. "Sorry! I'm OK."

Jack turned the ignition switch. A low humming, no start. Tried again, same. The third time was a charm; the old diesel came to life with a muted growl. The lines were cast off. Jack let the prevailing easterly blow the boat off of the pier, slowly slipping it towards the cove's center. The rain continued, heavier than before, making a racket as it drummed against the little pilot house. He had instructed the men that as soon as they got away from the wharf, they were to act as a bucket team from bow to him in the pilot house to relay sighting of the breakwater or other danger before they got to the open sea. The rain was so deafening, so intense and the night so dark, his visibility was near zero. Any communication had to be done by yelling into the ear. Despite this dangerous aspect of maneuvering blind in tight quarters, his fear of being spotted slowly disappeared. Relieved by the cover of the rain, he felt confident. The ocean was an old friend whom he hadn't seen in many years and rejoiced at the coming reunion.

Clearing the breakwater brought large waves at their beam, it rocked the boat violently. Jack was in his element and felt invigorated. The hardest part was over. We're out! Taking note of the time, he brought the boat into the wind, taking the sea slightly off its starboard bow, favoring a more northeasterly course to ride the waves better and get further away from the coast. The boat settled into a splashing rhythm of rising and falling; sea spry soaking the uncovered men.

Chapter Thirteen

Thursday, June 29, 1950 – Day Five of the Invasion
Suwon Airport – Twenty miles South of Seoul – Dawn

The deafening silence woke Wild Bill with a start. The lights around the plane shined brightly. After the death of his friend, Gene, Billy had dived into working on the plane like a man possessed. Swearing at anything and anybody who came near. All night, the banging and cursing carried on until the captain finally nodded off into a deep sleep.

He checked his watch, got up and walked to his plane. "What the hell!?" He stared at the lettering and image painted on its nose.

"*JUST DUE*," a robed creature holding a scythe wrapped the lettering. It was a picture of death calling.

"That's beautiful!" He called out. "My daddy would be proud! Who did this?"

Men stirred in the corner, then Billy's voice. "Jesus Christ! I just got to sleep!"

"It's time to get up, Billy! We need to leave today. Tell me you found the problem?"

"Goddamn it!" Billy got up and walked over to him. "Yes! I found it an hour ago while you were snoring."

"I'm glad I didn't have to shoot you. I'm just starting to like you. Thanks, Billy. Now, who did this?"

"I hope you like it." Said Arnie, as he came around the propeller.

"You captured my meaning perfectly, Arnie. He is one avenging creature. Good job!"

"He worked on it all night." Said Billy, "He wouldn't stop. Said it was important for you to show these bastards what they're in for."

"So he's ready to fly today?"

"Yeah, Captain. Just need to run a final check, but I'm pretty sure everything's all right."

"Let's get breakfast." Wild Bill again glanced at "Just Due" and smiled.

Arnie was left guarding the hanger. The line at the mess tent was crowded but moved swiftly. Billy and George ate hungrily as Wild Bill picked at his food and watched the excited officers near him. He wondered what was going on but didn't want to become visible. George got a tray for Arnie, and they all headed back.

Arnie was standing at the hanger entrance, arguing with a lieutenant. Captain Stands stepped forward.

"What's going on here, Lieutenant?"

"Sir, I just ordered this corporal to come fix some trucks so we can leave this airfield later today. He's refused."

"Who ordered you to come here, Lieutenant?"

"Major Griffin, sir, General Church's XO. He ordered me to round up all the mechanics I could find and that I should start at this hanger."

"I see. How many trucks do you need to be fixed?"

"Not exactly sure, sir, but I think we need four. We have five running, and the major said he needs nine. There must be twenty or more all-around needing some repair. Ought not to be too hard finding the quick fixes."

"Right. Tell you what, Lieutenant. I'll start getting things set up over here if you could round up a crew to tow these broken trucks next to this hanger. Make it ten trucks so we can find the easy ones. My guys will get right on it."

"Thanks, Captain, that'll help me out a lot."

Billy made a disgusted grunt sound as he grabbed Arnie and headed into the hanger. "We got work to do, Arnie." George followed.

The captain knew Billy was pissed, but he was on a mission. "Hey, Lieutenant, why is everybody all hopped up this morning?"

"Big doings later. The big man's flying in."

The captain had a blank look, not comprehending. The Lieutenant got it.

"General MacArthur, Captain."

"Here! He's coming here! Today!" He was incredulous.

"Yeah, in a few hours."

Back in the hanger, Wild Bill came up to the men working at the rear of the plane, near the tail. "Sorry about the extra work, but I had to do it. I already pissed off General Church, and we need two more trucks. I assumed you didn't want to join his merry band at the forefront of some operation he's planning. Might involve close in combat, if you know what I mean."

"Jesus, Captain!" Billy's demeanor changed. "I didn't think of that. Why do we need two more trucks?"

"How'd you think we're gonna move all this ammo and parts?" He pointed to the stacked boxes against the walls.

Billy turned and looked at all the crates, and his jaw dropped. "Shit! Captain, that's an awful amount of stuff to load. We'll need a lot of time and more men."

"Can't you dig up a forklift around here?"

"Right! Been pretty busy. I'll get Arnie to go look around."

"No. I'll hunt around for a forklift. Finish your check. Then get fixing trucks. They'll be arriving soon. While I'm out looking around, I'll see if I can dig up another trailer or two. Ask the truck drivers if they could help us find them. I want to take off no later than four, but I want to make sure you guys get off this base before I leave." He turned to leave. Over his shoulder, he said, "I'm off to see if I can get you an escort."

As he started walking out, he stopped and turned. "Billy! He better be ready in one hour, no more bullshit!"

76

Same Day – Same Time – Thursday, June 29, 1950 – Day Five of the Invasion
Korea – On the Ocean – Sea of Japan – Off the East Coast of South Korea –Dawn

The night had passed dreadfully slow. For JP, it seemed like he was being tortured, with agonizing pain. Unable to pass out, he tried mind games, they helped. The vomiting stopped after the first hour with nothing left to give up. He lay curled in a fetal position behind the pilot shack, moaning now and then. He didn't move all night. Greg and Phil held up well.

The seas were five to six but somewhat short, with a chop on top. Wind steady at 15 to 20 knots. Good sailing conditions, but not ideal for this boat and crew, Jack thought; thinking of turning off the engine and going to sail for the run south.

Two hours into the journey, Jack had cramped up, neck and legs screaming. The pilot shack was built for one regular size Korean. Although not a particularly big man, Jack was five-eleven, with a muscular, two hundred pound frame. He fit into the shack like a sardine, barely able to turn the wheel, it was so tight. To fit in, he had to bend his knees or bend his head over the wheel. Shoulders were wedged against the side walls. He had no fear of being knocked around by the rough wave action.

Greg was the first to relieve him. Simple instructions; get the feel of the boat motion and pressure on the wheel. It required constant small corrections as the irregular wave action would affect the angle through the sea. Without vision, feel was the only way of steering. Greg figured it out, did a good job. Phil took a little longer, but he too got it.

After another hour the rain stopped, supplanted by the spray from breaking waves. Outside the shack, it was unpleasant. Although mild, the temperature was in the high sixties. The ocean was cold; the men were drenched and the wind added to their misery. Each turn in the protected shack helped alleviate the shivering. Except for JP, he couldn't move.

77

Jack figured they were making three knots per hour. After three hours he decided nine miles out was enough to start heading more southerly. He turned to take the sea on the port bow. Same motion of the boat but now the boat angled to the starboard side. The men shifted positions to avoid the new direction of spray.

Black turned to gray, then light, as the sun started its ascent from the ocean edge.

Greg shouted out his joy. "Yea!!!!! You're a sight to behold! I love you!"

Another hour brought welcomed warmth. Jack decided it was time to head south. The maneuver would bring the waves on the beam. This was going to be tricky. Knowing the boat could take it but fearing the men couldn't. If he stayed under power the boat would swing violently, so he wouldn't. Time to raise the sail.

He instructed Phil on the maneuver. Taking the wheel, Phil turned directly into the waves as Jack untied the sail and boom pulley lines. He raised the sail, fluttering as it rose. Grabbing the port boom line, he wrapped it around a post in the port gunwale to control the sail as they turned south. He signaled Phil to turn, the sail filled and the boat heeled hard over. Jack secured the boom line with the sail adjusted to the best position, almost full out. The boat settled into their most comfortable ride so far. No spray. Jack was pleased with himself. So were the men. They could finally dry out. Jack turned off the engine.

Not bucking the wind or waves, Jack guesstimated they picked up speed to maybe four or five knots. He did his dead reckoning in his head, told the men that tomorrow they'd be in Pusan. They were euphoric. JP just groaned. Jack hoped Pusan hadn't been captured.

Same Day – Same Time – Thursday, June 29, 1950 – Day Five of the Invasion
Korea – A hamlet northeast of Seoul – Dawn

Joe checked his watch again. Almost time. His two-hour sentry duty almost up. The tree he lay by out at the approach road held no cover from the rain. The slicker provided by one of the town elders helped, but he was still soaked and cold. At least there was no trouble, he thought. What about today? The rain stopped.

"Joe! Don't shoot! It's Moose!"

"Jesus! Didn't you ever learn to be silent?"

"No! It keeps me out of dangerous missions."

"You're a goddamned Ranger for Christ's sake. You're always on a dangerous mission!"

"But never on point. Quiet, huh?"

"Nothing going on. Here's my slicker in case it starts again. Anybody up?"

"Nah. I put another log on, should be cozy for ya."

"Thanks."

The snoring noises masked his entrance as he went to the fire, stripped off his wet clothes and got warm.

Marty came in from a back room and came over. Whispering, Joe asked, "How long you been up?"

"A while." He sat down. "Was checking on the local, he was moaning a lot."

"He gonna make it?"

"Pretty sure. Maybe a concussion, fractured jaw, missing teeth, broken nose, that's about it."

Joe nodded, felt bad for the poor bastard but happy he wasn't in danger.

"How do you feel about our situation, Marty?"

"We're alive, aren't we? Never thought this would happen but it did. But so far so good. How about you? We're gonna make it?"

"Make it? Don't know, Marty. I'm a bad judge of predicting the future. Didn't think I'd make it past day one on Okinawa. Like you, guess I feel the same."

The men began getting up, going out the back to do their thing. Arron came to the fire, moving between Joe and Marty, and swung a pot of water over the fire. "You 'all got to move now, I got serious work to get done." He said in his usual southern drawl.

Foxy had learned the small village was called Sindap, some ten miles northeast of the capital. Two of the village elders had volunteered to guard the prisoners during the night, only after promising that they wouldn't shoot them. This accomplished Rusty's goal of not revealing that there were more than two Americans, which would have necessitated killing them. He still wondered what the village men might do. Not his problem, he concluded.

"Just getting light, Rusty. Looks like a clear day." Said Red, as he wrapped his web belt on. "We should leave soon."

"An hour, Red. Is that coffee?" He sniffed the air.

"Yeah! Arron dug up some of his secret stash. He's been holding out on us."

Frenchy came by, sipping a cup. Smacking his lips, he said, "He's better than a Paris chef."

Foxy came back from checking on the prisoners, came over to Rusty with a somber look.

"They didn't shoot them, as promised. But they did hang the captain."

Rusty had to smile at the take charge attitude of the villager's. "A well-deserved ending I'd say."

"We gonna leave the prisoners with these folks?" Concern in his voice.

"Foxy, they didn't do anything bad to them, only this nutcase, right? You told me these guys didn't like him anyway. We'll tell the people to hold them another day, then release them. Don't see another solution, do you?"

"Guess not. I'll go see if this stranger can tell us who he is. Marty says he'll be alright."

Lying on the floor, the beaten stranger was awake when Foxy knelt next to him. In Korean, he spoke to him. His eyes couldn't open, nor could he speak, but he moved his hand to his pants pocket and pointed. Foxy acknowledged, reached into his pocket and pulled out a medal, not just any medal, but the medal he'd seen two days ago, bestowed upon Captain Hui.

"It's Foxy, Captain! I can't believe it. You're all beat up but OK! You'll live, my friend!"

He moved his head in recognition as tears streamed from his swollen eyes. He raised his hand, Foxy grabbed it and squeezed tight.

"These are good people here, Captain; they'll watch over you. We must leave now, but we'll be back. You're critical to what happens next to your country, Captain. So survive!"

After each man visited with Captain Hui and said their words, Rusty led the men out of Sindap, assigning Tracker and Joe to point, and headed to their rendezvous.

Chapter Fourteen

Thursday, June 29, 1950 – Day Five of the Invasion
Suwon Airport – Twenty miles South of Seoul – Mid Day

"Goddammit, Arnie! Get that starter fixed! I told you to clean the wires."

"Billy! Get off my ass! I'm working on it!"

The trucks started showing up early and soon counted fifteen. The need for more trucks seemed to escalate by the hour. Billy and Arnie revived six trucks by noon. George had loaded most of their equipment and tools then went out with the drivers to help find and then tow two trailers back. Then he found a broken forklift and got another driver to tow it. Arnie fixed the lift in ten minutes.

Wild Bill showed up with a US Army squad of the 24th Infantry Division, part of the platoon assigned to protect General Church.

"Your escort has arrived!" Captain Stands announced proudly. "Probably help you finish loading if you ask them nicely." Then he saw the forklift. "Good deal! Glad you found one. Make sure you bring it with us. I understand they got less stuff than this shithole."

Billy was unbelieving of this help. "What the hell!? How'd you get all the men, Captain?"

"Billy. You must become a believer. My God is the right God. Your resurrection of *Just Due* will bring you fame and salvation. You must trust in the good, as it will explain all."

Billy was left stunned at this response. He had no idea of what Wild Bill just said, or its meaning. Just shook his head. He thought maybe the Captain's nickname should've been *Crazy* Bill.

They proceeded to load the trucks and trailers with the remaining P- 51 ammunition and parts crates. They were sure glad they had the lift.

Billy didn't know that Captain Stands had contacted Colonel Nelson, who contacted Howie at CIA, who then had issued orders to General Church advising him that this was a CIA "Black Box" operation and that he was to lend all assistance to Captain Stands on a priority basis.

General MacArthur's visit had lasted an hour. Much photographed, his presence projected the US concern and support for the South Korean government. The airport became a scramble to leave after his departure. Civilian dignitaries first, then the ROK military high command. All headed fifty miles south, to the city of Taejon.

The loading complete, the little convoy assembled outside, away from the open hanger. The Army squad rested around the trucks. The sergeant squad leader came up to Captain Stands.

"You must have some serious pull, Captain. Major Griffin was red faced, really pissed off when he ordered us over here. We'll ride in your trucks until we reach Taejon. We're ready to join the main convoy leaving in an hour. You need a jeep?"

"Thanks for your help sergeant. This is precious cargo, keep it safe. George Lopez, our sergeant, is in charge of this equipment on this move, you report to him. I'm going a separate route."

The captain had mulled through this last order. Billy should have been the leader. But Wild Bill knew he wasn't. He was good in an engine but useless leading men. After a brief chat explaining his decision to Billy, he saw the relief on his face and wondered why he even fretted over his choice.

Billy came out of the hanger. "You ready, Captain?" He called.

"Bring him out, Billy!" He turned to the squad leader. "Sergeant, could you spare a few men to help Billy bring out my ride?"

JUST DUE nosed out of the hanger, pushed by four soldiers on each wing.

The sergeant, standing next to Wild Bill, noticed the words and image for the first time. "She looks deadly! Beautiful!"

Wild Bill gazed at his war machine and smiled. "He is!"

Clearing the runway, the captain relaxed from his bliss and excitement at being back, at one, with his instrument of death. At last! In what he considered to be the best and most fearsome weapon of WW2. Pushing the throttle as he climbed, he took a hard bank north. He wanted to check out Seoul, twenty miles north.

At five hundred feet, he followed the highway and saw the fleeing hordes below. He climbed to a thousand feet as he approached the city and clearly saw enemy troops being ferried across the Han River on all sorts of rafts and boats. Most disturbing, though, was his view of the railroad bridge, a mile to the east of the destroyed main highway bridge he had witnessed being blown up. Nobody thought to disable this other bridge. Infantry were making their way across, albeit, under heavy fire from ROK positions on the south bank.

A long line of tanks and trucks stretched north from the bridge, waiting to cross. Construction crews were laying timbers along the outside rails, making a road bed for the tanks to cross on.

He got angry. Detesting stupidity, he cursed the idiots who left this bridge intact. The quick pass drew no flack. Executing a quick barrel maneuver, he angled back down onto the waiting vehicles. Remembering that he refused Billy's suggestion for loading bombs and rockets, he lamented further about stupidity. This time, his own.

As he dived on this column, that unbelievable feeling of exhilaration filled his entire being. He felt at home in his mind, in his skin, knowing his purpose and the reason why he had stayed in the service. This is what he was meant to do.

The plane shook as he raked the column with its six fifty caliber guns. Watching the tracers tear through trucks and raking tanks, he proceeded to stitch through troops crossing the bridge, then pulled up. Figuring he had expended most of his ammo, he kept going south. I'll be back, he thought. Next time I won't come light. Revenge is mine, you Red bastards!

Same Day – Thursday, June 29, 1950 – Day Five of the Invasion Aboard USS Juneau – Off the East Coast of Korea – Sea of Japan – Late Afternoon

"Captain! Radar picked up a small surface blip ten miles off the coast, heading south, making four knots, and twenty miles to our Port. Radar thinks it's a fishing junk. Should we check it out?"

The Captain called the Admirals' stateroom, alerted him to the news and asked for direction.

"Be right up, Captain."

"I don't like it, Captain. We haven't picked up any coastal traffic for two days. Could be an infiltration attempt. Send the *Gurke* on my orders. I want a close-up. But I want clear enemy ID before any engagement."

The USS Gurke (DD-783) was a new destroyer, commissioned in May 1945. Fast and heavily armed, sporting six five-inch guns, twelve Bofors 40 mm AA guns, and assorted other weapons. Its Captain, F. M. Randel, was an experienced veteran. He was an ensign aboard the USS Dale at Pearl Harbor on 12 7 41. As acting commander during the attack, he sortied the ship out of the harbor for anti-submarine screening. His ship was credited with shooting down a Japanese plane at the harbor entrance.

The *Gurke* went to General Quarters, proceeded to flank speed of thirty-five knots, peeled off from its escort duty of the *Juneau* and headed to the sighting.

Captain Randle was anticipating his first enemy encounter of this new war. Just promoted to command this ship in March, he, and his ship weren't quite in sink yet. But it was going well, so far. He loved destroyers; loved his new ship and liked his crew. He was aggressive but not reckless. His men respected his experience and appreciated his demonstrated concern for them during his brief command.

The *Gurke* was further away from the contact then *Juneau*, cruising north and west of her. ETA on their new contact was forty minutes.

Ten minutes into their new heading. "Captain! *Juneau* just advised us of a new contact. Fast surface small boat is coming from south of Yangyang heading south towards our contact. It just showed up on our radar."

Captain Randle suddenly realized this situation could alter his career. Turning to his XO, he ordered, "Ted, plot an intersecting course on that fast boat. Get us to three miles. We'll have good visual and be in engagement range."

"Aye, aye, Captain."

A few minutes later. "Sir, ETA in fifteen minutes. What do you think is going on here?"

"Not sure. Somethings not right, XO. I'm sure this fast boat is a North Korean coastal patrol boat. Nothing else it could be. So why is it going after the slow boat? We'll find out soon enough. I want Fire Control to focus on that fast boat on a continuous track, be ready to fire on my command."

As the minutes passed, the fast boat was confirmed as North Korean. The intersection point was close.

"Captain, range four miles, it's turning directly towards us."

"Ted, open fire on that patrol boat."

At the same time - aboard the sailing Junk.

Greg was in the pilot house. Near the end of his one-hour shift, exhausted, he kept thinking of lying in the sun, maybe even going to sleep, something that's been elusive. The routine of holding the wheel with the steady rise and fall of the boat at the passing waves became trance-like, his eyes closing and head nodding, only to shake himself awake again. He checked his watch, five minutes to go.

Jack was asleep, curled in the aft corner on the Port side. Phil was worried about JP. He hadn't moved in two hours. Still breathing, he hopped JP was sleeping.

BOOM!...BOOM!....BOOM!

Jack jumped at the firing. He saw the ship a few miles away, firing north, opposite his direction. "OH! Baby!" He yelled. He ran to the pilot house.

On the "Gurke."

"Two fish in the water! Captain! It's got two more tubes!"

"Then I guess you better get her soon, XO. Hard to starboard! Take evasive action!"

Every four seconds, a shell fired from each of her six five-inch guns. The guns Automatic Fire Control system brought deadly accuracy within a few minutes. The boat was bracketed by explosions and lay dead in the water. Smoke and flames were pouring out of her amidships.

"Nice shooting, Ted! What's our junk doing?"

"Odd, she turned into the wind and dropped her sail. She's under power but not moving. She's just holding her position into the sea."

"Doesn't seem like evasive action to me. Let's get close."

Chapter Fifteen

Friday, June 30, 1950 – Day Six of the Invasion
Japan – Eighth Army Headquarters – Colonel Nelson's Office
– 0200 – (2:00 am)

Exhausted, he sat back at his desk, trying to put the crazy events of the day in some perspective. Some good news, lots of bad news and then the news that drove him crazy….no news.

The unstoppable cascading of events has, as he predicted, brought America to the brink of war. Unprepared, as she may be, he knew it was only a matter of time and many needlessly sacrificed soldiers, until this aggression is beaten and turned back. When? When will we fully commit? It better be soon, he thought.

The military machine was now fully engaged in assembling resources to answer that call when it came. Agonizingly slow, the clogs were, at last, starting to move in unison.

The report that Air Force Command staged bombing raids on two North Korean airbases was encouraging. Air transports were arriving, a Navy transport ship arrived late today and Eighth Army heavy equipment of artillery, tanks and ammunition were being assembled in California for sea transit. He then lamented at the ten days or more it would take to get his Army up to strength.

Frustrated, he knew they didn't have ten days. Focusing on the problem of time, he revisited his earlier plans of delaying the enemy.

His thoughts were interrupted as Major Jarvis abruptly entered his office.

"News, Colonel." He was excited and exuded that it was good news. "Just got in a dispatch from Admiral Joy's command! Says they have our four guys from Post # 4 on the Destroyer **Gurke**. They plucked them from a stolen Junk after sinking a North Korean patrol boat in their pursuit."

He sat staring, assimilating his words, not fully comprehending. Then it hit him. "Oh God! Thank You!" He recovered quickly.

"Major, let's get over to operations, I've got some ideas." On the way over to the Staff Operations building, the major filled him in on the condition of the Post men and details about their rescue.

"Hank, I've got to do something. Assemble your staff. I want to hear about what we got so far. I'll be a few minutes."

Even at this hour of the morning, the Operations Room was busy, almost entirely manned. Major Jarvis went off to gather his new key staff people and brought them to a side conference room.

Nelson moved through the large open operations center to the far wing that housed the liaison officers and went directly to the Air Force section. A young captain viewing aerial photos spread across his desk looked up as he approached and recognized the colonel from a prior meeting.

"Sir! You're up pretty early. How can I help you?"

"I need some info, Captain." He pulled up a chair and sat to the side of the desk.

"Shoot, Colonel, whatever I have is yours."

"I'm trying to figure out how to slow this onslaught enough so that we'll still be in the country when enough force can be brought to bear. So, I want to know how effective the Air Force has been and what it looks like it can do in the next week or so."

"Jeeze, Colonel, I'm a Captain, not a soothsayer."

Nelson had to laugh. Asking impossible questions of ordinary dedicated staff were his stock in trade. He knew, however, that he'd get an honest, straightforward answer. His experience with intra-service information sharing reinforced his belief that the higher you go up the command structure, the more BS you got.

Smiling at the captain, with that all-knowing look, he spoke some military wisdom. "Predicting the future is your job, Captain. Your major depends on it. Get it wrong, and it's your fault, you get fired, not him. It follows all the way up the chain."

The captain leaned back in his chair. "Colonel? Can I transfer to your command?"

They both chuckled, then got down to the serious business.

"Colonel, from what I can see so far, we don't have what we need and we're doing a piss poor job with what we have. Our jet fighters are interceptors, not designed for tactical support. We've sent our only squadron of B-26 bombers over Seoul to knock out the bridges and breakup force concentrations on the north bank. They've been ineffective. Awful weather, inadequate training, old planes and not enough of them has resulted in crew losses and little or no results. The only B-29 bomber squadron available has just started targeting North Korean airfields, with mixed results."

"Do we have any P-51's available?"

"Yes and no. All we have in Japan were designated as interceptors and reclassified as F-51's. This meant that all supporting bomb racks and rocket brackets were removed, along with their controlling instruments. We have five squadrons, composed of about eighty operational planes. These have just been ordered to be refitted back to their original tactical fighter-bomber status. This will take days, or longer. My guess, longer. I don't even know if we even have the equipment or ordinance here in Japan for their new role."

"Trying to get some encouragement here, Captain. Do you have any good news?"

"As you said earlier, it's coming. But slowly. For example, tomorrow, the Navy Carrier, USS Boxer, is leaving San Diego with one hundred and fifteen originally fitted P-51's with full ordinance and experienced pilots. She's expected here in ten days."

"So nothing that can slow these guys is showing up now?"

"Well, I've heard it said by my dad, who was a Marine in the last war, that the guys in the trenches are the only force that can stop a determined enemy."

"Your dad, being a Marine, has a clear assessment of the truth. I'm afraid that what he says is true. Thanks, Captain."

He stood up. "Captain, I like your style. You're Air Force, but if you're serious about transferring to my command as a… don't know what right now, but I'd facilitate that. I'm good at cutting through red tape. I'm always looking for bright, honest leaders. Just let me know."

As he ambled back to his staff, Nelson ping-ponged through his reconfirmed incite on the desperation of their situation. No help was coming in time. He knew he had few if any choices. Ordering men to their almost certain deaths was abhorrent to him. He'd done it. Always justified by the greater good. But it didn't lessen the burden, or subsequent grief, about losing men you knew. This situation was bad. Real bad. He was getting angry.

Nelson entered the small conference room. His new staff sat around a table. He'd not met any of them; having relied on Major Jarvis to put the team together over the last day. A lieutenant was talking and fell silent as he entered.

Major Jarvis rose. "Colonel Nelson, let me introduce you to your new staff leaders."

"Sorry, I'm late." He crumbled into a seat, looking angry and worried.

"Sir, to your right is First Lieutenant, Larry Cole. Next to him is Captain Sam Haran. Master Sergeant Nick Beloit rounds out the first team."

Nelson assessed each, nodding at introduction, but his mind wandered, then refocused.

"I don't know you yet nor do you know me. What I do know is that you've been dropped into a maelstrom. I hope you're up to the task."

He looked again, at each for a few seconds, then said.

"Please continue."

The lieutenant started over. "Our objective, to slow the enemy advance should focus on two main choke points. They are a) The Han River crossing area and b) The east coast rail and highway. These attack fronts, if left unchecked, form a pincher to attack and envelope Pusan. Pusan is the last stand for whatever defense we can muster."

Nelson looked at this young officer. "Any specific recommendations?"

Sheepishly, the young man shook his head. "Not yet, sir. We've just started our planning."

With an angry voice and a raising red complexion, Colonel Nelson gazed around his staff. "You need to plan faster! Strategic assessment without operational details is meaningless!"

No sound in the room, except, maybe if you were a dog and could hear the pounding of heart beats.

He got up from his chair. Pissed off that he had to make some horrible decisions, he paced, thought about leaving.

Major Jarvis had never seen his commander in this state. Knew his frustrations and concerns. He interjected.

"Boss!" He'd never called him that before.

Nelson spun around to face Major Jarvis.

"Sir, you need to hear the rest of the briefing."

Composing himself, pissed that he lost control, he sat. "Please proceed."

Major Jarvis nodded to Captain Haran. He appeared as a Liberian but was a math professor at MIT that, in 1942, decided he wanted to make a difference in the war effort. So he left the mundane chore of teaching and quickly rose to the Army Staff Planning section for Pacific operations.

Captain Haran was intimately involved in the planning of many Island invasions and received two citations for his extraordinary efforts. He was plucked by Major Jarvis to this G-2 section yesterday. Colonel Nelson didn't know a thing about him.

"I've studied the terrain around Seoul in detail. I drew an arch, twenty miles in circumference from its center. Amazing things popped out that might help us."

He got up and went to the back wall where a large reconnaissance photo hung and pointed to a ridge that sloped down from the high mountain range to the northeastern side of the capital and the eastern edge of the Han River. It appeared as an encrusted lava flow from an ancient volcano.

"For instance, the distance of this ridge, from this mountain peak to the edge of the Han River, is twelve miles. Ending exactly one mile east of the railroad bridge."

Pausing, he saw the questioning look on Colonel Nelson.

"This is no ordinary ridge. Other, more detailed Aerial photos reveal many deep ravines throughout its width and most of its length. The width is what's amazing; it varies from a minimum of one hundred and fifty yards to three football field lengths."

Colonel Nelson started to get impatient. Decided he didn't need a geography lesson. "Please get to the point, Captain."

Captain Haran and Colonel Nelson were close in age. He wasn't about to be as intimidated as the young lieutenant.

"Colonel, please bear with me for a minute or so! Few officers grasp the significance of terrain as it affects strategy without being led through the process. I'm getting to the good part."

Nelson's face went beat red. Major Jarvis almost burst out laughing. He'd never seen a smack down so eloquently put to a superior.

Captain Haran pointed to the mountain peak. "You see, this peak is home to a South Korean signal team that is scheduled to rendezvous with our Post Team, Rusty and his band."

Colonel Nelson was stunned and stared at the captain. The full implication hit him.

"Holy Crap!"

Nelson realized the ridge would provide excellent cover, be lightly patrolled and end up a mile away from the most important target they had to slow the enemy's advance.

"Captain, what of the mile to the bridge? What about protection around the bridge?"

"We're working on that, Colonel. The enemy is reacting to our small air raid efforts by bringing in substantial anti-aircraft batteries. Things around the bridge are chaotic. Few NK forces have crossed the bridge so far, but a small enemy pocket has been established on the south side of the bridge. Only strong resistance by the ROK has prevented a major breakthrough here."

"When can you have a plan, Captain?"

"Soon. Later today I hope. I'm waiting for the latest batch of yesterday's surveillance photo's to arrive so I can assess conditions around the bridge, and, most importantly of all, we're waiting for contact confirmation of The Post team. Further, we need to know how much explosives we need to do the job. Then, how much C-4 the Post team have. Thinking they don't have enough, how do we get them enough? Of course, then there's the matter of getting to the bridge. Finally, planning their escape."

Colonel Nelson saw hope.

"Please move faster, Captain. Good job!"

The room felt like a small amount of air was let out of an exploding balloon. Everybody sat back, breathed easier. It didn't last long.

Nelson fidgeted, this new information was like a starburst in his head. He thought of a million things he needed to do now. Decided to leave. Started to stand.

"Colonel!" Major Jarvis sharply called out. "You need to stay. We're not finished with the briefing yet."

It was like he'd been slapped awake, came out of his head and looked at his second in command. Didn't know what to say, so he sat back.

"Master Sergeant Beloit has focused on the eastern coast threat down the peninsula. Please start."

An impressively handsome, somewhat short, young thirty-something, crew cut blond, rose, slid a crutch under his arm and stumped to the wall map, revealing in the process, his missing right foot. He held the look of a determined man, not cowered by his disability nor even aware that he had any. At the map, he turned to talk directly to Colonel Nelson.

"Colonel! This is our first meeting. I hope you come to understand that I'm a grunt. My foxhole buddies mean everything to me. These men and I here all work for you. We would do anything for you, and have, over the last day or so. Many of us have had only a few hours' sleep in this time. These are my foxhole buddies, Colonel."

The room got tense. Major Jarvis didn't move. Colonel Nelson stared blankly and thought how impressive Beloit was. How about his balls? Man, I like this guy. He got focused now.

"So, Colonel, I want to point out to you that Lieutenant Cole was instrumental in directing us to the specific locations we were to concentrate on, without him, we would've wasted a lot of time floundering around."

Colonel Nelson recognized courage and loyalty. He also recognized intelligence and flaws, the last of which, he now saw in himself. So he stood and addressed his new staff.

"Nothing better than being straightened out by a grunt!"

The small group was surprised, then laughed. Beloit thought he was about to get fired, or worse when he saw Nelson rise. He hadn't cared. It needed to be said. Relieved that the Colonel he'd heard so much about was now present, he relaxed.

"Thank you, Master Sergeant Beloit." They nodded at each other.

Nelson paused and looked at each team member.

"We meet for the first time under dire circumstances. I've been at this for a while. I've lost good men in the last few days and face the loss of many more in the days ahead. It's a heavy burden on my mind."

He sat down.

Leaning on his crutch, Beloit half turned to the wall map and raised the pointer to the east coast.

"It seems simple. A sort of straight rail and highway going down along the coast. It's not. First off, it's not straight. Secondly, the enemy has moved to mostly night travel because of interdiction efforts by the Navy. The Navy's efforts have proved to be largely ineffective. The enemy has a large force of repair laborers or troops to restore any damage to the road bed within hours."

He then pointed to two locations on the big map at his back.

"Here, in North Korea, twenty miles north of the 38th parallel, is a rail tunnel that feeds into the southern rail system. The tunnel is two miles long. We should target this tunnel. Over here......"

An uproar from the open operations area interrupted. Like at a football game when the home team scores.

"What the hell?" Colonel Nelson was closest to the door. As he rose, the door swung open, and General Walker pushed in like a charging bull.

"At ease!" He said as the group started to stand. He reminded one of an Edward G Robinson gangster movie character from the 30's. Short, stout and built like a fire plug. Rugged face with hard features. He usually had a chewed up cigar sticking out of his lips, but not today.

"Thought I might find you here, Colonel." As he checked his watch. "At two-thirty in the morning. Please sit."

As he moved to the wall map, he nodded to Major Jarvis.

"Glad I found the A team together. It'll save time. The President just ordered the Joint Chiefs to fully respond to this North Korean invasion with all available forces. The 24th Division has just been ordered to Korea. They'll be under General Church's command for now."

He paused, turned to the wall map, grabbed a marker and put a big circle on the southernmost harbor city of Pusan.

"That, gentleman, is our Alamo. This time, though, I expect a different outcome. You here will be the reason for our success. Unless we can do something to slow this enemy, I won't have time to set this defense. I, nor Eighth Army has ever been defeated. It won't start here. I'm relying on you."

He moved to the door to exit, then turned to Colonel Nelson. "I don't know where you got Lieutenant Cole, but he has worked with Operations on an in-depth defense scheme for Pusan that is brilliant." He left.

For the second time within a half hour, Nelson was left feeling pretty stupid about his earlier assessment of the young lieutenant. He got energized, stood up.

"Master Sergeant! Nick, right?" Nelson asked.

Nick Beloit nodded.

"Please sit. We'll pick this up later. I want a detailed action plan on taking out that tunnel from you ASAP. Tomorrow if possible. Is that doable?"

"Yes, sir! It will be very late, though. I'm working with my foxhole buddies on planning the Han Bridge operation first." He responded with a smile.

The Colonel nodded. He knew that this team, his team, knew what the priorities were. He stepped to the map and faced his staff.

"The General put it right! You're the A team!"

Turning to Major Jarvis. "You exceed my every expectation of you, Hank. Thank you, for bringing this exceptional group together."

Turning to the group, he continued.

"The fog has now lifted. We're at war. Our mission is clear. We will defeat this enemy, no doubt about it. The price we pay for this victory, however, is on *our* shoulders. All of us, right here in this room. What we do or don't do determines how many live or die. I'm glad I now share this burden with you. As our Master Sergeant...Nick, has put it so well, we are *foxhole buddies!*"

Everybody recognized the moment and started clapping; felt somewhat strange doing it but knew something special had just happened. Colonel Nelson joined in, clapping for his A Team.

97

Chapter Sixteen

Friday, June 30, 1950 – Day Six of the Invasion
ROK Signal Unit Mountain Hideout Northeast of Seoul
– 0315 – (3:15 am)

Mario leaned against the rock wall, turned to Snake, sitting next to him. "Doesn't look much like a hideout. More like a bus stop on a Friday at five in the afternoon in New York."

"When have you ever been in New York? Besides, we just got here. Maybe there's a penthouse."

It wasn't a cave. More like an arcade overhang of a small town movie theater. Kind of reminded Mario of that Eastside Seattle movie house where he and a friend cut class to see *The Dawn Patrol* with Errol Flynn. That's when he decided he never wanted to be an officer, didn't like the idea of ordering men to their deaths. It was raining hard, and they had to wait under the arcade till it opened. What a movie! It was worth getting detention for a week. He was fourteen, remembered it like it was yesterday.

"I'm going to sleep." Mario leaned into Snake's shoulder.

"Me too." Snake rolled his head back, found a comfortable position against Mario. They both fell into a deep sleep.

Meanwhile, Sergeant Chan-Jae, in charge of this ROK signal unit, huddled with Rusty, Red and Tully at the outer edge of this overhang. A slice of moonlight filtered light through the cloud cover that was becoming denser by the minute. Another bout of monsoon appeared imminent.

This rendezvous had been set up days ago by Colonel Nelson and Colonel Pyung OH, Nelson's counterpart in the ROK Army. The ROK sergeant was his nephew, spoke English and was highly trained.

"Didn't know you had so many men!" The ROK sergeant said.

"Is it Chan, Jae or Chan-Jae? Can't call you Sergeant. Most everybody's a sergeant." Said Rusty, having just met him.

"Call me C J. Makes it easy. How long you been on the move?"

"Four days since we left The Post at the border. How long you been here?"

"Same. We thought we might be able to help in the defense of Seoul as a spotter for artillery or maneuvering our troops to attack points. But they came so fast. Overran most of our forces farther north. We haven't done much but watch them take the capital. We have no artillery to spot for."

"You still have communications?" Rusty asked.

"We lost contact two days ago. There's been continuous heavy shelling on our positions on the south bank. I fear the worst."

"Why are you still here?" Tully asked.

"Waiting for you. I would have left days ago but for my uncle. He told me your mission was critical and I was to guide you. He told me to wait three days. If you hadn't shown up, I would have left today."

Red leaned in. "Who's your uncle?"

"Colonel Pyung OH, General Staff, head of Army Intelligence."

Rusty nodded. "He's a good man. I met him once. My colonel is close with him. Well... that explains a lot."

C J was anxious to know why he risked staying here two days instead of leaving to join in the fighting at the south river bank. "So, what's this mission you're on?"

He could sense the undercurrent of the question. Rusty thought how he'd feel. So he went with his gut. "It's going to blow your mind, C J. Probably mine too when I find out. But right now, I haven't a clue. We haven't communicated with our boss for a few days."

C J didn't say anything, just glared at Rusty with that *I can't believe you just said that,* look.

From the moment they had arrived, Larry and Foxy started setting up the VLF communication system. Foxy asked one of the ROK signal guys where he could see the mountain circled on Foxy's map; the one with the receiving tower. The soldier recognized it and pointed out the spot where they could get a clear line of sight shot to it. It was too dark to see anything, but it didn't have to be very accurate to get the signal to the cone on the tower.

Their location wasn't particularly high, nor was it at the mountain peak, but it jutted out towards Seoul, like a fish hook, giving them a clear view of the next group of mountains flowing south.

After setting the small cone in the general direction of the tower, they assembled the sender/receiver box, the Morse code like tap sender and the portable electric generating cranking device. They got Moose to start cranking. To their amazement, after being dropped and banged around on their long journey, everything seemed to be working. Larry started sending the connection codes and passwords to Colonel Nelson.

"Rusty!" Larry yelled. "We're connected!"

The four men hurried over.

It was over in fifteen minutes. There was good news about the US finally committing to getting fully involved. And bad news about the current situation, which appeared dire. Worse, there was no news about what they were to do.

Tully was troubled. "Rusty, why the questions about how much C-4 we have? Why do we have to wait? We followed his orders to get here so we could hook up with C J to get us to Osan. Why the change?"

Red was thinking about how jumpy they were from the long trek through no man's land, to finally get here. It's a miracle they had made it at all. Now the frustration of not knowing what's next.

"Tully, this is no time for a Ranger to be throwing a hissy fit, so shut up and think for a minute. The world has changed since we've been playing in the rocks and mud for the last few days. So, whatever our mission was when we started, has changed. I don't even think our colonel has decided which of the horrible choices is the most critical. So give him a little sway. Alright?"

"Red's right, Tully," Rusty added. "It's obvious he wants us to blow something up. But ten pounds of C-4 we have ain't going to blow up much of anything. So maybe he's got a plan B or C and needs some time to work it out. He said he'd be back to us in a few hours."

Rusty turned to find Arron and saw him against the wall nearby. "Arron! Any chance you got some of that special *sock* coffee fixin's?"

Arron jumped up and made like a Civil War era Florida servant, bending over, shuffling about; "I hears you mas'er, yes sir! Been cart'en around you' al favorite nectar for some time now. Jus-a-wait'en fo your call."

He lightened the men's spirits; made Rusty laugh.

The men had been up since before yesterday's dawn, walking, crawling sometimes. Traversing streams, rice paddies and finally climbing up over seven hundred feet on this mountains steep path. And here comes another dawn. Most decided to sleep, some ate unheated food, then slept. Some couldn't do anything but think.

Joe was one of those thinkers. So was Frenchy, sitting next to him.

"You're from upstate, right?" Asked Joe.

Frenchy rolled his head against the wall. "It's complicated, Joe."

"What? Where you're from?"

"Yes. You see, although I was born in upstate New York, my town was two miles from the Canadian border. Champlain, a no nothing town. Most folks spoke French. My dad's French. I grew up thinking I was French and Canadian. It was common to speak English and French, so I didn't know what I was. I think I was four or five when I learned that I was an American, and honestly, I didn't know what that meant."

"Frenchy! You're weird. A straight answer would've been, yes, I'm from upstate. But you need to go on about your French Canadian heritage. Why?"

"Are all Brooklyn people so simple? We are defined by our past and then are judged by how we overcome it. Don't you see?"

"See what? I grew up in a shitty area. You grew up in, as you say, a *complicated place.* I don't get it. Let's drop this. Sorry, I asked."

"Come on Joe. I bet Brooklyn had many languages, too. Didn't you ever feel like you didn't know who you were?"

"No. My dad and mom came from Italy. They learned English. Dad told me early on that America was the greatest country in the world. As a kid, I looked around, I lived in Flatbush, and it sucked. Couldn't fathom what he meant. Of course we had all kinds of strange people around. Crazy Jews, Irish, Slav's, Greeks. Christ! Brooklyn was an early United Nations back then. But I knew who I was. Truth be told, though, I had no idea of anything about life or other people until I joined the Army and saw things first hand."

"Is that when you learned to talk like a human?"

"Careful! I can laugh about it now, but it's not funny. Speaking Brooklynese was not easy to overcome, took me awhile."

"And you did a good job of it. You talk like you're from someplace in the Midwest."

"Benny was my teacher. He didn't really teach me; he just talked a lot. From Peoria. From the moment I heard him speak, I told myself that that was how I wanted to sound....like a real American. By that time, I was sick and tired of being kidded about my Brooklyn dialect. I committed to change. We went through boot camp together and became friends."

"I thought it was something like that or maybe you went to college somewhere. Were you guys in the same outfit? Fight together?"

"We were replacements. Yeah, we both caught up with the 96th Infantry after their Philippine campaign. Then Okinawa. Benny didn't make it." Joe shook his head. "Only ten of my platoon made it."

Frenchy also knew a lot about loss, said nothing.

Rusty grabbed a cup of Arron's sock coffee and sat down next to C J against a corner rock. It was still pitch black, with a light rain starting to fall. The air was still, the temperature mild.

"I've been thinking C J. My map shows two bridges across the Han nearby. They could be our next target. What can you tell me about them?"

"Been watching them closely. Two spans of the main road bridge were blown up the day before Seoul was captured. That's gonna take some time to repair, but they're working on it. The railroad bridge is almost a mile away, closer to us. Nobody thought to blow it. We've had a few artillery strikes on it that caused only minor damage, but it's intact. Some troops have crossed and set up a small bridgehead on the south bank, maybe only a company. I think it's to guard against us trying to blow it up. They made a try early on to penetrate our lines, but our guys managed to put up a decent defense. That'll change when they finish laying planks so that they can get their tanks across."

"Can we reach the bridge from here?"

"Yeah. You'll see when it gets light. Depending on the route, the rail bridge is maybe fourteen miles. We have only two access avenues. So yes, we can reach it. The easiest route is down the mountain slope to the river. It's like a lava flow, stopping about a mile from the rail bridge. Then it gets damn near impossible without a boat. There's no clear river edge to follow. Swamps and uncertain terrain fan off to the north."

Rusty frowned. "What's the other approach?"

"Like how you got here. But at the base of this mountain, we go southwest. Similar problem with swamps and bad terrain but not nearly as severe. It's also a little shorter route. This, I'd say, is the best approach to the bridge."

Red was sitting nearby, overheard their discussion and decided to get up and join them. As he sat, he said. "C J, you're accent has bothered me since I first heard it. You kind'a sound like an Aussie. Where'd you learn English?"

In his best Aussie imitation, C J started. "Well, you're quite the bloke, ain't ya? Good ear! Born and raised in Melbourne." He gave a cynical laugh at his little routine. "I go through this often when I speak English. I know! Now you want to know how I got here? That's a long story for another day. The short answer is that my family comes from Osan, not far from here. I came back with my uncle after the war. I'm fluent in Japanese, English and of course, Korean."

Rusty looked at Red. "Seems like we have another world traveler amongst us."

"Good! Ain't seen much of the world except from foxholes and rice paddies of late. A new perspective is certainly welcomed. C J! You got any combat experience?"

Rusty interjected. "C J has stayed here behind the lines to help us. It's obvious he's brave."

"Red. Right?" C J wasn't sure of the names yet. Red nodded. "To your good question, yes and no. I, like you, would want to know about who was guiding me through enemy lines and most importantly, could I trust him in a tight spot. So I respect your question."

C J turned to Rusty. "I've only just met you and your team. But I can only wish that I could have a support group like yours to command."

Red wanted an answer; wasn't belligerent, just firm. "What the hell does yes and no mean? Either you've been in action or you haven't. What is it?"

C J reflected. "You have no idea of the chaos and horror that went on here after the war. I got into the new Korean Army at the beginning in '46. Your Army was here, but this Country was screwed up. You guys pretty much let the shit fly. Can't blame you, this was a civilian problem. All those years of being oppressed, Koreans were pissed at everything. The Nip caretaker oppressors were first to be hanged. Then the grudges started. Then the rich organized the political parties into paramilitary organizations. That's when the real bloodshed began."

C J stopped, wondered about what side he was on. Again, he confirmed to himself that he was on the best side in a bad choice.

"Then it became you guys against the Communists. This is an ignorant country and easily swayed. My people were energized, as I, for trying to reestablish our rights that were long taken away for many decades. So civil war broke out. I was instrumental in putting it down."

C J leaned back against the wall. It was noticeable that he felt uncomfortable speaking about this.

"So yes, I've killed. Many! Hand to hand combat, and stealth. I've taken out men from behind."

C J paused, had a sad look. "So Red, I hope you can trust me with your life, as I, trust you with mine."

Rusty was impressed. "C J, if I didn't know better, I'd say you were running for President."

C J smiled at Rusty. "I'd like that. Maybe I can earn your vote."

The rain intensified. It hid the pending dawn.

105

Chapter Seventeen

Friday, June 30, 1950 – Day Six of the Invasion
Japan – Eighth Army Headquarters – Colonel Nelson's Office
– 0500 – (5:00 am)

Despite not having slept, Colonel Nelson was ecstatic with the news that Rusty's team had made it to the rendezvous point. Hope for some event to slow the enemy advance now seemed possible. With just the two of them in the office, Major Jarvis started his briefing, this time leading with bad news.

"We confirmed with Rusty that they only have ten pounds of C-4. Nowhere near enough. Since our meeting, our team has focused on this bridge, assuming it is the very best way to have any immediate impact on slowing their advance. The team is working on a plan."

The reality of the situation darkened his mood. "I can't wait, Hank. Let's go over to the team now. See what they got."

They proceeded to the Operations room. Entering the big room, they met three officers that were headed out. Nelson recognized his old friend, Lieutenant Colonel Charles Smith. He stopped.

"Charlie! What the hell you are doing slumming with the intellectuals?" They shook hands, made introductions.

"Haven't seen you in a dogs' age, Jim! Guess you've been staying out of trouble?"

"Yeah. I find it easier if I don't hang out with you!" They laughed. "So what's up, Charlie?"

"Just got orders to fly into Pusan. Been checking with Planning and Logistics."

"Your whole 1st Battalion!? We got enough transport for that?"

"Jim! We got nothing but six C-54s! Three of which aren't here yet. They'll be in by mid-morning tomorrow. Only half the battalion's going, plus some other stuff. The rest of the regiment's going by boat in a day or two. Gotta go, Jim. Good to see you."

"Give'em hell, Charlie!"

They moved through the room towards the side conference room they had used earlier, Colonel Nelson shaking his head and mumbling all the way.

Major Jarvis wondered what was wrong. He thought that US troops moving to Korea would be good news.

"Colonel, what's wrong?"

"Don't you see? We're sending five hundred men that may or may not be in position for three or four days to stop thirty thousand North Koreans. And those Commies got tanks!"

"Shit!" Major Jarvis was frustrated. He thought of his War College class about the **Spartan** defense at **The Battle of Thermopylae.** He hoped his team would come up with something other than the slaughter of the brave defense he knew LT. Colonel Smith would put up. He pinned a face to a name now. Determined, we'll find a way, he thought, as they entered the small room.

Lieutenant Cole was at a projector on the center of the conference table, its image magnified on the blank wall at its front, where the map had been. A bird's eye view close up of a railroad bridge showed every detail of this four hundred yard span.

Captain Haran was working on a side wall chalkboard. Lines, drawings of structures and calculations were visible.

Both turned to the entrance as they entered. Captain Haran nodded, "You're early!"

"And you're late!" Colonel Nelson barked. "Got anything we can kick around yet?"

Nelson walked up to the wall projection and looked at the bridge that he thought held the key.

"This was taken yesterday morning." Captain Haran stated. "It's the best shot we have of the construction of the bridge. The

107

Japanese built this like a brick blockhouse. I wish it were a shithouse, but no, this baby is way over built. Like those pillboxes we encountered in the Pacific Islands. Ten feet thick concrete, steel reinforced. Well, this bridge isn't much different. They didn't want this bridge to go down without a significant effort, and it won't."

The Colonel saw the incredibly thick walls under each of the spans. The steel girders, close and interlacing, supporting a rail bed with two-foot steel beams that were also supported by additional cross steel members.

"I'm impressed." Nelson said and talked to Captain Haran. "So? How do we take it down?"

"That's the easy part. It's just math. What I mean is that we know what'll bring down a span. With a margin of safety, four hundred pounds of C-4 ought to do it. One hundred pounds under each support beam end on the same support column."

"Jesus!" Nelson decided to sit. Everybody but Lieutenant Cole sat as well. Nelson noticed the master sergeant was missing. "Where's our grunt? I hope Nick brings back some coffee."

The Captain got up. "He's checking something out. Larry's got an idea he wants to go over with you. I'll get coffee."

Major Jarvis also got up. "I just thought of something I need to check out. Be back in ten."

Nelson looked back at the Lieutenant, standing next to the projector. God he thought, I was exactly like him. What? Ten years, maybe fifteen years ago? You thought out of the box then. You could see the big picture and yet, could focus on solving a very specific problem. Yeah. And I often did. Can Cole do the same? I sure hope so!

"What'da you have Cole?"

"Sir, we rounded up a thousand pounds of C-4. Almost everything we have in Japan. It's being delivered to Itazuke Airbase, as we speak. Don't need it all for this operation, but probably will need more as we get rolling. Getting four hundred pounds to the bridge area is the problem. That's what Nick, Master Sergeant Beloit, is trying to solve."

"What about the Air Force? I didn't have much luck. Did you get anywhere?"

"No, sir. The air resources are not adequate, and they're downright resentful we should insist on tactical ground support. USAF Far East chief, Lt. Gen. George Stratemeyer has a plan to bomb the NK's back to the Stone Age, using the conventional WW2 strategy of hitting cities and major hubs. It didn't work then, and it sure as hell not going to slow them down anytime soon. Besides, even if he should decide to go tactical, all he has is a few heavy bombers and a bunch of limited range fighter Jets. Not a fighter-bomber in Japan. They just have no weapons for tactical support. The Air Force, right now, is useless to us."

"I know all of this. They all got caught up in the *Atom Bomb thing.* No more ground wars! Idiots! If they'd let the Army keep our air force, we wouldn't be in this mess!"

Nelson was frustrated, shook his head. "What do you want to kick around?"

Captain Haran came in carrying a tray of coffee and some buns. "I brought reinforcements." As Master Sergeant Beloit crutched in behind him.

Colonel Nelson brightened. "Damn glad you could join us *Grunt!* We need some down and dirty assessments. Well, coffee too. Thanks, Captain."

They all grabbed a coffee and sat at the table.

Lieutenant Cole looked at his cohorts. "I haven't briefed Colonel Nelson on our thoughts about the bridge operation yet. I was hoping you might be able to make these options easier. Did you find anything?"

Captain Haran straightened. "I've got background. I should start."

Master Sergeant Nick Beloit interjected. "You should, Sam. You and Cole led us down this path."

"Tell me, Sam."

Besides Nick, it was the first time the Colonel used a personal name in the A team. They took notice.

Sam stood, went to the projector, looked through a few films and selected one. Put in on the light tray and the view from the two thousand foot airborne image of the southern Han River appeared. It was crisp, taken on a bright day. It showed the northern bend of the river as it turned into Seoul, the railroad bridge at its extreme upper left-hand corner. The mountains to the east of the river clearly dominated for a quarter of the frame. Further south, the river split at a large junction. The main flow coming from the northeast tucked in close behind a mountain before turning north. Tributaries went south and east. A vast tidal plain extended southwest. A few hamlets were visible on the southeast bank.

"This picture was taken a few years ago when we were mapping our new UN Protectorate."

He addressed Colonel Nelson.

"I think this is our key." He paused. "Hard to fathom. In our modern times that we know so little about so much. I communicated with some of my friends at universities, geologist, anthropologist, etc. It's a mind bender that nobody knows much of anything about this part of the Han River. The only thing they can find is that it was a major trade route before the Japanese took control in 1905. They then essentially closed the country. No more information. For forty years."

"I'm intrigued, but what's so special about this area?" Asked Nelson.

The Captain put another film sheet on the projector. This was also a high altitude photo, but with a closer focus, showing what looked like plane wreckage just off the east bank of the river.

"What the hell?" Colonel Nelson strained to get a fix on what it was.

"I'll take over from here, Sam." Said Nick, not moving from his chair. Sam sat down.

Colonel Nelson saw the interaction of his team and their fellowship of common purpose. He smiled to himself.

Nick continued. "We couldn't figure it out either. But it sure looked like a plane and a big one at that, so I dug around. Making a long story short, this was a B-29 bomber that went down in June of '44, coming back from the first raid on Tokyo, from a base in China."

"I didn't know we flew B-29s out of China." Nelson was curious but getting agitated. "But what does that have to do with anything?"

"Well, graves registration picked up on this wreckage when they did this mapping project and launched a remains recovery effort. It's that report that's interesting. They couldn't figure out how to get into this remote area. No roads, terrible terrain. Almost impossible. They first tried running a coastal boat down from Seoul, some forty miles away. The river current was swift and against them. They ran aground many times, finally lost a prop and gave up. That was after making only fifteen miles."

Nick paused, wondering if the punch line would excite the Colonel, as it had him.

"Somebody on this team was thinking. Came up with the idea of using the river to fly in a PBY Catalina and use rubber boats to get the bodies. That's what they did."

He saw the start of a smile on the Colonel. Knew he had him.

"And that's what we think will work for us now." Nick smiled.

Nelson was beaming as he looked around at his team. "That's good work! Really damn good work!"

Pausing a moment, Nelson squinted, "Any downside to this idea?"

Nick looked over at Sam. He nodded a go ahead.

"Colonel, there was one problem the body recovery team encountered. The PBY hit a sandbar powering to the crash site. It didn't cause any damage because they were going very slow. But it made them search their projected takeoff path on the river and found numerous hidden sandbars. Eventually, they did find a clear runway. Of course, we don't know at what stage the monsoon season was for this recovery, which would affect the river depth. So the landing part of this operation could be a problem.

111

"That's a serious problem, Nick. Anyway we can get around it?"

"No, sir. No other way to get in there."

Nelson frowned. Lady Luck again, he thought. I'm getting tired of relying on you. You're too damn fickle.

"OK. I see no choice. Please continue."

Then Major Jarvis filled Nelson in on a rough sketch of their plan.

After he had finished, the Colonel sat back in his chair, thinking for a bit. Then he turned to his XO, "Hank, go ahead and draw up the plan. Keep it flexible but focused. I want to run it up the command ASAP. It's an all Services operation, so let's call it **Operation Halt.** I'm going to brief General Walker now."

"Don't you think you should wait a few hours until we get this tighter? We don't even know if we can do any of this yet."

"Hank! We don't have a few hours. A lot of this is gonna be done on the fly. But it must start immediately. I want you all here to **ACT AS IF**. Start the wheels in motion. This needs to be executed tonight!"

Chapter Eighteen

Wild Bill had arrived first, yesterday. His first sortie against the enemy kept him in a jubilant mood; that is until he landed at the new airfield. The lack of everything appalled him. But the reception he got from the ROK troops was nothing but triumphant. Excited by seeing an American fighter plane at their base, they did anything he asked. So the first thing he did was to clear out one of the two hangers. Two spotter planes were moved to the side of the field, and the ROK unit that was taking shelter inside moved out. Then they got him food.

Billy and the convoy arrived a few hours later. They backed in their three trucks and trailers and started unloading Billy's tools and spare parts for ***Just Due***. After much praise from Captain Stands on the great work they did on him, they pushed the P-51 into the hanger and Billy, and Arnie started maintenance but promptly quit, deciding they were exhausted.

The new morning was in full swing with Billy and Arnie hard at it. George was offloading ammunition skids using the forklift, driving them into the hanger. Trying to position them in neat stacks, he realized the skid he was hauling had two large canisters, not the usual four one-hundred pound bombs. Being infantry, he didn't know anything about the different types of ordinance for planes. He was curious.

"Hey, Captain!" He yelled. "Got a strange looking bomb here! But don't think it's a bomb. Can you check it out?"

Wild Bill walked over. "Good job George! Your right, that's not a bomb. It's a napalm canister. Hot dog! Got any more of these?"

George knew what napalm was. Saw it action. Deadly stuff, he thought. "Don't know, Captain. Still got plenty of skids to take off. I'll let you know."

Wild Bill moved over to Billy, who was working on the engine. He yelled up to him, "Billy! We found some napalm canisters. Is *He* equipped to handle them?"

"Napalm! No shit! Yeah! No problem. Should go right where the bomb racks are. I'll check it in a few minutes. You want us to load the canisters if we can?"

"Absolutely! Nothing like fire and brimstone to bring our enemy to the great reality that they fucked up."

They loaded *Him* up with ammo, rockets and the two canisters were added to the under mount wing racks.

They finished late that morning. Seeing the Captain standing by the hanger entrance, George walked over to him. "Captain, can I talk to you for a minute?"

Wild Bill had expected this again from George after their last conversation. He remembered how time seemed to increase the loss of friends. How Georges' survival instincts and experience had sheltered the inner feelings. The lack of a new direction for George from Colonel Nelson, other than to stick with his new found team, was affecting him. He was frustrated and angry. He wanted to avenge his fallen buddies, not load ammo. A third wheel. Not really needed, and he knew it. Captain Stands braced himself.

"Of course, George." They angled off to the side of the hanger.

George leaned against the open hanger door edge, not caring about the light rain coming in on him. He bent his head, looking at his feet, then came up and looked straight into Captain Stand's eyes.

"I want to kill these bastards, Captain. I know you do too. I'm happy to help you do it, but it's not the same. I lost my whole team,

114

my friends." George hung his head and whispered. "My only family. You have no idea how I feel. I want to get back in this fight. Can you help me do that?"

It brought back so many memories for the Captain. He hadn't thought of the emotional response of George and how it might affect him. It did. Deeply. He remembered his nightmares. He tried, over the last five years to forget. It was always there. Here it was again, in his face. A fellow griever. A lost soul, seeking justice, revenge or what? Redemption? He didn't know.

The Captain drew near, put an arm around his shoulder and moved him to the inside corner of the hanger, out of the rain.

"George, I know what you want. Be patient. Your time will come. Let's sit. I want to tell you things I've never told anyone."

Captain Stands told him about a mission that he led in the War. As a new squadron commander of a fighter group in England that was escorting B-17s, and was lured away from his mission of protection by a faint attack of German ME-109s. He fell for it and led his squadron in pursuit. That left the bombers unprotected and open to the main Nazi attack of Flocke-Wulf 190s. He shot down three of the ME-109s, adding to his two previous kills, earning him his first Ace in that battle. He told George how he felt after realizing that because of his decision to go after the first attack, eight bombers were shot down. Shot to shit by the main attack force. Eighty men, dead. He blamed himself. Told George how, from then on, he wanted to die to avenge his mistake. Then he talked about his lost friends and more.

"George, I don't know if you got a damn thing out of what I just said. But I sure as hell did. Thanks."

Not waiting for an answer, the Captain got up and walked away, alone with his thoughts.

The rain started in earnest. It made a racket as it pounded on the tin roof. Arnie got a stove going and made coffee.

Captain Stands grabbed a cup, walked to the front and looked out at the rain and the airfield.

It was a field, not much else. A few buildings sat at the north edge. Two small hangers off to the northeast side of the field. A big pole with a wind sock stood at the far end of the dirt runway. A rusty truck, a small plow on its front and a big drum attached to its rear, sat by the side of one of the hangers.

The city, however, was big and spread out. Mostly one story buildings that sprawled out south and east from the airfield. The center had multiple two and three story concrete structures, housing government agencies, commercial businesses and a hospital.

And then there was a two-story blockhouse that was the communication hub, home of the Korean Cable relay station. The one above it, fifty miles north, was in Suwon. The next one, fifty miles below it, was in Pusan. The Japanese built the Korean Cable in the '30s. It ran from the northern tip of Korea to its southern tip in Pusan, then continued to Japan through an underwater cable. The cable was instrumental for the Japanese in waging its war against China. It was constructed well and now became a strategic necessity for this new war, if South Korea was to survive as a country.

Taejon was strategic in another way. It was a transportation hub. Two rivers flowed around it at its far edges. Two railroad lines from the south converged here, then continued north to the capital. The main highway from Seoul passed through town and split to both ends of the southern coasts.

It was now the new displaced Capital of the country.

"Billy!" Wild Bill cried out. Billy looked up, startled. He had fallen asleep, still exhausted from the late night's work, was laying on the floor, against the side wall of the small hanger.

"What is it, Captain?" Billy called out in a near panic, thinking that maybe they were under attack.

Wild Bill, standing near the open hanger door, looked sternly at him. "Are you a praying man, Billy?"

He didn't know what he meant but concluded that something must be seriously wrong. "Yes, sir! When shit hits the fan, I've been known to start praying like a mother...." He didn't finish, didn't think it was right to say that.

116

"Well good! Start praying for God to end this hell inspired rain to stop. I know he's on our side. This rain is preventing me from killing our enemies. He must be distracted or something. So remind him of his duty."

Billy almost laughed but wasn't sure if the Captain was joking or serious. Relieved that there was no immediate threat, he played along. "Right! I'll start straight away, Captain!"

Chapter Nineteen

**Friday, June 30, 1950 – Day Six of the Invasion
ROK Signal Unit Mountain Hideout Northeast of Seoul
– 1000 – (10:00 am)**

Tully was pacing like a Lion waiting to pounce. Everybody was on edge. The last communication said to wait and study the railroad bridge for a possible operation. More info later.

"What's later?" Tully wanted to know.

Red went off. "Tully! If you're not shooting somebody you get irritated. God damn Rangers! Calm down for Christ's sake. The Colonel's working on it. We're going to blow things up and cause mayhem before too long, so start preparing."

C J was taking this all in. He was sliding down, emotionally. Feeling more despondent at the sudden collapse of his country's army and watching, helpless, as his capital was captured and pillaged. The arrival of the Americans had boosted his moral, but still, he felt his country slipping away. Losing touch with his HQ added to his feeling of hopelessness. Thinking about trying to destroy this bridge, he laughed to himself. Impossible!

In a whisper, C J said to Rusty. "This is suicide, can't be done."

Rusty didn't respond. Thought about how he'd feel, sitting on a hill overlooking Washington, DC, watching Nazi's rampage through **my** city. How would I feel knowing America was about to be overrun.

Stunned for a moment, he made the connection between Korea and his own country's civil war. Different! What's different? He asked himself and thought for a moment. I don't give a good crap! He finally said to himself. I'm in the right! They've in the wrong.

Rusty leaned into C J. "Tell ya something C J. My team knows that an impossible mission sometimes can't even be conceived, not less accomplished, without some divine force. So you must believe. Red does. So does Tully. He's just impatient. And I, down to my toes, believe! We have a force of nature behind us that's hard to imagine, C J. I hope we all get to see it played out. It'll be something."

C J reflected on Rusty's words and nodded. "I too, believe. Although I sometimes doubt, Rusty. I don't want to die in a ditch. But I won't run and hide. If I must die, it will be for my family and my country."

Red, ever the listener, moved closer to them and chimed in. "Nobody's dying here, C J! These bastards are going to die for their country. We're going to live for ours. Screw them!"

He scanned Rusty, C J and Tully, met each of their eyes. He looked fierce as he was. "You remember that. We fight to win and live. C J, you're new to war, but the three of us here have seen more of hell than most mortals. We've seen bad death, and we've seen our share of miracles. But great leaders? We haven't seen many. We've met a few, though, our Colonel Nelson is one. He'll figure this out in the right way. By that, I mean that if he orders us on a potential suicide mission, it's an extraordinary situation that may save many, many lives, and I'm good with that. I'm pretty sure he'll tell us that in advance. Knowing him, he'd probably ask for volunteers. That's our leader, C J! Have faith!"

Tully sounded off. "Jesus, Red! Are you trying out for Ranger Academy?"

Maybe it was the tenseness, but he started laughing and continued. "Rusty, you better watch out. Maybe there's a local election of some sort going on."

It broke the tension. They smiled. C J marveled at his new, strange fellow warriors. That's how he viewed them. Like his uncle, who he adored, but much younger. His contemporaries in age but

119

not experience. Their eyes showed all to him. He wondered that if he survived this war, would his eyes also mirror the sorrow of loss and long forgotten dreams.

Rusty broke the momentary silence. "Seems to be a lot of electioneering going around. Let's quit the bullshit. Let's start thinking about this bridge."

C J started. "This rain will break at some point. These bands suddenly stop and the sun comes out for minutes or hours, very unpredictable. It will happen, though. Then you'll see the bridge and its surroundings."

Although it had been light for hours, the intense rain rendered visibility to less than a mile.

"What about your guys, C J? Can they help us?" Tully wanted to know.

C J thought about the question, been asking himself the same thing. "Don't know, Tully. Never fired a shot together. They're good guys. Loyal and tough, but they're signal troops. Not combat trained. I can't tell you how they'd react under fire."

Tully pursued. "Will they follow your orders?"

C J thought for a second, knowing what Tully was really asking. "Yes. I believe that they would under stress."

The weather broke a little later. The sun didn't shine but the rain stopped and visibility became adequate to see Seoul and the bridges. The foursome gathered around the two tripod mounted high-powered field glasses. At a fourteen mile distance, they could make out a face on the bridge. Rusty and Red got first to look.

Red came away first. "Holly crap! These are German, right!"

Tully replaced him. "Jesus!" But he was looking at the structure. Then he looked back. "Yeah, Red. Very German. Best goddamned optics!"

Rusty called over from his position. "Tully! You got the bridge and side banks. I got the north shore."

Tully focused and went back to scan the whole bridge. Then both banks. He studied every detail, for the next half hour until the rain returned.

They regrouped under the overhang.

"I've seen worse." Said Tully, thinking of his Normandy assault on the hundred foot cliffs of Pointe-Du-Hoc.

"Yeah." Rusty frowned. "But this is different." He stood up, started slowly pacing around. Red and Tully were surprised, seeing Rusty act like this. Rusty knew what he saw, its significance, and asked himself if this was where he would meet his end. Felt this a few times before, Rusty thought. And I don't know the answer? But for whoever is in charge up there, I'm not going down without a fight....and Oh! He said to himself; you're not taking my boys without my permission, either. He stopped pacing, looked out into the rain. Can we do this? How many times have I asked that question and got the same answer? This is different! Suicide! He shook his head. And that's what he'd always concluded.

He smiled.

Refreshed from his thoughts, Rusty looked around at his inner circle. He wondered at the gift of these great men that have been through so much and decided now was a good time to talk to all of the men.

He turned inwards to his men standing and lying about further in, under the overhang. The rain intensified.

He called to them. "Hey!" He yelled. "Come around. I want to talk to you 'all."

Arron picked right up on the southern slang and yelled back. "Not going all southern on us Mr. New Yorker, are you?"

Rusty had played enough with Arron to know.

"No Arron!" He yelled back. "We're not surrendering Southern style!" That got a laugh, even from Arron.

Then Arron yelled back. "They didn't have me! You do! We'll keep kicking some ass together!"

A big cheer went up.

Rusty stood proudly, glad they were in good spirits. He smiled, as he gazed around at their faces.

"Yeah, Arron. We are going to kick more ass together! Very soon!"

121

The men knew what that meant and drew closer.

"Don't know exactly when yet. Don't even have a definite target. But I got a good idea of what it is and I want you to start preparing for it. Because it will be our toughest mission ever."

The sound of the outside rain resounded through the total silence of the sheltered gathering. Rusty slowly paced then continued.

"That river down there," pointing towards Seoul, "is the only thing holding up this enemy tidal wave. But it won't last for long. When they finish laying a roadbed on that railroad bridge so tanks and trucks can cross, resistance on the south bank will collapse. The rest of Korea will be overrun in a matter of days."

"Have they started on it?" Joe shouted out over the pounding rain.

"Just!" Rusty replied. "It looks like they're waiting for more material, but yeah, they started. It won't take long to finish once they get the material."

"Can we do this, Rusty? We ain't got shit here!" Larry called out, knowing his ten pounds of explosives wouldn't do much of anything.

"No, Larry, we can't. Not with what we have."

He stopped pacing.

"Here's the thing. Colonel Nelson's one smart son of a bitch." That got a couple of *that's rights.*

"I think he's put a hold on us so he can put a plan together. He knows what we have, and he'll find out what'll take to accomplish this mission. I bet he does!"

"What can we do now? You know, to get ready." Arron asked.

Rusty saw an opening, couldn't resist. "Well, Arron, in your case, maybe you get us a mountain goat and prepare a feast for us." That broke the building tension. Even Arron didn't have a comeback; he was laughing so hard.

"Seriously. What I want you to do is pair off into groups around C J. and his men. They're locals and have been watching this bridge for a week. I want you to learn every detail possible about this area.

122

The bridge, the river, the banks, approaches anything that might help. C J's men don't speak English, so Foxy and Frenchy will translate in their groups. I want everybody to sit with each one. Everybody has a different take on surroundings, and I want you to get it all. Then I want each man to spend time at the high-powered glasses when, hopefully, the rain lets up."

"This is going to be a night mission, right? You think maybe tonight?" Mario called out.

"Can't imagine a daylight assault. Unless we've somehow discovered a secret potion that makes us like that *Invisible Man* guy in the movies. Now that would be fun!"

"Can you see it?" Quipped Frenchy, with a smirk.

Rusty, serious now. "When? This is so critical that I think tonight, early tomorrow morning. So let's get ready and oh yeah, get some rest."

He turned to Red and Tully, standing near. "Let's draw up some plans."

Chapter Twenty

Now known as the A Team, LT Larry Cole, Captain Sam Haran and Master Sergeant Nick Beloit sat around the staff table with Major Hank Jarvis and Colonel Nelson.

"The weather sucks." Sam started. "All over! Korea and Japan. We pretty much have the ground aspect covered, but the major part of our *Operation Halt* plan totally depends on fly-a-ability access and diversion tactics. This is our major problem, and I'm not sure how we address it."

Abruptly, Colonel Nelson stood up.

"You need to know something! We invaded Europe in a near God Damn hurricane!" He was aware that he exaggerated but wanted to make his point.

"Nothing! I repeat! Nothing will get in the way of this mission. Do you read me!?"

Everybody nodded.

He sat down, just looked at his team. "Larry, what's Air Force saying?"

"Just bullshit, Colonel. They don't like the Army, want no part of an operation they didn't plan. I'm getting nowhere."

Turning to his XO, "Hank, get General Walker." The connection was almost immediate. He handed off the phone.

"General, I'm pissed, and you should be too." Nelson started. "**Operation Halt**. I briefed you on this earlier. The Air Force is key to this plan, and they're not cooperating. It's being stonewalled!" A pause. "Yeah, the usual intra-service bull. General! I need your help!"

A few minutes later he hung up.

"Nick, how's your operation? You okay?"

"Yeah, boss. Had some issues but just waiting for more critical elements to come together. It's a crazy operation, sir. I got guys running all over Japan getting stuff. I'll have that nailed soon, pretty sure I'll be ready for the deadline."

"What's the issue, Nick?" Asked Major Jarvis.

"Things got a little FUBAR this morning. None of the trucks made it to the PBY Naval Station on time. So the plane left, per their orders, to get Jack's team. It turns out it was a good thing. That plane was an older model, wasn't retrofitted with the bigger engines. It wouldn't have been able to carry all the weight we need for the full operation. From there I had to improvise."

"What'da you do?

"First, my guy in charge of getting all this stuff together and meeting the rescued team also didn't make that flight. Had to get him out with whatever he had on a C-47 a little later. He didn't have much. Most importantly, I had to find a newer PBY. I did, but even so; we're in the process of stripping it down some to lighten it. But, like I said, I've got it covered. You don't want to know the rest."

Major Jarvis picked up the blinking phone.

"General Walker, Colonel."

"Yes sir, General." The Colonel listened, a smile spread on his face. "You did?" Pause. "Really!" Pause. "Politics be darned, right General!" Pause. "God bless you, General. Maybe this will give you a chance!" Pause. "Right." He cradled the phone and grinned.

Looking around at his A Team, he broke into a full smile.

"General Walker came through! This is an order directly from General MacArthur himself. I quote the Supreme Commander.

125

Operation Halt has the highest priority of all operations in Korea. Every Allied Command will follow this directive. Unquote."

"Hell of an order! That should open some doors!" A smiling LT Larry Cole said.

"Never heard an order like that." Captain Sam Haran bellowed.

"You're right, Sam! You and Larry are going back to your Air Force people and open those doors. If you meet any resistance, kick in that door! Make them listen and make them act. We got one chance here. There will be NO excuses...NONE!"

In unison, as if by command, Sam and Larry answered. "We won't let you down, boss!"

Nelson relaxed. He liked his new nickname.

"No! I don't expect you will. Let's meet back here in two hours."

**Same Day - Friday, June 30, 1950 – Day Six of the Invasion
Aboard PBY 276 – Approaching Pusan Harbor, Korea
– 1130 – (11:30 am)**

Flying at one thousand feet, buffeted by the rain storm, the craft shook violently as it changed altitude. They were five miles out from Pusan harbor. JP was strapped into a seat next to the big Plexiglas side window and was vomiting profusely in a bag that Jack had brought along, just in case.

126

Jack yelled over to him, "You're not going to die, JP! You're not getting away from this shit so easy!"

Jack didn't believe what he just said. He had to say it. Saying it, though, relieved him, probably more than JP. He'd never been in a small plane before. Actually, he'd never been in any plane before. He was scared shitless.

"Man this is fun!" Yelled Greg, lying on the floor, on the right of JP, next to the big window.

Phil, lying next to Jack, holding on for dear life, was stoic. He was an engineer; had linear thoughts about life and death. He wondered if this was it. Not afraid, just curious.

There was no intercom warning as they felt the first bounce. It was a big one. Felt and heard vibrations and loud noises from the planes hull as it interacted with the sea. Then a series of smaller bounces, and then, the engines and the harsh sounds of water against the hull.

After receiving a priority flash message from the *Juneau* earlier that morning, they, and the men of the *Gurke* had scrambled to get ready. The rescued Post # 4 team were to leave. The crew set about to guide the approaching flying boat to a rendezvous point and then lower the utility boat for the transfer. It went smoothly. The seas were calm, the rain moderate.

Yesterday, after their rescue and onboard the *Gurke*, JP's condition had improved immensely. IV and seasickness drugs stabilized him almost immediately. Although the ship moved, the seas were moderate and didn't generate violent movements. The rich Navy food helped all the men regain their strength.

The new experience of being heroes, expressed by all of the crew, reinvigorated them. Having never been on a Navy ship, they were curious. The captain allowed free access to all but a few places, one being the anti-submarine cube. The few hours of free time they had, was enough to excite their experience.

Jack went to the bridge, spent time with the captain. Greg covered the deck, inspecting the five-inch guns he saw in action, then went below to see how it all happened. Phil found his way to the control center, where radar and all things electronic happened. JP found himself going into the engine room. He didn't know why but followed his instinct. Maybe it was because he was told that the ship swayed less here? He didn't know. Standing at the top of the walkway, looking down at this maze of pipes, engines, and incredible noise. The crew was scurrying about as he realized how helpless these guys were to a sudden attack. Jesus, he thought, it's like rats in a trap. Glad I'm infantry.

It took a few minutes for the plane to motor down the channel. It then glided past a short, dilapidated pier. With engines revved high, it climbed onto land via a concrete ramp that ran into a big boatyard work shed. It cut engines in front of the big open doors. Hatches and the big Plexiglas side window were opened by the crew.

JP followed the first crew guy out of the window exit. He didn't wait for a ladder and dropped five feet to the ground. Ignoring the rain and the big puddles, he went flat, hugging the ground like a long lost lover.

Jack and Greg grabbed him by his arms and lifted him up; he wobbled a bit.

"It's all over bud!" Said Jack. "I'd like to say dry land at last, but, I guess, *no motion* land will do. Let's get out of this rain."

Standing inside the shed, Staff Sergeant Thomas Leyden watched the show and laughed to himself. He had almost upchucked himself, flying in earlier from Japan.

"You guys look pitiful! Squid clothes and all. Who's Jack?"

"I am! Who the hell are you?"

"I'm your welcoming committee and Brooks Brothers representative, asshole. Come to the back, got coffee on. I'm Tom."

Three old fishing boats on blocks lie against the right side wall of the huge warehouse, much in need of repair. A big military truck sat towards the back, on the left side, facing forward. At the rear, a few American soldiers were standing about a makeshift fire pit in a small drum with a kettle hanging above it.

Tom led the way back. Jack called, "Hey, Big Tom! Oh, can I call you Big Tom?"

Tom turned back to him. "Why would you be different? Everybody calls me that."

He wasn't a particularity big man at six one and two hundred pounds. Oddly handsome with a large face and bright red hair. But he had this presence.

"So, Big Tom, what's going on?"

"I don't know shit! Other than you guys are some very special VIPs."

They grabbed some tin cups, helped themselves from the steaming pot of coffee and found a crate and a barrel to sit on. Jack was thinking about Big Tom's remark.

"We're survivors, bud. Don't know diddly about any VIP crap. You better tell me something I can understand."

Big Tom looked across at Jack. He saw a hardened combat veteran, like himself, no bullshit here, he said to himself.

"I was kind'a hoping you'd fill me in. But since you know less than me, I'll tell you what I know. Oh, but first, in the back of the truck, you'll find Army clothes, full combat gear, boots, everything. They're in tagged bags. You probably want 'a get out of those Navy rags. We've got a schedule."

Jack sensed major trouble and had since the big rush started to get them here.

"You better start talking to me."

Greg knew it was time to get out of earshot. Heard about the new clothes, didn't want to get involved in more of this. "Come on guys, let's get some fighting clothes on." Phil and JP followed him to the truck.

Big Tom saw that these guys were savvy too. Felt for JP, still wobbly.

"Ok, about four hours ago, I get a call from my boss's boss, telling me that we have an emergency operation. I'm to spare nothing to accomplish my mission and if I encounter any objections from anybody, I'm to call this Colonel Nelson's XO, a Major Jarvis.

So this guy gives me a list and tells me that I and everything on his list has got to be on my flight that leaves at 1000 (10:00 am) from Ashiya Air Field. Well, screw all when I discover this airfield is in at the end of the world, right at the asshole bottom of Japan. But it was near a big city, the one we destroyed with the A Bomb, Hiroshima."

"Man, do I love a challenge! I got excited. I had the power to get something done, too. Never had that before. I started calling around, threatening officers if I had too. Damn! I was telling them to get stuff I never heard of. Must 'a had a couple of hundred guys running around. They didn't all come through, however actually only one did. That'd be your stuff in the truck. Got it and me loaded on a waiting C-47 on time."

Jack was confused. "Backup! So? You work for Colonel Nelson?"

"Aren't you listening? Come on Jack, is your mind scrambled?"

"Maybe. It's just that I need to know the players. I've been on the run since the invasion! I'm out of touch."

"Don't know anything about where've you been, only that you're a VIP. This is a big time operation coming up my friend, and you're one of the main players, like it or not."

"So fill me in on your roll, how do you fit in."

"The world changed but a few days ago, Jack. Eighth Army HQ went into overdrive. That nothing staff exploded. I got a call from my buddy, told me that I was now assigned to Eighth Army Intelligence, in the special operational section, whatever that means. Damned glad he called so far. Been different. My boss is ok, but his boss is the friend that got me in. We go back a while, did some work on Saipan together."

"No shit!" Jack shook his head. What a strange world, he thought. "I saw a little bit of fun there myself."

"So maybe you know Nick Beloit?"

"No, I don't know you or Nick from Saipan. Most of the guys I remember from there are dead. Who's Nick?"

130

"That's my boss's boss who called me. He's a master sergeant now. Best damn infantryman and friend. He was brilliant in assault planning. He'd get the orders from our LT for an operation, and after a brief study, he'd go to the CO and get them changed. His ideas saved many, not just our platoon, but the whole regiment. Probably why he's still around."

Big Tom went on, remembering the most exciting time of his life.

"I gotta tell ya. I watched that crazy bastard charge a Jap tank, throw a satchel charge under it, spin around and kill six supporting Jap infantry. He got a Silver Star for that, but I can tell you many more stories about him. Then he stepped on a mine."

"He lived! How's he still around?"

"Nick's a guy that's hard to describe. Nothing and no one will get in his way when he sees' what should be done."

"I like this Nick already. How does he fit in?"

"All's I know is that he's in this A Team, directly under this Colonel Nelson, head of Eighth Army Intelligence, and Nick is a guy you want on your team."

"I know Colonel Nelson. A smart guy. Sounds like he got us a good guy in this Nick. Are you gonna join this new operation, whatever it is?'

"I like you, Jack. Be honored to join this merry band of yours, if that's in the cards. My fingers are itchy. Don't much like much what's been go 'in on. These Red guys are crazy. Like the Japs. Only way to stop'em is to punchen'em out. So, I'm hope'n to do something like that."

"I read you, Big Tom. Glad you have a death wish….like all of us here, I guess."

"Nah! I got a live wish! Only death wish I have is for anybody who gets in the way of my *Live Wish*."

"I like you're style. Hope you join us on whatever's next." Pausing, "And what the hell is next?"

"Only thing I know is that there's a shit load of stuff coming our way. Should be here midafternoon."

"Then what?"
"We wait for orders."

Chapter Twenty One

Friday, June 30, 1950 – Day Six of the Invasion
Japan - Eighth Army Headquarters – G-2 Operations Section
– Conference Room - 1215 – (12:15 pm)

Captain Sam Haran was telling the gathered A Team about his and LT Cole's journey up the Air Force chain of command, finally ending successfully at General Stratemeyer's office and his chief of staff. Since no written orders had been issued as yet, he had to call General MacArthur's HQ to confirm the ***Operation Halt*** order.

"After that, all the doors flew open." Sam went on. "We managed to cancel an afternoon B-29 bomber mission so that they could fly our mission tonight. Also found B-26's from Third Bomber Group that were starting to prepare for a late night mission. We got them to change that mission and the bomb load."

The team was relieved at the news.

Master Sergeant Nick Beloit was worried. He still had a lot of loose ends that hadn't come together yet. But the key element of the Air Force diversion was in place. "Sam, you think you have enough to make this work?"

"Yeah, Nick, providing they get near the target and some bombs actually hit close to the bridge."

"Considering the weather and night time mission, aren't you expecting a lot?" Asked Nelson.

Nick responded. "I agree, Colonel. Bomber Command's track record isn't so good, but we've provided some help for them. In the stuff getting to Pusan are two RDF transmitters that, when positioned, will guide the bombersg."

Major Jarvis saw Nelson's skepticism. "OK, I guess it's time to get into the details of this plan."

Amidst numerous interruptions, they spent the next hour finalizing the plan.

Major Jarvis left to formalize orders. LT Cole and Captain Haran left together, headed to the Air Force section to see if they could find more bombers.

Watching them leave, Nick appeared anxious. Nelson addressed his fidgeting.

"Waiting sucks, Nick. It's the hardest part of this job."

"Yeah, boss, it is. But that's not why I'm jittery. This is the first combat mission I've been involved in since Saipan, and I'm not in the field. Never will be. I guess it finally hit me."

"I read your file, Nick. I think you're exactly where you should be. I know you were great in combat, but you saved more men with your brains than with your rifle. I'm glad the Army saw fit to keep you involved in another role. But it must've taken some serious pull, though. I know this man's Army, and I don't think they're that smart. So who was your Rabbi?"

Nick smiled. "You're a pretty savvy boss, Colonel. Don't get me wrong now; I love being here. I think I can do some good. My Rabbi, as you put it, requires a story."

"Good. I like stories."

"We were into our third week on Saipan. My unit was supporting a Marine division on our right. Both of us were getting chopped to pieces. Late in the afternoon, me and Tom are in a foxhole on the line when this officer and a radio guy jumps in with us. I see he's a Marine and he's angry. What fucking outfit are you, he yells at me? I'm kind'a busy shooting at advancing Japs, so I ignore him. His radio guy gets shot in the head. I tell him he'd better grab a rifle because it looks like we may be overrun. We manage to stop the attack on account of heavy mortars someone called in.

"He's pissed his radio guy is dead, asks us if we know how to operate it so he can call in a mission. Of course, we know how and I say it, as he pulls out a map. I'm looking over his shoulder as he's pointing at a location. I tell him we're not there but over here, I point. Are you sure sergeant? He asks, very skeptical.

"Yes sir, positive, I say, we've been fighting here for two days. OK, he points to a map and asks me if ordering an attack on this Jap flank position will work. I tell him we made two attempts and both were a disaster. I then suggest another route, say my company commander turned down this suggestion a day ago. He saw the benefit and ordered it on the radio.

"That's when I learned this guy was Marine General Holland "Howlin' Mad" Smith, the guy in charge of the whole Saipan operation."

"No shit!" An amazed Nelson blurted out.

"It gets better....and worse. A Jap tank comes out of nowhere, charging at us, forty feet at our front. I had a satchel-charge, so I ran out, threw it under the tank, it blows, then I shoot a bunch of supporting infantry. I'm running back when I step on a mine. I won a medal but lost my foot. But I made a friend. General Smith visited me on the hospital ship. Told me he'd do anything he could for me. His friend, Major General Jim Lester, was promoted to head up the 24th Division right at the end of the war. He got me into division planning when I left rehab; been there ever since. We've often spoken since then, hell of a guy, that Smith. Even though he's a Marine, he's OK in my book. Did a lot for me."

"That's quite a story. You should think about writing about it. Why don't you have a prosthesis?"

"I do, but it got messed up. Been waiting for a new one. Should be ready soon."

"Good. Now tell me about this Tom. Is this the same Tom that's on our team in Pusan?"

"Yeah. Same. We've been friends since '43."

"Why did you put him in charge of the bridge mission?"

"Easy. Because he's the best combat team leader I know. He's one stubborn son of a bitch. Nothing gets in his way. Besides that, he's resourceful and has great tactical presence. Jack's still his team's leader. I read his file and he's good, but Tom has more experience. Besides, I know Tom. I think they'll get along just fine."

Nelson leaned back. "How come Tom didn't go for the Jap tank?"

Nick smiled. "He would have if the satchel charge had been on his side."

Same Day - Friday, June 30, 1950   Day Six of the Invasion
ROK Signal Unit Mountain Hideout Northeast of Seoul – 1400 – (2:00 pm)

The rain bands had been intermittent, clearing out for good visibility intermittently. Everybody studied the terrain during these breaks.

During Arron's turn, he called out. "What the hell!?"

C J and Rusty came running. C J bent to Arron's glass to look.

C J got up and shook his head in sadness. "They're just killing the anti-communists, or folks they don't like. Been doing it for a while."

Arron was pissed, looked at Rusty. "I ain't seen anything like that. Women and kids. Must 'a killed twenty. It ain't right!"

Rusty was dismayed at the horror. His mind clicked back to France. His unit had just liberated a town. Saw the locals do unspeakable atrocities to perceived Nazi sympathizers. But they didn't just line them up and shoot them. They shaved their heads and hung a few that killed fellow countrymen. But this was much worse. More like the Nazi hatred. Damn it! Again!

He went over to Arron, steered him away so he could speak to him privately. Put his arm around him.

"You know what this is all about, right, Arron? You've been there. It's hatred and jealousy, revenge and just downright stupidity.

136

We can't change the world. We can only do what we can, that's all."

Arron lifted his head, eyes misting. "I know Rusty. Just can't fathom killing woman and kids. Never will. I hate these guys and yet, I know where that goes, too. Maybe I've just seen too much innocent death."

"I know. We all have. Just remember that you're a good man, doing his best."

Foxy was nearby and overheard what was said. He knelt down and said a silent prayer for his Grandma and his cousin. Every day he wondered and prayed that she heeded his warning to leave Seoul on the noon train.

"Got incoming!" Larry yelled out. He was on the VLF set. Moose at his side, cranking away at the generator.

Joe took his position, Rusty his. Red and Tully gathered around. Foxy and C J found a spot off to the side. The rest of the men drifted over.

It took a long time. It wasn't a message. It was an order.

Joe translated the code as it came in. Larry wrote it down. In the end, nobody spoke.

Reflective, Rusty knew what he signed on for, just didn't think it might end like this. He thought that if he were Colonel Nelson, he'd do the same. Pull out all the stops! Has to be! All out! Do or die!

Tully broke the icy silence. "This is one mother fucking plan!"

Red looked at him. Not knowing if he should cry or laugh. "You don't do it justice, Tully."

Foxy had done a lot of combat planning but nothing on this scale. He shook his head.

"Lota moving parts!"

Standing next to him, Arron was incredulous. "Moving parts! My ass! This got more shit going on than General Lee had staging his troops at Gettysburg!"

Arron always expressed himself so well; Rusty thought and laughed. "Arron! How the hell do you know anything about General Lee's plan anyway?"

Arron looked sharply at Rusty. "I read, you know!"

Rusty thought of the craziness of the moment. Couldn't let the chance slip by.

"No Arron, I didn't!"

The joshing cut through the gloom.

Then Rusty called out. "Listen up! General Lee had a piss poor planning staff and inferior leaders. We don't! Now let's dissect this plan and make it better!"

Chapter Twenty Two

Friday, June 30, 1950 – Day Six of the Invasion
Pusan Harbor, Korea – Boatyard - PBY Landing Area
– 1415 – (2:15 pm)

Outside, the PBY engines started up. Everybody jumped. Tom flew off his crate in a flash. "What the crap?" He ran to the front. Jack followed.

The plane started turning, doing a circle powering one engine, preparing to go back down the ramp.

Tom was waving his arms, trying to get the pilots attention. He didn't. The engines increased speed, slowly the plane entered the water and kept going out to the channel, finding a clear takeoff path. The rain had stopped about an hour ago; visibility was fair with low clouds still threatening more rain to come.

He and Jack watched as the PBY cleared the water and lifted out of the harbor.

"Any idea, Tom?"

Still looking off to the plane, Tom spoke to the disappearing PBY. "Maybe they got scared! We are a nasty bunch, you know, to most regular pansies. I think they found out about this mission and decided disobeying orders was a better alternative. But, basically, Jack, I don't have a goddamned clue."

"What'd we do now, big guy?"

"I got another delivery due in by truck soon. Maybe they'll know something. But I'm counting on somebody noticing we got no wings. After all the trouble of setting all this shit up? Can't imagine they'd forget!" He thought a moment about that, reconsidered. "Then again, *this is* the Army."

Jack was mystified and upset. Not used to being this much out of control. "You're something! You really know how to instill confidence. No wonder you're a Tech Sergeant. Are you a plumber or something?"

Tom turned to him, ruffled. "My dad was a plumber! And you have no God damned idea what I am or what I do! Be careful, Jack. I sense a budding relationship here. Don't screw it up!"

Jack knew the situation had nothing to do with Tom. He was at a loss, just like him.

"I think, Tom that if we were back in the neighborhood, I'd say, let's get a beer."

Tom smiled. "And I'd say, I'm buying!"

Same Day – Friday, June 30, 1950 – Day Six of the Invasion
ROK Signal Unit Mountain Hideout Northeast of Seoul
– 1530 – (3:30 pm)

Rusty had been sitting and planning for the last hour with his team of Red and Tully. Then they brought in Foxy, Arron, Tracker, Joe and C J to get their insights. It was a grim gathering.

"I still don't like this suicide part." Said Foxy.

"Which one?" Asked Arron, not trying to be funny.

Foxy continued with his objection. "I know we need diversions. Hell, we got at least three. But bringing down bombers on our heads? That's just nuts! We'll be in the open. Our body parts will be all over Seoul."

Joe nodded. "I'm with Foxy. Crazy is what this is! On Okinawa, my unit was dive bombed by our own damned planes. Dropped only one hundred pound ordinance, thank God, but it sure was terrible. These bombers are probably gonna drop five hundred pounders. That's like a hurricane compared to a breeze. We'll be slaughtered."

"Only if these guys are really very, very lucky." Added Red, with a scowl. The men looked at him like he had lost it.

"Some of you Europe guys might remember when we were stuck in the hedgerows outside Normandy just after we landed, in July '44. Two thousand bombers were sent to carpet bomb the Jerries' at our front. *Cobra* was the operational name. We had set up a series of RDF transmitters along the line so the bombers would know when to release. Our division, for additional safety, had pulled back a mile from the front that morning. In bright daylight, they came in at ten thousand feet. My division got creamed by our own bombers. Three thousand American soldiers were killed or wounded in an hour."

Joe and Arron were the only ones not present at this battle. The rest acknowledged this tragedy.

"So, what I'm saying is that bombers are good at twenty mile wide targets, like cities, but they just suck at hitting anything precise. I'm for this. They won't come close to hitting anything near the bridge. I don't care if you put a damned lighthouse on top of that bridge. It's a good diversion and we should feel safe."

"You continually amaze me, Red!" Tully said, smiling at him. "I thought I'd have to fight with you on this. But I'm in total agreement with you. The only chance of this mission succeeding is with diversions. I'm not sure that we have enough!"

"I agree." Said Rusty.

Shocked, Tully looked at him. "You do? You never agree with me!"

Rusty ignored his comment. "You got another idea?"

"Yeah! Two. One to save our ass and another to cause more confusion. But I have to admit, both need more work."

Rusty greatly appreciated Tully's creative and aggressive mind but relied on Red to ferret out the dangerous nuances. He has found that bringing more input into a situation has contributed to their survival so far. He hoped that adding most of his original Post Team would add critical help in this major operation. It paid off immediately.

"Chief!" Tracker called out to Rusty, interrupting Tully. Without waiting, he talked. "Rangers are God-like. Tully being exception." He said with a grin.

Rusty, surprised at Tracker's lead, had to laugh at the comment.

Tully, respecting him for what he'd done so far with them, had never even talked with Tracker. Forgetting about his quip return, he thought about how serious their situation was. Then he made that connection. An American Indian! Damn! That's what we Rangers have always emulated, right! Against all odds, we shall prevail. Screw our Ranger motto, he thought, yeah, he thought, we'll always lead, but it should be that we'll overcome. He listened.

Tracker, very serious, continued.

"Indians have fought against impossible odds for a very long time. I know I did, in many ways. Cunning was always the answer. Indians took many scalps because our enemy always underestimated us. Thought we were on the defensive, running from the relentless rape of our land. But we always planned, setting traps, and killing many."

Arron got exasperated. "Jesus, Tracker! You sound like me and my Confederate War shit. What's your point?"

"Many diversions! That's my point! We make *like* a big counterattack.... *from the rear*!"

Tully, mindful that he was stepped over by Tracker, said, with a grudging respect, "Sure glad I was born late and didn't have to go up against any Indians. And I'm damn grateful that white folks had a lot more warriors than you guys."

The sound was unmistakable. They heard the roar of high bombers. It wasn't raining, but light clouds obscured the view of the planes. Tully and Arron ran to the edge, picked up a pair of high powered glasses. After a few minutes, with no ground detonations, Tully pulled back, returned to the group. Arron continued to watch.

"That's a good sign. We're attacking." Said Rusty. The men settled back.

"Let's get back. Tracker, I like what you're saying." Tully was just sitting down.

"What were you gonna add, Tully?" Asked Rusty.

"Tracker's got the right idea. Though first, I want to say, this idea of trying to escape south is bullshit. We'd never get through the ROK lines. Even if they're waiting for us and don't shoot right away. Too many things can go wrong and they will. It's going to be chaos, dark and unfamiliar."

C J jumped up. "Tully's right!" He said. "My troops holding that bank are green, scared shitless and disorganized. Can't believe they've held so far. This plan wouldn't work. We need to go north, not south if we want to survive."

"Hey! What the hell's that?" Arron called out.

Rusty spun around. "What?"

"Don't know! Shit's floating down! A lot of shit!"

Everybody got up, went to the edge. "What is it?" Asked C J, thinking it might be some secret weapon.

Joe recognized it immediately. "Leaflets!"

C J, not understanding. "What's leaflets?"

Joe looked at him. "It's nothing! Damn waste of time! You'll see." He was disgusted. Moved away from the edge.

"Must be millions of 'em!" Added Arron. Watching as the cloud of leaflets disbursed over the entire Seoul area and south of the river. Eventually, some flew into their lair.

"What's it say, Foxy?" Shouted someone.

Foxy turned to the group. "It calls for the people of South Korea to have faith and hope. America and many other friends are coming to defeat this aggression."

C J, could not understand how we would waste bombers to drop leaflets instead of bombs. He looked at Rusty. "Are all Americans crazy?"

Rusty, having been here before, addressed him directly.

"Americans are unique, C J. We are a culture that has never been seen on this planet before. We're naive and stupid sometimes. But we have good intentions. Have faith!"

Rusty yelled. "OK! Let's get back."

As the men reassembled, Rusty thought about some of the most difficult decisions he had ever made. Looking at his team, he stopped at his most trusted advisor.

"Red! Thoughts?"

"Yeah! We need a better plan…and fast!"

Chapter Twenty Three

JP was back in full form. A stable platform made all the difference. The IV, drugs and great food onboard the *Gruke* prepared him for normality. Jack and the rest of his team weren't sure about his return to normal. They kind'a liked the lack of strife. On the other hand, all recognized his valuable input to their survival. After all, it was his idea to steal a boat.

The team had changed into new fatigues. Wondered how somebody got it all right, down to boot sizes. No helmets, just caps. Lots of ammo slings, grenades, Tommy guns and combat belts and carrying pouches filled with various stuff lay piled on the floor.

"Looks like somebody's got an idea about our next assignment. Sure you don't know what it is, Tom?" JP said in his usual accusatory manner.

"You ain't seen nothing yet." Tom looked at his watch again for the umpteenth time. "I'm hoping!"

"Son-of-a-bitch!" Jack yelled at him. "You do know something!"

"No, no! I've been straight with you. I don't have any idea what's go'en on. Just that I didn't tell you what's on this next shipment. Should 'a been here an hour ago."

"OK, so what's in this shipment?"

Just then, a truck pulled up to the front of the shed, and a soldier jumped down from the shotgun position, looked around, uncertain about this location.

"Looks like you're gonna find out right about now." Tom moved quickly to the truck guy and called out. "About goddamned time! Where the hell you been?"

"You Leyden, Sergeant?"

"No! I'm MacArthur, you asshole! Pull the truck in the shed. Be quick now!"

JP was the first into the covered rear. He recognized the stacked bundles immediately. With panic in his voice, he yelled out. "Not liking this at all, guys!"

Greg came to the rear. "What's wrong? What is it?"

JP looked like he was about to puke. "They're boats! Tiny, rubber, rolling type boats!"

Tom hadn't known about JP's water aversion. He started laughing. "Never saw that kind'a reaction to deflated rubber boats before."

"It's a long story, Tom." Said Jack, as he got close up to Tom. "Mind telling me what the hell we're gonna do with these?"

A lieutenant came around to the rear of the truck. He was the driver. "Got orders for Sergeant Leyden."

"Here!" Tom signaled to the officer.

"You must be pretty special, Sergeant. Hand deliver only, I was ordered." He passed Tom a large sealed envelope marked **TOP SECRET.**

"I'm to wait for your reply, then go to the relay station and communicate with a Colonel Nelson in Japan. You know him?"

"No, sir. Just know of him."

"Yeah, me too." Said the LT. "Funny though. These orders came from a Master Sergeant Beloit, works with this Colonel. Not used to being ordered by a non-com."

"When'd you get out of the Point?" Tom asked innocently.

The LT pumped himself up. "A year ago Sergeant. Got here a few days ago."

146

Tom opened the envelope, moved to a table, pulled up a crate to sit. "Come Jack, let's read this together."

They read the two-page order.

Tom looked up at Jack. "It's still your team, Jack. You got a problem with me being in charge of this mission?"

"I've been in shit, but not like this. If Colonel Nelson trusts you, then I'm good! Kinda relieved in fact."

"Don't get all complacent on me, Jack. I go down, it's all yours!"

Phil joined Greg who was rummaging through the truck. JP wanted no part of it. He'd seen enough. Feeling sorry for himself he got down and went over to sit in a corner. He was thinking about being in a little rubber boat and big waves on the ocean.

Greg found a bunch of walkie-talkies, then let Phil take over from there.

"Alright!" Phil yelled, as he then found the two RDF transmitters. "About time we got some electronics!"

"What are they?" Greg asked.

"Signal homing devices. Radio Direction Finders. Used to direct planes and ships to a target. These are pretty new, battery powered. Wonder what we're gonna do with them?"

"Lots of questions here, Phil. I'm starting to feel like JP. Queasy. Find anything else?"

"Yeah!"

"I don't like the sound of your voice."

"Well, whatever the hell we got ourselves into," pausing, "involves blowing up something enormous!" Pausing again.

"Got a shit load of C-4 here."

The PBY announced its presence a short while later. Its engines roaring as it climbed the ramp, got to level and then spun around to face reentry into the bay, then cut its engines.

Tom and Jack went to the shed entrance. A Navy commander climbed out of the cockpit. By his gate, they knew this pilot had

147

been there. Probably not more than thirty, he looked seasoned, determined.

John Muzich had seen much in his ten years flying PBYs. His Navy Cross, awarded to him for his near suicide attack on Japanese landing craft trying to land behind Marine positions on Saipan, didn't justly reward him for the many acts of valor he performed. He was a quiet man. Unlike most, he was modest, deferential. He was centered, simple. Knew right from wrong. You just didn't want to get in his way when he had a mission.

"Who's in charge here?" He demanded, knowing full well who he was to report to.

In all fairness to the Navy commander, he had been ordered here without any detail. But first, his PBY had been stripped at his base in Japan. Seats, machine guns, bomb racks, mostly everything not necessary to fly. And then his crew, out of eight, they were reduced to four. The forward gunner with the only armament left aboard, he, his copilot and the navigator. None of the men on the ground knew this.

"You must be our ride?" Tom said, not taking any shit from him.

"You must be Leyden. This better be something, Sergeant. I don't do transport."

"Come with us, Commander, I've got something to show you."

As they walked back into the big shed, Tom yelled over to the LT in the truck. "You need to get that truck to the PBY and start loading cargo onboard." Yelling over to soldiers milling about. "You there! Jack's team! You do the grunt work. Get to it now! Don't dick around! We leave here in an hour!"

Moving to the back of the shed, Tom turned back to Jack. "I think it's crucial that you supervise the loading. Our success depends on it."

Jack peeled off and followed the truck to the plane.

After reviewing the mission orders, Navy Commander Muzich was stunned. The orders: ***Operation Halt***. Explicit. Signed off by the Supreme Commander himself.

148

"You're shitting me!" He looked up at this Sergeant. "Who in hell are you guys!?"

"Nobody you want to mess with is who we are." Said a stoic Sergeant Leyden.

"So? Are you gonna give us a ride into hell?"

Navy Commander Muzich liked this Sergeant's style. He'd seen a lot of assholes, though they were mostly officers. Didn't think this Sergeant was one.

"Let me tell you something Sergeant. I've never had orders to ride into hell before. I did it on my own! Twice! My choice. And NOW! It's still my choice! Right?"

Leyden realized he didn't know anything about this Navy guy. Assumed he was a know nothing pilot of a PBY that did reconnaissance missions. He'd been hasty in his assessments of men before and had regretted it. Now, he wasn't sure about this one.

"It is your choice, Muzich." Big Tom, was deliberate and defiant. Knowing that speaking to him without his rank was derogatory. He wanted no officer to enlisted man bullshit. "I've seen this shit before."

Muzich stared at him.

Tom saw a hesitation, felt, maybe he was trying to back out.

Tom walked around the table, got close to the Navy commander.

"Got to tell 'ya, Navy boy, if it wasn't for one of your PBY guys on Saipan, I'd probably have to pull my gun. You know! So you could do our mission. Do I have to?"

Muzich kept his composure. "I flew into that shitpit. Saipan! I was there, you asshole! Lost a crew and almost my life. Back off!"

Incredulous, Tom backed off. "You were at Saipan?"

Muzich was recognized as an equal.

"Yeah, I was there, Sergeant!" Muzich said in a somber tone.

"Damn!" A memory came back. "There was only one PBY involved in the Saipan thing. I watched it get shot down."

"Yeah! That Zero came out of nowhere. Must have been cover for those troop barges I destroyed."

149

"Holy shit! I was on that beach! If you hadn't taken out those troops, we would've been toast."

Deadpanning. "You're welcome. I lost eight of my crew."

"Sorry. But you saved hundreds."

Thoughtfully, Muzich scanned the map again. "Kinda like our current situation?"

"Kinda! Your call? You know what they say Commander; *three's the charm*!"

"Yeah. Three's a winner!" Muzich said, thinking that this crazy plan might be the right thing to do. But also thinking it probably would be his last mission.

"I need to go over these charts." He moved to the table.

The loading process wasn't going smoothly. The truck was backed up to the biggest opening on the PBY, the rear side Plexiglas bubble window, and it wasn't very big. This was not a cargo plane and was never designed for heavy capacity. Even so, the basic internal configuration of the plane lent itself to internal storage. Jack knew what the sequence had to be, tried to visualize the end process, what goes in first comes out last. And through it all, knowing his team had to fit in there and get this stuff out of the same window. Maybe under fire.

Damn! Jack thought I've never been involved in a big operation like this before; where I'm crucial. He was relentless in positioning the cargo. With his early boat training, he was good at exacting every available storage space.

Back at the map table, Tom asked, "Can you get us there?"

"I've flown into... well, you can't imagine. Of course, I can find this river. What I don't know is if we'll survive the landing."

Tom was surprised. "What'da mean?"

"I got nothing here on the river depth. Sandbars, nothing! I'm blind. When we hit the water, we'll go down at least four feet, maybe more with our load. We could just disintegrate if we hit a sandbar or worse, rocks. This is a suicide mission."

"Sounds like we'll need a bit of luck." Tom drew back from the table. "I don't believe in God. Can't believe anyone could run

150

things as mucked up as earth. And I don't believe in destiny. So tell me, Commander Muzich, what do you believe in?"

Although taken aback by his tone, Muzich respected this Sergeant. Thought about his question, one he has asked himself for many years.

"After my plane was shot down and I bobbed around in the water amongst the wreckage and my crew's body parts, I wondered why I didn't die. Didn't even have a scratch. I still ask that same question. The only consistent thought that makes any sense to me is the Theory of Random Luck. My own invention, although it's somewhat based on The Chaos Theory."

"Have you gone all section eight on me? What the hell are you talking about?"

"Sorry! Sometimes simple questions don't have simple answers. I tend to think more than I should sometimes." He paused, choosing his words carefully.

"I believe in luck, Sergeant. And I believe in following orders. I'd like to believe we have a choice sometimes, but, mostly, we don't."

"Even though you're a Navy officer, I think we'll get along just fine, Muzich." Tom moved off to find the truck lieutenant. He needed to contact Colonel Nelson's office.

Chapter Twenty Four

The small conference room finally just got four more phones installed. Now each of the team could be connected at the same time. The timing couldn't have been better. It was going to be a long night.

As each team member came in, they nodded at Nelson and smiled approval at the new phones. Nick came last, saw the phones, then looked around and turned to Colonel Nelson. "Boss. I think we need a coffee maker to go along with the new communication stuff. Any chance?"

The tension in the room melted into laughter. Nelson appreciated the distraction. "Grunts know what's crucial!" He turned to his XO, "Hank, could you arrange to get us one?"

Major Jarvis grinned.

Captain Haran at the other end of the table stood. "Sir, it would be my privilege to bring pleasure to the needy." On the way out, he turned, "Please start with Larry, I know everything he knows."

"Go, Larry!" Said Nelson.

"This may shock you, but the Air Force guys think we're crazy. Don't like being directed by the Army and being put on the carpet. If it weren't for those orders from *el supremo,* we'd be sucking air. As it is, I'm concerned about their commitment. Bad weather, finding the target, low-level attack. They have a ton of outs if they want and have expressed them all and more. That *all for one and one for all* crap didn't find its way into any conversation."

Nelson nodded. "Got it. Larry, that's why we got those orders. Don't worry about them shirking their duty. As you said, they're on the carpet. Lots of important folks are interested in this mission, and they know it."

"Right! So, we got eighteen B-29s loaded with incendiary devices. They're out of Kadena Air Base on Okinawa. They'll be first in. Hopefully, they'll light up Seoul near the bridge."

"What altitude did they agree to?" Asked Nick.

"They didn't at first. Sam finally had to get tough, told them no fifteen thousand feet bullshit. They were going in at seven thousand feet, period! If they wanted to call MacArthur about it, we'd wait. Sam figured that no way were they going to call him on this. Sam was right. He did well!"

"Amen!" Nick said. "Probably wouldn't have come close to hitting Seoul from fifteen."

Larry continued, "The second wave of sixteen B-26s is coming out of Ashiya Air Base, from Japan. Loaded with one hundred pound conventional bombs. Their command also proved difficult, but less so. Once they got past the interservice BS they were more enthusiastic about the mission, and in fact, they suggested they attack from three thousand feet, not five. We jumped on that."

Nick, focused on the tactical aspect of the mission, "I don't know about bombers. What's the bomb load of these babies?"

"I didn't either." Said Larry. "They're impressive. The B-29s carry twenty thousand pounds, and the B-26s carry four thousand pounds."

Nick smiled, "Yeah, I like it!"

"Good job, Larry. Is that it?" Asked Nelson.

"No, sir. Sam was the key on this. He deserves the lion's share of the credit. I just went along for the ride."

"Got it, Larry. Any loose threads?"

"Two things, sir. The exact timing needs to be established. We talked about midnight over target for the first wave. Secondly, they want to confirm the RDF transmitter frequency to home in on it. They suggested one; we just need to give them the Ok. Otherwise, we're all set."

Captain Sam Haran pushed through the door carrying a big open box, filled with supplies and a coffee maker.

"Now that's service! Thank you, Sam!" Said Nick.

"Did I miss anything?" The captain asked as he set up the coffee maker.

"Yeah, you did." Nelson cracked a smile. "You missed the part where I complemented you on doing an outstanding job with the Air Force."

"Maybe I'll go out and get some donuts or something. I seem to do well when I'm not here."

"Now that's another great idea!" Nick cracked wise.

Nelson ignored the remark. "You're up, Nick. What's the tactical situation?"

"Fluid, sir. I've been back and forth with Rusty on the VLF. His team has suggested some changes to our original plans along with reservations about some others. Mostly, I like his ideas. He's on site and knows what's happening. I'm in favor of going with his conclusions."

"Give me the high points."

"Basically, they want to split into four teams. The demolition team at the bridge, a north river bank team at the side of the bridge, a swamp team at the eastern edge of the NK positions and a rear team up towards the valley in the northeast. You told me these guys are good and I have to agree. Between the air attacks and these changes, nobody is going to be focused on the bridge."

"So, what's the problem?"

"Boss, they think it's suicide to escape south. They want to go back north, up the Uijongbu Corridor. Then double back to their ROK hideout on that mountain."

"And?"

"Not a problem with me, boss. It's just that Rusty's team will still be fighting behind the lines."

154

Nelson paused. "That's their job, Nick. That's what they signed on for. Like you said of your friend Tom. Rusty and his team are beyond exceptional. They get it done. Trust that they'll survive."

Nelson knew this mission was different. His men were going into the spear of the enemy, big elements, not a platoon or company, but the advance of an army. He feared the worst. But he was driven by the need to slow them. Yes, he said to himself, to save a country. I don't want to order this, but I must. Rusty, you son of a bitch, you better pull off some of your magic here.

"What about the key to this mission, Tom and Jack? If they don't get there, we're screwed. This will all be for nothing. Do you know this pilot?"

"This is my biggest concern, boss. Everything's in place, ready to go. Random luck that we got a decorated combat pilot. But the pilot raised some issues about landing blind in the river. You know, like hidden sandbars or rocks, even the depth of the water. This is the X factor, the hated unknown."

So did Nelson. Old lady luck again, he thought. She's totally indifferent. Luck or no luck.

"Nothing we can do about that, Nick. Anything else?"

"That's it for me, boss."

"OK. Unless anyone else has something, let's finalize timetables and get orders out."

Major Jarvis snapped up. "Colonel, Captain Stands called earlier. He wants a mission. Say's his, and I quote, *his warbird is ready, locked and loaded, ready to bring fire and brimstone on these heathens.* He said his P-51 is fully loaded and has two napalm canisters. I told him to stand by, that we'd be back to him."

Nelson shook his head, grinned. "Wild Bill is something! Let's think about how he could join us on this mission. Now let's get back to planning."

155

Chapter Twenty Five

Friday, June 30, 1950 – Day Six of the Invasion
Pusan Harbor, Korea – Boatyard - PBY Landing Area
– 1745 – (5:45 pm)

Tom and Jack had been in town at the cable relay facility, going back and forth on the phone with Nick Beloit. Getting agreement on the final orders, they hurried back. They needed to leave soon.

Phil was playing with the RDF transmitter when they came in. Jack went right to him.

"Here." He handed Phil a piece of paper. "Set these transmitters to this frequency. The Air Force needs this. Any problems doing it?"

"Who are you talking to, Jack? That's a stupid question! If I had the right materials, I probably could make us a small A bomb."

"Do this first, Phil! You'll have your shot at the big bomb later."

Then Jack moved away to face the whole group.

"Listen up! Lot's of shit been going on. Here's the skinny. First off, Tom is in charge of this mission. You and I take orders from him. That goes for you too, Navy boy." He looked at Commander Muzich.

"Second, the order comes straight down from MacArthur." He paused. "That makes us very special. Or very stupid."

No one laughed.

"Third, we leave in an hour. Our mission is to blow up the Han River Railroad Bridge. We're going to hook up with the Post team and some Rangers. They know the area and will lead us to the site and support our withdrawal. I've got maps and details on the table. You got thirty minutes to review them. Then we load up." He turned to Tom, "You want to say something?"

Tom stood tall, addressed the men. "We got a lot of fingers in this pie. Jack is your boss. I'm here to help him. But I want everyone here to be clear about this mission. We will accomplish it!"

JP frowned. "That was inspirational! Thanks, Tom."

"You are such an asshole!" Said Greg, really pissed. "You just can't keep that mouth of yours shut!"

"Screw you all! We lose most of our team, survive like animals then do a high seas escape where I almost die. And now we're going into a convoluted stealth type crazy mission we know nothing about. With a new leader we don't know. And you're calling me an asshole? Sorry! But this is beyond comprehension!"

Jack shook his head. "You're such a God damn cry baby, JP! If I didn't know better I'd think you were afraid. But I know the only thing you're worried about is getting into those rubber boats and being on the rocky seas again. So let me put you at ease. It's a river JP! No waves! No rocking. Easy!"

JP looked at Jack like he was Moses and had just revealed the Ten Commandments. "Really? A river? No rocking?"

Navy pilot Muzich, stunned by this whole dialog, decided to interject. "I don't know you or for that matter, anybody from shit, JP, but being that I'm flying you guys in, it's definitely a river and it's certainly flat. There are no waves."

Relieved and revived, JP looked at his new boss. "So, Tom, let's go over the maps."

A half hour later they boarded the PBY.

JP was bitching throughout the boarding. "Jesus, it's cramped. Why do we need four of these inflatables? You sure we can take off with all this shit in here?"

Jack had enough on his mind, about surviving the landing. Good thing JP, nor the others, knew about that danger.

Tom had had enough. The last one in, he barked, "JP! Shut up and tie yourself in! The rest of you do the same! It's going to be a bumpy ride."

They had no idea..

Same Day - Friday, June 30, 1950   Day Six of the Invasion
ROK Signal Unit Mountain Hideout Northeast of Seoul – 1600 – (6:00 pm)

Rusty and the men gathered around in a big circle. They all had heard the translation of the VLF transmission by Joe as it came in. They were relieved that Colonel Nelson had agreed with everything they had suggested. Rusty wasn't. He was just determined. No matter what, he was going to follow his plan anyway. At least now he wouldn't be going against orders.

Earlier, when making the team assignments, Rusty had questioned C J about his three men. He knew they didn't speak English but wanted to use them in this operation.

"These are good men, Rusty. Loyal and smart. Fully trained with light weapons. Excellent marksmen. But, no combat experience."

"Can they kill silently, from behind?"

"Don't know. Most men can't do it, but they certainly know how."

"Fair enough. I need them for my rear team and I need them to guide us there. Can they do it?"

"They got you here, didn't they? Of course they can take you to your position. They know this area well. You just can't understand each other. I don't foresee a lot of communications going on anyway, do you?"

"No, I don't."

"Got an idea." C J called his men over. Talked to them for some time.

"OK, Rusty." He pointed to the man on the right. "This is *One*." The man bowed, in accented Korean, he responded, "*One*, Rusty." C J repeated the process for *Two* and *Three*. "So now you know them and they now know you, the rest is sign language. I've told them where you want to go and showed them. They know what to do."

"That solves a major problem. I think you got my vote if you ever decide to run for office."

Rusty started the final assignments. He sought confirmation and began.

"C J, are you sure about the timing to get to the river?"

"I've done it many times. The back path down this mountain is an easy trail. The river winds behind and is much closer than straight from here. It's less than two miles to the river. Should take about two hours if we go slowly."

"Mario, you're positive you can scale the base? It's a hundred feet high?"

"It's higher, Rusty. But yeah, I could do this in my sleep. The Matterhorn was a much bigger challenge. I wish I were doing that rather than this bridge right about now."

Growing up in Seattle, Mario had been an amateur mountain climber since his youth, perfecting his skills as he traveled with the Army after the War. He was well recognized in the climbing community.

Tully chimed in. "You climbers are all crazy!"

Mario laughed, "Look who's calling the kettle black!"

Rusty interjected. "OK, ok. Personally, I think we're all crazy."

Everybody was too tense to react.

"I've had second thoughts about the machine gun. I think it should be assigned to the Rear team. That'll be our big deal to make sure we can escape. What do you think, Red?"

"Damn it, Rusty! You want to take away my team's major weapon and want me to agree? No! I can't! You're not reading this right. I'm in the middle. If shit's gonna happen, I'll be the key to guarding the bridge and bank teams. If we hit any resistance, my position will bear the brunt of the fight. If I fold, your position is meaningless."

Red paused, focusing his thoughts then continued.

159

"You know me, Rusty. I am a tactical conservative. Your position is key to our safe exit, but my position allows us to get there."

Rusty nodded agreement, "I forget how good you are."

Rusty called over to C J, "Tell *Three* he's with Marty and Red. Introduce them. They've got the machine gun."

He turned to the men, "Good! Any questions?"

No one responded. They'd been through the plan many times.

"Saddle up then. C J! You're in charge of getting all the bridge teams out. That's your main responsibility. Stay low."

C J nodded.

"Good luck!"

Rusty watched the men gather their equipment.

"*Three!*" Marty pointed to the machine gun. *Three* repositioned his rifle strap around his neck and picked up the machine gun. He went for the base tripod but was intercepted by Marty, who grabbed it, nodded to him. Then Marty grabbed some of the ammo belts and hauled them up around his neck. Moose came over and grabbed the rest of the belts.

The men followed C J out and down the path.

Rusty turned to his rear team.

"Arron! You got the bazooka. *Two!*" The ROK soldier came forward. Rusty gave him the backpack with the four remaining rockets and pointed to Arron. He nodded.

After much debate about leaving the hideout unmanned and leaving the top secret VLF equipment, Rusty made the call. They were going to get back here. Larry was assigned to ensure that if they didn't return, and somebody stumbled onto the hideout, they were not going to leave with this equipment. Larry, being incredibly talented in all things devious and explosive, set elaborate booby charges around the VLF equipment.

Rusty felt he had covered everything. Time to go.

"*One!* Let's go!" He pointed to the exit.

Chapter Twenty Six

Friday, June 30, 1950 – Day Six of the Invasion
On Board Navy PBY leaving Pusan – 1800 – (6:00 pm)

They ascended to cloud height, about six hundred feet. A slight drizzle allowed decent visibility of the ground. Not everybody had strapped in right away. Some looked out the big windows, watching the takeoff. Finally, they all settled down and strapped in, hard and tight. They used rope and web belts to secure themselves. The cargo was stacked against the bulkhead behind the navigator's seat, leaving only a small space for the access door to his and the pilot/copilot section.

Commander Muzich had timed everything. Normal for him, especially with the lousy weather. It was all plotted out in his mind. An exceptional pilot, he had an innate ability to feel what was right or not. It was bumpy, flying slow and low under the clouds, but manageable.

JP was holding up well. Maybe because he figured it was only going to last for about ninety minutes. The two hundred mile flight on the slow PBY was the least of JP's worries, though. He kept thinking of the river, and the rafts. Despite what they told him, he kept thinking about those ocean waves. His stomach churned.

They flew north to intersect the main highway south of Suwon. That would put them twenty-five miles west of their river destination. It was a solid plan, with a known point of reference to proceed onto a remote spot in the river.

"John! We just passed over the highway!" Said the copilot.

"Good eyes! I missed it." It was starting to get dark. He turned north, picked up the highway and followed it. "Shouldn't be long now." He checked his stopwatch. "Suwon airfield is southeast of the city; we'll see it first."

A few minutes later they did. Muzich's plan was to skirt the airport, hit his stopwatch to start the timing run to the river, then make the final turn east. It didn't quite work out that way.

White puffs appeared in front of the plane. Anti-aircraft fire!

"Oh shit!" Muzich yelled. He pulled a sharp left and dove the plane. It saved his life and the plane. A blast engulfed the cabin on his copilot's side. Debris and the sudden rush of one hundred and twenty miles an hour rain soaked wind whipped through the cockpit and the entire plane. The bulkhead behind the navigator's seat blew outward, and the access door exploded off, narrowly missing Jack, sitting near.

Muzich was momentarily shocked. Sharp pain in his arm quickly revived him. The plane was diving. They were low to start with and didn't have a lot of room before impact. Muzich immediately started pulling up and turning. After a few tense moments, the plane responded, leveled off and started climbing. Another minute and they would've been all dead.

With total presence of mind, Muzich hit his stopwatch and turned to his planned heading.

The blast occurred just below the copilot's seat, shielding Muzich, but instantly killing the copilot and the forward gunner, who was lying in his crawl space in front of the copilot. The navigator and radio operator that sat directly behind the co-pilot were also unprotected and died from the explosion.

JP, already queasy, was so tied in that he couldn't turn and vomited his last meal all over himself. Jack was freaked out seeing the cabin door fly by within inches of his head that he was transfixed, frozen in place.

Tom immediately knew what happened. Thought this was it for him. But when the plane came out of the dive, he acted. Unstrapping himself, he went to the open hatchway and had to fight the wind to get through, finally deciding the only way was to crawl. Stunned at the sight of the mangled bodies and a gaping hole in the plane to his right, he saw Muzich at the controls. A large piece of metal jutting out of his right arm made the scene that much more bizarre. But he'd seen worse.

He came up behind Muzich. He had to yell over the incredible noise. "A fine damn mess you got us into! You OK!?"

"Hey! Swell! Nice for the support. How're your guys?"

"They're all good. Your guys weren't so lucky."

"I figured. Don't know why I'm not dead?"

"You have a mission, Muzich! That's why!"

"What's this shit in my arm?"

"I'm no expert, but it's about six inches long and looks like a horrible medieval weapon."

"The bastard is heavy. Can't move my arm too well. Take it out."

"Oh! Before I forget, how long till we land?"

"You're a determined bastard, Leyden. I'll give you that. See that stopwatch hanging from that knob, what's it say?

"Six minutes left."

"Take this damn thing out of my arm, or I'm not sure about this landing."

Tom knew a lot about wounds. What he didn't know is if this metal piece had severed an artery, removing it would threaten Muzich's life. He leaned over and grabbed the dead copilot's pants belt and ripped a strip of cloth from his uniform. He wrapped the belt around Muzich's arm above the wound, wrapped it real tight and pulled out the metal shard and wrapped the cloth around the wound.

Tom knew that it had to be painful, Muzich had just flinched but only said. "Thanks. Now go back and tie yourself in tight. This landing is going to be interesting."

Muzich could barely make out the river. He made a dead reckoning approach and hoped the hole in the plane didn't go below the water line. There was just enough light to see the river but not

163

much else. He wouldn't be able to spot a boulder sticking up if there'd been one. He prayed.

The first bounce was normal. The second was jarring when they must have hit something; then the plane settled into a smooth slowing glide until jolted to a very abrupt stop.

Unbeknownst to them, Suwon Airbase had been strafed by North Korean fighter planes fifteen minutes before they approached. The irony was that they were hit by the only anti-aircraft gun in all of South Korea. It wasn't an American gun or Japanese, but German. A captured Nazi weapon the Russians had used against the Japanese at the end of the War but abandoned when the Russians pulled out.

When the plane jarred to the sudden stop, everybody moved. Tom went back up to Muzich with his medical stuff, Jack opened the big window and organized the men to unload the inflatable's first and then start loading them. They couldn't wait to get out of the plane.

Tom wrapped Muzich's wound with a proper field dressing. Although a deep wound, there was no blood spurting. "No artery hit, pilot! You're a lucky bastard!"

"You call this lucky?"

"Damn right! You got us down safe. Don't know how you did it! I'm starting to think you've got some special powers, Muzich. What do you eat?"

"Beats me! But I do like rice and beans."

"That's encouraging, so do I. Bullshit aside, thanks! You saved our asses up there. Hope you got more of that *rice and bean* luck because you're coming with us."

Tom didn't often acknowledge excellence because he expected it. Not only of himself but from everybody else. But sometimes, he overcame this when he recognized something beyond his comprehension of achievement. He had a new respect for Commander John Muzich.

"Come on, Navy man, let's get out of here."

The nose was up on a sand bar. Water outside the big side window was three feet deep. It made the plane easy to unload. They got the first three inflatables out and inflated. The last one was stored up against the bulkhead. It was damaged by the blast, ripped apart, useless.

Not completely dark and no one was shooting at them, they started off-loading the cargo directly into the inflatables. Silently the men did this in earnest. They had a timetable and every minute counted.

As planned, two boats were each loaded with eight twenty-five pound bundles of C-4 and two coils of two hundred feet of rope. One of two inch and one of one inch thick. The third boat was loaded with the rest of the cargo. It all went pretty fast.

Finally, Jack emerged with an outboard motor. It was a small ten horsepower type.

"I hope this baby is a lot quieter than the ones I'm used to." He said to no one in particular, as he placed it in the first boat transom. All three boats were tethered, and finally all six men climbed in the first boat. After shoving off, the three boats moved together in a haphazard way because of the fast river current. Jack started the outboard and got the boat train straightened out.

Tom and Muzich were sitting in front of Jack. The outboard had been modified and was thankfully silent, emitting just a purr.

Jack whispered to Muzich. "Did we land where we should have?"

His arm was throbbing now, but he ignored it. "Pretty sure. Not positive."

"Okay. We'll find out soon enough. Another twenty minutes I think. Do you know what happened to the plane?"

"Oh, yeah! Somehow, the ROK found some anti-aircraft guns. Must have thought we were the enemy."

"Our guys! Damn! Sorry about your men, Muzich. Tom told me what you did to save us, thanks."

Greg leaned over the bow, trying to see ahead for any significant obstructions. It was futile. Dark now, he couldn't see much but the faint outline of the shore. Although it seemed their progress was slow, they still moved at a fast clip with the current, moving around six knots. The signal light Greg was looking for was at least another fifteen minutes away. Still, he kept looking.

Chapter Twenty Seven

Friday, June 30, 1950 – Day Six of the Invasion
Taejon Airfield – Fifty Miles SE of Suwon –– 1900 – (7:00 pm)

The day had passed slowly. A truck arrived from Pusan around noon carrying barrels of aviation fuel, along with food and a large cooking stove.

Wild Bill got a ride from the leaving truck to the communications building, as the Korean Cable relay station was now known. He asked the driver about how things were in Pusan. It was a short ride, but he wanted to know what was going on.

"It's crazy, Captain. I've never seen so much ammo being piled up; trucks and bulldozers were being offloaded. Only got two ships in this morning, but they were full."

"Any tanks?"

"No, sir. Didn't see any heavy stuff. Some men, but I think they were engineers, but I was busy."

He was dropped off and called Colonel Nelson's office, spoke to Major Jarvis. Got an update and asked for a mission. Disappointed after being told to hang tight, he walked back to the airfield. Pleased that the weather had changed to cloudy with intermittent light rain, he still felt useless but hopeful that something might develop.

He thought of going up on his own. He'd done that a few times but thought something really big was developing that he didn't want to miss.

Wild Bill went back again around three o'clock to call and was told again to stand by. This time by a Master Sergeant Nick something. Angry, he returned, fumed for another hour then decided to go back to give it another try.

"Major Jarvis here."

"Stands here! I'm tired of waiting, Major! Is my Colonel there? I need to speak with him!"

"Hold!" He pressed the hold button. Nelson was sitting next to him at the operational conference room table, along with the rest of the A Team. Holding the phone, Jarvis said, "Colonel, Wild Bill is insistent and angry. Wants you."

Nelson picked up his phone, hit the inline. "So you don't want to miss a fight, Captain?!"

"About time! I was starting to think my favorite Colonel was avoiding me. You know what I want! I can contribute to whatever you got concocted. So what gives?"

Nelson had thought about this expected interchange for a few hours. Knew Wild Bill would live up to his reputation and confront him. He'd been avoiding him for sundry and convoluted reasons. Mostly, because Wild Bill was amongst his longtime cohorts in surviving ridiculous odds. And, more importantly, he was a friend.

"This is going to be a long war, Bill. No use getting all huffed up if you miss one battle."

"One battle my ass! I know that if we don't do something big, right now, this thing is over. Don't dick with me, Colonel. I know you got something going on and I want in."

"You are a pain in the ass, Bill! Maybe why I love you as I do." Nelson paused, feeling the emotion rise. "OK. I'll fill you in. Maybe at the end, you could help out?"

After the brief by Nelson, the Captain was on cloud nine. About damn time! We're finally moving. He ran back to the airfield, chanting, *"We're just, and **JUST DUE** will prevail."* Returning, he ordered Billy and the crew to get as many vehicles as they could and line them up on either side of the field in case he's called out.

168

With their headlights on, he could take off, and hopefully, return at any hour of the night.

George realized Billy wasn't competent to fully understand this order. There just wasn't enough vehicles on the field to do what was needed, so he yelled over to Arnie, "Come here. We're taking a ride."

They drove around the area and stole two trucks and four jeeps, kept going back out and forth. Finally set them up on either side of the field, enough, George thought, to get enough light to get the captain up and out and get him back.

A feeling George hadn't experienced for a while overcame him. For the first time since his friends died, he felt he was contributing, not just surviving. Smiling to himself, he gave thanks, felt his revenge was finally coming near.

Chapter Twenty Eight

It started out rough with light rain and dangerous terrain. It got easier when they got further down, then made a cut to the river. They started to pick up speed.

Arron, fourth man back in the line carrying the bazooka, was the first to gripe. "Hey up there! Men, not horses back here."

Larry was at his front. Not one to say much, still he turned, "Arron, you Confederates were assholes a long time ago. Please don't be one now."

Arron mumbled something.

Rusty tapped *One* on the back, signaled him to stop. He moved down the column and spoke low. "This is not a goddamned excursion! No talking, no griping, no sounds at all!" He walked back to the front. They moved out.

The rain stopped. The thick cloud cover lightened, increasing visibility. The terrain changed again into lava rock and swamp. This was a tidal wash area. With the rains, it became a quagmire. Weeds grew to four feet in places almost overnight. Water varied from six inches to three feet. Progress slowed considerably.

Eventually, Rusty started doubting *One's* navigation and halted the column again. He cursed himself for not learning Korean and not remembering Foxy's cheat sheet of common phrases. He tried sign language. *One* seemed to understand his concern and indicated OK, and that they'd be there soon.

Rusty checked his watch again. Another hour or so. We can be a little late, he thought. The show won't go on for a while yet. He moved them out.

After slogging through the swamp for another hour and crossing a deep stream, Rusty saw the glow of campfire lights to the north, maybe a hundred yards away. He and everyone froze. They were standing in seven inches of water and didn't know where the next dry bank was.

One signaled to come forward and follow him. Soon they found the end of the wetlands and reached a low dry bank. Small huts were nearby and appeared abandoned. More campfires were seen farther back behind the huts.

They were very near where they planned to be. At the edge of a harsh, poverty zone and knew from observation that further west were a few hamlets that expanded to the city edge. These were the far outskirts of Seoul with broken flat land of rock and streams. It was time to lay low and wait. Rusty signaled the men to spread out along the bank. He then knelt next to Arron, whispered. "I need you to scout this area. Start northeast." He pointed. "There's a tank park in the trees, off the road. Remember seeing it?"

Annoyed, Arron nodded, "Rusty, I know as much about this area as you! I know what to do! I want *Two* with me."

Rusty was surprised. "Why *Two*?"

"He's smart and playful."

Rusty was quiet for a moment. Tried to think of something to say or ask, but couldn't.

"Your call. Go when you're ready."

Rusty waddled over to Larry. "Take the bazooka from Arron. I'll get *One* and the rockets. Show him how to load it."

Addressing each man as he moved down the line, he ordered them not to make a sound, and that this was **not** their final position.

Rusty sat down next to Larry on the bank, took out his hi-powered glasses, scanned, and waited.

Arron took out his special knife; he carried two. This was a Fairbairn. He got it from a dead SAS British guy, Bernard, a friend,

171

with whom he was on a special operations mission. A fierce weapon, the Fairbairn was a double-edged seven-inch dagger. He kept it razor sharp. It would cut through anything with ease except metal. That would take a bit longer. He called it his *Bernie*, in deference to his fallen friend.

He showed it to *Two*. Made signs indicating to use no sounds to kill. *Two* understood, nodded. But raised his hands and shook his head, indicating that he had no knife. Arron nodded and pulled out his second knife, a seven-inch Bowie, handed it to him. *Two* grinned and nodded.

They moved out north. Skirting the empty huts, they reconnoitered and plotted their escape route. The ground was solid with good covering brush. The trees and a few campfires gave the tank park away. What arrogance! They have no idea! Arron thought I might die today, but you idiots will pay big time.

Passing around the tank park, they came to a general assembly area of supporting troops, trucks and supply vehicles. No guards. He checked his watch. Good. They started back, this time they circled closer to the main road. The enemy were all spread out. Not a care in the world. Vehicles parked off the highway. Troops are cooking nearby. They had gone up into the corridor maybe two miles and then turned back. As they got closer to the bridge, things changed. They moved cautiously.

They slid close by Artillery batteries. Three, Arron gauged. Grouped close. He counted eighteen guns. Anti-aircraft positions were laced through these and further on towards the bridge. He couldn't see that far. He signaled to *Two* that they were going back to do a check of the huts that they had by-passed.

There must have been twenty huts in this little hamlet. Arron didn't see any activity and wanted to go back. *Two* insisted they check them. Arron nodded. *Two* started entering the huts. On the third one, yells and a female scream bellowed. Arron ran in, saw *Two* lay down a soldier, blood spurting from his neck. A young naked girl, in shock, lay on the floor.

Two yammered away in Korean at Arron. Arron grabbed his collar, brought him close and smiled. Gave him the universal thumbs up. *Two* had never killed before. Felt relief that an American would give him support of his action.

Two talked to the young girl, told her to run and hide. She calmed down, nodded to *Two*, said words of thanks and left.

They continued to search the rest of the huts. Having found all abandoned, they returned to Rusty's position and reported.

Rusty checked his watch.

Arron watched *Two* go over to *One*, kneel beside him and bow his head a few times as he spoke. Arron didn't know what he said but had an idea of what this young man felt. To his credit, Arron watched *One* cradle *Twos* head in a loving gesture of comfort.

Chapter Twenty Nine

Friday, June 30, 1950 – Day Six of the Invasion
The PBY team in the lead boat on the river – 2030 – (8:30 pm)

They all saw it; a faint flick of light. Then another. Jack couldn't judge the distance but knew it was close. He throttled back and shifted his heading. Five minutes later, another light, a little brighter. Followed again by another quick flash.

"That's our signal!" Jack whispered to Tom.

Tom leaned forward, whispered to Greg and Phil at the bow, "Be ready! Hopefully, they're our guys."

Muzich and JP were prone, their Tommy guns pointing out. Tom joined them. Another set of lights flashed. They were very close. Jack hit his flashlight button three quick times and saw the answer flashes. The shore came up fast and he cut the engine. They bumped.

"Must be the crazies from Post four!" Red called out low.

"Son of a bitch!" Jacked whispered back.

The tail inflatables followed the current and continued drifting, coming even with them, potentially pulling them off the shore.

Jack called out in a muffled order, "Pull us up Red!" JP tossed him a rope. "Tie us to a tree or something."

They got the boat train secured. The tethered boats swung to their side on the bank. They piled out, greeted each other. Most of the Post teams had met before deploying. Red liked Jack; they'd had some laughs together, thought he was a real cowboy.

"You're safe now, Red. I've come to save your ass."

The rest of the men greeted one another. Jack hugged Red.

Red pulled back, still holding Jack's shoulders, he barked at him. "Didn't you ever learn not to volunteer?"

Jack shot back. "You big lug! I'm as stupid as you. Think we're related somehow. You got relatives in Mississippi?"

They hugged again. Red said, "You're such a jerk! Glad you're here!"

Tully didn't know any of the new guys. Assessing the situation, he grew angry. "Who's Tom?" He called out, louder now. They felt safe in this spot.

"Who in hell are you?" Tom sniped, taking an immediate dislike.

Tully didn't answer the question. "We're supposed to have four boats! What the hell? Can't you count?"

"You tit sucking pansy! We got three boats! Deal with it. You're lucky you got any goddamned boats at all! So screw off and do your job!"

Red came over to them. "Tully, figure this out. You must be Tom! We got a mission you two! Get on with it!"

Tom got quiet and looked at Red. "I got an extra guy I can't take. Our pilot, a Navy guy. Good man! Saved our lives. Wounded in the arm and can't climb. Otherwise, I'd want him by my side. You got him, watch out for him!"

Red knew Tom's type, only met a few like him. Liked him immediately.

Red pulled Tom aside. "I know Tully comes off like a blowhard, and he is at times. But he's brilliant and fearless. Despite the fact that he's a Ranger, get past the bluster. Realize he's the real deal. You can trust him."

Tom nodded. "Jack told me you're hot shit! I'll take your word on Tully. Oh, is Rusty here? I got something for him."

Red, curious at the question, answered. "Rusty's not here; he's with the rear team. What do you have for him?"

"An envelope passed directly from Colonel Nelson. Not directly to me you know, through a few hands."

175

"I'm Rusty's second; it may be important, so give it to me."

The small envelope was thick and squishy. Red opened it. Read the note, laughed. He looked around, spotted him.

"Joe! Need you!"

Joe came over.

"This is Tom, comes from Colonel Nelson's new team. He's delivered a message directly from Colonel Nelson for Rusty, to give to you. Hope you don't mind, but it may be a while before we see Rusty." He bent down again, to shield the flashlight so that he could read it to Joe.

"Thanks, Joe, for being on my team. You've displayed incredible valor and leadership. Never thought your encounter with that lieutenant deserved what you got. But it did bring you to me, so I'm grateful. As a catching up matter, enclosed are your restored First Sergeant's stripes. Well deserved. Also, I'm putting you in for a few medals. I know you don't care about that, but I want to pin them on you. You know, alive, in front of me. Wish I'd met you before this started. Congratulations, First Sergeant Joseph Cappanela. Best, Colonel Nelson, G-2 Staff, Eighth Army."

Joe smiled then laughed. Sitting there, on the river bank, thought about the craziness of life, and how he liked this Colonel Nelson. How strange, he thought. A colonel writing me a personal note!

"About time Joe! Hated seeing you a private." Red handed him his new stripes.

"Thanks, Red. Didn't think it mattered much. Did you?"

"No. Nor did anybody else around here. But it shows respect, for you! Our colonel does shit like that. Congrats!"

Tom, having listened in, interjected. "How long you been a private, Joe? And what the hell happened to you?" Tom saw the string of stitches across Joe's forehead as Red read the letter.

Joe shrugged at his questions. "Jeez! Seems like a long time, but it wasn't."

Joe reflected on knocking out his lieutenant. Had no regrets about that, actually brought him a smile. Then the payback. Busted from platoon first sergeant to private, with a good chance of going to Leavenworth after a Court Martial. That was, what? June 20th. When I hit him. Lost my stripes on the 21st and got here the next day. He did a quick calculation.

"Nine days on being a private, Tom. The stitches? Well, I met some wood leaving a burning date."

Tom half laughed, wondered about the burning date thing. "I can see why you're liked. Glad you're back making the big bucks."

Red got back to business. "Who's leading the first boat, Tom?"

"Jack's Post team are all in the first boat. Where's your climber?"

Red found Mario kneeling near the boat. Signaled him to come then turned to Tom, "Mario is one of Tully's Rangers. Mario this is Tom, your boss on the bridge. You'll be with Jack in the first boat."

Knowing what his job was, he quipped, "Climb any mount, Tom, just tell me how high." He went over to Jack, introduced himself, got in the boat and started sorting through the ropes. The rest of Jack's Post guys got in and started talking with Mario.

Phil was busy going through the bag of blasting caps for the third or fourth time. He wanted to ensure no mistakes might happen. He had the wire to connect everything to the detonator. He also had the British pencil timed detonator sticks. This bridge was going to blow, one way or the other. He shifted half the blasting caps and half the pencil detonators into separate bags. He also had two wired detonators that he also separated. I'm ready, he thought.

Tom checked his watch. Red checked his. They had time. Everything had gone well, so far.

"Brought four portable radios. Same old War shit you know that had limited range, but they'll be good for our mission. Also got a few things you wanted and they're in your boat. Some M-1s and a bazooka with four rockets. Ammo for your thirty caliber machine gun and extra grenades."

"Thanks, Tom. Why're you alone in the second boat? You sure that's smart?"

"I think it's the best plan. Jack's men got the lion's share of the bridge shit. I only need to tie up the C-4 bundles at the other pillar so Jack can lift them. Then I climb up. Easy, right?"

"How many times have I heard that?" Red shook his head.

"I need to talk to the pilot. You said he's wounded? Is it bad?"

"I'm no doc, but it was a deep wound in his arm and is still oozing through my makeshift patch job."

Red saw Marty was sitting on a rock nearby. "Marty!" He low yelled, "Bring your bag!"

Tom brought the two of them over to Muzich who was sitting nearby, holding his arm. Red sat down next to him, introduced himself and Marty.

"Rough trip. How's the arm?" Marty didn't wait for Muzich's response as he lifted out his flashlight from his pack, cuffed it to focus the light on his arm and inspected the blood soaked rag on his arm.

"Still attached, so I'm grateful, but throbbing like a son of a bitch. I still can fire a weapon, though. I want to contribute in this battle. I won't hold you up."

"If I hear right, if it weren't for you, there'd be no battle. So forget that crap. You got any weapons training?"

Marty stuck his hand in. "Take this! One pain pill, it'll help. Won't mess you up!"

"Thanks!"

"I had lots of weapons training. Had a boat load of free time in Japan. I went to any Marine infantry training school they let me into, which was most. It covered a lot of stuff. So I'm no recruit, Red."

"You're sure you can handle a rifle?"

"It's my goddamned arm, not my trigger finger."

"What do you think Marty?" Asked Red.

"Best guess? He'll live for twenty-four hours. Not sure after that unless I clean that wound. I don't want to change the makeshift dressing now. It's a very serious wound."

"We don't have time now. You'll be with my team. We move out in ten."

Red, Tully and Tom had worked out how two boats initially assigned would be one. It was Tully that had to combine with Red's team. They worked it out by figuring out that the ten man inflatable would probably hold twelve even with all the extra ammo and weapons.

It was Tom who prioritized the operation before they left, and addressed all the men.

"We're to blow this bridge, period! That's our job. All teams are to support this effort. The bridge comes first! Everybody understand?"

The men knew exactly what that meant.

Tom continued, "The portable radios are all sequenced on the same frequency. Air Force is keyed in on it as well. Let's set our watches. I've got 2110 (9:10 pm) coming up in five seconds, hit it. OK, the air show begins at 2230 (11:30 pm). Stay low and quiet. Let's go!"

They got organized, passed out the radios, Phil set the RDFs and started broadcasting.

The men manned the boats and shoved off. The big wait, for the big show, had begun.

Jack, on boat one, started the outboard and headed the boat train out towards the center of the river. They had a twelve-mile run to get into position.

Boat three, now overloaded and riding very low in the water, brought up the rear of the water convoy.

Chapter Thirty

**Friday, June 30, 1950 – Day Six of the Invasion
On board B-29 "Stick in the Eye" - Group Commander
–Colonel Mark Haines – Flight out of Okinawa
– 2130 - (9:30 pm)**

The pressurized cabin allowed for comfort and regular speak without oxygen masks. Colonel Mark Haines appreciated the experience since flying B-17's. Twenty missions over Germany had changed him. Couldn't think of returning to a normal life, so he stayed in. He was only twenty-nine years old. But old before his time. He'd seen much.

A new war mission. Five years! How can that be? He wondered. Yet here he was, at it again, carrying a firestorm to a population of mostly civilians. He prayed he was in the right.

His copilot, Captain Neil Hazell said, "We're at the halfway point, Mark! Two hours out."

They'd been together for two years, had become close friends. Arriving yesterday from a grueling flight from California, they were still tired. This was Neil's first combat mission, and Mark was a little concerned.

"You Okay?"

"Yeah sure, Mark." He paused. "Well, I've been thinking about our bomb load. Why incendiary? Aren't we supposed to knock out the bridges? Why are we going to burn the city? Aren't civilians still there?"

"Jesus, Neil! For someone you say is Ok, you sure don't sound like it."

"Just been thinking about it. Some things that we did it in the big War bothered me."

"Me too! But we have our orders."

"That's my point, Mark. The Nazi's followed orders too! We hung them because they didn't refuse to obey those orders!"

Colonel Haines had ridden this conundrum and had come to grips with most of it. He believed his side was more right than the other side but knew each side did barbaric things. The Nazi's killed for prejudice, ethnic cleansing and whomever they didn't like. And we fire bombed cities and killed civilians. Then we dropped one bomb on each of two cities in Japan and killed two hundred thousand civilians in one moment.

Colonel Haines had studied the bombing tactics of Japan after the war and discovered that no aerial bomber attacks had occurred throughout the entire war on Hiroshima or Nagasaki, none of which had any strategic value. His gut had retched at the understanding.

"Captain, let me remind you of the tenacity of both the Nazi's and the Japs. They just wouldn't give up. And Captain, I want to think that we, as Americans, did our goddamned best to save as many lives as we could, be it our troops or our enemy, civilian or soldiers."

The Colonel wasn't sure he believed everything he said but wanted to think it was so.

He continued, "Besides, they told us Seoul was mostly occupied by the North Korean Army. And, need I remind you that this mission has the highest priority, straight from MacArthur."

"You really believe one and a half million people had gotten out of Seoul before it fell?"

"Neil! It doesn't matter what I believe!"

"Hey, Colonel," Said Randy, who came up behind Mark. Randy was the mid top chief gunner, in charge of all the guns and the gun crew on the plane. "You think we'll be hit by night fighters?"

181

"You heard the briefing. They don't have night fighters. They have flack, and we're going in low."

Randy didn't move. He was nervous. "Colonel, you're the only one on board that's experienced combat. So, how bad is flack?"

He didn't know how to answer that question. Thought about the first time his B-17 got shot to hell over Germany. Just making it back to England on two engines. Then the second time. He stopped thinking.

"Don't worry about it; they said they don't have many guns." He prayed it was true.

Chapter Thirty One

Friday, June 30, 1950 – Day Six of the Invasion
The Han Bridge teams on the river – 2200 – (10:00 pm)

The Bridge team was in two boats. # 1 team was the first boat with six of the men and all the climbing and lifting ropes, along with the two hundred pounds of C-4 for their target on the left pillar.

Bridge # 2 team was Tom with the other two hundred pounds of C-4 for the right pillar.

Bank # 3 team was Tully and his three men. They were to land close to the north end of the bridge along the bank to ensure the Bridge was not attacked from the north and defeat the mission.

Swamp # 4 team, with Red in command, had eight men positioned one mile east of the bridge on the river bank.

Each of the teams had a portable radio, and their team number was their call sign. Both Tully and Red's team had an RDF transmitter.

Rusty's Rear team was # 5. Two miles northeast of the bridge and didn't have a radio.

The moon cast a sliver of dim light between irregular waves of low clouds. The rain had stopped but didn't look like it would stay that way for any length of time. The air was dense with little wind.

When the boat convoy made the bend and started heading west towards Seoul, the river widened considerably. Vague lights were off in the distance, the concentrated grouping of lights was assumed to be Seoul. Much smaller light speckles appeared haphazardly throughout the northern shore.

Jack followed C J's directions and maneuvered the boat convoy toward the north shore and hugged the dense weeds and marsh that trailed off to the north. About a mile from the bridge, C J signaled Jack to head into the weeds and cut the motor. They grabbed paddles and got in deeper. Boat # 3, now free of its tether, followed their lead and paddled in up next to them. Tom, alone in boat two, swung into the raft up.

C J whispered to Red. "Paddle in as far as you can, only maybe about a hundred feet, then get out and walk. Only two feet of water from here to the bank." Turning to Tully, he said, "As planned, you bring the boat back to the weed edge and paddle another half mile or so, do the same. There's good cover along the bank right to the bridge. We're staying here. We'll check in when we're set to go."

Tom was on the other side of the three boat raft. He leaned in and whispered to Tully. "Hey, Tully! Remember, you're our backup to blow the bridge if something happens."

Tense, Tully took instant offense to Tom's presumption that he might forget his part in this most important mission. He caught himself.

He was focused on all the possible things that could happen and how he should respond. Although impulsive, his Ranger experience always brought clarity. He knew Tom had the toughest assignment and probably wouldn't make it out alive. He knew that Tom knew it, too.

Tully leaned into the middle boat, trying to get closer to Tom, on the far end. He whispered, "You'd make a good Ranger, Tom. I got your back!"

Tom was surprised at the comeback. Thought he'd catch some Ranger bravado. Reflecting a moment, it seems the reports about Tully and his men were accurate. A first! He smiled.

Tom gave Tully a thumbs up, and they nodded to each other as boat # 3 moved away.

Red had signaled to stop paddling. The weeds were getting thick and higher. He stuck his paddle in the water to check the depth and confirmed it was about two feet.

Red nodded at Tully. He whispered to his team, "Time to leave our shipmates." He grabbed a few of the thirty caliber belts and put them around his neck. Foxy shouldered a few of the new M-1s, strung a few bandoliers around his neck and then hoisted up the RDF ten pound satchel. Muzich got the other M-1 rifle and more bandoliers. Moose grabbed the bazooka. Snake picked up the satchel of four bazooka rockets and a knapsack of grenades. Marty and *Three* struggled off with their weight of the machine gun, tripod and more ammo belts. Tracker grabbed Larry's special bag of tricks knapsack he'd been entrusted with, and just slid off the boat, with not a sound or ripple of water.

The river bed was solid. Walking through two feet of water was easy, quiet and slow. In the dry season, which had ended a week ago, this bed was exposed, dried out. The Monsoon Season raised the river a few feet and had flooded the marshlands.

Distant noises, of equipment moving and mental banging, set a constant murmur through the still night as Red reached the bank and signaled the men to halt. Quietly, he dropped the belts and bags he was carrying and moved up the three-foot slope. After lying still a minute, hearing no threat nearby, he popped his head up and scanned his front.

Seeing no danger, he signaled the men forward, dropped down and checked his watch. An hour to go.

Visibility ebbed and flowed with the passing clouds as the men spread out and sought the best spots to set up at the bank. Red now surveyed their area with his hi-powered glasses.

Foxy placed the RDF transmitter and pulled out the antennae, then checked to make sure it was working. The dial showed it was transmitting.

What they had anticipated at their front was mostly there. A few new small anti-aircraft guns got emplaced since they last viewed the area five hours earlier. With rough terrain and great difficulty to access, this area was considered a no threat zone for any serious counterattack and so was lightly defended by the North Koreans.

Red liked the position, thought it was perfect.

Earlier that day, he, Rusty and Tully had wondered why the North Koreans had slowed, almost stopped their advance at the Han River after capturing Seoul. They had the South on their heels. Nothing of substance was at their front. American troops weren't here! Why stop? They bandied about a lot of theories but concluded that these guys from North Korea were like Corporal Hitler, who ended up running the German Army, and like him, they didn't know shit about warfare.

But they were grateful. Despite the horrific slaughter of civilians going on in the capital, the delay was giving the South Korean Army and America a small window of time to get organized.

Red ordered Foxy and Snake to reconnoiter, with a caveat, no sound, and no attention. They were pissed he had to say that to them, but Red was Red, always cautious, they let it go.

Tracker was angry he wasn't picked, gave Red a disgusted look. Red nodded, almost smiled, gave Tracker that *don't worry you'll get your turn look*. Tracker acknowledged, gave him a thumbs up.

Foxy and Snake crawled out. Neither had their Tommy's. But they had their primary stealth weapons, multiple knives. They also carried a .45 automatic pistol in their shoulder holster.

A few hundred feet out they saw the first emplacement, then the next. They knew about these, machine guns and mortars. As they scouted straight out, they came to a new position. A big gun. Foxy knew it at once as a German 88mm cannon. A fierce anti-aircraft weapon.

Then they saw the rest of the battery of four guns spread out. A radar unit in the background showed its cone going back and forth. This battery must have just come in.

Foxy cursed silently. He knew these 88 mothers were the most effective and fearsome weapons in the Big War. Russians captured hundreds of them and sent many to their friends after the war. They kept most because they were so superior in many roles and modified them to be better. Foxy mulled the thought of the hated Nazi's still haunting him.

They decided to split. Snake moved north. He slithered off, as only he could. They were a mile south of Rusty's Rear # 5 position and a mile northeast of the bridge.

Foxy went south. Encountered a few known positions then stumbled upon a new unit of mounted infantry on half-tracks. A platoon. Jesus! He thought, six armored vehicles! Thirty men! Right near our guy's line of escape. He started thinking fast. He checked his watch, realized it was time to get back.

Snake and Foxy drifted in, reported to Red.

Snake told them he found a perfect spot where they should reposition. It was just northeast of the 88's and not too far back from the half-tracks Foxy encountered. Snake had covered a lot of territory.

Red called the men together and made an improvised plan.

187

Chapter Thirty Two

Friday, June 30, 1950 – Day Six of the Invasion
Tully's team # 3 on the Han River – 2300 – (11:00 pm)

After leaving Red's team, Tully's men paddled with the current navigating amongst the weeds. He could make out the contours of the bridge and the high grass on the bank. Tully guessed the spot and pulled into the thick weeds until the boat couldn't go any further.

The air was still. They knew there were manned positions around the bridge entrance, a few hundred feet away. Occasional roaming guards had been observed yesterday. Small moving lights on the bridge had also been noted, indicating guards on top walking the rail. Communications were now going to be by hand signal.

Just as C J had said, the water was not deep. They exited the boats. After grabbing his stuff, Joe was left to kill the inflatable. He opened the valves slightly to start deflating the boat, then knifed the two sides to guarantee the boat would sink.

The team moved slow and quiet. Tully had the RDF unit. Frenchy carried an extra M-1 with two bandoliers. Dean brought up the rear with more bandoliers and pouches of grenades. Tully moved another fifty feet through the weeds and came to the river bank. They were a hundred yards from the bridge. They nestled into the high grass at the top of the bank and checked for enemy activity. Nothing. Joe caught up with them a few minutes later, gave Tully a thumbs up about sinking the boat.

Tully signaled for them to move closer to the bridge. The ground along the bank was soft and noiseless. Weeds on top of the bank were three feet high. They moved unseen. Two hundred feet from the bridge, they stopped and took up positions. Each knew their assignment.

Tully set up the RDF transmitter. Dean started searching the bridge with his sniper scope.

Watching him set up the transmitter, Frenchy squirreled in next to Tully. More out of nervousness than anything else, he whispered, "Why two RDF's?"

Tully was focused on so many things that he got caught up short by the question. Then turned and whispered.

"Backup! Just to make sure."

Dean whispered over to Tully, "Got a guard, three hundred feet, at our end of the bridge. Another, mid-span, he's smoking." Pausing to move his rifle scope, "One on the far bank. He's smoking too, and I think he's taking a piss."

Joe was at the top of the bank. He turned and whispered back to Tully, "Same as we figured, no change up front."

Tully turned to Frenchy at his side. "Be careful. Go!"

Tasked to scout the area, Frenchy knew what he had to do. Smart in sneaky ways, quick to improvise and he spoke Korean; he moved off through the high grass.

Fifty feet out, crawling around a prepared machine gun position he heard a step or a sound that seemed like it. He froze to the ground. Another sound. The distinctive sound of water flow hitting the ground. A guard's pissing! For Christ's sake, he thought. Maybe I won't kill him, long as he doesn't piss on me. He heard him move away, then Frenchy moved forward.

He made a half circle to about two hundred feet out. The area was getting crowded with soldiers trying to sleep just outside of semi-prepared positions. Didn't think they planned to stay too long. He's seen enough. No surprises, he headed back.

Chapter Thirty Three

Friday, June 30, 1950 – Day Six of the Invasion
Bridge team # 1 on the Han River – 2310 – (11:10 pm)

Jack had his hand in the water trying to gauge the speed of the current. He knew they were off the main flow, a tidal wash to the side. But his experience gave him an edge on estimating the real flow in the main river. The approach around the river bend gave him some indication of the speed, but then they swung so far towards the north bank they got out of the central current.

The rain in the last few days kept adding to the volume of water. It had been a few hours since the torrential downpours had ceased, but the unrelenting flow from the mountains kept increasing.

His dead reckoning on the open seas was excellent, and this wasn't too different. Estimating tidal flow and timing were crucial in navigating on the water, any water. Jack thought about his assessment of the timing.

If he didn't get it right or even close, they'd be all dead, the mission a failure.

Last minute craziness, Jack said to himself. His brain is shouting at him. Get a grip! Trust your instincts! He focused on the details. One mile away from the bridge and mid-channel. In his head, he did calculations on estimated speed and distance. Less than ten minutes.

Mario sat in the middle next to the C-4 bundles. He knew he would make better time climbing with bare feet. He removed his boots, tied them loosely together, stuffed his socks in them and put them around his neck. Earlier, wanting to climb without too much weight, Mario had tied the ends of the one-inch rope to the two-inch line and now tied the one-inch rope to his web belt. Setting his Tommy across his back, he reflected. Waiting! All the demons come out at the moment of truth, as they did now to him. He shuttered, silently cursed them away.

Phil eyed the C-4 bundles next to him, grabbed onto the pouch containing the detonator equipment that hung across his shoulder. Can't lose this, he thought, it was the key. Felt weird. Been here before. It hinges all on you. He kept repeating it. He finally forced his mind to focus on a single thought; *don't fall off the damn rope!!*

Greg didn't think he'd make it out of this mission and silently said his goodbyes to his Mom and Dad.

JP hadn't said a word, felt queasy but determined. He decided that the last many days of horror he'd been through was because of these Red bastards. He was looking for some payback.

Tom was alone in boat #2, rafted up and sitting astride Jack's boat. Both kept checking their watches and hadn't spoken. Waiting for the bombers! They despised waiting.

At 2320 (11:20 pm), an air raid siren started wailing. Then another.

Surprised, Jack grabbed his field glasses and scanned the bridge. He still saw a few small lights, but they weren't moving.

"We go now!" He barked and started the outboard, gave a high sign to Tom and moved out from the weeds with Tom in tow. Phil had the portable radio and notified Tully and Red that they started the assault.

B-29 Bomber Attack – All around the Han Bridge
– 2320 - (11:20 pm)

The sirens startled the teams. No previous air attack had triggered any warnings. They all concluded it must be new equipment that was just brought in. The scouts from Rusty's team # 5 and Red's team # 4 had reported new anti-aircraft positions only minutes ago, but still, they didn't anticipate the early warning.

The bombers had started their approach at twenty-five thousand feet but quickly descended to an operational height of seven thousand feet five minutes before the drop. They hoped the maneuver would confuse or delay any radar automated ammo fuse settings. The RDF signals from the target were clear, easy to hone in on.

All the teams heard the distant approaching bombers, like a train starting its descent down an incline. Only a few of the men had ever heard B-29's before. But certainly, no one had heard anything up close and personal like this. Not many had ever experienced a low-level attack by heavy bombers and lived to tell about it.

Enemy anti-aircraft guns started firing. They were mostly German 88's that were rapid firing, semi-automatic cannon shooting shells with height adjusted fuse detonation (Proximity fuse). There was no need to hit a plane, just get close and let the shrapnel do the damage. Three batteries of four guns each started firing.

Jack angled his approach across the river, steering to the right center span - the third buttress bridge support of the bridge, Tom's boat was the first to be dropped off.

Jack got to the right bridge support just as the sounds of the bombers were almost overhead. Tom threw a line around a pole sticking up from the bridge base as Jack unfastened the towing rope, turned back into the current and headed to the other pillar. Noise from the nearby anti-aircraft guns and approaching bombers was deafening.

Minutes later, C J quickly secured the boat as Mario jumped out onto the bridge base and started climbing the stone-faced wall. He knew the wall was going to be very rough, not the climb; the large rock edges made the climb uneventful. But of the effects the sharp rocks would have on cutting his bare feet would. But speed was essential. He ignored caution and the awful pain and raced to the top.

Same Time - Tully's Team #3 - At the Bridge Bank

Everyone jumped at the sound of the sirens, totally unexpected. The siren was near and loud. The teams knew the first air attack was to be with incendiaries, not bombs. Joe wasn't afraid of much, but he sure was terrified of anything dropped from the air. He'd seen the results of air attacks using various munitions on enemy positions directly at his front; napalm, phosphorus, rockets, light and heavy bombs, it didn't matter. It gave him a feeling of utter helplessness. He yelled, "Get into the water!"

He didn't care if the enemy heard him, although that was a slim chance with the sirens blaring. He just wanted to save his team.

The reason that going to the water was important was a combination of experience and the last communication with Colonel Nelson where he told them that the bombers were going to drop M-69 incendiary canisters, the primary weapon used against Japanese cities. We had a lot of these munitions left over, so these were tasked for this mission. He told them about the water.

The M-69 was a horrific weapon. Each B-29 carried forty of these cluster bombs, with a total of 1520 M-19 bomblets stored in each canister. These small bomblets were filled with jellied oil and white phosphorus, known as WP. The canisters opened up at about 2,000 feet to release all. After separation, each of the 3-foot tubes had cotton streamers to orient their fuse downwards. Upon impact, the timing fuse burned for about five seconds and then a white phosphorus charge ignited and propelled the incendiary filling up to 100 feet in flaming globs. The globs stuck to anything and burned everything.

Except if the bomblets landed in the water.

Water significantly dissipated the effects of the detonation as it diminished the dispersion of the lethal jelly, and, depending on the depth of impact, might entirely prevent dispersal into the air.

Tully should have acted first but was stunned by the air raid warning. He quickly recovered after Joe's call out.

Tully confirmed. "Follow Joe to the water! Now!"

Frenchy followed Joe and Tully followed Frenchy. Dean didn't move. He'd been scoping the bridge and been following three guards on top of the bridge walking the rail. He hadn't seen another sentry on the bridge. Dean had flinched at the sirens but had kept his sniper rifle focused. He patiently watched, scoping the guards and then the bridge center base span. Surprised the guards hadn't moved by the air raid alert, he stayed with them and finally saw Jacks little convoy appear approaching the right center bridge base.

He re-scoped to the guard above the raft to see him looking down, apparently spotting Jack's raft. He braced his rifle on his knee and took aim.

Dean made a quick decision and shot him, then quickly moved his scope to the guard nearest him. The guard reacted as if he heard something, turned and looked back to center span then looked down into the river. Then Dean shot him. He then turned to the far side guard who must've decided the bridge wasn't a good place to be and followed him as he ran to the south exit off the bridge.

Counting on the warning sirens and anti-aircraft fire to hide his sniper rifle reports, he none the less checked his immediate front. Nobody had been alerted, then he too, ran to the water.

Same Time - Red's Team # 4 -   2320 - (11:20 pm)

Red checked his watch again. Ten more minutes! Maybe? He knew shit happened. Wouldn't be the first time something got fouled up. He'd seen many FUBAR's, some costing his friend's lives. Hoping this wasn't going to happen here, he said a silent prayer to anyone who might be listening. *Please bring the bombers in on time.*

Just then, the air raid signal started.

Red bowed his head, said a prayer. "Thanks, now please keep my boys safe!"

Red knew about the incendiaries and called out for his men to move back into the water.

Chapter Thirty Four

Friday, June 30, 1950 – Day Six of the Invasion
On the Bridge with Team # 1 - 2330 – (11:30 pm)

As the bombers roared overhead, Mario reached the top. There was a four-foot clearance between the base and the steel H beams of the rail bed. Not looking around, he unhooked the one-inch rope from his belt and started yanking the rope up.

Many things started happening. Action exploded!

Pops and extreme light flashes illuminated the night. All around the bridge fire filled the air. The first wave of bombers was just passing over, heading West. Detonations started as munitions from a gun position hit in the raid started cooking off.

Mario shut out all the distractions and focused on his tasks. He grabbed the end of the one-inch line tied to the two-inch rope and untied it, then fastened the two-inch rope to a three-foot-thick steel H-beam above his head, then yanked on the thick rope twice and got a confirming two pulls back.

He sat, put his socks on his bloody feet, then his boots. He then coiled the two hundred feet of one-inch line and put it on his shoulder.

C J climbed the thick two-inch rope quickly and lifted himself up next to Mario. He had another one-inch line attached to his belt. He removed it and attached it to an overhead beam, then tugged it twice. Receiving the confirming signal, he nodded to Mario for him to go.

Mario moved to the edge and climbed to the top. As he swung up, he hit a body. "Jesus!" The body lay half on the inside rail and half on the outside. The head shot was revealing. Must've been Dean he thought. Man, he's good. Not hesitating, he lifted the dead soldier's legs into the center of the rail tracks.

Mario took off for the other column, careful to step on the wooden cross ties and not fall between the six-inch gaps. The bombers were now directly over the entire north bank. The noise was insane. Continuous flashes all around, as thousands of incendiary bomblets ignited, anti-aircraft cannons firing, flak shells exploding overhead and bomber engines roaring.

C J began pulling up the twenty-five lb. blocks of C -4. The explosive bricks were stacked and taped and easy to handle. As the first load came onto the top support, Phil swung himself off the thick rope and dropped to his knees, panting heavily from the climb.

Greg was up next, saw Phil. "Don't die on us now old man. You okay?"

He nodded. "Haven't done that shit in a while. I'm good. You can stow that old man crap!"

"Yeah, you're good! Just don't let the Rangers see you like this. You'll never hear the end of it!" With that said, he climbed to the top and headed over to help Mario.

C J pulled another bundle in, untied it and tossed the line down. Fully recovered, Phil carried the first stack to the far end of the support and placed it under the steel beam. It was going like clockwork.

Mario got to the right bridge support, took a second to see the shit hitting just off the bank to his east, where he knew his men hid. He was a Ranger, determined, yet still felt the horror of being killed by your own. He prayed they took good cover as he climbed down underneath the rail beams to the base. Immediately uncoiling his line, he tied it to a steel support and fed it out down the column. He couldn't see Tom, didn't want to just drop it on his head. Seconds later, he felt the tug and started hauling it up. As before, the two-inch line was pulled in, untying the lighter rope, he secured the thick one to another beam and then dropped the smaller one to pull up the explosives.

Greg hopped down to join Mario. At the edge of the city, about a mile away, thatched huts and larger houses were burning, casting an amber hue around them and along most of the upper bridge.

"What about the dead guy up there?" Greg asked.

"Don't know. Think our sniper took him out."

The line Mario was holding yanked twice. He started hauling it up. When he pulled it in he said to Greg, "You take over, I'm going up top."

He checked his watch; they had forty-five minutes till the next bomber attack.

Same Time - Rusty's Rear Team # 5

Two miles away, Rusty watched the progression of shell bursts as they headed towards him.

The bombers flew in waves of four, in staggered formation, left and right. Flashes started lighting up the sky in the foreground. Big, continuous waves of fire and small popping sounds filled the distant north shore. Seoul started burning. Ammo from ground installations hit was detonating.

Seconds later, closer detonations flashed. The eastern section around the bridge where all the teams lay hidden erupted in flames. The eruptions continued moving north, towards his position. It happened fast.

"Holly shit!" He yelled, "Everybody! Move back into the stream. Spread out! Now!"

His men were watching this thing unfold and didn't hesitate. Arron grabbed *Two* and dragged him back. *One* was alert enough to follow Rusty. They hadn't thought to pick up anything. They ran with what they had in their hand and ran as fast as they could. They knew what was coming their way and they only had seconds.

The stream wasn't far away. They dove into the three-foot water with seconds to spare. Flashes started engulfing the area just vacated. One splash, three feet away from Rusty, caused his heart to almost stop. He started shaking. Then a dull blurb, nothing.

As the bomber wave passed, Rusty, got hold of himself. Larry, lying next to him, said, "Nice party you brought me too, Rusty! You okay?"

He shook his head,"Yeah. I'm good. Rest of the men?"

Larry nodded, "I'll check." He moved down the stream amongst the team. Small flames lighted near the positions they had just abandoned. The small hut village at their front was ablaze.

They all were getting up as Larry moved down the line. Except one. He lay still in the water. Moving to him he saw the reason. The body was aglow, burning from underneath with a small fire coming out of a hole in its back.

"Crap!" He said.

Arron was nearby, just starting to get up, looked at Larry and then at *Two,* lying, burning, still in the water.

Arron had experienced much hardship and witnessed an enormous amount of pain and death in the Big War. He formulated a protective persona about his Confederate families past early on as he made up a continual personal battle against the American Norther States in his belief that deflection and cynicism was the best defense against revealing personal feelings.

"I liked him, Larry!"

"I think he saved your life, Arron. Sorry, buddy." Larry stuck out a hand to help him up. "Thanks."

Nothing had hit their position directly, but small fires burned in the fields nearby. Further out, the huts were burning like a wooden match just lit. Still further out, north and south random fires burned. In the far distance, Seoul was on fire.

198

Chapter Thirty Five

Saturday, July 1, 1950 – Day Seven of the Invasion
Midnight at the Han Bridge – 0001 – (12:01 am)

Under the left bridge span, the eight bundles of C-4 had been placed where the steel was secured to the rock and concrete base. Phil and C J started to wire them up. J P came up from the boat and checked his Tommy. Jack, still below, opened the valves on the inflatable, punctured the two sides with his knife and watched it deflate. Then he untied the lines and watched it float off with the current and disappear below the surface.

Climbing the rope, Jack heard the beginning of silence. Crackles and some pops in the distance but relative calm. He didn't like it.

At the top, Phil was setting the detonators. Jack called over to him, "How long?"

"Ten minutes!"

C J had already moved up to the rail top to take up a defensive position.

Jack turned, "JP, you stay and help Phil. I'm going up. Hurry!"

As Jack rolled over the top, C J warned, "Lights coming!"

Jack looked down the south approach and saw small flashlights fifty yards away, three. He crawled over to C J, encountering the dead body as he did. "Who's the dead guy?"

"Unlucky." Whispered C J.

"No shooting, C J. We need to take'em quiet." A pause, "I'll go right and crawl behind. Think you can get them close?" He only met this guy a few hours ago. No idea who he was or his experience. And he was Korean.

"Unless you fall or make a lot of noise, yes."

Jack wanted to laugh. But this was a high threat situation he'd experienced before. Maybe, that's why he thought it funny. Funny, in that he survived them all. Hard to believe, he thought. Is this where luck runs out? He concluded his thoughts by thinking of his best friend, Rick, who, after the War, was killed when his tractor overturned in a ditch, on his farm. No! Not me. Jack thought. Not going out that way!

C J moved to the dead guy, found his helmet, put it on, picked up his rifle and stood up. He hoped it would be enough.

Close now, a Korean voice called out. C J responded. They came closer, three men, not very concerned, weapons up. They were looking for their guard.

C J chatted them up some more as he moved closer. Jack moved slowly along the far back rail, got to their back and angled over the rails. Knife in hand he squatted up behind the last man, grabbed his mouth, pulled his head back and sliced his throat in a fast cut. He held him a few seconds as he bled out. Not a sound, except for the exchange between C J and the NK leader.

The sound of Jack putting the body down caused the first and second guy to turn. C J reacted by grabbing the lead guy and thrusting his combat knife into his heart. The second guy got a double whack as Jack and C J both stuck him, front and back. With a horrid, gurgling sound, he collapsed.

"Good job! C J." They moved the bodies to the center of the track and lay them prone, waiting for a follow-up.

Jack checked his watch, almost thirty minutes for the second bomber wave to attack. He whispered to himself. "Damn, that's a long time."

Below, Phil finished wiring up the charges, adding the timed British pencil remote detonators he'd carried for insurance. He used the sixty-minute capsules. "Let's go JP!"

JP carried the hard wired charge reel as Phil, making sure the wire didn't get stuck, brought up the rear. Popping up onto the rail bed, they saw Jack and the bodies. Phil gave Jack the high sign and moved out. They both scurried across to the next pillar. As they got near, JP saw Mario laying in the rail tracks, Greg on the other side, guarding the approach from the north shore. JP nodded to them as he stopped to play out lots of wire before he climbed down. Phil, following, gave them a thumbs up, then he too followed JP down the undercarriage of the rail bed onto the support column.

After lifting the C-4 bundles, Tom killed his boat as Jack had, climbed the thick rope and joined Greg. They stuffed the packages of C-4 as instructed, then Greg had gone up to join Mario.

Tom checked his watch as Phil climbed down, then JP. Twenty minutes to go. "You set, Phil! Don't mess this up!"

"Tom! Take a hike! I don't make mistakes!" Phil started hooking up the detonators. He was pleased with how the charges were placed around the steel beams.

He didn't turn to Tom but called to him, "You actually can follow instructions, Tom. Quite surprising."

"Asshole! I was taking instructions long before you could read. Now, work fast!"

Things were going well, Phil thought, just want off this bridge before the next bomber raid.

After a while. "How long?" Asked Tom.

Phil looked at him, didn't say anything and then continued setting the wired detonators at the far end of the support column. He then pulled out his remote detonators from Larry's gift bag, and placed two, but didn't set them.

Tom was watching him. "What the hell is that?"

"Insurance! They're called Pencil detonators." He worked as he spoke to Tom. "These little beauties are one of the major contributions the Brits made in the War. Besides capturing the Enigma coding machine and breaking the Nazi High Command coding orders that made our victory possible, this little innovation in remote detonation did wonders for the Allies resistance."

"I don't give a shit as long as they work. No wires? Did we use them?"

"Even the German High Command used them. The attempt on Hitler's life in '44 was a prime example of its use. It's a simple two-part chemical tube with a detonator. Break the vial and the chemicals mix, eating away the neutral wire. They premixed the chemicals based on the time needed to eat the wire. The whole thing is the size of a pencil, easy to use and pretty time accurate."

Tom watched him work as he didn't skip a beat while talking. "Thanks for the history lesson. So, how long?"

"Ten minutes!"

"That's all we got left! See if you can pick it up. I don't want to be on this bridge when the next wave of bombers come in."

"Ya think I got a death wish?"

On board B-26 Bomber "Lady L" – Group Commander Colonel Joe Lowe – 0020- (12:20 am)

"Got Suwon airport lights, Joe." Said his copilot. "Turn to compass heading zero fifteen. Got a hard lock on the RDF signals."

"Turning now. Have the Group execute the plan."

Colonel Lowe flew twenty-nine missions against Germany. Had refused to stand down after twenty missions. He volunteered to continue. He'd been assigned to special operations after demonstrating extraordinary planning capabilities. Winning a few medals for successful assignments and minimum plane losses, he was an unassuming, quiet man. His wife and two children were killed in an unexplained house fire in the winter of 1943. He embraced the Army Air Corp for his personal survival. He loved flying, felt personally responsible for his men and always planned hard for his missions.

This one was no exception.

Knowing that North Korea had been heavily supplied by Russian captured German 88 anti-aircraft radar activated automatic fuse cannons, he developed a plan to hopefully confuse the enemy, at least for a few crucial seconds.

His Group would approach Suwon Airport at ten thousand feet, fifty miles from the Han Bridge. From then on, the surrounding mountains would not be a safety issue, as it was a straight shot to Seoul.

It was a ten-minute run.

Colonel Lowe's plan was that when he reached Suwon, the trailing V formation of four would slow but maintain their height of ten thousand feet. The remaining flight of three V formations of four would dive to three thousand feet. The low formations would come in first, like an arrow, spread wide.

The last high-flying formation would, at the target, veer off left and execute a circle dive to three thousand feet heading north, up the corridor, trying to hit the tank park.

The fires at the Capitol soon became apparent. Not a conflagration, but enough to see. Colonel Lowe knew there were American troops on the Han Bridge. He wasn't told this. But he knew. Orders were to drop just beyond the bridge. Why else, he thought.

"Open bomb bay doors!"

Chapter Thirty Six

Saturday, July 1, 1950   Day Seven of the Invasion
On the Han Bridge – 0020 – (12:20 am)

JP had pulled out enough wire so Phil could tie off the connections to the two piles. He climbed up top, unfurled the wire and crawled towards the north side of the bridge, getting a jump toward their exit off the structure. It was a long way off.

Phil finished hooking up the wire on the last detonator on the last stack of C-4. He jumped when the air raid sirens started again.

He didn't notice Tom flinch as well.

"Let's go asshole!" Tom yelled.

Phil didn't respond. He ran across to the other stack, pulled out a crimping tool and broke his preset Pencil fuses. He ran back and did the same on his just finished wired pile. These were thirty-minute fuses.

Phil shouted as he turned. "Tom! Why are you still standing there? Move!"

Tom went up first, Phil right behind.

As Tom hurled himself onto the rail ties, he heard automatic weapons fire to his rear. Not loud, but loud enough to be heard above the air-raid warning sirens.

Tom called out to the prone men, "Follow JP! Make sure the wire doesn't get tangled up! Get off this bridge! Follow the plan! If we're not off after ten minutes of your arrival, blow it!"

Mario and Greg started north with PJ when Phil came up. They led the way. Their orders were to ensure that nobody interfered with getting the wire safely across. PJ had three reels of wire hanging off him as he moved slowly across the rail ties.

Phil picked up the wire and took off after JP. Each reel had three hundred feet of detonator cord. His job was to connect the wire at reels end so as not to slow JP from getting off the bridge.

Tom turned to the continuous sounds of fire coming from Jack's position to his rear. Quickly he walked over the ties towards the sound. Getting a sense of the distance between the ties, he picked up his pace.

A Little Earlier

Jack saw a flood of lights coming from the south. He figured the NK thought something might be wrong. One guard was missing, then three men missing, so now they'd send ten. That's what I'd do.

No time for stealth now, Jack concluded. Only brute force. His mission was to keep them away from the set charges for as long as possible. Then escape. Wonderful! He considered scenarios where he might have a chance, then stopped.

The lights were one hundred feet away. The figures were cast in a dull amber shadow from the burning city.

Air-raid sirens started blaring.

Lying prone, Jack yelled out to C J, "Now!"

They opened fire with their Tommy's, immediately dropping a few. The NK, now also lying prone, returned fire.

As he approached behind his men, Tom saw the action taking place. He stopped, knelt, and assumed a throwing stance. A star quarterback many years ago, he reached into his pouch, pulled out two grenades, aimed, and threw. One, then immediately another. His old skills hadn't deserted him. Of course, he'd practiced throwing grenades a lot over the last many years.

The first one exploded just to the rear of the enemy group. Lots of adrenaline in that throw, he thought. The second landed like a touchdown pass. Right in the middle of the bread basket. Boom!

Jack and C J ran forward, firing. One soldier was wounded but still got off a few rounds at them. C J finished him off.

Suddenly the air-raid sirens stopped.

The oncoming sound of a monster rising from its lair replaced the sirens in the now almost quiet night, as the low-flying bombers approached.

C J turned to Jack, but he wasn't there. Then he saw him in a heap, lying across the tracks. Tom came up and bent over the body.

"Through the heart! Never felt a thing. Shit! C J, give me a hand." Tom grabbed Jacks arms, C J grabbed his torso and lifted the body onto Tom's back.

"You lead! Let's get out of here." Said Tom.

Jack's weight slowed Tom until he adjusted for the new weight and balance and readjusted to the intervals of the rail beams and increased speed.

Shaken, Tom cursed himself. If only I had released the grenade a second or two earlier, Jack would still be alive. He knew this reasoning was a waste of time. Just as it had been so long ago when he missed a throw to his open wide receiver as he crossed the goal line and he lost the biggest game of his life. A second too soon or too late. Timing! Luck! Fate! No, he thought; I fucked up!

They got to the end of the steel bridge support just as the anti-aircraft 88's started firing. Fifty caliber machine guns at their front chimed in. It was deafening. The bomber's engine noise swelled in the background.

It was a twenty-foot drop to the elevated riverbank below. Tom knelt and laid Jack to the side of the rail. He looked at him and whispered, "Jack, I'm sorry, but I can't climb down with you on my back. I know you won't feel anything, but damn, I hate doing this!" Tom then lifted Jack to the edge and pushed him over the side. He couldn't hear the thump above all the other noise. He started climbing down. C J witnessed the whole thing, just shook his head and followed.

They hit the dirt as the B-26's screamed overhead.

Twelve bombers were in the first wave, each releasing forty, one hundred pound bombs. At three thousand feet, they would be released in sections. Rear loaded first from the bomb bay in eights, until all five units of eight were released, two seconds apart. They would hit in tight clusters spreading north; twelve planes, four hundred and eighty bombs.

There was a considerable amount of enemy activity farther north amongst the emplacements of soldiers and weapons. Fires roared from vehicles and among soldiers previously hit by the jellied fire spray. Munitions were still cooking off. Soldiers trying to put out fires or save their wounded friends now scurried to find cover from this new air attack.

Sniper Dean focused on the near threat. Soldiers manning a machine gun position close to the bridge exit had become agitated during the air raid sirens, pointing at the bridge. They must've seen something, he thought.

As guns fired from the ground at the bombers, Dean started his relentless, highly exacting 99% accuracy rate of fire. A totally unemotional killing of his enemy. The first targets were the soldiers at this machine gun emplacement. Then shifted to concentrated positions along their intended escape route. He aimed, shot, and killed. Bolted another round in his 1913 Enfield sniper rifle and began again. Three seconds, total. No one counted how many scores. But him.

The bombers roared in.

At Rusty's Rear Team #5 – 0020 – (12:20 am)

Rusty scanned the bridge front until the sirens started. Then he switched his focus to the center bridge span. Although cast in a faint light, from two miles away he couldn't see any detail. The tiny flashes of what he thought was gunfire on the top of the bridge alerted him to something bad happening. Then he saw a bright flash and another. Grenades he believed. Ours or theirs? He started to worry more than he had.

207

When the anti-aircraft guns opened up, he raised his hi-powered glasses up to see the low flying bombers approaching. Cast in shadowy light from the nearby burning buildings and vehicles, they looked like hawks descending on their prey. A long line of planes, spreading west. He was glad they were on his side.

Rusty watched it unfold, like an old film reel in slow motion. He was mesmerized. Now clearly visible, the bombers were over the bridge.

The detonations started one hundred yards north of the bridge. Clusters. Rapidly speeding north, like a wind-swept fire in dry woods, but in seconds, not minutes. Then it was over. The rumbling sound of the bombers faded.

But the anti-aircraft 88's didn't stop firing. He then saw another flight of bombers appear diving towards him. He panicked and yelled at the top of his voice, "Take cover!"

Of course, he didn't. He was wrapped up in this scene and couldn't move.

The diving four planes executed a turn north, just at Rusty's front. A stunning four plane formation, tight. He could see their bomb bay doors open but didn't see the bombs drop. Detonations began shortly after that, just north of his position, where the tank park was. He smiled. It was a beautiful sight.

A little earlier - At Tully's Bridge Bank Team #3

Tully wondered where the rest of the Bridge team was. Mario told him that Tom had gone back to Jack and C J, that there'd been gunfire.

Tully had seen the flashes of explosions and wondered if they'd gotten off that bridge section. He didn't know these men. They did sound capable in their brief meeting, but so what, he thought, he'd seen many capable men die.

Scanning through his hi-powered glasses he saw movement, men moving fast. Was it them?

Tully yelled over to Mario, "Get to the bridge. Make sure it's our guys coming down!"

Mario grabbed Greg, "Come on with me!" They were only fifty feet away but it was dimly lit by shadows.

Figures above were seen as a shadow, as they were backlit from the burning city. No clarity. Some movement, then a thump and sand spray two feet from where they knelt. Both jumped, thought it was a bomb. Two seconds later, they crawled over and found a body. It was face down, lying at an awkward angle.

"Don't shoot!" Yelled Tom, as he approached them.

"You scared the shit out of me!" Said Greg, visibly shaken by the two surprises.

"Who is it?" Asked Mario.

C J then joined them. Greg looked at C J, knew it was his boss who was dead.

C J grabbed Greg's arm, "Sorry, Greg. Jack fought right to the end. My fault, I should have fired faster."

"No one's fault!" Tom hoisted Jack up and followed Mario back to their position.

As the bombers passed overhead, Tully turned to Phil and yelled, "Now!"

Phil pushed the plunger.

The blast wave was felt. The sound, although muted by the cannon fire and bomber noise that was intense was heard. Four hundred pounds of C-4 going off at the same time will do that.

Then the bombs started exploding two hundred feet in front of them. The ground shook, the noise deafening. The men got as close to the ground as possible.

Tully watched the last bomber group sweep across his front and head north up the corridor. He turned and scanned the bridge trying to see if the span went down but couldn't see through the cloud of smoke.

"Time to move!" He yelled.

C J moved to the front of the column, followed by Joe and the rest of the men. Tully waited, as each passed him. He was going to bring up the rear. Tom neared him and saw the body he carried.

"Is he dead?"

Tom kept moving passed him. "Yup!"

Tully followed him, wondering what kind of man Jack had been. Shit! He thought, if he was here, then I know what kind of guy he was. Brave and stupid, like the rest of us.

Chapter Thirty Seven

Saturday, July 1, 1950 – Day Seven of the Invasion
Bridge and Tully's Teams moving towards Red's Team #4
– 0045 – (12:45 am)

Phil radioed Red with a quick, "Moving to you now."

They moved out fast along the bank, C J at point with Joe close behind him. They moved toward Red's swamp position. Secondary explosions were kicking off from the west and north of them. Then a few big bangs and flashes came from up north in the corridor.

A few seconds later, Joe grabbed C J from behind, whispered "Stop! Get down!" Like a traffic light at a busy intersection, the in-line men got real close to the next guy and slammed on their breaks, got still. Tully waddled up to Joe and C J and whispered, "What's the problem?"

"Something's wrong," Joe said. "Get Frenchy up here!"

Tully knew about Joe's ability to sense danger and wasn't going to mess with it. He went back to get Frenchy, telling the men along the way to be ready for action. Phil got on the radio to Red, "Something's up. We halted about a half-mile away from you. Checking it out."

"Roger that." Red responded.

Returning, Frenchy got in close to Joe and C J. "What's my Brooklyn friend got cooked up?"

Joe liked Frenchy, smiled. "You and C J are going to find out what's around here that's giving me the willies."

From behind them, Tully interjected, "You guys don't know shit about Joe, but he's more right than wrong! So go!"

"Someday I hope you will show me Flatbush Ave." Frenchy said, as C J just looked on, not knowing what either man meant. Then they got up and slowly moved forward.

The rest of the men got into two man fire teams and spread out. Dean and Greg went into the water, moved out about twenty feet then silently walked waist deep parallel to the bank in the weeds.

They heard them before they got too far, chattering low speak. Two? More? Frenchy didn't know but took a chance that it was only two guards, so he took the initiative, spoke out loud in Korean. "You'd be all dead if I was the enemy!" He and C J slowly moved closer.

A gasp! "What? Who are you?" Someone called out, still too dark to make out details.

Frenchy knew the Korean mindset and played it to the hilt. "Captain Jong! Security! I ask questions! Who are you?"

A sergeant responded, saying they were part of a mechanized unit parked nearby. His squad wanted to get away from the bombers, so they came to the river bank for better cover.

Then this enemy sergeant lit them up with a flashlight.

"Shit!" Frenchy said as he and C J opened fire with their Tommy guns. The bright light had temporarily blinded them, so they sprayed the area around the flashlight and dove to the sand.

They heard cries, sounds of a body falling and then crawling noises from the area. C J lobbed a grenade. The bright flash illuminated the area for a second, allowing Dean, who was in two feet of water and thirty feet away, to fire one shot at a fleeing soldier, then he and Greg moved fast towards the position.

Joe and Tully were on top of the river bank in high weeds when the firing began. Too far away to make a difference, they moved further away from the bank towards the action, thinking they might cut off any retreating enemy. They heard noise in the distance but couldn't see anything.

C J and Frenchy crawled forward, heard labored breathing, then a deep cough, then nothing.

Near them, Dean called out, "Any alive?"

Frenchy responded in typical fashion, "Qui! Only good guys!"

They found six bodies and another on top of the bank that Dean had shot. C J said it first, "A few got away. We need to move!"

A few minutes later, not far from them and above the background noise of sporadic explosions, big engines started up.

Same Time - Red's Team #4 at the Swamp

Alerted by radio that the escaping team was facing a situation, Red told Foxy and Snake. "Our guys are in trouble! Go to that spot you found, set up like we talked about."

Snake nodded. Moose, nearby, let out a whisper, "Okay!" Foxy grabbed the bazooka and told *Three* to follow them as he was carrying the backpack with the four bazooka rockets. The four of them crawled out with Snake in the lead.

Red said, "Tracker! Now's your time. You roam out, get behind them, but don't do anything unless shit flies!"

Tracker smiled and left.

Red signaled Marty and Muzich to follow him out to their position in the high grass midway between Foxy's new position and Tully's team at the river bank. They set up the machine gun. They had lots of ammo belts.

Red had accessed the tactical situation should something like this go wrong, planned it out with his team so there would be no surprises. His men knew their roles.

His guess was confirmed as gunfire erupted in the area where he thought Tully's team were stuck.

Everyone knew the fight to escape, and survival had started.

Foxy's new position

Foxy followed Snake into the position he'd found earlier. It was a shallow crevice in an open field. Activity was all around, but it

213

seemed dysfunctional with no immediate threat. Then firing at the river over by Tully's team got them sharp.

The noise of a big engine starting up got their attention.

Moose than moved to the edge of the crevice and set his BAR. He called over, "I got the infantry! Just get the Armor!"

Then more engine ignitions fired. They were close, maybe a hundred yards. The night was dark but distant fires and munitions cooking off allowed for decent profiles as they saw the half-tracks pull out of a culvert, infantry forming at their side, moving toward the river bank and their fleeing bridge team.

Tracker moved like a Hollywood movie Indian, fast and silent. Being a real red-blooded American Indian that was raised in the wilderness of his reservation on the Michigan shores, he was in fact, a long lost warrior who still had his native skills and keen instincts. Like his ancestors, he showed no mercy to anyone trying to do harm to his tribe.

Skirting through disorganized troop concentrations, Tracker knew where Foxy's position was and angled a little north of it. These were scared soldiers, waiting for the next potential air attack, putting out fires and carrying wounded and dead men away. He knew where the real danger to his men were. Armored vehicles with mounted troops. He followed the engine sounds.

Chapter Thirty Eight

Saturday, July 1, 1950 – Day Seven of the Invasion
The Battle at the Han River Bridge - 0100 – (1:00 am)

Red had a bird's eye view of how this was developing and didn't like it. He grabbed Muzich, who now had the radio. "Tell Tully's team we deployed out to the northeast; we'll cover their flank. Tell'em to move fast along the bank."

Glasses up, Red got a good look at the oncoming vehicles. "Fucking Nazi's!" He said out loud as he recognized the infamous German halftrack. "We're fighting these same bastards all over again." Red was right.

As with the German 88mm cannons, the Hanomag -251 halftrack was, by far, the best mechanized infantry vehicle in the War. Noted for its innovative slanted topside armor, extended tractors, troop capacity and a mounted heavy machine gun. It could traverse almost any terrain. The Russians captured hundreds and repurposed them to their friends.

Sensing that if these enemy troops got organized, he'd probably lose his men. Red thought about his own demise. That vision flashed thru his mind. He saw it again, as he had in the past. His prayer was fierce. No! Not yet!

Red leaned over to Muzich, "Get help! See if you can contact Air Force for a tactical run."

Muzich switched the radio to the Air Force channel and started calling. He wasn't optimistic. The range of the radio was limited to a few miles at best, but he also felt that tingling feeling of death. He kept at it.

Foxy's New Position

Snake had already silently killed two enemy soldiers that strayed too close to their position. They were very exposed in their crevice, but the enemy hadn't noticed. Thankfully the enemy was too preoccupied with the air-raids and now the river bank. Foxy's team focused on the armored vehicles and infantry crossing at their front.

Foxy hated the sound of tracks, his stomach turned. He'd been there. Fighting through his fear he immediately loaded a rocket into the bazooka as he showed *Three* how to do it for the next time. He brought up the bazooka, got up into a textbook kneeling stance that was totally against Red's instructions and fired on the first halftrack nearest him.

Even the old 2.5mm bazooka would make short work of a thin skinned halftrack, and it did, as Foxy's round hit dead center.

A first time hit for him, Foxy yelled, "Jesus! I'm good!" Then turned to see *Three* reloading, he refocused, knew he had to do it again. Then he dived into the crevice and hit the ground.

Secondary explosions from up the valley at the tank park added to the general confusion, but the halftrack exploding got all the nearby troops' attention. Some had seen the propulsion fire as the rocket swooped past in front of them. Others saw the rocket flash from the bazooka. All reacted immediately and dropped to the

216

ground, brought up their weapons and started firing on Foxy's approximate position.

Moose, off to the side, fired back with his semi-automatic rifle. It kept them down.

The next halftrack in line started to turn to come at them directly. With the enemy now firing at them, Foxy remembered Red's warning about firing the bazooka without being exposed to enemy fire, so he stayed prone, aimed at the turning halftrack and hit the driver's door, sending a plume of fire and smoke ten feet in the air. Since all the enemy had watched the bazooka fire, they now knew exactly where Foxy's position was and began pouring on automatic and rifle fire in response. Moose's gun jammed.

Then about thirty soldiers got up and charged them.

Red's team.

Red liked firing the light machine gun. Even with the tripod mount, the gun jumped a bit but his strength was able to keep it pretty steady and hence, more accurate. He and Marty had worked together on the team weapon a few times and had developed a chemistry that's hard to describe for anyone that never experienced a superior force charging at you. Hell bent on killing you.

Seeing the action unfolding, he was proud of the *take charge attitude* of Foxy. He would have done the exact same thing. The burning halftracks now backlit the charging infantry. Nice! Red said as he opened fire on them from a different position. Scores of soldiers went down before the charging enemy realized they were being raked from their flank.

At the same time, Foxy's team began firing on the charging enemy. Moose's BAR weapon, now unjammed, laced them with a continuing torrent of rapid death.

Two more fast moving halftracks came into the field, heading straight toward Foxy's position. More soldiers started advancing from the bridge area. A tank appeared approaching from the north and fired, the boom of the tank fire registered on Red. The shell missed everything but the event spelled out the hopelessness of their situation. They had kicked the hornet's nest and the bees were mad.

"Muzich! Tell Tully we're pulling out! He's on his own. He's to move to Rusty."

Then Red reached into his bag of grenades and found the Berry flare gun Muzich had given him and fired it. Igniting a few hundred feet in the air as a bright red star. It signaled Foxy and Tracker to withdraw.

Tracker – before the flare

Hearing the battle noise, Tracker got to the halftrack culvert. The first four vehicles pulled out. It was time for his enemy to die as his tribal instincts and military skill took control of his action. He was like a walker on water that didn't show a ripple.

Some soldiers were racing about, rushing to do what they were ordered to do. They were preoccupied and acted in shaded, flickering light from nearby fires.

Crawling around the enemy position, he got to the far end where the remaining two halftracks were getting ready to pull out. Soldiers climbed aboard both vehicles and got into the armored open bed and got down behind the protective steel sides, ten man squad per halftrack. Additional infantry in the culvert ran to its front to support the halftracks on their flank. They were exposed, on foot; it was their assignment.

The rear of the culvert was deserted. Tracker slid in, got real close behind the first halftrack just starting to move out and threw a grenade into the open troop compartment. He did the same to the second halftrack just as the first grenade went off. The explosions were muted and didn't garner any surrounding attention. But they were effective.

He crawled out of the culvert and ran north to the 88mm gun sandbag emplacement not far away and dove to the side of it. He looked up and over. A stack of shells was ten feet away, a big stack. Anticipating the next air attack, the gun crew was preoccupied.

Searching amongst the grenades in his carry bag, Tracker found the small block of C-4 Larry had given him, along with two short timing pencil fuses. He crawled over to the stacked shells, slid over the emplacement and placed the C-4 among the shells, crimped the fifteen-minute detonator vial to start the chemistry burn, climbed back over the emplacement then moved away around the gun emplacement heading north.

The red flare went up as Tracker, hunched low, rounded the north corner of the gun emplacement and came face to belly with a guard, rifle cradled in his arm across his chest looking up at the flare. The guard made the first move, trying to bring his rifle to bear. Tracker dropped and spun low to the side as he pulled out his tomahawk and in one long swing motion hit the guard just below his knee with such force that it cut straight through the leg. The guard fell like a stone. In shock, he didn't make a sound. Tracker didn't hesitate. He swung the ancient weapon into his neck. The blood shower from the squirting artery hit him square in the face.

Foxy's Team

Foxy figured they'd done their job. Staying longer would accomplish nothing. He ordered his team to withdraw, silently, with no returning fire. The red withdrawal flare confirmed his decision as they made their way to the swamp.

Tully's Team

As their firefight ended, Tully knew their chances of getting out were questionable. Red's moves were bold. A Ranger, if I ever I saw one, he thought. Tully went against every instinct, a classic case of bravado, versus stupidity, versus survival. Decided that they needed to get the hell out of here and not go to support Red.

C J led the team along the river bank to the marsh area where Red's team had originally come in. The battle raging near sharpened Tully's decision. He felt Red was smart enough to know what to do.

Meeting in the swamp

Trackers C-4 explosion of shells ignited a huge fireball to the north of the swamp. Secondary cook-offs added to the now, very confused enemy. They didn't know what was happening, nor where it was coming from.

Foxy's disengagement went smooth after Red's team opened up on his charging enemy. Red stopped firing after he sent up the flare. Then he withdrew back toward the swamp. Near the swamp edge they stopped.

"They're not pursuing, Red." Said a surprised voice from Marty.

"That's called a Hail Mary! Marty. We prayed they wouldn't, that they'd be confused, maybe they even think that the ROK were staging a counter-attack. I think they went into defensive positions."

"I may have to learn this prayer."

Muzich radioed Tully that they were at the swamp, that the enemy wasn't chasing them, reminding him not to be trigger happy when they got close.

Tully's team quickly caught up to Red's. They were on the run, knew it and kept moving.

Further along, they heard. "Foxy here!" Came a low call from the left.

"You got balls, Foxy!" Came the familiar voice of Red. "How'd you know?"

"Who else would be mucking around in a swamp on a night like this?"

Meeting up with Red and now Foxy, Tully was relieved. They instinctively fell into a column, following C J into the deep swamp.

"Where's Tracker?" Snake asked Red about his friend.

"Doing his thing out there, on his own. He's the best, Snake, he's fine."

Red moved up the column and got to Mario when he saw Tom in front of him carrying a body. He didn't know anybody had been hit. He grabbed Mario, "Who is it?"

"It's Jack."

Red didn't say anything, felt that sickening churning in his stomach that had become all too familiar after losing someone close. Resigned to the fleeting bond of soldiers in war, he kept moving. Because he had too. For his survival. No time to grieve. Yet he did.

Now deep in the marshes well away from the action and any potential pursuit, they stopped at a raised spit of land. Putting his machine gun down, Red came up to Tom and said, "Thanks for bringing him out. Let me take him from here."

"No! I got him killed! I'm carrying him!"

Red had not expected that. Knew guilt when wrongfully placed. "I don't know you from a hole in the wall, Tom. But what I do know about you is that you're a great leader. So back off with that guilt shit! You lost one! Think about how many you probably saved?"

Hardnosed Tom knew Red was right but was not consoled. He'd taken a real fondness for Jack in the very short time they spent together and felt he made a mistake that caused his death.

Still seeing the anguish, Red came close to him, "Please, he was my friend, I want to carry Jack."

Tom understood. Tully was nearby, heard everything and came over to help transfer Jack to Red's back. Tom picked up Red's machine gun and started off, and the column picked up their pace.

As he walked through the marsh, Frenchy turned to Dean. "How many did my favorite sniper get?"

Dean grunted. "Not enough."

"I counted around twenty-five shots. You fired all through the bombing. Didn't stop."

"Not even close." Said Dean.

"Miss any?"

Dean didn't respond. But thought, yeah, I did. Missed two. Must've been the bombs got me riled. And it was forty. But who's counting! Yeah!...Nobody! Just me!

At Rusty's Position

C J kept the lead through the swamp heading toward Rusty's location. Another fifteen minutes he calculated. His mind went into rewind, thinking about Jack and why he died. Did I freeze for a second? Maybe? It all happened so fast. When the second grenade went off, I got up and charged, thinking all were dead or wounded. Then the prone guy fired. Was it one or two shots? Can't remember. Which one got Jack? Why him? I was closer? His mind accelerated. Shit! It could have been me! Reflective, he whispered to no one, "Thank you, God…"

After a tense moment of recognition, Rusty greeted CJ and pulled him aside. Rusty saw something in his eyes, knew something was wrong but didn't ask because he had sadness to tell him.

Rusty put his arm around C J, "Thank you for bringing back my men! C J, I have bad news for you. *Two* didn't make it."

C J snapped, "Did he suffer?"

Rusty didn't tell him how *Two* died, just that he didn't see it coming and that it was instant. C J went off to see his men and bury *Two*.

Tom walked up. "You Rusty?"

"You must be Leyden. Colonel Nelson said you'd be in charge at the bridge." They shook hands.

Tom looked expectantly at Rusty. "So?"

Rusty didn't understand. "What?" Then he realized that Tom didn't know what happened. Did the bridge go down? "Sorry!" He smiled. "Great job, Tom! Knocked that center span right into the river. They won't be crossing that for a while."

"Damn!" Relieved that something went right, Tom walked away.

"Who are you?" Muzich had followed Tom in. Rusty looked perplexed. "Is that a flight suit?"

"I'm the pilot. We crash landed. Navy Commander John Muzich at your service."

"I'm Rusty." He was about to shake his hand when he saw the bloodied right arm at his side.

Marty was right behind Muzich. "Got to take a close look at his arm, Rusty. It's messed up."

Rusty nodded to the pilot. "We'll catch up later." Rusty moved to meet the rest of the men coming in.

Marty removed the dressing and confirmed what he felt with one look at his arm. His flashlight showed the ragged wound and cloth edges hanging out. No major vein puncture, but cloth means infection? It's got to be cleaned! Marty stilled his mind. He hated this part.

"Come over here, Commander. Lay down." Marty looked around. "Arron! Moose! I need you."

The returning men were subdued, silent. Like men feel when a major stress event had passed and all the adrenalin faded from the blood stream, leaving the body fatigued. Strange, though, Rusty thought, feels like something else is going on. Then he knew. Men are dead. Who? How many? Is it Red? Please! Not Red! His mind raced with the possibilities.

Then he saw Red carrying someone. Dread turned to joy. Red was alive. Then he went cold, realizing it was Jack Red was carrying. He knew Jack, not as well as Red did, but liked him a great deal. He was a friend.

Jack's team gathered around Red and took Jacks body to where *Two* was being buried behind their position.

Marty had immediately given Muzich a heavy dose of antibiotic and pain pills. "Pilot! The pain pills will kick in later, but I can't give you morphine now. You need to walk out of here with us. What I have to do now is explore your wound, make sure there's no debris in there. Then I'm going to pour in antiseptic. Finally, I'm going to stitch the wound." He paused. "This is going to be a bitch! And I mean, really hurt! But I want to save your life and hopefully your arm."

"Doesn't sound like I have much choice. Can I ask you for your medical credentials?" He grunted.

"Arron! Hold the flashlight on the wound, cup it to shelter the light. I've done this a few times, fly-boy. But, I've had mixed

223

results." Marty's turn to grunt as he cleaned the outside of the wound.

"Moose! Hold his arm and body steady! He's gonna jump and squirm." Marty reached into his bag and brought out a half inch thick rubber strap and quickly put it in Muzich's mouth. "Can't have you screaming. Sorry! Bite down."

The muffled screams were heard throughout the group. Muzich passed out.

Tom walked over to Jacks men, sitting next to his body. He knelt down, said to all, "I didn't know him well, but I liked him. Sorry for the loss of your friend."

J P lashed out, "It was that Korean got him killed, wasn't it!?"

Tom was surprised. Felt shame. "No! C J led the charge. It was my fault. I threw that grenade a little too far." Tom bowed his head. "I'm responsible! I got Jack killed. I'm sorry."

The entire group surrounded both internments.

Tracker appeared out of nowhere next to Red, startled him. Then Red smiled and somberly said to him, "Didn't think you'd miss this. Glad you made it."

They were shallow graves, marked and honored.

Tracker was the only one who voiced, whispering something that no one understood. The melody of the whisper was soft, like he was saying good-by.

Chapter Thirty Nine

Rusty signaled Tully and Red to join him.

Tom saw it. He was not going to be left out and walked over and joined the huddle.

He spoke up. "My orders were to make sure that the bridge went down, and I was to work **with** you, Rusty. It didn't say I was to work **for** you. But as far as I'm concerned, you're my boss. I still expect an equal seat at the table."

Rusty confirmed. "This is no time for bullshit, or ego's, so thanks, Tom. Just not adjusted to another talented leader yet. All input is welcome, and I want yours, but I consider myself the final decider amongst equals. Welcome to our team of ABTL's."

Simultaneously, Red and Tully said, "What the hell does that mean?"

Rusty laughed. "It means, *Asshole's Behind the Lines.*"

Tully and Red laughed, Tom joined in. Skeptically, he added, "So I guess you found out about some of my past issues?"

It would be the last of smiling for some time.

"Tom, you weren't privy to our early plans of what comes next, so I'll open this discussion by stating that we did really good tonight. Based on that, we planned to go deeper behind their lines and further screw up their plans in the corridor, disrupting road traffic and causing havoc."

Tom liked the plan so far.

Rusty continued. "We planned to split up. Most would go north, up the valley. A few would go back to our starting hideout at C J's outpost and be a communications hub, directing interdiction to where it was most useful. That's where we are now. Splitting up. Got any thoughts?"

"Yeah! You're all crazy!" Tom looked around at them, smiled. "And I like crazy! I'm in. Whatever you say is good with me!"

Tully grinned, "Sure you're not a Ranger?"

Tom chuckled, "I would have joined had I known they accepted deranged guys."

Tully smiled. Rangers liked being called crazy. It meant fearless. Which he knew in his heart was stupid. Every man was terrified of dying, or worse yet, being maimed or tortured. Rangers just went forward. Overcoming their fears with every step.

"Enough! Let's go over how we split up."

Red was always the stopgap, conservative yet flexible. "Nothing's changed, I say we go with the plan. Let Tom decide which way his guys want to go."

Tom reacted, "Let me be clear, these were Jack's men. I was imposed on Jack for the bridge thing. That's over. They're your responsibility now."

"No!" Rusty stood. "All the men are our responsibility! We work together. I may be the final decider, but we all contribute. We all volunteered to be at this party and we'll do our best to stop these bastards, and that's what we've going to do. So talk!"

Tom did something he rarely did. He didn't react. Looked at Rusty, reflected a moment and nodded his understanding.

"I don't know shit about what you men have experienced in the last few days, but I know you've been through a lot. I've spent all of twelve hour's with Jack and his men, so I have an extremely limited perspective on their capabilities. I'll offer you this, though. All of his team performed, excelled actually. Phil is an expert technician and bomb expert. J P is as brave and fierce a fighter as I've met. Greg is the ultimate *charge the walls* kind of guy, just point. I would be proud to fight next to them in any engagement. But I'm not their leader, Jack was. They loved him. It is very evident."

"What about the pilot?" Rusty asked.

"He's a true hero, Rusty. I saw what he did at Okinawa. And I saw how he kept his cool and saved our ass from going down. Not only is he a great pilot, but he's also smart.

Red added. "He knows weapons and tactics. We talked about a couple of options waiting for the bombers. He's good. I like him. I hope Marty was able to help him."

"As long as he can walk, we're good. Okay! We need to finalize our plan. Red, you first."

"I think the only thing we need to decide is who goes back to communications at the hideout. It's obvious to me that we need Larry to run the VLF equipment. We need a translator, so either, Foxy, Frenchy or C J. I vote Foxy. Next would be local knowledge, so I'd add C J's *One.*"

Rusty looked at Tully for his assessment.

"I like it. Covers our needs and gives us max firepower in the field."

Rusty looked around at the men, "Any other suggestions or thoughts?"

Nothing.

"Then we need to go. I'll talk to Foxy, give him a portable radio, and confirm our previous plans."

Before this attack on the bridge, much discussion had ensued amongst them about what to do next, and how to escape. Not a person wanted to escape to safety. All thought it an opportunity to inflict more damage, disrupt the further progress of the communist invasion.

They headed out.

C J was instrumental in leading them to a spot they'd discussed. His *Three's* cousin's village, three miles up the corridor.

On board B-26 "Lady L" – Group Commander Colonel Joe Lowe – 0130- (1:30 am)

"Any contact with Hawk?"

"Nothing since his Mayday, sir."

"Time check and heading?"

"Colonel, he was the last to dive. Dropped his ordinance up the valley and turned. Not sure of his actual heading when they initiated their Mayday. They didn't say; it was quick."

"Shit! Alert any offshore assets for a ditch."

Same Time - On board B-29 "Stick in the Eye"- Group Commander Haines – 0130 - (1:30 am}

"Sir, Dave is falling behind, has hydraulic problems and is starting to lose altitude. Thinks he was hit."

"Crap! Tell him to divert to nearest. I'm thinking Japan. Have him send out the rescue signal, just in case he has to ditch."

Taejon Airfield – One Hundred Miles SE of the Han Bridge — 0200 – (2:00 am)

Wild Bill had paced the hanger for hours. Waiting. Nothing. No word had come. He sat on a crate feeling useless. He was feeling down about not participating in the Han Bridge mission but then thought positively. If they didn't call, it must mean it went well. Good! Colonel Nelson's words rang in his head. "It's going to be a long war." I'll have my opportunity. Maybe today! He felt better, decided to turn in.

In the hours since his return from the cable connection office in town, high activity had occurred at the airfield. Flatbed trucks had arrived with construction equipment and at least a platoon of Army engineers and communication specialists. They started working as soon as they arrived and hadn't stopped.

228

Direct linkage with the Korean cable in town had been established at the hanger in short order. George woke the captain with the news. He tried getting through to Colonel Nelson, but the line was busy, gave up and went back to sleep amongst the noise of heavy equipment working on the airfield.

Chapter Forty

Major Jarvis had volunteered to wait out the long night in the conference room, knowing no information would be available about the mission until either the VLF at C J's hideout was activated, or dawn would reveal results to the ROK forces on the south bank. A dawn Air Recon sortie was also scheduled to get detail pictures of the bridge and its surrounding area.

Master Sergeant Nick Beloit arrived first, then the rest of the A Team came in a few minutes apart. They grabbed a coffee and sat. Nobody said a word. They looked like shit, thought Jarvis. I'm sure I do as well. Waiting! It was the worst thing! All the plans, all the hours! It came down to luck and other men's determination and ingenuity. And their sacrifice. It was maddening.

Colonel Nelson pushed through the door, had an angry look on his face and said, "Got an early causality report from Air Force Command a few minutes ago. A B-29 went down fifty miles off of southern Japan two hours ago. Rescue ships are responding. One of the B-26 Bombers called out a mayday after its run over the target. It was a quick message, with no known heading or condition. No word on that, as yet. They're presumed lost."

He slumped in his chair at the conference table, thought of the air crews. Eleven on the B-29, seven on the B-26. Eighteen men! He hoped it was worthwhile. Then he thought of his men at the bridge. How many?

"Goddamn waiting!" Nelson barked.

Major Jarvis got up, went to the coffee pot and got the Colonel a hot cup.

"Yeah, Colonel, it's a bitch!"

Except for Nelson and Jarvis, the other three leafed through maps and notes, and occasionally jotted something down. They waited in their own way.

His mind racing, Nelson kept looking at the wall clock. What if it's still up? What's next? That hit him hard, like a jolt from a lightning bolt. Rusty came into his mind; how competent he has led his men through terrible shit. His team was inspiring. Why the hell am I thinking this way? The adage *of hope for the best and plan for the worst* hit him as it had in the past. Screw that! He said to himself. Not appropriate here. My men and my team are the best!

Nelson stood up. "Hey! A Team! We got ourselves into a funk. We have a great group out there. Let's assume they knocked that bridge down. Now what? This is going to be a long campaign! Let's get a jump on events."

The group responded. Doom became bloom. Waiting inspired loss and failure. One always feared the worst. Turned around, positive thinking freed the mind to think beyond the moment of perceived loss, but instead, focused its attention on future success.

And, as a group, they did.

"Boss," said Nick. "I don't know your Post guys but they sure as shit have impressed me with what they've done. But I know Tom and think this bridge is Kaput, and it'll buy us some time. But we need more. Captain Sam and I have studied the supply routes coming down from the north. I never got to finish our analysis of the East Coast North Korean spear. Right now, it's unopposed except for some naval interdiction and small ROK units fighting a rear guard action. I see this as a significant threat to holding onto the country. Pusan is our only deep water port where we can bring big ships in and land heavy equipment. The east coast highway and the rail line lead directly into this harbor city."

Nelson remembered Nick talking about a North Korean tunnel, but nothing else.

"I recall the start of this but can't remember any details. What are you getting at?" Nelson asked.

Captain Sam Haran spoke up. "Colonel, this is as important as the Han Bridge. Maybe more so. Nick is the lead on this; you need to hear his full report."

"What are you working on Sam?"

"Sir, Lieutenant Cole and I are working on defensive lines for the 24th Divisions initial deployments. We're working closely with Army Staff Operations."

"Good! Okay, Nick, I want the full story. You ready?"

Nick stood, grabbed his crutch and started hobbling toward the projector. He said, "Yes and no."

Nelson stayed quiet, reminded again of Nick's injury and the courage it took for him to claw his way back to being a leader again.

Nick placed a film in the projector and turned it on. "Larry, could you hit the lights!"

A high altitude look down image appeared on the front wall. It was sharp, taken on a crystal clear cloudless day. It showed a long stretch of the East Korean coast. An irregular marker line was hand drawn across the bottom third with a notation that this was the 38th parallel, the border between North and South Korea.

Nick started. "Like I said when you asked if I'm ready. The yes part is right here. Taken about a year ago, what you see is a fifty mile north/south shot of the coast and about a ten mile east/west view. Railroad tracks are visible running from the very top through the bottom of the picture. Most of the rail line runs less than a quarter mile from the coast. The east coast highway runs parallel to the rail line."

He raised his pointer to a spot just north of the border marker at the 38th parallel.

"This was the terminus of the line before the country was divided. It's a big rail yard, now 100% in the North. Tracks through the border were removed after the separation of countries but now have been reinstalled after the invasion and supplies are moving steadily, replenishing and supporting the east coast advance south."

Nelson interrupted. "Isn't the Navy shelling the coast highway?"

"They are Boss, but so far their efforts have proven to be largely ineffective for two reasons. They don't have enough ships and second and more importantly, the enemy has shifted to mostly night travel which limits significant damage to supplies. In daylight, we destroy the roadbed and rail sections for a few hours, but the enemy has a large force of repair laborers to restore any damage within hours."

Nelson heard this same story before. Germany was notorious for employing slave labor to repair rail and bridge damage within hours of a bombardment. "So where's this tunnel?"

Nick raised his pointer, "Here! Twenty miles north of the border. It's a two-mile long tunnel through a mountain that juts out into the sea. The southern exit is five hundred yards from the coastline. We close that tunnel and we stop substantial support for their advance. This will slow them down significantly."

"Good presentation, Nick." The lights came up. Colonel Nelson continued, "Now for the fun part. How? And how soon?"

As Nick tottered back to his seat, he said, "That's the '**No**' part of my answer. I don't have a plan for this yet. I have only one idea of how this can be done but no details."

Nelson leaned in. "I like how you think, so give me what you got."

"The quickest, probably safest and most assured way of closing this tunnel is by submarine."

Nick paused to let this sink in.

"The water off this coast gets very deep real fast. A mile off, the depth goes to two hundred feet. This is perfect for an insertion of a small team. The tunnel is close by. The team can escape back to the sub, and the tunnel will be closed for quite a while."

Stoic, Nelson stared at Nick. He was thinking. "Do you have a team? Shit! Do you have a sub!?"

Nick grinned, big. "Colonel, I'm a grunt. I need doors opened for me. What you did for the Han Bridge mission is what I need to get this done."

As tense as Nelson was about this past night, he laughed. He said, "I now fully understand why you're here Nick. Can you get this done?"

"Sir, I can move a mountain, just tell me which one. This mission can only be hampered by bullshit that I can't navigate alone. Give me the wherewithal to overcome that, and this tunnel is dead!"

Nelson nodded, turned to his number one, "Hank, you work with Nick on this. I want this done. Fast. I want a full mission proposal on this so we can go to MacArthur. I want full mission authority just like the Han Bridge. Any roadblocks, you come to me."

Major Jarvis skeptically looked at him. "I got nothing if we weren't successful at the Han."

"You're not paying attention, Hank. Of course, we killed that bridge! We just don't know it yet!"

Nelson returned his attention to Nick. "When are you getting your prosthetic?"

Nick was taken aback by the question. "Boss?"

"Just wanted to know when you might be eligible to go on a mission." Nelson smiled at him.

Nick lowered his head. Composed himself, "Boss! I dream of that every night."

The phone rang. Hank picked up immediately, "Major Jarvis. What? Yes! Be right there!"

"Communications! Just got a VLF message from Rusty's team!"

As a group, they all jumped up and hurried to the VLF station, twenty feet away.

The importance of the call had telegraphed through the whole operations center. Scores of men not immediately engaged in something were gathered nearby at the station. General Walker was there too, sipping a cup of coffee, at least it looked like coffee.

Colonel Nelson slipped in next to the VLF sergeant at the station. "What did they say?"

"It's a confirmation message, Colonel. You know, so we know who they are. I sent the receiving message and told them to stand by, waiting for you."

"OK, send the waiting to receive message."

He started tapping. Then they waited. Not long. The tapping started back.

The sergeant recorded as the taps came in. Suddenly it stopped. It was a shorter message than Nelson had anticipated. He grew anxious.

The sergeant read the message. "Foxy coordinating at C J hide. Successful in mission. Rusty heading up U Valley to disrupt. Radios coordinating. Can advise targets."

Colonel Nelson mumbled in relief, "Thank God!"

Nick was pumped, and yelled, "They did it!"

Everyone knew what that meant. A roar of success filled the room, if only for a moment. They clapped.

Nelson leaned over, "Ask for a causality report."

The response came a few seconds later.

The sergeant read it.

"Lost three crew of the PBY. Commander wounded but OK with us."

"Jack from Post 4, KIA."

"One ROK member of C J team, KIA."

Nelson got up, walked away. Major Jarvis said to the sergeant, "Tell them, great job! They are to wait for new developments."

General Walker saw Nelson slip away, knew something was wrong. He decided to catch up with him, and did, by the Operation Room exit doors.

"Wait up, Colonel!"

Nelson turned and stopped. Walker saw the blank look. He stood close to him.

"How many did you lose?"

"Five, General. Four I didn't know and a close friend."

"Come with me, Jim, got something for you. Time to honor some heroes."

To anyone who knew the General, that meant a stiff Scotch...or two.

Chapter Forty One

Major Jarvis wasted no time worrying about Colonel Nelson. Knew he'd quickly pull out of his grief as he'd done before. But the war demanded constant attention. He figured Nelson knew he had a safety cushion to lean on, if only for a brief moment. That would be him and his A Team. We'll not disappoint you, Colonel, he affirmed to himself, as he reassembled the team in the conference room.

"Okay, we had our ten-minute celebration on our first successful mission. Now on to the next. Larry, you alright going it alone for a time on defensive planning south of the Han River?"

"Major, sir," The lieutenant was somewhat put out as he responded. "Haven't finished the Pusan defense area as you know, and just got this new assignment a few hours ago. Got some initial stuff done but yeah, I can handle it."

Jarvis stood up, felt Cole's anxiety, and knew he and the rest felt the same. "We will all be overwhelmed by events! You will become the best jugulars, dealing with each ball thrown in the air and do the best you can."

As he started to leave, he said, "I've got a few things I gotta do. I'll be in the building but away from here. I don't want to lose a minute of planning. Keep at it!"

Then he looked at Nick.

"Nick! You got the big ball. That tunnel is going down. Figure out how!"

"On it, Major!" Nick replied with a smile. He'd been thinking about this for some time and had a direction already laid out in his mind.

Jarvis headed off to the Air Force liaison section. He found a captain writing at his desk, introduced himself and pulled up a chair.

"You work for Colonel Nelson, right?" The Captain asked.

Surprised by the question. "How do you know that?"

"Just met him yesterday." He paused, "Maybe the day before, don't remember. It's all becoming a blur. Anyway, I asked if I could transfer to his unit. You're lucky working for a man like him. I mostly deal with pompous assholes. Please don't repeat that. Sorry, but what I can I do for you?"

"Your refreshing, Captain," he looked closer at his name tag, "Captain Lewis."

"That's not what my boss calls me. But thanks, I think?"

"Oh, it was a compliment. Now I've got a few questions for you. You got a recon mission this morning over the Han River Bridge, and I need to know what time it is and if it's got an escort?"

"Been working on that, Major. Finalized it just a few minutes ago. TOT (Time over Target) scheduled for 0630. Two photo Mustangs. No sir, no escorts scheduled."

"Do you know why no escorts?"

"No. I can only surmise, Major. Like I told your boss, we've got very little here. The brass has realized that our jets are no match for their jets, so they don't want the number of our jets shot down to get too public. They're holding back on their deployment, mostly using them to escort the bombers. But that's another issue. Anyway, the P-51's we do have are all being retrofitted from fighter interceptors to fighter bombers. FUBAR, sir. That's why I asked for a transfer. You guys seem to know what you're doing."

"Captain. I think the Air Force needs a guy like you. Hang in there, make a difference."

He pushed through the conference room door, determined to ward off a premonition he had, hoped he was wrong but wasn't going to let this feeling slide. Larry and Nick were on calls. He sat down and called the Korean cable section. Told the operator he wanted to speak to Captain Stands at Taejon Airfield.

It took five minutes but finally got a ring.

"About time someone called me!" A half-awake Wild Bill answered.

"Major Jarvis here. I assume this is Captain Stands?"

"Where's my favorite Colonel?"

"Captain, he just lost a good friend, crap is raining down, and I need your help!"

There was a pause. In a somber voice Captain Stands said, "I understand. That's why he's my favorite Colonel. He cares." Another pause. "So you're picking up the slack. First, I want to say *fuck you* for not calling me last night and secondly, I'll do anything I can to help you now. So what do you need?"

Jarvis first thought a fight was in the works. Realized Wild Bill just wanted to be part of the solution. He was humbled by this crazy three-time Ace who only wanted to fight.

He told him what he wanted the Captain to do.

Reconnaissance Flight of Two P-51 Mustangs out of Japan – Flying Seventy miles south of the Han Bridge 0620 – (6:20 am)

Flying at five hundred feet, they followed the main highway north. Visibility was excellent with only moderate high cloud cover. The sun was up on the horizon but had not risen fully past the eastern mountain range.

Captain Hurst pressed his mike. "Pisser! Remember. You got Seoul! Split left near the bridge. Follow our plan."

"Are you trying to Pisser me off?" He laughed into his mike at his well-worn quip on his call sign. "I know my job, Nosepicker! Just do yours!"

239

Captain Hurst's P-51 had a large painted human nose on its front with bullets entering its nostrils and flames coming out its side. Hence his Call Sign, as he often boasted that "I could shoot the snot out of a Jap at 500 feet." He regularly backed up that claim over Okinawa and Japan in the War.

"Pisser! Five minutes and we execute."

Pisser, AKA Captain Reynolds, was Captain Hurst's long time flight buddy, almost a brother and also an Ace, but only a one time Ace, as his friend often kidded him. His twice Ace standing was often rebuffed by Reynolds as downright luck. They loved kidding each other and reveled in their general disrespect for all things bullshit.

Accepting their new role, transitioning from Army Air Corp to the new Air Force, had not been easy. Forced to take this assignment or leave, they opted to keep flying in any capacity they could.

Captain Hurst wasn't quite used to shooting pictures instead of bullets. He had never gotten comfortable going on a mission without any weapons. He believed his recon missions would create more destruction for his enemy than he could do with his warbird fully loaded. At least he talked himself into believing this.

The Recon P-51's were based out of Itazuke Airbase in Japan. Specifically, the 45th Tactical Reconnaissance Squadron. These planes were perfect for tactical photo recon; fast, agile, and with long range capabilities.

The planes were stripped of all weapons and retrofitted with three cameras; two side views and one bottom. Each camera shot two frames per second with incredible clarity.

This mission bothered Captain Hurst. He knew what happened last night. The enemy would be on alert, maybe have fighters nearby. They've flown two missions a day for the previous five days and been jumped once, by Russian jets with North Korean markings. If it hadn't been for low cloud cover, they probably would've been shot down.

No cloud cover today, he thought. He hadn't felt fear on any mission before this. It was creeping into his being. Always the superior warbird in the sky in the past, now he was the prey, and defenseless. He hoped his plan would get them in and out fast. A low approach and then a fast up, take the run, then dive low. Classic stuff. He didn't invent it but knew it worked and hoped it would today. He prayed there would be no jets.

The thrill of flying four hundred miles an hour at treetop level was something few people will ever experience. Captain Hurst relished this like it was his first because it always felt so special. His fear gone now, accepting his fate as a God with special powers that may end in seconds, he pressed his plan.

Five miles out, he turned his cameras on and started his steep climb. The eastern sun now revealed its beaming light fully over the eastern mountains. At two thousand feet, he began a slow right roll up the valley. Then he executed a sharp left heading west, diving to five hundred feet over Seoul. Snapping pictures all the way. He didn't expect to meet up with Pisser at this point but maybe later, after they cleared the South Korean coast.

Earlier At Taejon Airfield.

After receiving that call from Major Jarvis, Captain Stands acted like a madman. Screaming at Billy and Arnie to remove the Napalm canisters from *Just Due* so he could get him ready for dog fight duties. He was in the air by five-forty-five for the half hour flight to the Han Bridge. It was still dark as he climbed to seven thousand feet and throttled back to a slow cruise. He was early, wanted some extra hang time to check out the area.

The Major had sounded very apprehensive about the scheduled recon flight. Funny, he thought, that an Army guy would think of Air Force guys. But after hearing the story about what happened last night, and the fact that no escorts were riding shotgun, he had the same misgivings.

241

Current Time

Wild Bill followed the west side of the central mountain range, just clearing their tops. As the sky lightened to the sunrise, he had an exceptional view of the valley north and the sea to the west.

He saw the recon plane climb over the bridge and up the valley. Now he was at max power and steady at seven thousand feet heading north. Wild Bill followed the photo plane below as it started to make its turn at three thousand feet in the valley.

The action happened fast.

A spot appeared as reflective light off the rising sun. It was at the same height as *Just Due*. The enemy didn't see him. Maybe the sunlight prevented the enemy from spotting him as the Captain was further east into the sun.

The Captain thought it had to be a jet because of its speed. Saw it start its diving attack on the recon P-51. Wild Bill was out of position to do anything. Hoped the enemy pilot wasn't experienced, that the recon guy was special, and that he had exceptional luck.

Captain Hurst, *Nosepicker,* now coming out of his photo shoot, saw a light sparkle from a reflection off to his right. Reacting, he pulled a hard right into the light and climbed. The move saved his life as the diving jet swished by his front.

He clicked his radio. "Pisser! Jets! Get out of here!" The climb initiated a barrel roll. At the top, he started his dive. He hoped this maneuver would get him in a spot where the jet couldn't find him. Looking back over his shoulder, he saw the enemy plane near the top of its barrel roll, not far off. Told him he wasn't going to shake him.

"Damn! I'm dead!" He said out loud into his mike.

Wild Bill got lucky on all three counts. The recon plane made a sudden maneuver just as the jet came into shooting range. It caused the jet to overshoot its target. The Captain knew what the jet would do next. Wild Bill was now in a position to plan his attack. He put his plane into a slight dive anticipating when the jet would climb and complete its barrel roll so as to start another attack from behind.

At the top of the roll is when it would be at his slowest speed and be most vulnerable.

The jet didn't see him diving. With the enemy caught in mid-turn at the top of its roll, and with perfect timing, **Just Due** let lose a three-second burst of its six fifty caliber machine guns into its belly.

The shells tore into the plane. Large chunks flew off and smoke immediately poured out of the exhaust tail. On fire, it started its death spiral. No chute.

Anticipating the jet now on his tail, Captain Hearst looked back again. "Jesus Christ!" He yelled as he saw the flaming jet spiraling down. He still had his mike on.

His radio called out, "Nah! Just a friend! Wild Bill at your service!"

A smiling Wild Bill pulled his plane close beside the recon and waved through the canopy. "If you ain't a God fearing man, I'd say today would be a good day to start! You got Major Jarvis at Eighth Army to thank for saving your ass! And you owe me a beer! Now you have a nice day!" The plane veered off.

Captain Hurst hadn't recovered yet from thinking of his imminent death. He clicked his mike a few times, didn't know what to say. Finally, "Make that two beers!"

Getting his wits back, he wondered. Who the hell is Wild Bill? Then he thought, Eighth Army! What the hell? They don't have an Air Force!"

Wild Bill opened the throttles and dove. He let out a howl; more like a scream. Success - after five years! He thought. And against a jet. It looked like a Nazi Jet he'd seen in Germany after the war, but much sleeker. Shit! These babies look fearsome. I hope I don't have to meet one in a fair fight.

Authors Note

The P-51 fighter plane was considered the most dominant fighter plane in WW2. Then the emerging technology of jet propulsion cast a dark shadow on all things propeller. In 1950 all the major powers had jets.

Except some were better than others.

What showed up from our American opponent was a new radical leap in fighter design and manufacturing. The Russians copied it from captured Nazi German technology and made it better. America had it too but decided our defense corporations were brighter, they weren't.

The Russian Mig-15 was a total shock to America. It outperformed any jet we had. It was the best fighter plane over Korea for more than two years.

*The P- 51 was two hundred and forty miles an hour **slower**. Six hundred and seventy vs. four thirty. No dog fight here. If you were uncovered, you died.*

Chapter Forty Two

Saturday, July 1, 1950 – Day Seven of the Invasion
Outside the Village of Yangiu, Three miles northeast of Seoul
– 06:30 – (6:30 am)

On their arrival at C J's number *Three's* cousin's hamlet, the lights and commotion in the small village signaled Rusty's team to take defensive positions on the outskirts. Obviously, North Korean troops were in the village. How many or why were unknown.

Their journey had been challenging. First, bypassing the tank farm by a wide margin into swamp and marshland, then across rice paddies and finally through rock and uneven terrain. All in darkness.

Three was mystified at what might be going on. His cousin was a vocal anti-communist, and this village was supportive of new independence with the elected government. But this was a closed little community; no one outside of it would have known the people's leanings. That's why he thought it would be a safe place to hide, maybe even be the base to conduct raids along the main highway only a few miles away.

A spirited debate ensued. Stay or go?

The sides were predictable. Red wanted to withdraw to a safer area. When another area could not be agreed upon other than maybe the mountains eight miles away, where no operations could be easily carried out, his option expired.

Tully decided they should stay and fight. He argued that they were a strong force, had ample weapons and if necessary, could fade back into the marshland going back the way they came.

Rusty mulled the options and decided he needed more information. He went to his best.

"Tracker!" He called out in a whisper. The word passed, and Tracker appeared.

"We need to know what's going on in there, but no killing!"

Tracker whispered back. "I promise chief! No scalping."

Amazed at Tracker's response, Rusty wanted to say something funny but couldn't think of anything.

Tracker returned later, plopped down next to Rusty, Red and Tully. C J came over and knelt, forming a circle.

"Bad stuff happening. Counted twenty soldiers, one officer. Two trucks and a jeep. I think most are drunk. They're raping women in the huts; men tied up. Got one man hanging from a tree near the village entrance. Think they're going to kill everyone when finished having fun."

Horrified, Rusty wasn't sure what to do. If he waited too long, he'd have a dead village haunting him for the rest of his life. Or he might risk the death of his entire team to save a village. Shit!

Tully was first. "That's enough for me." He said, "Not guns blazing but stealth. I've seen what evil can do and I vowed never to shirk from facing it. I say we go kill them all, slit their throats."

Red was solemn, "Tully's right. I couldn't live with myself if we left them to be massacred."

Rusty realized he had no choice and issued orders.

Before he left, Tracker whispered to Rusty, "Scalps this time!"

At this point, the team was a well-oiled machine. Men were assigned perimeter positions. No one was going to escape, and nobody was going to approach them without a firefight.

Mario, Tracker, Snake and Frenchy were the stealth preeminent killing teams. Like ghosts gliding above the earth on a soundless zephyr, they floated into the village from the east.

246

Although difficult to compare to the best of their team, they were the best of everyone else.

Tully, Arron and Joe entered from the west.

It didn't take long. Tracker was right. Most were drunk. As planned, they wanted the officer alive, if possible. They found him passed out, half naked on a bed, next to a strangled young girl.

Light of Sunrise pushed the darkness away as the men assembled in the village. A new day was beginning. But not for many in this village.

Cries and wails arose as villagers found their loved ones. Some abused but alive. Others should not have been seen.

C J's *Three* entered the village from the north side at the entrance. He saw his cousin hanging from a tree and puked, then wept. C J was with him. He had anticipated the worst. He knelt with *Three*, tried to comfort him.

Tully dragged the officer out into the village center. The freed villagers began assembling. Frenchy was talking with them, trying to figure out what happened.

The story was the same. Around midnight, this group pulled in and rousted the entire village. But they asked specifically about *Three's* cousin. Found him and dragged him to the tree. Then the soldiers started drinking, that's when it got ugly for the people.

A story emerged about a jealous rival of the cousin who was rebuffed by the young girl the cousin was seeing. He left the village two days ago and hadn't been seen since.

After some persuasion, the enemy officer confirmed the betrayal of the young man, who had told him the village was plotting sabotage and were outspokenly anti-communists. Nobody likes a coward or a traitor, even the communist. So this young man was conscripted into a labor battalion.

The officer subsequently died from the persuasion techniques employed, but not before he told them the unit was to stay in the village for a few days, for some R & R.

Convinced this unit wouldn't be missed or ever traced, Rusty directed removal and burial of the bodies away from the village. The vehicles were moved and hidden. Lookouts were set.

Rusty ordered that the nearby highway be monitored. Knowing the flow was the key in determining how they could interrupt it. All the men were exhausted. Those not on watch slept.

Chapter Forty Three

"How'd you know, Hank?" Asked a slightly tipsy Colonel Nelson.

The action reports on the early air recon mission had just arrived. The earlier call from Captain Stands, thanking the Team for giving him a chance to fight and the outcome details, alerted all to Major Jarvis's initiative.

"I didn't. Just had a strange feeling something bad might happen."

"Well, keep those instincts coming. That was a hell of a call!" Nelson paused. "And it got Wild Bill occupied to good use. Damn, he did good! A jet, no less!"

Grabbing his third cup of coffee to mollify the effects of General Walkers two stiff Scotch's, he proceeded. "Now! What's been going on since I had my little pity party?"

No one acknowledged the remark. Thought it showed a human side to the Colonel they'd rarely seen.

"Sir!" LT Larry Cole spoke up. "Captain Stands mentioned a swept wing jet he shot down. I checked with our Air Force liaison officer and they're not aware of any Russian made fighters like that. Fact is, they're not aware of any Russian operational *jet* fighters...anywhere."

Nelson nodded. "They're good at keeping secrets, these Russians. Wonder why a lone plane would reveal a weapon like that?" He thought about it for a second and continued. "Only explanation I can come up with is that a Korean or Russian *Wild Bill* wannabe did his thing, against orders. Have you passed this intel on?"

"Yes, sir!"

Nick stirred, "Boss! I've got things going on about that North Korean tunnel."

"Let's hear it!"

"Things are coming together, real fast. Found a Navy UDT Team here in Japan. Only six men, but perfect for our tunnel mission. Then I found a submarine. A fleet boat, just docked at Naval Base Sasebo, where our Navy UDT guys are."

Jarvis and Nelson smiled at each other.

"Jesus, Nick! That's amazing!" Said Major Jarvis, really proud of him. He had taken a chance bringing him into the A Team. Realized how lucky he was to do it.

"Have you got them on standby?"

"No, boss. Haven't been able to get the Base commander. Fleet Command won't even talk to me without specific orders from MacArthur's headquarters."

Nelson acknowledged. "You seem to have a lot of high-level friends. Got anybody you could call on to help us until we get these orders approved."

Nick smiled. "I might."

"You got a name for this operation?"

"Boss, I thought *Bowie.* You know, like the knife; cutting the enemy's lifeline."

"*Bowie* it is then!" Nelson turned to Major Jarvis, "You've done well Hank! Hell of a team!" Holding his gaze for a second, he continued. "Now get this plan off to MacArthur's Headquarters and get it approved."

Japan - Naval Base Sasebo – Base Commander Wyle's Office – 1000 – (10:00 am)

"Are you looking for a section eight, Sergeant?"

Nick was a bulldog, pushed through doors and assholes like they were butter. He had a way. Usually found a method to get what he wanted.

"Sir! That would be Master Sergeant Beloit. And, no sir! Not looking for any trouble. Just looking to save American lives. I'm calling from Eighth Army Headquarters, Colonel Nelson's G-2 section. I need your help."

"Go through channels! I don't talk to sergeants!" He was angry.

"Sir! Before you hang up, you should know that I got your name from Admiral Sloane, a friend of mine, your boss, I think? Please call him to verify. But I don't have a lot of time to mess around. I need you to ready the submarine **USS** *Catfish* for immediate departure on a secret mission, code-named *Bowie.*"

"What?"

Ignoring his attitude, Nick continued, "Sir, that's not all I need. You have a UDT Team on your base that will go along on this mission. I need them to get ready."

"You're serious?"

"Commander, if you knew how serious I was you wouldn't go out at night. You'll be getting orders to this effect shortly. And that would be the big guy himself, you know, General Mac. So now Commander, move! Protect your ass." Nick hung up, disgusted at the BS.

Later at the base, after a few calls, Commander Wyle put the sub and the UDT team on alert. He took a chance. He sensed something important was developing. The timing was fortunate as the *Catfish* crew were about to go on an extended shore leave.

251

Japan - Naval Base Sasebo – UDT Three - Barracks – Same Morning - 1100 – (11:00 am)

"What the hell does this mean? Prepare for an immediate mission?" Chief Petty Officer Drew O'Malley was mystified.

"Commander Wyle is not our boss, and this notice isn't orders." He paused in front of his four men.

"What a God stupid time for the LT to break a leg! I told him it was unnatural to jump out of a plane. Him and his crazy ideas about how we had to change our warfare methods. Nuts!"

Seaman Ray Albert hadn't heard about this before. "What do 'ya mean Chief? I thought he just wanted to learn how to parachute?"

"Well, he talked to me about how the UDT mission had to adapt to the new realities of warfare. He didn't think landing on heavily defended beaches was ever going to happen again. But parachuting into a lake or river behind enemy lines might be just the ticket."

"Jesus, I hate heights! Hope that doesn't happen."

"Ray! I think he was thinking further down the line then next month!"

"Good!"

"OK! Enough bullshit! The LT's not here, and that's that. I'm not going to mess around with our base commanders orders, legit or not. We have a goddamned war going on, and maybe we're up! So get your shit together. Bobby, you and Ray get to the shed and get our equipment out. Handy, find a truck, bring it to the shed. Matt, go to the explosives bunker, get our stuff organized, we'll be along shortly with the truck. I'm going to see Commander Wyle."

O'Malley, universally known as **Chief**, was originally a Seabee, joined the Navy in 1939 and came up from the ranks. Born in San Diego, he took to the sea like a baby took to suckling. His impressive frame made him an exceptional swimmer.

After the disaster at the landing at Tarawa in 1943, word came down about a new unit forming that required skilled swimmers.

Seabees were first to be recruited, and O'Malley had jumped at the opportunity.

Underwater Demolition Team Three had seen much action in the Pacific fighting the Japanese. At its peak, the unit numbered sixty. Frogman, as they were known, became infamous for their bravery and spectacular successes in recon and clearing beach obstacles. First for their underwater work, but their legend grew when they came onto the land and helped the guy on the beach who faced a bunker and then blew it up.

Chapter Forty Four

The men were studying the recent arrival of the recon photos of the Han River Bridge area.

The phone rang. "Major Jarvis!" A pause as he listened. "No, sir! We're not trying to take anything away from staff planning." Another pause. "No, sir. This is not pie in the sky stuff." Another pause. Major Jarvis turned red, face bulging with anger. In a calm and an even controlled voice, he answered. "Sir, I don't have time to do that. Not only that, but I resent your implication. I don't know who the hell you are Colonel, but I want to speak to General Almond, and I want to speak with him now!"

The line went dead. Jarvis exploded and pounded the table in frustration. "Moron!"

The table was silent for a moment until Nelson let out a belly laugh. "So, Hank! Welcome to my world."

The Major looked at him for a second, then laughed. The rest of the A team joined in, venting their own frustrations.

"I'm going over to MacArthur's headquarters," Nelson said as he rose from the table. "Come on, Major! Let's go have some fun."

It was a twenty-minute drive. Majors and colonels were sitting in the spacious waiting area. Near the doors to the inner sanctum, a very attractive brunette sat at a large reception desk on the back wall.

They walked up. Nelson leaned in and in a quiet voice said, "Ma'am, I'm here to see General MacArthur about preventing the slaughter of American troops in Korea. It's urgent. And no, I don't have an appointment."

She was startled, stared at him. "Yes sir, I get a lot of that here, Colonel," she looked at his name tag, "Nelson!" Without his dress uniform, she couldn't identify specifically what unit he was with. He only had an Eighth Army arm patch. "What unit are you with, Colonel?"

"General Walker's Eighth Army Staff, ma'am, I'm head of intelligence."

"I've heard of you."

Nelson didn't know if that was good or bad. He continued. "I've made an urgent request for confirmation of orders for a secret mission, and I'm being stonewalled by a colonel on your staff. I need to speak with a superior, preferably General MacArthur or General Almond."

She became noticeably anxious. "Right!" She looked around the waiting area, then back at him. "Well, neither general is here, and I don't expect them back today. I suggest you go through proper channels."

Nelson was enjoying this repartee. "Who's in charge of Staff Planning? You know, in the General's absence." He felt he hit a cord with her, of what he wasn't sure, but it looked like someone who might want a little payback.

She looked up at the Colonel. In a very small voice, said, "Colonel, I need this job. I think you're an honorable man. At least I'd been told that. So I'm going out on the limb here. Who you want to see is Colonel Ashburn, and he's in. But I must warn you that he's got major political connections." She hesitated a second. "And he's a complete asshole."

Nelson wanted to let out a belly laugh but just smiled. Then leaned over the desk, gave her a wink, and murmured, "You'll always have a job with me if the shit hits the fan." He saw her name tag and added, "Veronica."

She blushed. "I may have to take you up on that, Colonel." She turned and picked up a phone. "Colonel, I've got a very upset colonel here with orders from General Walker. He says he needs to see you immediately." A pause. "No sir, he says this is an emergency and doesn't have time to go through channels." Another pause. "Yes sir, I told him both generals were out. But you're in charge sir, right?" Another pause. "Yes, sir, I know you're busy." She hesitated for just a moment. "Sir! There's a war on. This man has a field mission that needs approval. It sounds urgent. Could you spare him a moment?"

The call ended, and she rose from her desk. "Gentlemen, please follow me."

"Speaking frankly Veronica. That took a lot of guts." Said Nelson, as he followed her down the hall.

She turned to him. "My friends call me Ronnie."

"Well, Ronnie, my friends call me Jim."

The meeting was intense. Colonel Nelson threatened him right off the bat. Told him he didn't give a shit about his connections or anything else he could do to try and hurt him. What he had to do, right there and then, was to get approval for this mission.

Ashburn was obstinate, refused intimidation. He was not going to stick his neck out and threatened to call the guards and remove them from his office.

Nelson laughed at this and went to his chair, pulled him up out of it by his collar and dragged him to the near couch. "Sit and shut the fuck up!"

"I'll have you thrown in Leavenworth!"

"Another word from you and I'll break your jaw!" Nelson said calmly; his eyes told Ashburn that he was deadly serious.

Nelson sat down at Ashburn's desk, pressed the secretary's button, "Veronica, could you get me Admiral Turner Joy, Commander of Naval Forces Far East?"

"Right away, Colonel."

He smiled to himself, thinking where he could bring this ballsy woman into his staff.

Connected, Nelson gave a brief explanation of his dilemma to the Admiral. At first, the Admiral was upset.

"You're calling me from where?"

"Sorry Admiral, but I've perhaps gone beyond accepted bounds as I've taken over MacArthur's acting third in the office circle, Colonel Ashburn's office."

"That asshole! Maybe now we'll get something done. What do you need from me?"

"Besides being at my Court-Martial, I need you to contact my second, Major Jarvis. He has an operational order named **Bowie** that needs your initial approval to speed things up. Then I need you to forward this plan to General Almond for MacArthur's final approval. I need this done quickly."

"This better be damn important! Give me a hint!"

"It's about a small operation that will cause a major impact on slowing the enemy's advance down the east coast."

"Sounds worthy! Just heard about your **Halt** operation. Good job! I'll get right on this. Now don't shoot this Ashburn character, although he probably deserves it."

"Thank you, Admiral!" Nelson hung up the phone, stood and looked at Colonel Ashburn. Major Jarvis just looked on in wonder. He hadn't said a word since they entered the building.

"Ashburn!" Nelson said without deference to rank. "I'd advise you to go back to Kentucky or Georgia, or where ever the hell you're from and continue to screw the small folk. If you ever get in front of me and stall something again, I'll nail you to a cross. Your friends will spit on you and I think your daddy will renounce you. Because I think he's like you. None of you have any God damn balls."

He and Major Jarvis left the office. Going down the hall, Nelson softly laughed. "Now see, wasn't that fun?"

Jarvis's had to smile. "Colonel, you got a pair!"

Still smiling, he said. "Hank, you just have no idea of how many politicians have filled our ranks. Time to get rid of them."

Japan - Eighth Army Headquarters – G-2 Operations Section – Conference Room – 1210 – (12:10 pm)

The call from Major Jarvis had just come in. Nick was on cloud nine at the approval of operation **Bowie** by Fleet Command. Time was short, didn't know how long it would take to get formal orders out, so he decided to call back to Sasebo Naval Base Commander Wyle. The call, surprisingly went through, being lunch hour at most places, he didn't think the commander would be available. He liked pleasant surprises.

After the acknowledgments and complements by Nick of the commander's awareness of the situation and his cooperation, he asked if he could speak directly to the **Catfish** commander and the leader of UDT Three Team. He was told that both were in the building awaiting Fleet orders.

"Hold a few minutes, Master Sergeant. I'll get them."

A few minutes later. "Master Sergeant! You still there?"

"Yes, sir. Are they with you?"

"I've got this new speakerphone setup on my desk that I'll try to use. Only tried it once, but we'll all hear each other if I get it right, switching now." A click. "OK, I'm hands-free. Can you hear me?"

"Loud and clear, sir. Although you kind'a sound like you're in a cave."

"I am in sort of a cave! Let me make the introductions. Master Sergeant Nick Beloit of Eighth Army Staff Intelligence, please let me introduce you to Lieutenant Commander Wayne Milligan of the **Catfish,** and Chief Petty Officer Drew O'Malley, of UDT Three."

Uncomfortable speaking through this new speakerphone, they exchanged greetings.

Nick began. "From here on, please call me Nick. But you may want to call me something else out of earshot after I tell you about this mission."

"I only know blunt, so I'll give it straight. We need you to demolish a railroad tunnel, on the east coast, twenty miles north of

258

the South Korean border." He paused. "And we need it done before dawn tomorrow."

Silence.

"Good! I got your attention. Fleet orders will be forthcoming. How soon can you get Catfish underway Commander?"

"I have enough fuel and provisions for only a four-day deployment, that's why I'm in port."

Nick got a little tense. "I didn't ask you that, Commander."

"Sorry. We've been on standby ever since Commander Wyle issued his orders earlier, so we're ready. We can cast off in half an hour."

"Chief, what about you?"

"I've got my shit on a truck, ten minutes from the dock. Men are ready." He faked a cough, to buy him a moment. "Nick, my LT is on leave, I'll be in charge."

"Chief! You got a few years under your belt, I think. You know your men?"

"Yeah, to both."

"Ever blow up a mountain tunnel before?"

"If it's anything like the command bunkers on Okinawa, I'd say yes."

Nick laughed. "I don't think this will be as difficult. How much stuff you got?"

Now it was the Chief's turn to laugh. "Got enough! Not to worry, Nick."

An interruption. Nick overheard somebody entering the room saying, "Sorry sir, got a flash message from Fleet Command on operation **Bowie** that you've been expecting."

"Hold on Nick, just got the orders." Said Commander Wyle.

A few seconds passed.

A very anxious submarine commander called out, "Nick, how am I to find this beach landing zone. I've got longitude and latitude coordinates, but shit, that's a wide area. I can't drop these guys off within a few miles of the target. You got anything?"

"I thought so!" Said Nick. "Somebody left out the specific tell on the landing site. Not an issue. Commander, at these coordinates, on radar, you'll pick up a mountain jutting out to sea. At the southern edge of that mountain is a small cove. The tunnel is five hundred yards due west from that cove."

They signed off.

SS-339 Catfish cleared the base at 1315. (1:15 PM)

They had to do a surface run of fifteen hours at flank speed of twenty-two knots, for them to be on station by 0500. (5:00 AM)

Chapter Forty Five

Saturday, July 1, 1950 – Day Seven of the Invasion
On Board SS -339 Catfish - 1600 – (5:00 pm)

At flank speed of 22 knots, it took a four-hour surface drive to get to the Korean East Coast through a six-foot ocean swell. Up and down mostly, but swaying as subs do. These are mild sea surface conditions at this heading. Submarines are at their fastest on the surface but don't ride well for its occupants. With the bow planes above the water line and with the small rear fins designed mostly for steering underwater, the boat swayed and lurched, even in the most serene of ocean swells. It was like riding in a giant cigar with flaps.

Having just cleared the edge of the Korean peninsula, they turned north. The ride of the boat now changed radically. The ocean swells came at them on their beam, and the side to side movement increased dramatically.

In the forward compartment, UDT Three tried to relax in their tiny space. Having never been in a submarine, they were unaccustomed to the claustrophobic feeling and staleness of air in the cramped compartment. Sea noises against the hull added to the overall sense of entombment.

"Does this get any better, Chief?" Asked Seaman Ray Albert, who started looking a little pale.

"Ray, I hate to tell you this, but it's going to get a whole lot worse."

"What do you mean? We're almost there, right?"

"You're not paying attention, Ray. We're only out four hours. We got, maybe, ten or so hours to go. Hang in there, buddy. This is a stout vessel, goes underwater, just like us. Besides, ain't nobody shooting at us? Right!"

"You think they got some grub, Chief?" Asked Petty Officer 3rd Class Irwin Handler.

"You little shit! You should be three hundred pounds, Handy. Didn't you eat before we left?"

"That was hours ago!" He snapped. Handy became his moniker because he could do most everything, and it worked with his name. At five foot eight and maybe one thirty, Handy's ability belied his stature. He was relentless. His *never giving up* attitude had gotten him into the UDT unit.

Chief smiled. "We'll get chow in a bit. You know our Navy always provides. Any questions about this mission?"

Petty Officer 1st Class Bobby Grill, second in command spoke. "Chief! I for one am grateful we're not blowing up some sunken ship to clear a channel or unexploded ordinance on a resort beach. I joined this outfit to do some good, you know, like save lives, so I like this mission."

"Bobby, whether you were told or not, you and I, and the rest of our team have saved lives. The past many years we've done a lot of good shit that did that. Taken away the stumbling fool from dying because he stepped on a land mine or swam into a beach obstacle with a contact mine."

The Chief paused. "Knowing this, I'll tell you square. There's no feeling that can describe the HIGH you get from blowing up something that fucks up the enemy. Nothing!"

Petty Officer Third Class Robert "Matt" Mayhew chimed in. "Chief, I've never done a beach landing in the dark. What should we expect?"

"Good question. Our beach landing zone is a little unclear. Meaning we have no fucking idea of the conditions at the beach. Rocks, high waves, nothing."

"Nothing like a challenge! Right Chief?"

He nodded. "Listen up! We're the best of the best! Nothing gets in our way. I don't give a shit if we crash on the rocks at this beach. We will recover and kill this tunnel. Many hundreds, maybe thousands of our men depend on our success."

The lurching of the boat got worse.

Korea, Village of Yangiu, Three miles north of Seoul –Same Time - 1600 – (5:00 pm)

"Are the men rested?" Rusty asked Red.

"Too much, I think. After that breakfast feast they fed us. Crap, I slept like a baby."

"Who's been on the highway watch?"

"First it was Mario, then Arron, then Tracker, then Moose. C J's been out there for the last hour."

"OK, send Joe out now. I want C J back here to go over our next move. Get Tully and the rest of the lookout men. We'll meet out back, under the big tree by the chicken pens." Red went off.

Rusty wandered to the south end of the village, stood under a beautiful tree and gazed down the valley towards Seoul. Smoke was visible from the city to his right. C J's lookout mountain was also clearly outlined. The sky was turning to a moody gray as a new front formed from the east. It matched his temperament. Undecided on what to do next, he fretted about the many options.

"I hate watching you burn up all that gray matter. You're gonna lose it all too soon." Tully said good-naturedly, as he came close.

"That's why I got my special council!" Rusty said as he turned to him. "Keeps my burn rate down."

Red and the day's lookout men came in and sat around in a circle. The clucking sounds of the chickens nearby was the only distraction.

Red started. "The lookouts all reported constant traffic on the highway. Troop trucks with trailing artillery, construction equipment, armored vehicles, and marching infantry. You name it. All, almost uninterrupted."

263

Tully commented. "I was hoping we'd see big breaks in the flow. This doesn't lend itself to any intervention, except for some suicide mission."

"I was afraid of this." Rusty nodded at Tully. "We're not doing suicide!"

C J suggested they call Foxy at the lookout mountain hideout since they hadn't checked in since early morning.

"Somebody's thinking!" Said Red, as he grabbed the radio.

He spoke with Foxy for a few minutes, mostly listening and signed off.

"Nothing good to report," Red said to the group. "Activity around the Han River is intense. Small boats are ferrying enemy troops across. A pontoon bridge for troops is being assembled, and repairs to the bridges are proceeding rapidly. He spotted a barge with a big crane being towed in."

Thoughtful, Rusty said. "It seems our enemy has realized that South Korea is not surrendering after the fall of their capital. Now they're gonna have to work to get the rest of the country. Colonel Nelson was right! This is going to be a long war."

A far off rumble was heard, like from a distant stampede of buffalo. They all looked south and up into the sky. The gray clouds had not closed in yet so they could see the entrails of approaching bombers through the breaks in the sky. They were high up, maybe forty thousand feet. A big formation.

"All right!" Yelled Mario.

"What's that?" Arron pointed off to the north, revealing similar contrails heading towards the bombers, but going much faster.

"Jesus! Looks like jets. Not ours!" Red called out. "This looks bad!"

And it was.

Four specks split off and dove through the bomber formation in a flash. They circled, two going high, two low and attacked again. The bombers were just coming over the capital, about five miles away.

"Must be forty or fifty!" Mario called out. "Jesus, they're going slow!"

They heard the dull cascade of explosions as the bombs started impacting on the river banks around the bridges, then moving north into the city. The ground shook with the vibrations.

Then they saw a bomber break formation, starting to lose altitude. A second followed, then a third. All began to go into a death spiral. No parachutes were visible.

The bomber formation disappeared into the clouds a few moments later. The men were quiet.

"Never saw anything like that before." Said a subdued Arron. "And I hope I never see it again."

"I didn't see any escorts." Tully said in a flat voice.

Rusty didn't like what he saw either. Felt like he'd been sucker-punched. "Not sure it would've mattered, Tully. I don't think we got anything like those jet fighters."

"Let's hope we do; maybe we've just been keeping it secret." Red wanted to be positive, but even he had his doubts. "Enough of this!" He said. "Let's get back to our situation."

Chapter Forty Six

Saturday, July 1, 1950 – Day Seven of the Invasion
Japan - Eighth Army Headquarters – G-2 Operations Section
– Conference Room – 2000 – (8:00 pm)

Refreshed after a few hours rest, the A Team had reassembled three hours ago to review the latest developments.

Operation **Bowie** was in progress.

Communications with Foxy, at C J's lookout, was ongoing and was the main topic of current debate.

Captain Sam Haran, now nicknamed the Professor, was discussing the Han River bridgehead.

"The enemy is expanding their foothold on the south bank. Somebody seems to have woken up to the fact that there's not much of a defense in front of them. The Red's don't have any armor across yet, but they sure as shit have artillery and a finely trained assault force. To their credit, the ROK have stiffened their resistance. But, essentially, they got nothing but light weapons."

"I got bad news." Lieutenant Larry Cole joined in, "And bad news."

"Just got Air Force Command results of the last bomber mission over Seoul and the Han River Bridge area. They lost four B-29's, five more heavily damaged. They're suspending all daylight bomber activity until further notice."

Author's note:

*The B-29 was considered safe for high-level bombing missions of forty thousand feet and above. No known fighter could operate at that altitude, or so they thought. On this day, American Bomber Command discovered that this new Russian jet could indeed operate at very high altitudes. We finally were able to match its capabilities with our swept wing F-86 F Saber jet in 1953, **two years later.***

Major Jarvis said, "This is bad! Really bad! This confirms Foxy's last communication that we got creamed. These new enemy jets broke up the bomber attack to such an extent that little damage was done around the river. A waste!"

Colonel Nelson was dismayed. "There'll be more of that Hank until we get organized. Right now, we're just throwing shit against the wall. Maybe something sticks if we get lucky..... But mostly men die."

He paused, looked around the table at his A Team. "You're all doing a great job, don't forget that. Many, many more of our friends will die, but we must focus on the big picture."

Nick had been thinking of the downed aircrews, forty, maybe fifty men, dead. Then, about his **Bowie** mission. Had he ordered these men into a death trap? He looked at Nelson. "Boss! You forget! In the foxhole, you don't give a shit about the big picture."

Nelson nodded. In a low tone said, "Nick! I forget sometimes. But you know, somebody has got to stick his head out of the foxhole and see how to fight back. That's our job!"

Nick pulled out of his funk. "Yeah, boss! You're right!"

Nelson looked over to LT Cole and Captain Haran. "Have you come up with a defense plan for the ROK or us, further south of the river?"

The Professor led. "Been working with Planning trying to get a handle on 24th Division deployment schedules. It's a mess Colonel. Only one organized force is being landed, and that's going slowly. Your friend, Lt Colonel Charley Smith, arrived earlier today with part of his unit. They'll be first up. They should be able to move out tomorrow or Monday. Where they go depends on what happens at the Han River."

"Any help from the ROK on reinforcements at the river?"

LT Cole answered. "I was able to speak to your ROK G-2 counterpart, Colonel OH, earlier. He's been at Suwon rounding up stray units to send back to the river. The situation isn't encouraging. A mile or so south of the river is a small industrial town on the main highway. He hopes to have enough troops to put up a house-to-house defense in the town, says he's got nearly two thousand soldiers that'll move up tomorrow. Oh! Almost forgot! He thanked me for keeping him informed about his nephew; he's been apprehensive. I told him what a great job he'd been doing. He sends best regards to you, Colonel."

"Poor bastard! He reminds me of the story about the little Dutch boy hopelessly trying to hold back the bursting dike by sticking his fingers in the holes."

Nick looked up. "At least he's trying, boss."

"Right! He's a good man, gives his all. Hope he survives through the next few months." Nelson paused. "What else we got?"

The A team looked around at each other, searching for somebody to say something.

Major Jarvis jolted up. "Holy shit! Sorry! I forgot to update you all on Foxy's last transmission."

"Calm down Hank." Said Nelson. "A lot of stuff's going down. What happened?"

"He reported Rusty's team encountered constant traffic going south on the main highway in the valley. Didn't think it was a survivable mission to try harassment on the road or anywhere nearby. They're returning to C J's lookout mountain tonight. They want a new mission."

Nelson just smiled. Early on, he had recognized that Rusty had exceptional talent. Damn glad, he thought, that he survived so much crap. Critical, sound decisions happen when you allow input from your team. Rusty was the best of the best in bringing out his team's most crucial ideas. He was a leader that allowed his team to lead.

He smiled to himself. He needed to remember that thought.

"Okay! A team! Finally! Good news! We got people out there that can think. Let's help them as much as possible. Any ideas?"

The Professor stood up. "Got one!"

"Let's hear, Sam." Nelson said, recalling his team in Europe. They were good but not as good as these men.

"I'm a logic person." Said the Professor. "An engineering type, but I got a creative angle at times. Think I was dropped by my mother to get that. Anyway, I don't see anything that can stop this juggernaut, or even slow it for a while. The Han Bridge helped, and Nick's tunnel destruction will help in a few weeks because it's strategic. But, we don't have a few weeks!"

He paused. "Unless we can start pulling some rabbits out of our ass we're done! The country will be overrun."

Nick interjected, **"Boss! It's time to slug it out!"**

Nelson nodded, hearing what he felt but didn't want to hear, then asked, "Tell me, Sam, why do you feel so strongly about this?"

Sam looked at Nick then back at Nelson. "Nick's right. That's why I'm pessimistic. The Air Force decision today, suspending daylight heavy bomber attacks, was telling. For the first time, the Air Force admits it doesn't have air superiority. That means our troops must totally rely on their resources. No help from above, and I think, it will take some time for us to reestablish ourselves in the air."

"Further, our buildup is slow. We just landed our initial force this morning, all six hundred troops! Won't be fully on the ground until tomorrow. They don't have anything heavy, not even a halftrack."

Nelson had had enough of the doom and gloom. He looked around the table in a composed manner.

"This reminds me of the winter of 1945 when the Nazi's hit us with a surprise attack. The Battle of the Bulge. I was there. They had the overwhelming firepower of tanks and men. On paper they should have crushed us. Driven on to the coast and possibly ended the war in the west."

Pausing in his deliberate speech, "The Nazi's should have, and could have! But for one thing….the American soldier! Against all the odds, he fought! And fought! Until he stopped the Nazi's cold! Our men suffered greatly for their bravery. They'll do it again, NOW!"

After a long silence, Nick spoke up. "Sir, I agree with you. The grunt mentality is simple, given no other alternative, they'll fight rather than die. But I think it's our job to give them more options."

Sam stood up. "Colonel! If I've given you or anyone here the impression I've become negative and given up, well I apologize, because I haven't."

Sam paused and looked at the team. "Nick's got it nailed. It's gonna get real ugly in the field. Our men are going to die in big numbers until we here can figure out how to bring our very meager forces to bear on exactly where they need to be. That's our job, and I'm fully there!"

"Never thought otherwise for a minute, Sam." Said Nelson, "And I'm sure no one else did either." Looking around, "Anybody?"

Major Jarvis spoke up, "Based on what we know so far, the area around the town of Osan could be our first engagement of US forces with the enemy. We're working on that defense. I think we should instruct Rusty's Post team to get into that area."

"I agree, Hank." Nelson continued, "Anyone have another opinion?"

Silence.

Nelson remembered his orders of only a few days ago for Rusty to move south, to Osan. Then things happened.

"Okay, Major. Get Foxy back. Order the whole team to move south, to the Osan area. They're to call here before they leave. Tell'em US troops may be in the area."

Chapter Forty Seven

Saturday, July 1, 1950 – Day Seven of the Invasion
Korea, Village of Yangiu, Three miles north of Seoul
– 1900 – (8:00 pm)

Rusty's team had agreed that the best they could do now was to get out of Dodge. Decided it best to go back to C J's mountain hide while the getting was good. Packed up and heading out, *Three* paid his respects to his cousins' family. C J followed, then wished the villagers well.

Three led the team out. Joe brought up the rear, with Frenchy in front of him.

It was twilight with cloud cover. Distant lightning in the east, then a deep rumble of thunder alerted them to the coming storm.

About a mile out, Joe froze in his tracks. Frenchy kept walking.

"Hey!" Joe whispered. Frenchy stopped and turned. Alerted, he saw Joe's concern.

"Did you hear that?" Joe whispered.

Frenchy moved back to Joe. "Hear what? The thunder?"

"It sounded like a truck, back at the village."

"I only heard the thunder. You sure?"

"No. But I got a bad feeling. I think we should go back and take a look."

Frenchy didn't hesitate. By now, all the men well knew Joe's reputation for sensing trouble.

"Stay here!" He ran up to Dean, who had kept walking and softly called out, "Dean! Stop! Then he whistled further ahead to Red who was next. He signaled to the next man then came back quickly. Slowly the column stopped.

Red huddled with Frenchy and Dean. Frenchy filled him in on Joe's intuition, told Red he and Joe were going back to check things out.

"OK, I'll tell Rusty. We'll hold here."

Frenchy started to leave. "I'm coming!" Said Dean.

Frenchy looked at Red. Red nodded.

Joe, Frenchy and Dean headed off to the village. Joe's anxiety grew as he approached it. He knew something was terribly wrong.

They circled the village, came in from the west side. Loud voices were heard as they crawled between the huts and houses, eventually finding a small rock wall that had a complete view of the village square.

To their left, at the road entrance into the village, was a truck and a jeep. The jeep was more into the square, had a funny looking flag on its side that they couldn't make out, and a stand-up soldier, holding a mounted machine gun, pointing at the assembled villagers in the square.

Twenty feet at their front were ten soldiers, standing, backs to them, facing the people. Not in formal order, they appeared relaxed; rifles laid haphazardly in their arms.

An officer stood in the center of the square, talking to the town's mayor, his wife and young daughter at his side.

The men made a few hand signals then slipped off. Joe moved off to the far right of the wall so he could get a proper shooting angle to the open square away from the people. Dean backed off a bit and found a big vase where he could kneel behind and rest his rifle on and have a clear shot at the guy in the jeep. Frenchy focused on the standing soldiers.

Frenchy couldn't hear what the officer was saying or asking, but knew, by his tone, it was very threatening.

Joe raised his Tommy gun, had a great angle on the officer.

272

It happened so quickly. Afterward, the three wondered why they had hesitated. It would haunt them.

In one motion, the officer lifted his machine pistol and killed the mayor and his family.

Dean immediately shot the jeep guy, Frenchy jumped up firing at the standing soldiers.

Joe sprayed the officer's legs with a burst from his Thomson.

The villagers screamed at the first shots and scattered.

It was over in a few seconds.

The men came out and checked the bodies. Joe went directly to the officer. He was still alive, but lots of blood was out on the ground. His thigh wounds had severed an artery. Maybe he had a few minutes before he bled out.

Frenchy came over and knelt beside him, spoke softly in his language, gave him a sip of water, he bent to listen.

The officer spat the water back into Frenchy's face.

Frenchy pulled out a knife and stuck it in this pricks wounded thigh, below the major wound, and twisted it.

The officer screamed.

"Now tell me! Or you will cry until you die!"

He told Frenchy what he asked, then died.

Rusty and the whole team entered the square from all sides. Rusty walked over to Joe.

"You saved this village!"

Joe moved off, shaking his head, still wondering why he waited to shoot this officer.

"Rusty!" Shouted Frenchy, "Come here!"

He came over to Frenchy, kneeling over the now dead officer, a captain, as Frenchy was wiping his knife clean on his uniform.

"See this patch?" The dead officer's arm insignia was a *Grey Dragon*.

"Holy shit!" Rusty was stunned. "These bastards are still operational?"

"Yeah!" Frenchy said. "Before he died, he talked. Said a full company was nearby, scouring the area for anti-communist. They've orders to kill them all. This village was going to die."

C J and his *Three* went to the dead family sprawled on the ground, knelt down to them. *Three* screamed in anger and agony; he knew them, they were alive only moments before.

The scene moved Rusty. The raw feelings of hate engulfed him. Glancing around, he eyed the jeep nearby, saw the small flag flying on its side, and walked over to it. The townspeople started to gather around and watched him.

The flag was attached to a foot and half thin metal shaft. The flag was six by six, showing the circled Grey Dragon. He pulled the pole out of its holder and came back to the dead officer in the square.

"Frenchy! Tell these people what we know about this unit. That they'll send more men."

Then Rusty bent down, screamed at the dead officer, "You fuck!" and thrust the tip of the flag pole deep into the dead officer's throat. Most of the flag hung out of his mouth.

"This is a sign to these bastards." He said to Frenchy. But actually, he said it to no one.

"Frenchy! Tell them they must abandon the village. No time! They must leave."

C J and *Three,* after learning of this enemy units past and what the captain had said, joined Frenchy and convinced the people to leave. They listened and scattered into their homes to gather belongings and food.

Red was standing next to C J, watching the people get organized. He asked C J, "Where will they go?"

"They're Korean, Red. Generations have suffered through many rulers. They're resilient. They'll go into the eastern mountains. It's wilderness. Of no interest to anybody. They'll survive."

Rusty came over and instructed Red to contact Foxy, tell them what they encountered and relay that to Colonel Nelson.

It was dark when they left. Thunder and lightning brought the rain.

Taejon Airfield – One Hundred Miles SE of the Han Bridge — 2100 – (9:00 pm)

Over the last day or so, the airfield had been extensively modified and extended. C-47s, the two engine transports, were now able to land, arriving slowly at first in the morning and picking up throughout the day. Ammunition crates they carried became too much for the small force at the airport to unload. Some planes had to be waved off, for them to circle. They couldn't turn the planes around fast enough. At noon, a ROK platoon in trucks showed up. It helped relieve the pressure of unloading the planes.

Frustrated all day that he couldn't return to the fight, Wild Bill watched the slow buildup. He still wondered where the Air Force was and what the hell was happening. Ammunition! No fighting soldiers! No fighter planes! It was not looking good, and he got mad whenever he saw an opportunity missed.

Sometimes he recognized reality, as he did now and realized how small a clog he was in this grand theater playing out. Remembered this same feeling of helplessness in Europe.

He screamed. "I make a fucking difference!"

Nearby, Billy did a double take at the sudden outburst.

"Captain! You Okay?"

"No, Billy, I'm not." Wild Bill turned and walked away.

Chapter Forty Eight

Sunday, July 2, 1950 – Day Eight of the Invasion
On Board SS -339 Catfish - 0430 – (4:30 am)

Boat commander Milligan entered their compartment. Chief yelled, "Commander on deck!"

The men stumbled out of their bunks and got straight.

"Relax! I'm here to wish you good luck. I've never been involved in an operation like this. Feels good to know you make a difference. I have great respect for you men. I'm just a taxi driver, and you do the shit work. If I were you, I'd worry about the taxi taking you home. So I'm here to reassure you that I'll not leave you on the beach. That's my promise to you."

The men stared at him. Chief broke the silence. "If you leave Commander! I'll come back and kill you every night in your dreams."

Milligan was surprised at the response. "I'll wait for you, Chief!" He turned to leave, "You got twenty minutes!"

"He'll wait for us." Said Bobby.

"I know." Said Chief. "Just wanted some insurance."

They pulled their gear on, wetsuits, special boots that fitted into swim fins they carried. Strapped on waterproofed weapons and checked the watertight bags of demolition charges and sundry other tools.

Catfish was dead in the water but slowly rocked as they entered the deck. A seaman brought them to the assault craft entrance ladder next to the side of the sub. Their raft was inflated and preloaded, in the water, ten feet down. They couldn't see it. The rope ladder lashed to the hull fed down and disappeared into the blackness.

"Jesus!" Said Handy, "Can't see shit! You sure our boats down there?"

"Go Handy!" Said Chief, "Navy doesn't screw around."

"Good luck!" Said the seaman near the edge.

It was a ten man UDT rubber boat they climbed into. Good thing it was only the five of them as the weight of the one thousand pounds of C-4 brought everything in balance.

As they cast off, Commander Milligan strained to follow them from the conning tower but couldn't. The deck crew had already secured the hatches and gone below. On the intercom, he called for a partial submerge of thirty feet, enough to bring the hull of the boat below the sea but leaving the conning tower fifteen feet above the waves. He wanted to actively scan the area with radar and be able to see any trouble on the beach. He was committed to his promise.

Rain poured. Seas were down with little wind and no chop. It was black. They paddled. No need to check the compass heading anymore, Chief thought, as the following seas moved them right along directly to their intended landing spot. Although he wished he could see something, Chief gave into fate because he knew they'd passed the point of their control of events. As the waves gradually grew, Chief called out. "Closing in!"

The sound of breaking waves was sudden. The boat lifted high, then crashed onto the sandy beach, flat on its bottom, jolting the men with a teeth-jarring impact. The next wave broke over the stern, soaking them, filling the boat and pushing it farther up the beach.

"Out!" Shouted Chief. They removed the bags and weapons, then started removing the five blocks of explosives. Grabbing straps, one man at each end, they lifted the two hundred pound blocks out of the boat and then up to the grass line.

Finished getting everything out, they dragged the boat up onto the beach.

"Get me the radio!"

"Got it, Chief." Said Ray, as he unpacked the watertight bag, unwrapped the walkie-talkie and handed it to Chief. He clicked send, then clicked twice and spoke. "Okay! Good job!" Commander Milligan acknowledged with two clicks.

"It's 0515," (5:15 am) said Chief to his men. "Making good time so far. Ray, Handy, put a block on my back."

They had discussed this on the Sub. It was a tricky problem getting all that weight to the tunnel. Five hundred yards doesn't sound that far, but five football fields! In the dark! Over what? Grass or rock, maybe through heavy bushes? They had no idea. Chief was the only man capable of carrying that load alone. The blocks had straps for carrying, but it also had a harness that a man could wrap around his arms and chest. If Chief could bear this one, then the rest of the team would only have to make one trip back to the beach to bring the rest up.

They strapped on the block. With a grunt, Chief rose up. "Bobby and Handy lead, I'm in the middle."

The rest of the men took an end of each of the two, two hundred pound blocks and advanced.

Bobby knew Chief loved American Western stories. Told him that, as a kid, he had fantasized about himself as a leader on a wagon train, going through the badlands. A thought suddenly popped into his head and couldn't resist it.

"Go west young man!" Said Bobby.

Chief had his own thought. "Bobby! You lead us to the Little Big Horn, and you won't have to worry about Indians, I'll scalp you."

Bobby grunted.

"Just find the damned tunnel!" Quipped Chief.

The rain masked any noise they made stumbling through low brush. Mostly flat, they moved rapidly. Then Bobby stepped on gravel. Stopped. Knelt to feel the rocks. Crawled forward and met the rail.

They followed the track north. Not far along, Bobby stopped, whispered over to Handy to lay the bundle down. "What?" Handy whispered back.

"Look!" Bobby pointed. A tiny twinkle of light showed through the rain.

It wasn't obvious at first. Handy had to strain and finally saw the flicker. "Got it! Hard to tell how far."

Chief came up. Bobby pointed out the light.

"Get this block off my back." Chief whispered.

Ray and Mayhew joined them. They huddled. Chief made his decision. "I'm sure that's the tunnel, and we got company. I'll stay here. Drop your bags. You guys go back and get the rest of the bundles."

They dropped their bags containing their tools, hand grenades, extra ammo, wire, detonators and plunger and started to move off.

"Hey!" Whispered Chief, "We got no time to fool around, you know your way back?"

In the near total darkness, Bobby whispered back, "Easy! Due east until we hit the water, then due west, to the rails. Just be a few minutes or so." He grunted. They left without a sound.

The rain hitting the wrapped blocks of C-4 lying next to Chief, made the only noise.

Needing to know what he faced, he slow crawled up the rail towards the light. He didn't have to go far. The tunnel opening was visible, fifty feet, he thought. The light was deeper in the tunnel. Maybe a heating stove for coffee or tea. Breakfast? He had no idea.

The back glow of the fire put the two entrance guards in definition. One on each side, in the corners, standing, just inside the entrance, behind small sandbag protective barriers. They were sheltered from the rain and appeared very relaxed. He took out his hi-powered glasses but couldn't see further in. The tunnel looked like it curved slightly, hiding the western side from view.

Shit! Now what? Chief thought through the options. How many were in there? I can't take the guards without firing! I'm running out of time!

Then he thought of his Marine Drill Sergeant Mac. It was 1947. UDT members and any new recruits had to undergo Marine combat training. Not basics, but advanced infantry tactics and field exercises. Mac was a prick. Hated non-Marines, thought they were inferior. But he respected UDT vets like him that had seen action. On an exercise, they faced a challenge. A ravine at their front, blocking the main attack force behind them. They had no intelligence about the position. Only a small number of identified enemy troops were visible.

"What!" Said Mac to his assembled charges, "Do you do now?"

There was no response.

"I'll tell you what you'll do!" He shouted. "If you can't sneak up on them and kill'em quiet like. Then you get as close as possible and attack with everything you got. Then hope for the best. Uncertainty! My children will surely kill you before any bold action."

Yeah! Right on Mac! Chief thought. Uncertainty! He decided what he was going to do.

Chief checked his watch when the men returned. Almost 0600 (6:00 am). The rain was steady, not real hard, but a good sound covering rain. Perfect for what Chief wanted to do. He briefed the men.

Chief and Bobby rose, got their Tommy's chambered, safety off, readied for full auto, and moved down the track, Bobby to the left, just off the rail, Chief, to the right.

Handy, Mayhew and Ray were moving down the center of the tracks, slightly behind them, their Tommy's shouldered. Each had a grenade in their throwing hand. Another grenade hanging from a cross belt.

The group walked soundlessly toward the tunnel entrance. They heard chatter between the guards. One was smoking, leaning against the tunnel wall. The other had his rifle slung in his arms.

Ten feet. The guards weren't looking out. Might have seen them if they had. They just heard the rain.

Chief's firing signaled the start. Bobby opened up on the other guard. The three centermen pulled their pins and tossed their grenades as far as they could into the tunnel. Running forward to the lip of the shaft, the three men threw their second grenade farther in.

Waiting until the smoke cleared, they now entered the dark opening and listened. No sounds.

"Bobby! Recon the tunnel! Don't want any surprises! Be careful!"

"Right!" He headed inside with his flashlight, passed six bodies of other guards, quickly stopped to make sure they were dead and then went further into the black hole. He slowed. Moved off the gravel to dirt. Hugged the wall as he moved into the dark and listened carefully as he walked.

They moved quickly now, rushing to finish before the rapidly coming dawn.

It was all preplanned by Chief. Having come from the Seabees, he knew about blowing up rock. Surface or mountain, rock was rock. Start a fissure, increase its size by breadth and the result was X times the input. He couldn't remember the exact amount but knew it was big.

Having placed the two hundred pound bricks every fifty feet from the entrance, they brought in their tools. They set their lights and with hand held rock pickers; they hammered out holes in the wall, four feet off the ground. Holes big enough to place a one pound C-4 block. Then they banged in a metal spike to support the two hundred pound brick they tied to it.

Every man knew how to hook up the explosives, and they did, in earnest. Almost finished, Handy grabbed the five connecting wires and started tying them off to the detonator wire.

"Mayhew!" Chief yelled. "Go south down the tracks a hundred yards or so past the entrance and plant a pressure mine under the tracks, cover it real good."

Mayhew opened the big bag, grabbed the twenty-five-pound mine, picked out a small shovel and ran down the tracks, counting his steps. Stopping at one hundred yards, he knelt next to a wood tie and started digging under it with the shovel. In two minutes, the hole was big enough to place the mine directly under it, nice and snug. He covered it well.

The pressure detonator on this mine was preset for four hundred pounds.

Ray, now finished, called out. "Where's Bobby?"

Chief didn't know where Bobby was. He hadn't come back.

Handy, who also just finished, started playing out the detonator wire and was coming out of the tunnel.

"Handy!" Chief caught up with him. "Listen! You are to blow this mother in five minutes! I don't give a shit if I'm in the tunnel or not! You do it!" Chief went into the tunnel.

Handy couldn't possibly kill his friends. Did what most soldiers did. He wasn't going to obey his orders unless his life or his mission was threatened. He checked his watch.

Chief ran back deep in the tunnel, and shouted as loud as he could, "Bobby! Bobby!"

"Come 'in!" He heard back. Bobby ran into view, stuck his flashlight in his pocket.

"We got three minutes!" Said Chief. They sprinted.

Chief, relieved at finding Bobby, was also angry and yelled at him as they ran, "Asshole! Almost got yourself killed!"

As they exited the tunnel, both saw a single light far down the tracks.

"That's a train!" Bobby called out as they cleared the entrance and turned east.

"You're good!" Chief being snide. "Keep moving! We're close!"

Handy heard them first. "Here!" Handy yelled. They changed direction slightly and dropped down next to Handy, Ray, and Mayhew. They were now two hundred feet from the tunnel.

The sound of the oncoming train vibrated through the earth; it was coming in fast.

"Do you think that they know we're here? Maybe a rescue train?" Said Ray.

Chief ignored Ray. "Handy, wait till Mayhew's mine goes off. If it does?"

"Damn you, Chief! I set it right!"

The thundering of the train and its vibration became a power unto itself. The steam engine was going thirty miles an hour pulling a train of empty box cars and flatbeds, traveling home to reload under the last cover of darkness.

The ***boom*** of the mine explosion was faintly heard, but distinct.

Chief witnessed the whole scenario. Mayhew did it right. The locomotive kept moving beyond the explosion point, not unbalanced at the detonation under its middle section. He watched as the trailing boxcars started to pull away and slant to the left as they hit the explosion hole with no rails.

Chief yelled to Handy, "Now!"

The tunnel explosion was louder but also muffled. Multiple things happened at the same time.

A tremendous cloud of rock and dust spewed out of the tunnel entrance as the locomotive charged in, now moving alone on the track.

The following cars were fully off the rails and impacting the ground and each other. They started piling up. Cars randomly moved in all directions, now to both sides of the track, as the pile grew bigger.

The men reacted in unison, some cursing, as they ran away from the maelstrom coming towards them. Dawns gray light was now adequate to keep them from stumbling; they raced to the beach. The terrible grinding, crunching and screeching sounds of wood and metal followed them to their boat.

"Jesus! That was scary!" Said Ray. "I thought we were goners!"

Bobby laughed. "Nothing like a train come' in at you to get your ass in gear!"

They moved fast, dragged the boat to the surf line, hopped in, caught a lull in the surf, and paddled like crazy to hit the next wave before it broke.

On board the **Catfish,** Commander Milligan watched from the conning tower. He saw the light of the train coming, saw the dull flash of the mine, heard the boom from the mountain tunnel and watched as sparks flew and heard the sounds like a giant crushing machine at work. Fires broke out in the wreckage.

The team appeared on the beach. Relieved as he counted all five men, he ordered the boat to fully surface and prepare to receive them.

Paddling out, Chief, at the bow, yelled to Bobby, "Where did you disappear to?"

"Oh shit, Chief! Don't break my balls! I lost track of time. Went to the end of the tunnel. Just wanted to make sure nobody was gonna sneak up on us. I ran most of the way back."

"Good thing you did!"

In silence, they paddled into the brightening dawn, in the rain, into the ocean swells, and towards the visible submarine and their escape.

"Proud of you all!" Chief shouted at his team. "Good work back there!"

Chapter Forty Nine

Sunday, July 2, 1950 – Day Eight of the Invasion
Korea - Pusan Airport – 0700 – (7:00 am)

Platoon First Sergeant "Whitey" Carlton Dillon sat on an ammo crate eating his first meal in twenty-four hours. He was grumpy. Having slept in a pup tent on the wet ground, he hadn't slept well. He was, however, grateful for the late arrival last night of the regimental field mess unit and equipment, as he was starving and fully enjoying his hot breakfast. Further review of his situation brought more encouragement as he was safely eating his meal, out of the rain, under a large open tent that had been newly erected. His platoon surrounded him.

Finishing his first full plate, he lifted his tin cup and sipped a great hot coffee and wondered how they managed to make it taste so good. Then he thought about going back for full seconds. He was feeling like a man having his last meal. Shit! He thought, stop thinking like that! But he couldn't.

Taking in his men, he was dismayed. None of them had ever seen combat. Wounded once, on his initial, and only experience fighting through the whole Okinawa campaign, he wondered how they would respond. They looked so young; kids really, like he was back then. Six years! Jesus! He thought, remembering how terrified he was on the landing craft approaching the beach. Then the contact, when the real killing began. The horror and fear that didn't stop. What do I say to them?"

Whitey's 1st Platoon of Company B, 1st Battalion, 21st Regiment, 24th Division was the last unit to land late yesterday. They expected three more flights today to fill out **Task Force Smith;** two heavy weapons platoons, consisting of machine gun and 60 mm mortar crews. Maybe bazookas. Maybe artillery.

Well, he thought, it ain't tanks, but it's something.

Same Day - Japan - Eighth Army Headquarters – G-2 Operations Section – Conference Room – 0800 – (8:00 am)

Colonel Nelson was last to arrive, grabbed a coffee and sat. Major Jarvis started on the review on the night's activity, some good but most bad. They still had no word on the **Bowie** operation.

The review was interrupted by a knock and then entrance by a sergeant who brought in a cable message. "Got a high priority here for Colonel Nelson."

LT Cole, nearest to the door, signaled him over, "I'll take it."

Still standing, he unfolded the message with great trepidation, feeling it was about the unknown results of the night's Tunnel mission.

"Colonel, may I?" He said with a straight face.

"Don't keep us waiting for another second, Larry."

"From Naval Forces Far East Command, Admiral Turner Joy," Cole read, "**Catfish** reports total success of **Bowie** mission. All accounted for. Great job! Keep it up, Colonel."

The A Team clapped.

Colonel Nelson stood. "It's your successful mission! And to you, Nick!" He raised his hand as a tribute. "Who put it all together?" The A team clapped again.

Nick blushed then grinned modestly at his team. Then stood and walked over to Colonel Nelson.

Astonished, the team watched him walk. No crutches! All realized the special moment. Larry started the chant. "Nick! Nick!

286

Nick!" The team joined the celebration chant and all clapped for Nick, finally getting his prosthesis.

He walked up to Nelson and stood at attention. The room fell silent. Nelson stood up, smiled at Nick.

"Colonel, sir! Master Sergeant Nick Beloit reporting for full combat duty!" He saluted.

Nelson returned his salute.

"Glad you ditched the crutches! But you've been on combat duty since you got here. Your ability transcends any fight you could add in the field. It's in your head, Nick. You are the fiercest fighter I know! You will kill many bastards. Not with a gun, but with your BRAINS."

The team broke out in applause. Nick returned to his seat.

Nelson remained standing and addressed the group. "Lots of good news so far today. Let's hold this memory for when it's not. Major. Please resume the briefing."

After some updates on troop developments at Pusan, the Major got around to Rusty's team, now back at C J's mountain lookout, east of Seoul.

"They confirmed receipt of our orders for them to move south to the Osan area. They plan to start tonight, and expect to arrive sometime on July 4th." Jarvis continued. "The second action report at that village they left is what is most disturbing."

"Hold on Hank, I think we all saw that, but I don't think our A Team knows anything about this unit." Nelson looked around the room for confirmation. Sam, Nick and Larry nodded at him.

They had not been privy to the first encounter with this unit.

Nick smelled something suspicious. "What's this unit *Grey Dragon?*"

"I need to address that, but not now." Nelson said. Only Major Jarvis knew about this unit, but was told by Nelson to keep it under his hat.

On his way out Nelson asked that they press on. "Be back in a few hours."

Nelson went to his office and called the US Embassy, asked for the Military Attaché, finally connected with Howie.

"Damn it, Jim! You're clairvoyant! I was just about to call you. What's up?"

"Don't give me that shit, Howie. We need to meet. Now!"

"Serious Jim, I was going to call you because I need to see you now as well. How about the Imperial Hotel, still serving a great breakfast and the place is old and musty, just like us."

"Speak for yourself. If you're buying, I'll be there in half an hour."

"We at the State Department spare no expense for VIP's. See you there."

Right! Thought Nelson. As Station Chief of CIA Far East, I can't even dream of how big your expense budget is, Howie.

In the cab ride over, Nelson wondered what Howie wanted. Had the CIA finally cracked something open that he could use? Or is Howie trying to cover his ass about who knows what? He wanted something, that's for sure.

The rainy weather landed them inside, not on the beautiful garden veranda they preferred. Exchanging greetings, they sat at a corner table, away from any intruding guests, ordered coffee and the breakfast special that was designed primarily for the big eating Americans.

After coffee had been served, they got down to business.

"You called me. Go first!" Said Howie.

"I need your help. You know bad shit's happening fast. I don't know if we'll be able to stop these bastards before they overrun Korea and slaughter what forces we've sent so far. So, I was wondering if you got any of those radio intercept gizmos to give me. That's for starters. I got more. Your turn."

"As I said, I think you're clairvoyant, Jim. That's one of the reasons I was going to call you. I do have one available to give you. And, by the way, the gizmo is called the *Wide Array Spectrum Receiver Collector*. And it's still Top Secret."

"Is it the same unit the Posts had?"

"It's been modified a bit, has a little longer range but still has to be a hooked up to a direct source to us, in your case, the Korean cable. We can then translate the field orders that are not usually coded, and give you feedback on the tactical situation. We also have broken some of their codes, from division level. Still working on going higher up."

"That's good news, Howie. Of course I want it. You got another VLF setup to go along with that?"

"Of course!"

As breakfast was served they got quiet.

They started eating, and Howie picked it right up. "Where and when, Jim. They're ready now."

"My staff has increased, Howie. I'm going to have to share all this with them. You OK with that?"

"If you trust them, that's good with me. But I need them to sign a Secrets Act document. It's standard issue stuff. You know, if they reveal anything to anyone about this, they'll go to jail for treason. Just regular department requirements."

"Appreciate the confidence. I'll get you the details later. We'll probably pick them up on the way to the airfield tomorrow."

"You got people that can use this stuff?"

"Don't worry. I'll figure that out."

"Okay. Your turn." Said Howie, as he dug deep into his meal.

"I didn't tell you about something that happened with my Post team when they went off to fight gorilla style. On their special mission to destroy bridges just south of the 38th parallel, they encountered a unique Korean unit called *Grey Dragon.*"

"Stop Jim!"

Nelson reacted, surprised, "Why? You know about them?"

Howie laughed. "Jim, we got that Russian Embassy bugged so big, it would boggle your mind. We heard every bit of your conversation with Andre. Most importantly, we got the one on the outside balcony."

"No Shit! So you knew about this unit?"

"We didn't. But your conversation got us involved. We started searching. We alerted all our assets and particularly, our Russian Embassy staff in Moscow. It paid off."

"What'd you uncover?"

"Jesus, Jim. We share many secrets, but this is big. You can't share this with anyone. You agree?"

"Don't be an ass, Howie! We go back a long time. I know when to keep my mouth shut."

Howie finished his last bit of toast and washed it down with excellent coffee. Satisfied, he regarded his longtime friend, sitting across from him. He greatly admired Jim. Not only for what he has accomplished, sticking his balls out, tempting fate and always being aggressive. But he recognized his loyalty and most importantly, he knew his word was sacred.

"Jim, we cracked a couple of the Russian codes. Keyword Alert got us to *Grey Dragon.* It seems a few top dogs in the Kremlin aren't happy about this unit. Then, our guy in our Moscow Embassy overheard two generals at a party disparaging Stalin's promoting this Korean adventure. They mentioned this unit."

Howie paused to look around the big room and wondered how many Japanese generals had eaten here and talked about killing Americans.

He refocused on Jim.

"Yesterday, there was an auto accident just outside of Moscow. It killed a colonel in the First Directorship of the KGB. We don't know a lot about him. What we do know, however, was that he was a radical anti-American, anti-capitalist, and ruthless. We believe he led this unit but aren't positive."

Howie continued. "Andrey has been very cautious at the Embassy. He's smart, has use of the only room in the Embassy that isn't bugged by us or their security. Their safe room."

"Is Andrey safe?"

"No one's safe, Jim."

Nelson leaned in and whispered. "Howie, make it clear to your sources that this war will probably be short, maybe a year or a few at most. But I have a long memory. Tell them that if this unit isn't disbanded, I will personally execute all officers associated with this *Grey Dragon* command structure. I want that broadcast through your network, Howie. You got it? I need your support on this."

Howie looked grave, nodded. "Colonel, you probably have more back support than we do at the CIA."

Nelson stood, "I'm counting on that!"

"I want that new stuff tomorrow!" He looked down at Howie who was still sitting.

"Thanks for breakfast!" Pausing, he placed his hand on his shoulder. "Howie! I'll always have your back!"

Chapter Fifty

Back at the briefing table, Nelson got caught up on current events. Very little had happened since he had left.

"I got a few things to share with you all, but first, I need to know if each of you is willing to sign an official Secrets Act document. It says that you must not reveal anything that we further discuss, to any person not so authorized." He looked around. "Any objections?"

Nick piped up. "Is this like walking the plank stuff?"

"Worse! More like hanging from a tree." Nelson quipped and looked at them. "This is serious. I'm about to tell you secrets. I trust you, but the CIA doesn't trust anybody. It's their show. Papers are being messengered over, but I'm not waiting. So, if anyone has a problem, you must leave now, otherwise, if you change your mind, you'll be detained and isolated."

A strange quiet descended on the room. Nelson observed their reaction. Wondered if the entry into the inner sanctum was scary or exhilarating.

"I didn't think there'd be a problem. So let me start at the beginning."

He proceeded to tell them about his involvement with the CIA going back to WW2 and then the new equipment developments in VLF (Very Low Frequency) transmission technology and finely the other innovation about the ability to intercept a broad range of radio transmissions at distances of up to ten or more miles. All ultra-secret and all belonging to the CIA.

Nick was the first to recognize the potential. "You mean we can monitor unit communications?"

"Right, Nick, as long as they're not hard-wired. Only radio frequencies. But that is the bulk of Russian-oriented combat communication system preferences to field units."

Excited, Nick persisted. "What's the turnaround time between interception and relay back to troops in the field?"

Nelson saw the flaw immediately. "Nick. You ask the best damn questions! I don't have an answer for that. This system wasn't designed for tactical interaction. But I'm sure it can be jerry-rigged. I'll find out."

Nelson knew the importance of the answer to Nick's question and immediately called Howie at the embassy. After a brief coded introduction to his question, Howie replied, "Yes, my friend. We are aware of these crucial nuances. Our receiving staff has been greatly expanded. Each intercepted channel is personally monitored and fed real time into that sector's coordinator. We found out, actually through your listening posts, that there are three main frequencies used. Division to regiment, regiment to battalion and battalion to company. Some use codes that we've cracked. Battalion to company is usually open language, using coded map coordinates or coded operational mission names."

"Didn't answer my question fully, Howie. What is the turnaround time for the guy in the trench?"

"Too much I don't know, Jim! Shit! It depends on a lot of things, but I'd only be guessing! Everything's new. Even the distance intercept has been enhanced! We know we can pick up signals beyond fifteen miles. But how much farther? Depends on a lot of unknowns. Sorry to say it, Jim, you're the lab rat."

The call ended.

"They don't know, Nick, we'll be winging it."

Always optimistic, Nick said, "Well, something's better than nothing!"

"Got another one, boss." Nick persisted. "Who's gonna man this listening post at our end?"

"Got an idea." Said Nelson.

ROK Signal Unit Mountain Hideout Northeast of Seoul 1230 – (12:30 pm)

Larry finished writing the VLF coded signal he'd just received. "Huh!" He said, as he got up to find Rusty. He was in a huddle with Red and Tully.

"Got something interesting from Major Jarvis, Rusty. He's got questions." He sat with the three men.

"Go on!" Tully snapped.

"He wants to know if the PBY crashed landed and is it flyable. If so, is the wounded pilot able to fly it out? He also wants to know how we are to proceed to Osan."

Red wondered. "What's our Colonel have up his sleeve? I sense the beginning of our next mission."

"Yup." Said Rusty. "Red, find Tom and the pilot. What's his name?"

"Muzich." Said Red.

"Right! Also, get Marty."

A few minutes later Red returned with the men and joined the circle.

"How are you feeling?" Asked Rusty.

Looking around at the big circle, Muzich got anxious. "Jesus! Is this some hanging trial! I swear, I'm innocent!"

Tully had to keep this up. In a somber tone, he added, "That's what they all say."

Everyone laughed, Muzich wiped his forehead with dramatic flair with his left hand.

"Let me start over." Said Rusty, smiling. "We want to know about the condition of your plane. Is it flyable? Can you fly it?"

294

"That's better. Thought we were running out of food or something and the new guy had to go."

They chuckled, thinking he was close to the truth about the food.

"Marty tells me that if I haven't gotten a high fever by now, I don't have an infection. Which means I won't die. The arm hurts like a bitch but less so than I guess it would, thanks to Marty's pain pills. And it's still usable, probably for the same reason. He looked over at Marty. "Never told you thanks for saving my arm and probably my life. I sure didn't feel that way when you started. But I appreciate the honesty. So thanks! I owe you."

Marty was moved. But Marty being Marty said, "You owe me a beer. Maybe. But you and I are a couple of very lucky fellers. I'll leave it at that." Then he looked over at Rusty. "He's good to go. Although flexing his arm isn't recommended."

"What about the plane?" Asked Tully.

"We didn't crash land. Just hit a sand bar and bounced, then grounded on another sandbar. I took a quick look at the damage from the anti-aircraft hit. The hole was above the waterline, and it didn't seem to cause any structural problems. The plane should be flyable."

"Do you need a copilot to take off?" Asked Rusty.

"No. I may only need some help getting it off the sandbar, but maybe not even that. She's got powerful engines."

Rusty nodded. "Get C J over here!"

Red yelled out for C J above the sound of the rain. He was near and came over. So did most of the other men. Something was up. They wanted to hear it firsthand.

"C J. You never told us how we're going to get to Osan. We got the Han River to cross, and I think a few other obstacles as well. What's your plan?" Asked Rusty.

C J felt defensive. "I told you it would take two days, maybe longer. I know the route, and *Three* grew up in Osan. What's this all about?"

"Somethings come up. Just want to know how we get out of here." Rusty's tone was inquisitive but non-threatening.

"We have a boat."

"No shit!" Said Tully. "And you didn't tell us?"

C J shook his head. He thought, Americans! They must know everything!

"Would it have made a difference? I knew! And **One** and **Three** knew."

Rusty didn't like the direction this was going. "Okay, okay. You're right. It didn't make any difference then. But it matters now! So tell us about your exit plan."

C J relaxed. "It's a skiff, holds ten men, maybe a few more. There's also a good size raft that can be towed. I think they'll be able to take all of us. It's a three-hour walk from here around the back of the mountain to the river and the boat. We'd cross to the south side of the Han; then we'd row south down the side of the estuary, where the current going North is slack."

Collecting his thoughts, he continued.

"From what your pilot told me, he landed about six or so miles south of the junction from where we'll set off. Maybe it's farther. We don't know and it doesn't matter. We can't miss his plane and our final destination is much farther south. We exit the river forty miles from here. Cross a few miles of lowlands, climb two low mountain ridges and come out just east of Osan."

Rusty smiled. Red and Tully looked at each other.

Agitated, Tully asked, "How many miles from the river to Osan? How long?"

C J got defensive again. "Miles don't matter! Conditions matter! Two valleys, two mountains. Although small, these ridges are five hundred to a thousand feet. Will it continue to rain? Do we meet infiltrators? I don't know!"

"Calm down everyone!" Rusty sensed Red and Tully's unease. The tension of this next journey was reaching near climax.

"Let me remind you that C J concealed us, was instrumental in the completion of our near impossible mission, and now has a plan for our escape. I think we owe him some respect!"

Turning to C J, Rusty addressed him. "Our lives depend on you! You're not on trial! You have a good escape plan! We're just trying to figure out what's next!"

Then the men discussed time schedules and other tactical possibilities.

After a long while, Rusty motioned Larry over to his side. They walked to the VLF equipment.

"Larry! Tell Major Jarvis that the plane is okay and Muzich can fly it."

An hour later, Larry was alerted to an incoming VLF. He transcribed the Morse code and brought it to the waiting group.

He read his translation, "From Colonel Nelson. Tom Leyden is to head up team of Post # 4. Phil, Greg and JP. They are to proceed with Muzich to fly out of area, land east of Taejon, on south end of Lake, where they'll be met."

Larry paused. "I've got coordinates for Muzich here that I'll give to him."

He continued. "Further, if other volunteers wish to join this group, they would be welcomed. Notify as to expected arrival. As previous, rest of team to proceed to Osan area maintaining secrecy. C J and his team are ordered to Osan and assist, by approval of his commander, ROK Colonel Oh. Establish contact here on arrival."

"Son of a bitch!" Said Red. "I knew he had something going."

Rusty knew the war was turning badly against them, while dismayed at his orders, he never the less felt positive. Something good was going on, he thought. Otherwise, Nelson would've ordered all of us out. Or else he was desperate. Thinking realistically for a second, he decided on desperate.

"Get all the men together." Rusty said. Most were there already. The rest came into the big circle. The gloom of the rain offered a somber backdrop to the gathering.

Rusty stood. "You all witnessed the new spearhead across the Han River today. Troops, with artillery support, are crushing the ROK. In a day or so, they'll probably be able to bring tanks across. That's the end of any serious defense until US forces get involved. You've heard this before. We've done everything we could to delay them. We've done well. Extraordinarily well, I'd say!"

Rusty paced. He needed to inspire his men and thought of a quote.

"Winston Churchill once said, *Success is not final, failure is not fatal: it is the courage to continue that counts.* I think that's where we are right now!"

He relayed Nelson's orders and the offer, to any man who wanted out.

Arron raised his hand and asked if any bonuses were involved in staying. Men grunted approval, but nobody else commented.

Leyden spoke up. "I'm not one to run from a fight. I'll speak for Jacks team who'd I'd be proud to lead, but they, nor I, want to leave." Jack's team, nodded in confirmation.

Rusty respected their response. "Acknowledged, Staff Sergeant Leyden. But you're ordered out! Apparently, you and your men have more to contribute where you're going then killing a few men behind the lines."

That ended any further discussion, but the whispered speculations began.

The survivors of Post # 4, Phil, Greg and JP moved off to a corner. JP started. "I don't like this! We don't know Tom from a hole in the wall. I still think he got Jack killed. What'd you think we're gonna do?"

"You're a jerk!" Greg said. "Always whining, thinking up shit to worry about. Just shut up!"

"He's a good warrior." Deadpanned Phil. "Smart too! Takes no shit and's determined, just like Jack. I'll follow him!"

298

JP shuffled about, quiet. Then looked at them, "Just worried about where we're going. Guess you're right about him. He is a lot like Jack." Pausing, "Christ, I miss Jack!"

Marty sat next to Joe. "You heal really fast. Time for me to take those stitches out, buddy."

"Don't give me that buddy crap! I know that's gonna hurt like hell!"

"Yeah! It will. But if I leave them in too long it will leave a bad scar and be more painful taking them out. So, buck up, Brooklyn boy!"

"Hey! Did you sew my stripes on?"

"Yeah! Got lots of stitch stuff. You were sound asleep. Can't let a hero go on without proper rank."

Joe had to smile. "No hero! But thanks! Now do your worst, you New York wanna-be Jew doctor."

Marty grunted. "My first office will be on Flatbush Ave."

"Don't you want to go climb some mountain somewhere, Mario?" Asked Snake, as he packed his gear.

Mario kneeling next to him was doing the same, "No! All my life I've searched for a purpose. I thought it was climbing, feeling the thrill of overcoming nature. Then the Army gave me something inside. I can't really describe what it is, only that it's right for me. Makes me feel whole." He paused, "You know, this mission here, has been special for me. There's been no bullshit, good men all around. Great leadership. And I met my ultimate assassin partner, you. We make the best God damned team!" They laughed and slapped each other on the back.

Dean wandered over to Tom Leyden, who was leaning against the mountain edge of the overhang, looking out to the east, viewing nothing. Dean started talking into the emptiness.

"We snipers always wonder when to shoot. Especially if we miss and a friend dies. We hold it close. It starts eating at us from the inside. Doubt, guilt, remorse. Unless you can regain your humanity and realize you're not perfect, you'll descend into hell and

299

become useless to everyone, mostly to yourself." He then turned and walked away.

Tom wondered how in hell this man knew he had been dwelling on his fault in Jack's death. Then he thought of his words.

Rusty motioned to C J to sit with him. Red and Tully followed.

"We should leave now. What do you think?" Rusty asked C J.

"The weather is good cover for us to travel. I don't think the rain will let up today, so we could get a jump on getting to the plane. They could fly out first thing in the morning. So yeah, I think we should leave soon."

Rusty issued his orders.

Alone, Rusty thought of the past many days in wonder. How he'd survived, how this new team had come together and the good they'd done so far. His mind then moved to the dark side, thinking of his men who weren't here. Did they die for something? Christ! He didn't know...He just hoped!

Chapter Fifty One

Sunday, July 2, 1950   Day Eight of the Invasion
Taejon Airfield – One Hundred Miles SE of the Han River –
1400 – (2:00 pm)

It had been raining all day, Wild Bill and his crew laid around, watching the airfield grow from the constant construction expansion. Not far from them, a new metal building was erected during the morning.

These guys would work in a hurricane, Wild Bill mused. Hats off to them. *Battered Bastards of Bataan* flashed through his mind. Yeah, he thought about how Army engineers fought back in that great struggle. Delayed and delayed until the food ran out. Well, we're not running out of food. Thinking more about that line, he laughed to himself. We may, however, be running out of running room.

The Korean cable telephone line buzzed. Captain Stands picked up. "My favorite Colonel! I was starting to wonder if you retired." He listened, excitement turned to neutral. Stands made occasional acknowledgments, then asked. "When? Tomorrow?" Another pause. "Oh, he'll be real happy, Colonel. I'll call you when they arrive."

"Billy! Arnie! George! Come over!" They had watched Wild Bill on the phone from across the hanger but hadn't heard anything.

"What's up, Captain?" Asked Billy.

"We're gonna get real busy around here. That was Colonel Nelson telling me our role in this war is to become very active starting tomorrow." He filled them in on most of the details. Before ending, he looked at George.

"Sergeant Lopez!" He smiled at him. "You're finally going to rejoin Nelson's private Post Army. Survivors of Post # 4 will join us tomorrow and take up the same listening tasks you guys did at the border. This time, though, you'll use the info to kill the enemy."

George nodded, held back tears as he whispered, "Thank you, thank you."

Japan - Eighth Army Headquarters – G-2 Operations Section – Conference Room – 1600 – (4:00 pm)

Nelson addressed his A Team. "Everything is moving in the best possible direction. I want you all to get a well-earned time off tonight. We'll meet at 0600 (6:00 am) tomorrow."

Pausing, "Men! The next few days are going to be difficult, but the next few months are going to unbearable. Rest up!"

The End

Thank You for Reading
Fighting Behind the Lines

The Journey Continues

I hope you would continue to follow the series and all the characters into **Book Three**

America Attacks